PRAISE FOR
BAD LOVE TIGERS
Book 2 in The Bad Love Series

"A mind-blowing, historically correct, time-travel adventure seeped in danger and laced with conspiracy, intrigue, and the origins of Area 51!"

—Susan Keefe, *Midwest Book Review*, 5 Stars

"*Bad Love Tigers* is an enthralling book that kept me spellbound and excited to turn the next page."

—Dr. David Holladay

"A wild romp through time—with its own soundtrack! This book is drenched in meticulously researched historical detail. To me, the blend of imaginative science fiction with accurate fact is an unbeatable combination."

—Mike Ball, Erma Bombeck Award-Winning Author, 5 Stars

"*Bad Love Tigers* combines the nostalgia of teenage friendships with a playlist that will have you reminiscing about the good old days."

—Kimberly Love, Author of *You Taste Like Whiskey and Sunshine*

"This book is not just for adults. Teens and pre-teens will enjoy the adventure and it's a great way to teach kids some history! If you're looking for an enjoyable read, pick up a copy of *Bad Love Tigers*. You won't be disappointed. Highly recommended."

—Pamela Gossiaux, Bestselling Author of *Russo Romantic Mysteries*, 5 Stars

ALSO BY KEVIN L. SCHEWE, MD, FACRO:

BAD LOVE STRIKES

BAD LOVE
TIGERS

KEVIN L. SCHEWE, MD, FACRO

Jan-Carol
Publishing, Inc
"every story needs a book"

Bad Love Tigers
Kevin L. Schewe, MD, FACRO

Published June 2020
Broken Crow Ridge
Imprint of Jan-Carol Publishing, Inc.
All rights reserved
Copyright © 2020 Kevin L. Schewe, MD, FACRO

This is a work of fiction. Any resemblance to actual persons,
either living or dead is entirely coincidental. All names, characters
and events are the product of the author's imagination.

This book may not be reproduced in whole or part, in any manner
whatsoever without written permission, with the exception of brief
quotations within book reviews or articles.

ISBN: 978-1-950895-41-0
Library of Congress Control Number: 2020939293

You may contact the publisher:
Jan-Carol Publishing, Inc.
PO Box 701
Johnson City, TN 37605
publisher@jancarolpublishing.com
jancarolpublishing.com

DEDICATION

I have been a board-certified cancer specialist practicing radiation oncology for 33 years as of July 1st 2020. I am the youngest of three children and have two older sisters, Kathy Williams and Denise Bourg. My first novel, *Bad Love Strikes*, was dedicated to Kathy, who remains in remission from her breast cancer. This second novel, *Bad Love Tigers*, is dedicated to Denise Bourg, the middle child in our family of three siblings.

Growing up together, Denise and I were close enough in age to play games together (mainly Monopoly, Risk, and card games such as Go Fish and War). While we evenly divided our victories and losses in Monopoly and card games, Denise consistently suffered humiliating losses in the game of Risk for many years. Finally late one night when we were older, she won in a marathon game of Risk. With the curse broken, she called our family in the wee hours of the night, informing them of her victory! It was a hilarious ending to a long drought!

Denise has a true heart of gold and a passion to selflessly help and serve other people during her journey through this life. Devoted to her strong faith in God and to her husband, Curt Bourg, a retired airline executive, she has moved more than twenty times and is now happily retired in Virginia! She has worked as a math teacher, cheerleading coach, a florist, and a non-profit executive amongst other things. She has volunteered to help homeless people get back on their feet.

Being close in age, Denise and I negotiated for our favorite T.V. shows growing up together in the 1960s and 1970s. We found common ground with both science fiction and especially spy and espionage-themed shows. *Bad Love Tigers*, has plenty of espionage and science fiction to make it the perfect book to dedicate to Denise. She, her husband, and I are all graduates of the University of Missouri–Columbia. We are all tied together as "Mizzou Tigers"!

BAD LOVE
TIGERS

ACKNOWLEDGMENTS

For 33 years I have worked on the front lines of cancer care as a radiation oncologist in private practice. Receiving a diagnosis of cancer and then facing the realities of staging, treatment, side effects of treatment, and recovery are challenges that are larger than life. Living with a cancer diagnosis after treatment requires a new view on life and life's priorities. I want to acknowledge the thousands of cancer patients that I have cared for these past 33 years—all of whom have taught me valuable life lessons and have shown me courage beyond measure, sacrifice, love, humility, victory, real-life miracles, and acceptance. I am eternally thankful to all of these patients, their families, and loved ones—all who have shown me and continue to show me the meaning of life here on earth.

The writing of *Bad Love Tigers*, has taken place during my COVID-19 experience here in my beloved home of Denver, Colorado. While I treated cancer patients during this unprecedented global pandemic, my dauntless colleagues in medicine have fought an epic and courageous war against a vicious virus attacking our society and way of life. I want to acknowledge all the frontline responders to this pandemic who have sacrificed so much in a heroic effort to save lives. Our hats are off to you—your sacrifices and bravery shall never be forgotten.

AUTHOR'S FOREWORD

RECOMMENDED ACTION FOR ALL YOU TIME TRAVELERS!

In order to get the full sensory effect of traveling through time with the Bad Love Gang, I highly recommend that you download the 30-song soundtrack listed on the next page by using your Spotify, iTunes, Pandora, or Amazon Prime account. Alternatively, you can use YouTube to play each song as you are reading. As each song is boldly introduced throughout the novel, take the time (no pun intended!) to listen to the music and enjoy the full sensory effect of being an honorary member of the Bad Love Gang. Do not be afraid to lip sync, sing, and/or break out and dance, play your air guitar, or tap your feet as the music moves you!

Bad Love Tigers starts on New Year's Eve 1975 and will take you on a bonafide road-trip across America in 1945 and to 1942 WWII China as Bubble Butt and the Bad Love Gang play music from the late 1950s, 1960s, and early 1970s. There is never a dull moment in the lives of these 1970s adventurous teenagers as they interact with three different U.S. Presidents, the dawn of the atomic age, time travel, WWII history, and foreign espionage, and simultaneously tackle controversial topics such as racism and equal rights as they travel across America. Music paves the way as they experience their first, actual alien encounter in the dark of night in a south China forest while volunteering for the famous AVG Flying Tigers. Buckle-up for the ride of your life!

SOUNDTRACK TO *BAD LOVE TIGERS*

1. "You're So Vain," Carly Simon (1972)
2. "We're an American Band," Grand Funk Railroad (1973)
3. "Midnight Train to Georgia," Gladys Knight & The Pips (1973)
4. "Get Out of Denver," Bob Seger and the Silver Bullet Band (1974)
5. "A Beautiful Morning," The Rascals (1968)
6. "Can't No Grave Hold My Body Down," Sister Rosetta Tharpe (1956)
7. "Rock Your Baby," George McCrae (1974)
8. "Magic Carpet Ride," Steppenwolf (1968)
9. "Roll on Down the Highway," Bachman-Turner Overdrive (1975)
10. "Paranoid," Black Sabbath (1970)
11. "A Hazy Shade of Winter," Simon and Garfunkel (1966)
12. "Summer Rain," Johnny Rivers (1967)
13. "Already Gone," Eagles (1974)
14. "Kodachrome," Paul Simon (1973)
15. "Peggy Sue," Buddy Holly (1957)
16. "War," Edwin Starr (1970)
17. "Superstition," Stevie Wonder (1972)
18. "25 or 6 to 4," Chicago (1970)
19. "Tears of a Clown," Smokey Robinson and the Miracles (1970)
20. "Bang a Gong (Get It On)," T. Rex (1971)
21. "Knock Three Times," Tony Orlando and Dawn (1970)
22. "Rescue Me," Fontella Bass (1965)
23. "Kansas City," Wilbert Harrison (1959)

24. "Goin' Out of My Head," Little Anthony and the Imperials (1964)
25. "(I Can't Get No) Satisfaction," The Rolling Stones (1965)
26. "Thank God I'm a Country Boy," John Denver (1975)
27. "Radar Love," Golden Earring (1973)
28. "We Gotta Get Out of This Place," The Animals (1965)
29. "Stand by Me," Ben E. King (1961)
30. "That's the Way (I Like It)," KC and the Sunshine Band (1975)

MAIN CHARACTERS

THE BAD LOVE GANG FROM OAK RIDGE, TENNESSEE

1. **Kevin "Bubble Butt or BB" Schafer:** Age 16. Precocious, borderline genius, has one foot in reality and one foot in destiny. Great sense of humor. Loves strategy, adventure, and popular music (has a "music brain"). A pilot, he discovered the White Hole Project time machine with Bowmar. Plans adventures for the Bad Love Gang. The narrator of *Bad Love Tigers*.

2. **Nathan "Bowmar" Williams:** Age 16. Bubble Butt's best friend. African-American certified genius, with an IQ somewhere north of 140. Discovered the White Hole Project time machine with BB. Understands time-travel. Co-plans adventures with Bubble Butt. A walking, talking, human encyclopedia.

3. **Brianna "Cleopatra" Williams:** Age 17. Bowmar's sister, a total social butterfly with a high social IQ. Becomes the queen of any social circle she enters. Tries to keep her brother, Bowmar, grounded. Very independent. Crisco's best friend.

4. **Jimmy "Goondoggy" Blanchert:** Age 16. Bubble Butt's next-door neighbor from early childhood. Has absolutely no concept of fear. Loves the outdoors and adventure. Always ready for the next adventure, and will try anything at least once. Highly energetic and very smart.

5. **Billy "Willy" Blanchert:** Age 18. Goondoggy's older brother. A pilot who learned how to fly with Bubble Butt. The polar opposite of Goondoggy. Analyzes Bad Love Gang plans to try and calculate odds of success. Struggles to overcome caution and fear. Has a gentle spirit, and usually caves in to the group's plans. An audiophile who can wire anything for sound. Very smart.

6. **Donny "The Runt" Legrande:** Age 17. French-American, shorter in stature than the rest of the Bad Love Gang. Son of a talented aircraft mechanic. A resourceful mechanical genius who can fix or improve any and all internal combustion engines. Not afraid to take on a fight. Loyal friend.

7. **David "Crazy Ike" Eichenmuller:** Age 18. German-Irish American who can speak perfect German and English. Covered head to toe with freckles. A bit of a troublemaker who generally ignores rules/laws. Can steal anything and lie his way out of trouble. Smart, and headed to journalism school. Always entertaining.

8. **Karen "Crisco" O'Sullivan:** Age 15+. Irish-Catholic American and the oldest of 11 children. Overly mature for her age, a good athlete, and "street-smart." Interested in nursing and photography. Super cute with blonde hair, blue eyes, mature voice for her age, and a perfect body—except for a slightly disproportionate booty. Cleopatra's best friend.

9. **Frankie "Spaghetti Head" Russo:** Age 16. Italian-Catholic American, a relatively new addition to the Bad Love Gang.

Strong Italian family background. Speaks with an Italian accent and adds a Mafia-style touch to the gang. Has incredibly thick, curly dark hair. Good at calculating damage and destruction.

10. **Gary "the Pud" Jacobson:** Age 15. Great at doing tedious and/or time-consuming jobs. Understands wireless communication devices backwards and forwards. Got his nickname for being average in every sport as a kid. Resourceful, dependable, and reliable. Cynical sense of humor.

11. **Aaron "Meatball" Eisen:** Age 16. From an American-Jewish family. A jack-of-all-trades who can fix anything mechanical or electrical. Always ready to lend a helping hand. Has a true heart of gold. A problem solver and totally street-smart. A great cook. Fathered a child (Elijah) during the group's first time-travel mission.

12. **Paul "Waldo" Thompson:** Age 43. A Korean War Medal of Honor recipient. Works in procurement at Oak Ridge National Laboratory. A gun collector and firearms expert. Loves to camp, play cards, talk about everything under the sun. Married to Mary with no children. Together, they virtually "adopted" the entire Bad Love Gang and serve as surrogate parents. Their home is always open to the gang. Devoted to Mary.

13. **Mary Thompson:** Age 42. Married to Waldo and surrogate mom to the Bad Love Gang. Incredibly nice, sweet, and nonjudgmental: a peacemaker. Worries about the gang's adventures and encourages Waldo to "protect their children." Uniquely, never assigned a nickname by the Bad Love Gang. Devoted to Waldo.

14. **Danny "Tater" Ford:** Age 16. A southern boy to his core from a military family. Born in Columbus, Georgia; moved to Oak Ridge, Tennessee at age eight. The Bad Love Gang's continual source of Southern-fried humor. Terrific sense of humor and uncanny wit. Always entertaining. Always ready for adventure.

ADDED BAD LOVE GANG FROM THE 1944 RESCUE MISSION

15. **Jack "Bucky" Smith:** Age 26. West Point graduate, in 1940. US-AAF Captain and Special Forces WWII pilot. Personally chosen by President Franklin Roosevelt as the first White Hole Project test pilot. Has top-secret clearance to Area 51. Was lost in time on his inaugural time-travel mission, until rescued by the Bad Love Gang. Returned with the Bad Love Gang in November 1974 and has become BB's de facto big brother. Smart, courageous, handsome, great at strategy and hard to kill.

16. **Darby "Pumpkin" Nelson:** Age 22. British by heritage, from London, England. Adopted: parents both killed in a Nazi bombing raid on London. Navigator extraordinaire, and also trained as a pilot. Joined the Bad Love Gang along with Bucky during the Phantom Fortress mission, and returned with the gang to November 1974. Adopted Jewish orphan boy Benzion "Ben" Kaplan. Great British wit and total team player. Face turns orange when embarrassed.

17. **Benzion "Ben" Kaplan:** Age 8. Jewish orphan boy on the run from Nazi authorities during the Holocaust. Rescued by the Bad Love Gang in November 1944 and brought back to the future, along with Bucky and Pumpkin. Adopted by Pumpkin. Good at math. Wants to become a pilot. Represents part of the future of the Bad Love Gang.

TABLE OF CONTENTS

CHAPTER ONE:

THE BIG BANG IN 1975

"I know not with what weapons World War III will be fought,
but World War IV will be fought with sticks and stones."
—Albert Einstein

December 31, 1974 at 11:00 PM local time,
The White Hole Project in Oak Ridge, Tennessee

T he entire Bad Love Gang had decided to celebrate New Year's Eve
together at the White Hole Project. It was the very first time they
had all been assembled together in one place since they completed their
first White Hole time-travel mission to save Jews and Gypsies from the
Holocaust in November 1944. They had successfully rescued thirteen
souls from certain death in the Holocaust at Chelmno, Poland, using
a famous WWII B-17 Flying Fortress known in the history books as
the "Phantom Fortress." The group had returned from their inaugural
time-travel rescue mission just over five weeks ago, on November 21,
1974. Three new members had returned with the group as a result
of the rescue mission; USAAF Captain Jack "Bucky" Smith, USAAF
Sergeant Darby "Pumpkin" Nelson, and eight-year-old Jewish orphan
Benzion "Ben" Kaplan had all been added to the ranks of the Bad Love
Gang. Pumpkin had officially adopted Ben, and in addition Bucky,
Pumpkin, and Ben were all just getting accustomed to their new lives

1

"in the future" (to them) of 1974 Oak Ridge, Tennessee. Unbeknownst to the group at this very moment, Borya Krovopuskov (whose Russian first name meant "battle, war or fight" and last name meant "to let blood") had arrived dressed in full battle gear at the secret tunnel entrance to the White Hole Project.

Borya, known locally only by his American name "Russ Krovo," had an impressive and fascinating espionage lineage to the Russian KGB, dating back to his education at the Moscow D. Mendeleev Institute of Chemical Technology (MCTI). Of historic and related interest, Dmitri Mendeleev (the namesake of MCTI) was a Russian chemist and inventor best known for formulating the periodic table of chemical elements and the periodic law which he used to better define the properties of some known elements, not least of which was the valence and atomic weight of uranium. Russ Krovo, an outstanding Russian scholar/athlete from his youth, was believed to be a budding espionage superstar by his handlers. Fluent in English and five other languages, he was groomed and trained by the NKGB (People's Commissariat for State Security—a forerunner of the KGB) before he graduated from MCTI with an advanced degree in chemical engineering. Upon graduation in early 1944 at age twenty-three, he was sent to New York City to work directly under the tutelage of the infamous and notorious Russian spy, Leonid Romanovich Kvasnikov.

Leonid Romanovich Kvasnikov was also a Russian chemical engineer who graduated with honors from the Moscow Institute of Chemical Machine-Building in 1934, and joined the KGB in 1938 as a specialist in scientific-technical intelligence. He swiftly rose to become the chief of the KGB scientific intelligence section, and was one of the forerunners of work in the foreign intelligence on atomic weapons development in 1940. Kvasnikov, working from Moscow, supervised the initial KGB penetration of the British and American atomic bomb projects. Kvasnikov worked very closely with Pavel Fitin, the head of KGB's foreign intelligence unit, who was a strong proponent of and totally convinced that the Russia needed to develop nuclear weapons. In 1943, Kvasnikov was sent to New York City under diplomatic cover. He was a consummate professional who understood and could manage the intricacies of scientific and technical intelligence related to nuclear weapons development. Kvasnikov competently constructed an espionage group that included the famous spies Klaus Fuchs and Julius Rosenberg, who successfully passed secrets of the US atomic bomb to the Russians. It was Kvasnikov who personally trained Borya Krovopuskov (Russ Krovo).

Kvasnikov immediately recognized that he had someone very special as he trained Borya/Russ for his evolving role as a spy in America. Kvasnikov was immersed in espionage focused on stealing America's atomic bomb secrets from the Manhattan Project in Los Alamos, New Mexico. However, he had become quite intrigued by just a few snippets of intercepted and decoded American messages that suggested some sort of ultra-top-secret activity connected America's mysterious, remote, and well-protected air base (Area 51) in the southwestern Nevada desert to the Manhattan Project construction in Oak Ridge, Tennessee. Kvasnikov made the forward thinking and trend-setting executive decision to make Borya Krovopuskov (Russ Krovo) the focal point of his prototypical, long-term sleeper cell unit for espionage in America. He planned to assign Krovo to build a spy unit in Middle America and to try and infiltrate the Manhattan Project work at Oak Ridge, Tennessee with a longer-range goal of uncovering the suspected top-secret link between the secret airbase in the Nevada desert and the Manhattan Project in Oak Ridge. What neither Kvasnikov nor Krovo could have imagined was just how long it would take for Krovo to break his cover and spring into action.

With his paperwork, identity, and background successfully altered after spending invaluable time and intense training with Kvasnikov in New York, Russ Krovo, with his impressive academic credentials, moved to Oak Ridge in late 1944 and landed a job working at the K-25 plant. K-25 was the code name given by the Manhattan Project for the program to produce enriched uranium for atomic bombs, using the gaseous diffusion method in which gaseous uranium-235 (the fissionable uranium isotope for the atomic bomb) was separated from naturally occurring uranium-238 through an incredibly fine mesh. This separation process was extremely space-intensive, requiring a very large building. When it was finished in 1944, the mile long, U-shaped, K-25 gaseous diffusion plant covered 44 acres, was four stories high, and was the world's largest building, comprising over 1,640,000 square feet.

As the incredibly massive K-25 project was undergoing construction, the simultaneous undertaking of the adjacent White Hole Project went virtually unnoticed. The White Hole Project time-travel machine was constructed deep underground and required similar innovative foundation techniques as the K-25 gaseous diffusion plant. All those involved in its construction were told and made to believe that the White Hole was a necessary component of the K-25 plant functionality. The White Hole was connected to the K-25 plant by a long, wide, drivable tunnel, with adjacent narrow-gauge railroad tracks for transporting building supplies and heavy equipment. That connecting entrance tunnel was very heavily guarded, required high-level top-secret clearance to enter, and *was the only way to get building materials in and out* of the White Hole Project. There was one secret emergency exit tunnel for the precious few staff allowed to work at the White Hole, which was known only to a few on-site workers and not to be used except for a dire emergency event.

Captain Jack "Bucky" Smith was the first and only test pilot for the White Hole Project, and had the highest national security clearance of any US Army Air Forces (USAAF) officer in 1944-1945. He had top-secret access to come and go at Indian Springs Airfield (Area 51) in Nevada and the White Hole Project in Oak Ridge Tennessee. In the late morning of April 13, 1945, Bucky and two other American officers were walking through a long hallway lined with 1940's "computers" in the K-25 plant on their way to the heavily-guarded entrance tunnel to the White Hole Project. By chance, they happened to walk right by Russ Krovo, who was making his routine morning rounds to check on K-25 equipment operations. Krovo, for his part, had never before seen Bucky or this group of officers on the premises, and noticed that one of the officers was a tough-looking general, and the other a colonel who looked a bit young for the part. As his training had prepared him, Krovo tried his best to take mental pictures of the faces of all three men, despite the brevity of the encounter, and imprint those pictures in his memory bank. His desire to remember these three faces was enhanced even further because the very next day, for unknown reasons, the heavily-guarded entryway that these men had accessed was completely sealed off, closed for good—and no longer guarded. What he failed to notice was that Bucky took the same mental picture of his face, as he was looking hard at the other two officers.

On this New Year's Eve of December 31, 1974, nearly 30 years had passed. Borya Krovopuskov (Russ Krovo) was 54 years old, and held the record as heading the oldest and longest Soviet Union KGB sleeper cell unit in modern Soviet/American history. He was married to Catherine, and they had two children (Robert, or Bobby, and Natalie Krovo)—both of whom were now in college. Russ and Cathy lived in Knoxville, and Russ continued to work at the Oak Ridge National Laboratory (ORNL). Cathy Krovo, seven years younger than Russ and equally committed to their partnership in Soviet espionage, held a PhD in political science, and taught international studies along with both Russian and Chinese language classes at the University of Tennessee, Knoxville (UTK). UT Knoxville, founded in 1794—two years before Tennessee became the 16th state—functioned as the flagship campus of the University of Tennessee system. The top three home countries of international students at UTK were China, India, and Iran, all contributing endless possibilities to Cathy's role in expanding their Soviet sleeper cell activities in America.

Russ worked under the new director of the Oak Ridge National Laboratory, Herman Postma. On January 1, 1974, Postma was appointed director of Oak Ridge National Laboratory and was the first director not to have worked on the WWII era Manhattan Project. Postma was in the process of making drastic changes to the laboratory; Russ was in the thick of those changes, being able to provide valuable historic references to Postma regarding the site's continuous evolution since late 1944. Postma was focused on nuclear fusion (a nuclear reaction in which atomic nuclei of low atomic number fuse to form a heavier nucleus with the release of energy) research rather than fission (a nuclear reaction in which a heavy nucleus splits on impact with another particle, with the release of energy), to which the lab had traditionally been associated. This new priority switch from fission to fusion played well, insofar as Russ was concerned.

Russ Krovo had never forgotten or been swayed from his primary focus to determine a possible connection between what had come to be called Area 51 and the Oak Ridge National Laboratory. Nevertheless, he was already a living legend and a hero of the KGB back in Russia, for providing 30 years of continuous information from ORNL and creating an American espionage sleeper cell in that time frame. All of his original handlers had been handsomely promoted within the

KGB. They discreetly discussed among themselves how glorious the day would be when Krovo returned to Moscow. They would have the biggest KGB welcome-home celebration ever held.

Russ had made it his personal mission to systematically hike the backwoods trails around the K-25 site. He had done this for many years, both for exercise (he kept himself in great physical shape) and hoping by chance to discover anything unusual. The K-25 site property borders the Clinch River and originally occupied about 1,300 acres, with more than half of it still closed off by security fences. Earlier that day, while taking a New Year's Eve hike along the eastern and southern fringes of the K-25 acreage, he witnessed two motorcycles in the distance; they both seemed to disappear, both visually and audibly. Russ rubbed his eyes and ears, but the bikes were gone. He then made a beeline to their last location and came to a dry ravine, where he saw signs of motorcycle tire tracks going up and down both sides of the ravine. He quietly made his way down into the ravine, searching hard for signs of the two motorcycles. As he looked under two fallen trees, staring up the ravine to the hillside, he saw the outline of a closed hatch or entryway. Russ could certainly be utterly ruthless—but at that moment, he was concerned that he was alone, unarmed, and outnumbered. He proceeded to very quickly inspect the outside of the hatch, then decided to return that night properly armed, and with help.

At 11:00 PM on December 31, 1974, Borya/Russ returned to the entryway hatch. This time, he was dressed and ready for action in black army fatigues with a black mask to cover his face in the event that he did directly encounter people. He was armed with an M16A1 assault rifle and three 30-round clips, plus his new .45 caliber ACP Colt 70 Series Gold Cup National Match 1911 pistol and four extra clips. After living in America for thirty plus years, Russ had kept his cover clean, knowing everything about American firearms. He could hold his ground well when talking with the experts at local and regional gun shows. He also carried the Gerber Mark II fighting knife. His wife Cathy was likewise dressed in black fatigues and armed with her own Colt .45 ACP pistol; she was waiting in a Jeep on the dirt road nearest the entrance. His personally recruited and most-trusted local associate, Mikhail Smirnov (known locally as Michael Smith), was guarding the entrance from the ravine with his MI6A1 assault rifle while Russ proceeded to open the hatch and enter the tunnel.

As Russ entered the tunnel, there was no one immediately in sight. He cautiously began his walk, quickly noticing that he was walking on a downhill slope. He very carefully and slowly walked for nearly a quarter mile, stopping frequently to look ahead and listen carefully for any sounds of human activity until he encountered several Honda dirt bikes and one Harley Davidson dirt bike parked in the tunnel. He proceeded to systematically slit all the spark plug wires using his Gerber fighting knife. After rendering the motorcycles unusable, he then continued for about another city block and came to the end of the tunnel, where there was a very large door held shut by a wheel latch, like you might see on a submarine. It was 11:45 PM as he began to turn the wheel latch to gain entrance to the White Hole Project.

Inside the vault of the White Hole Project at the same time, the entire Bad Love Gang was present and celebrating New Year's Eve together. Yours truly, Bubble Butt (AKA BB or Kevin Schafer) was playing DJ—and I had quite a song list to play for New Year's Eve 1975! We were in a very festive mood, especially being all together in one place for the first time since returning from our incredibly adventurous and successful time-travel rescue mission, five weeks before. There were thirteen males and three females; unfortunately, we couldn't bring any friends or dates because the White Hole Project was top secret and known only to us—or so we thought—for these last few moments. Playing DJ using cassettes in my new 1974 Marantz Superscope CRS-152 boom box, I had just been ambushed by Karen "Crisco" O'Sullivan and Brianna "Cleopatra" Williams.

Cleopatra had called me out to the center stage of the lower race-track, which was covered with soft cushions and supported by the trampoline like floor. She started to remind me about how I had accused her and Crisco of having a "little bitch glitch" as we were settling into our roles aboard the B-17 Phantom Fortress, which we had named Bad Love. The thought occurred to me that everyone else seemed to be watching this developing encounter. I couldn't help but laugh because Cleo was acting all tough and serious with me, like she was some jacked-up female cop. Playing along, I announced we were finishing the 1974 Chinese zodiac year of the tiger in early February 1975, and that 1975 had been declared the International Women's Year by the United Nations. I commented on how the tigress Cleopatra was in step with the times, then loudly blurted out, "You know, Cleo, and you're such a Bad Mama Jama!" While Cleo distracted me, Crisco had snuck up behind me and got down on all fours. Cleo gave me a big shove and down I went, backwards over Crisco, who quickly sat on my legs as Cleo pounced onto my chest. Everyone else was busting a gut at these antics! Cleo quickly reached into her pocket and I thought she was going to put a toy gun to my head. Instead, she pointed a cassette tape at my face and said, "Play this, bitch boy!" At that point, my face was redder than Rudolph's nose, and the Bad Love Gang were all rolling on the floor with laughter.

By then I realized that this scene had been rehearsed, and everyone but me knew it was coming. I took the cassette and plugged it into the Marantz boombox. With their song selection, Cleopatra and Crisco were giving me a dose of my own medicine, for sure! I cranked up the volume and the song **"You're So Vain"** by Carly Simon started

9

to play. The song was written in 1971 by Carly Simon and released in November 1972, becoming a huge number one hit in the United States, Canada, Australia, and New Zealand. Interestingly, Mick Jagger provided backing vocals in the chorus; you can definitely hear his voice, if you listen carefully. Cleo and Crisco immediately started dancing together and lip syncing the words in a serenade directed at me. For a brief second, I mused about the meaning of having clouds in my coffee, which Simon had explained in a subsequent interview as representing the confusing aspects of life and love. While you can't see through the clouds of life and love, love itself seems alluring...until, like a mirage of an oasis in the desert, it turns into parched, dry sand. Within a minute, the entire Bad Love Gang was singing along, and I joined Crisco and Cleo to dance and sing together with them.

It was nearing midnight, and high time to pump up the jams just a bit. I invited everyone out on the center stage with the next song, to "play their air guitars, beat on fake drums, and dance our way into 1975." I plugged in a new cassette tape and started playing **"We're an American Band,"** by Grand Funk Railroad. It was the title song of the seventh studio album by Grand Funk Railroad, released on July 15, 1973 and certified gold a little over a month after its release. The single track "We're an American Band" became Grand Funk's first number one hit. The album's original label instructed the listeners to play "at full volume," a directive with which I had no problem complying. Nearly all of us were on the stage and to a person, we were shouting out the words, playing our air guitars, and dancing wildly. As we were rockin' out together, I noticed that Paul "Waldo" Thompson had disappeared from the group and assumed that he had to go "drain the main vein," as we Bad Love boys would often say.

The song was coming to an end, and I looked at my watch just as the clock was about to strike twelve midnight. Our world changed again at that moment. Fifty-four-year-old Borya Krovopuskov (Russ Krovo) threw the main light switch at the third-floor vault entrance above, and the White Hole vault went temporarily dark. He then fired three shots from his .45 caliber ACP Colt in rapid succession to get everyone's undivided attention. The music had stopped, and the echoes of the shots fired were deafening inside the vault. Nearly everyone had hit the deck, and they were lying face down on the center stage. Nathan "Bowmar" Williams, Bucky, and I knew the vault layout in our sleep; the three of us were all standing and staring at the third-floor entryway as Krovo threw the large light switch back to the *on* position. As my eyes came into focus, I saw a well-built man in all-black army fatigues with a black mask and piercing eyes looking down at us, with his assault rifle pointing directly at us. He said, "If any one of you moves from their position, I will not hesitate to kill just you, but every one of you." For a brief second, I could tell that he was staring directly at both me and Bucky. In Krovo's mind, Bucky and I both looked familiar, and he was mentally trying to connect the dots. He asked, "Who wants to be the spokesperson and answer my questions?"

I immediately replied, "I will answer your questions."

Krovo asked, "What is your name, and who do you all work for?"

Not wanting to give my actual name, and hoping everyone else would take my cue, I replied, "My name is Bubble Butt, and we all work for the Bad Love Gang."

Using his assault rifle, Krovo put a single round six inches in front of my toes and barked, "You will not play games with me!" I caught a hint of a possible Russian accent as he yelled at me.

David "Crazy Ike" Eichenmuller, who also caught the hint of Russian accent, was now on his feet. He looked red in the face (he was half-German, half-Irish, covered head to toe with freckles and had reddish-blond hair) and I could tell he was scared and pissed at the same time. Knowing him as well as I did, that was not a good combination of emotions for him to experience. Crazy Ike spoke German fluently from his childhood. He looked up and screamed at Krovo in perfect German (which none of us Bad Love Gang understood), "Listen here, you lousy piece of shit, we work for the Bad Love Gang. And if you kill us, there are many more where we come from who will find you, filet you like a Russian herring, and pour cheap vodka all over your bare bones, you bastard!"

Simultaneous to Crazy Ike verbally assaulting Krovo, Waldo (age 43), who was a decorated US Army Korean War Medal of Honor recipient for leading the repelling of an enemy attack in the Korean War, was on the move. Waldo had been in the bathroom when the first shots rang out. Waldo was quite the gun collector, and frequently "joked" with us about how he was "packing" on our various adventures and outings. The truth was, he frequently carried a concealed weapon— and certainly wouldn't go out on New Year's Eve empty handed. On this night, he had a Walther PPK pistol in his right ankle holster. He was now armed and moving up the steps, out of sight and planning to engage Krovo. One thing was certain: Krovo had an assault rifle pointed at all of us on the lower racetrack center stage, which included Waldo's beloved wife Mary. If any harm whatsoever was to come to Mary, God help the perpetrator; Waldo would not hesitate for one millisecond to take revenge or die trying.

The second Crazy Ike finished his German verbal lashing of Krovo, then Jimmy "Goondoggy" Blanchert (who never seemed to perceive the emotion of fear, since we were little kids) loudly echoed Ike's sentiments in English. Goondoggy had also perceived a hint of Russian accent from Krovo, and reflexively used the name *Boris* as a prototypical Russian name for addressing Krovo. "Hey! Butt-head Boris! Take that stupid mask off, drop the guns, and come on down here for a fair fight like a real man!"

Krovo was somewhat unnerved that Goondoggy had called him Boris; his name, Borya, is a diminutive of the name Boris. He first reacted to Goondoggy and said, "I look forward to either killing you or kicking your ass." Krovo, also fluent in German, was impressed with Crazy Ike's foreign language skills. Because of that, he had actually begun to wonder if Bad Love Gang was some sort of code name for the group. He then responded to Ike and me, using English. "I understand German perfectly well. I hate herring, and I love vodka. Bubble Butt, it seems you don't have much control over your gang here. I am going to give you one more chance to tell me who you work for, what this giant machine is designed to do, and how it is connected to Area 51."

Our unrehearsed delay tactics were working. Waldo had reached the third floor and circled around the balcony, staying low beneath the covered, waist-high railing. He was coming around to the right of Krovo and ready to confront him. Waldo had already determined that he couldn't risk a standoff and planned to come out shooting. He was hoping to wound and capture Krovo alive, then interrogate him. To Waldo's disadvantage, he could not risk trying to observe Krovo's stance or exact position prior to rising up for his ambush.

While shocked that Krovo had mentioned Area 51, I brushed it off, discreetly winked at Nathan "Bowmar" Williams and Captain Jack "Bucky" Smith, who was standing next to Bowmar. I answered Krovo firmly. "You know who we work for, and this machine is designed to process weapons-grade plutonium more efficiently than any machine in the history of mankind. No one on earth has even a remote chance of catching America's nuclear weapons development program, given this sovereign and superior technology. Killing the few of us will not stop a thing; you are outgunned by a nation that knows only one position."

Krovo enquired, "What position is that, Bubble Butt?"

"*First* place," I emphatically answered.

At that moment, the shit hit the fan again. Waldo popped up from his position to the right of Krovo, on the circular balcony of the third floor. Krovo was holding his assault rifle in his right hand; Waldo's first shot went through the back of Krovo's right hand, ricocheted against the rifle, and literally caused Krovo to drop the weapon. It was a fairer gunfight as Krovo swung his left hand around holding his Colt .45 ACP pistol, taking aim at Waldo. Waldo got the second shot off, which cleanly passed through Krovo's upper left abdominal sidewall as he was turning toward Waldo and crouching to a shooting position. Krovo, rapidly trying to get his first shot off, hit Waldo in the deltoid muscle of his left shoulder. Waldo immediately fired two more wild shots past Krovo, trying to confuse him as he ducked for cover. For his part, Krovo got a good look at Waldo's face and felt that he also knew that face; he just needed to process the picture. Krovo realized the gig was up. He knew he had been hit twice, but was running on pure adrenaline and training. He fired twice at Waldo's position, simultaneously pulled the large, third floor light switch to the off position, and headed out the exit tunnel.

I yelled for Bowmar, Gary "the Pud" Jacobson, Aaron "Meatball" Eisen, and Darby "Pumpkin" Nelson to get everyone off the center stage and safely under cover. I called out for Bucky, Crazy Ike, Goondoggy, Donny "the Runt" Legrande, Frankie "Spaghetti Head" Russo, and Danny "Tater" Ford to come with me and grab some guns. As we exited center stage in a hurry, I flipped on the lower level light switch to get the lights burning again. Waldo had stayed down until the lights came back on, and his left shoulder felt like it was on fire. Nevertheless, he ignored the pain and began to give chase after Krovo. I yelled up to Waldo, telling him that we were getting armed and we'd be right behind him. We ran directly to the firearms section of the wardrobe warehouse and grabbed guns, as well as extra ammunition. We all sprinted to the exit tunnel, trying to catch up to Waldo.

As we came through the hallway to the exit tunnel, we did see a small trail of blood, which we assumed was from Krovo's injuries. Krovo was in superb shape; despite suffering two bullet wounds (his right hand and left abdominal sidewall), he was outrunning Waldo by a good clip while firing his .45-caliber ACP pistol behind his back toward Waldo as he ran for the exit. As Krovo reached the outside hatch of the exit tunnel, he left the hatch open and screamed at Mikhail Smirnov to open fire into the tunnel. Smirnov quickly emptied the first thirty-round clip from his MI6A1 assault rifle into the tunnel as soon as Krovo was clear. Waldo was about halfway down the tunnel at a junction where the tunnel curved and had to stop. We were just catching up to Waldo when Smirnov started firing his second clip. It was like fireworks going off in the tunnel, only that was not the New Year's celebration that we had planned. Despite the craziness, noise, sparks and bullets flying, when I reached Waldo's position, I yelled at him. "Your big prostate saved our lives in there!"

"What the hell are you talking about, Bubble Butt?!"

I answered, "You know, your 'old-age prostate' and frequent urge to piss saved the day!"

"As soon as I kill this Russian bastard, I'm coming after you!" he quickly retorted with a smirk.

Outside the tunnel, as Krovo reached Mikhail's position, they looked at the tunnel opening and saw it was vacant, then turned and retreated quickly to rendezvous with Krovo's wife Catherine, still waiting for them on the adjacent dirt road with the Jeep running. The three of them were gone in a hurry.

When the shots stopped, we slowly made our way around the corner out to the tunnel exit and cautiously confirmed that the coast was clear. Bucky complimented Waldo on his bravery, and thanked him for confronting the enemy so decisively. Tater, in his typical southern accent, made the comment, "That guy was as crazy as a sprayed cockroach!"

"That Russian cockroach was a professional. Somehow I recognize his eyes, but I can't place him just yet. Gentlemen, we have some work to do—and decisions to make about the future of this White Hole Project," Waldo said soberly.

CHAPTER TWO:

HERE WE GO AGAIN

"Let us never forget that government is ourselves and not an alien power over us. The ultimate rulers of our democracy are not a President and senators and congressmen and government officials, but the voters of this country."
—Franklin D. Roosevelt

January 1, 1975 at 1:00 AM local time,
The White Hole Project in Oak Ridge, Tennessee

After we secured the exit tunnel and locked both the outer hatch and the entry door to the vault, the entire Bad Love Gang reassembled at the center stage of the lower racetrack of the White Hole Project. Crisco and I had first taken Waldo to the medical bay, where we had cleaned and dressed his left deltoid shoulder wound. While we worked on him, Waldo racked his brain, trying to match the Russian's eyes with a face in his memory bank. He was still drawing blanks, but not giving up. When we were done, we joined the rest of the group.

Everyone was talking a blue streak about what had just transpired. Nobody was the least bit tired, or eager to try and head home in the middle of the night with the possibility of armed Russian spies lurking about. All the motorcycles in the exit tunnel were temporarily disabled, but the Runt had extra spark plug wires at home, in his dad's workshop. We all would have had a major hike home in the morning, but Waldo and Mary had driven their Jeep to the White Hole that night, and parked on a dirt road on the opposite side of the ravine. It was not detected by our Russian visitors. Getting back to town at daybreak would take place in shifts, and the Runt and Meatball had committed to working together to get all the bikes running again later in the day.

We were all feeling the need to talk and vent, but what happened next was not exactly what I expected. USAAF Captain Jack "Bucky" Smith—the first White Hole Project test pilot, who had been instrumental in the success of our first time-travel rescue mission as the pilot of the B-17 Phantom Fortress we named Bad Love, and who had necessarily returned to November 1974 with us just over five weeks previously—stepped into the middle of the lower racetrack center stage and began to speak to the group as a whole.

"As the first test pilot for this ultra-secret White Hole Project, I was zapped in time from this very stage on March 14, 1945 on a mission to East Anglia, England, arriving there on November 14, 1944. My original global cosmic positioning device was freakishly damaged by the silent white lightening in that inaugural launch though the time travel tunnel. I was supposed to be recalled directly here to this stage in one day, or joined by others for a top-secret mission using the Phantom Fortress within three days. Three full days came and went, and nothing happened: no contact whatsoever. Then four days, five days, and six full days passed. I didn't understand what had happened, but for the first time in my life, I was truly scared and felt lost, maybe even dead but just not knowing it. After all, who knows what it is like to travel in time? I was the alpha test subject.

"The seventh day arrived, and that day we were scheduled to fly a mission to bomb the most heavily-defended oil refineries deep in the heart of the Third Reich. Pumpkin and I drove out to the plane that morning, and waiting there for us were Waldo and Bubble Butt. It was then that I first learned what had happened. Though I was scared, I was also relieved to know that there may be a way to get my life back. We flew an impossible mission, taking out a third of the heavily-defended Leuna oil refinery as a solo bomber, and then rescued thirteen precious souls from the Holocaust, all before being zapped back to this stage on November 21, 1974. Since then, you have all become my family. I am proud to say that I am part of the Bad Love Gang, and I love our motto: 'Live dangerously, have fun, don't die!'"

Everyone to a person had become quiet, focused on what Bucky had to say. He continued, uninterrupted. "It would be normal for some or all of you—anyone, for that matter—to want to go to the authorities after what happened here tonight." A few heads nodded in the affirmative and all of us were alert, wide-eyed, and carefully listening. "However, I need to tell you that I think alerting the authorities now would be a huge mistake because we are dealing with time travel, and there is something unimaginably bigger at play here than what meets the eye. I know for a fact that *I have seen that Russian agent's eyes before,* and that can only mean one thing: I saw those eyes on or before my inaugural time travel launch on March 14, 1945. If we blow this project open now, we will lose control over what happened back then, as well as what happens in the future with this White Hole Project. I had the nation's highest top-secret clearance in 1945, with access to what you now call Area 51, and to this White Hole Project when Oak Ridge was completely a secret city and surrounded by fences. I boarded the alien spaceship that crashed in Area 51 on June 17, 1942, and witnessed the aliens using a machine just like this to escape. The exotic matter that makes this machine work came directly from that alien ship. I know President Roosevelt and his top scientific advisor, Vannevar Bush, and personally shared the details of the alien ship experience when I met with them at the White House!"

Waldo, physically expended from the night's events and resting his head in Mary's lap while she gently caressed his head, neck and uninjured right shoulder, said in a low voice, "I also know that I have seen that Russian's beady eyes before, and I just can't place them with his face. I'm sure it will come to me sooner or later. I'd rather catch or kill that son of a bitch than trust someone else to do it for us!"

Bowmar, totally engaged in what Bucky had to say, asked the question that was also on the tip of my tongue. "If we continue to keep this White Hole Project our secret, notwithstanding the Russian spies who now know some important technology is here, then what do you think we should do next, exactly?"

Bucky did not hesitate, and replied passionately, "We have to go back to 1945, and establish the security and future of this project from that point forward! This breach in the White Hole Project security started thirty years ago; I am certain of that. Otherwise, I fear that tonight's events are only the tip of proverbial iceberg! Telling the authorities now will take this out of our hands for good, and I cannot help but feel responsible for this White Hole Project and what is happening to it."

Frankie "Spaghetti Head" Russo weighed in. "Me and my family, we've never trusted any 'authorities' with important stuff. The authorities will screw you *and* screw up what they're supposed to do, every time. That's why we supposedly have elections in America, to throw out the crooked politicians every few years! No, we trust *family*—and that's it."

Bowmar then enquired, "Going back to the origins actually makes perfect sense to me, but where do you start? This White Hole is a project of such gigantic dimensions."

I jumped in at that point. "My mother always taught me that anytime you want to get something done, start at the top!"

Bucky smiled and said, "Spaghetti Head and BB are both right. I trust all of you as family now, to deal with this. I recommend that we start at the very, *very* top, directly with President Franklin Delano Roosevelt. He knows me, and personally selected me to be the first White Hole Project test pilot. If we go visit him in late March 1945 or after, he will know that I have been presumed missing or dead since the inaugural time travel launch, and he will definitely meet with us."

Bowmar, our walking, talking encyclopedia, interjected with some vital history. "Roosevelt died in the afternoon of April 12, 1945 at the Little White House in Warm Springs, Georgia, of a sudden, massive, and rapidly fatal stroke. We would have to make the time travel trip sometime between March twenty-first and April twelfth of 1945, based on Bucky's assessment of best timing."

Tater couldn't help but add a word in his heaviest Southern accent. "Georgia is my home state, and I'd be happier than a tornado in a trailer park if I could get back there on a little time-travel mission. I'd be right at home there, sneaking around and trying to find these Russkie spies before they get a head start!"

As usual, Tater's remarks brought some much-needed comic relief to the group, making everyone laugh and relax a little bit. Crisco, always being street smart and practical, then asked a question that was on nearly everyone's minds, including mine. "If we don't tell the authorities, how are we ever gonna keep us and this place safe from this Russian spy or spies, who now know about its location?"

Waldo responded, "I estimate that there were a minimum of three spies involved here tonight: the one we engaged, whom we'll call Boris, as Goondoggy labeled him—" We all interrupted him, yelling out "GOON-DOGGY!" Goondoggy proudly stood and took a bow. Waldo continued, "The shooter outside, who unloaded two full clips into the tunnel as Boris cleared the exit, and a driver who was waiting to take them away.

Regarding Crisco's question, I really think that Boris was potentially planning to kill us all after he finished interrogating us; his eyes were too cold and calculating for someone who would have a problem with that." This comment sent a chill down everyone's spine. "Think about it; no one but us knows this place is here. We are out in the middle of nowhere, beyond sight and sound; he chose to directly confront us, rather than simply spy on us; he did not hesitate to fire rounds to get our attention; and he also put a round in front of BB's feet. I was totally convinced that he meant business in a bad way, and that is why I made haste to shoot first rather than try to talk him down. All that said, he wasn't expecting me and didn't know where I came from. I didn't kill him, but he was hit twice and is injured. He and his two 'friends' are not coming back soon. They are foreign spies in our country and they do not want to be recognized, caught or killed, lest their hard-earned cover is blown. I suspect they will report their findings here tonight to their superiors, and will be given instructions to lay low and remain undetected before making any attempt to reengage in some fashion. Bucky and I will take steps to increase the security here, but Boris and his helpers are off the grid for now. By the way, Crazy Ike, what the hell did you say when you yelled at Boris in German?"

Crazy Ike smiled, blushed a little bit, said he was really pissed-off that some stranger in a black mask was pointing guns at us and repeated in English his German rant directed at Boris. "Listen here you lousy piece of shit, we work for the Bad Love Gang and if you kill us, there are many more where we come from who will find you, filet you like a Russian herring, and pour cheap vodka all over your bare bones, you bastard!"

We all just busted a gut at Crazy Ike's rant. Spaghetti Head commented in his Italian accent, "I just saw *The Godfather: Part II* with my whole family, and I feel like I'm living in a movie! Crazy Ike, you would fit in just great with the Corleone crime family as a hired hand! We need to have you go make Boris and his friends 'an offer they can't refuse!'"

Cleopatra gave Crazy Ike a hug and said, "For being such a total white boy, I think my friend Shaft might even hire you!" We all laughed again!

Waldo added, "Actually, that was just perfect! Boris got that message in Ike's perfect German, and he understood every word. Basically, Ike told him we were not alone, and said it in such a crazy way that Boris couldn't ignore it. I'd say that we collectively put some significant doubts in his mind about this place and its purpose. So, BB, why did you tell Boris that this place processes weapons-grade plutonium?"

"I thought about telling him that it made weapons-grade toilet paper, and to stick it up his ass!" I exclaimed. "But I knew we were running out of time, and was thinking that his trigger finger was getting itchy, so I had to give him something plausible that fit in with our proximity to the Oak Ridge National Laboratory and nearby K-25 site. I was hoping he would report back to his superiors that we may have some advantage in nuclear weapons technology that they should lose sleep over. What blew me away was Boris mentioning Area 51! That means they suspect there's some sort of connection between this site and Area 51, and that is a scary thought!"

Bucky took over once again. "Area 51 and the alien spaceship that is hidden there are America's most closely guarded secrets from all espionage, both foreign and domestic. From June 1942 until today, you can bet that anyone spying on America wants to know exactly what is going on there! What is amazing, as BB pointed out, is that Boris knows or suspects a connection between this site in Oak Ridge and Area 51 in Nevada. It further cements the urgency that we get to Roosevelt for a discussion about any potential security breaches to the White Hole Project, especially as related to Russian espionage activity. I propose that Bowmar,

Bubble Butt, Waldo, and I design a time-travel mission correlating with Bowmar's chronology parameters, to meet directly with President Franklin D. Roosevelt and see if this breach in security started thirty years ago, as I strongly suspect. If we come up empty handed or reach a dead end, then we go to the authorities with disclosure of the White Hole Project and what happened here tonight. If we find favor with Roosevelt, if he shares valuable information and is supportive of our mission to protect the integrity and security of the White Hole Project, then we stay the course and continue to keep the White Hole Project our secret."

Truly amazed by how this entire discussion had unfolded, I asked the group for a vote. "All those in favor of proceeding as Bucky has described, say 'aye.'" The ayes were strong and unhesitating. "All those opposed, say 'nay.'" The room was silent.

Willy spoke up for the first time since the shots had been fired. "Oh, shit! Here we go again!"

As we finished our group discussion, Borya Krovopuskov (Russ Krovo), his wife Catherine (Cathy), and their associate Mikhail Smirnov (Michael Smith) had arrived at a Russian safe house, 25 miles to the east in Knoxville, Tennessee. A local Russian KGB agent/doctor had come to the safe house to deal with Krovo's bullet wounds from earlier that night. Using sophisticated encrypted communication technology at the safe house, Krovo transmitted a message to his designated Russian KGB office. *Made contact with suspected Volunteer (Tennessee) and Gambling (Nevada) nexus. Injured but will recover. Request a meeting.* Shortly thereafter, he received a response: *The Apples are delicious, you should try one.* Cathy commented, "I love visiting New York! *The Wiz* is starting at the Majestic Theater later this week. I will make that part of our plans!"

CHAPTER THREE:

FACE TO FACE WITH ROOSEVELT

"The only limit to our realization of tomorrow will be our doubts
of today. Let us move forward with strong and active faith."
—From FDR's undelivered Jefferson Day Address,
scheduled to be broadcast over the radio on April 13, 1945.

April 12, 1945 at 9:30 AM local time in Warm Springs, Georgia

B ucky, Waldo, Bowmar, Tater, and I (Bubble Butt) were zapped by
the White Hole Project time travel machine to a lightly wooded
area adjacent to the city of Warm Springs, Georgia and a short walking
distance to the entrance of President Roosevelt's Little White House.
Captain Jack "Bucky" Smith of the US Army Air Forces (USAAF)
was dressed just as he had been when last seen, at the time of the
inaugural White Hole Project time travel launch on March 14, 1945.
Paul "Waldo" Thompson maintained his now-cherished persona as
a US Army Air Force two-star major general. I continued in my role
as USAAF Colonel Kevin "Bubble Butt" Schafer, and Bowmar was
playing the role of Tuskegee Airman First Lieutenant Nathan Williams. The Tuskegee Airmen were the first African-American pilots in
United States military history, and they flew with distinction during
World War II. Finally, Danny "Tater" Ford, the son of a military family
from Columbus, Georgia, decided to break away from our USAAF

crowd and pose as a US Marine Corps officer, First Lieutenant Danny Ford. Marine commissioned officers are distinguished by their commission, which is the formal written authority issued in the name of the President of the United States that confers the rank and authority of a Marine officer. Commissioned Marine officers carry the special trust and confidence of the President of the United States. While I had reservations about Tater's motivations, I suspected that he could easily talk the ears off the Marine Corps sentry guards posted at the entrance to Roosevelt's Little White House while we met with the president inside. In addition, Tater had the knack of adding some levity to what would soon be an otherwise painfully serious task in front of us.

The five of us landed safely, and no one got stung by the silent white lightning during the White Hole time tunnel trip. From my perspective, it was a very quick, nearly spontaneous ride from Saturday, April 12, 1975 in Oak Ridge, Tennessee to Thursday, April 12, 1945 in Warm Springs, Georgia—especially when compared to my first time-travel trip to East Anglia, England the previous November. This particular day in history, Thursday April 12, 1945, was a hot day in Warm Springs and the locals were planning an early dinner barbecue, organized by the mayor and the manager of the Warm Springs Hotel in honor of the President. As we landed, for reasons I just can't logically explain, my "music brain" was already playing the song **"Midnight Train to Georgia"** by Gladys Knight & The Pips. Released in August 1973 and becoming a number one hit single, the song tells the story of a Georgia man who sells all his worldly possessions and leaves his home state of Georgia to try and make the big-time in Los Angeles, California. Things don't work out in L.A., so he heads back home with his lady friend to live in a simpler place and time in his beloved state of Georgia. Perhaps that is exactly what President Roosevelt was looking for when he discovered the soothing, warm spring water and laid-back life style of Warm Springs, Georgia in the midst of a grueling life of high-power politics—ending the Great Depression, leading America into and nearly through World War II, and facing continuous global drama of historic proportions.

Not surprisingly, as we shook our heads clear after the time-travel landing, Tater was the first to speak, with his classic Southern accent. "Man, it's great to be back in Georgia again, and I'm finer than frog hair split four ways! But it's already hotter than a billy goat's ass in a pepper patch out here. Which reminds me to tell y'all, as Roosevelt's VP, Harry Truman, would say, 'Never kick a cow turd on a hot day!'"

I'm sitting there simultaneously laughing and trying to process what the heck Tater just said, and Bowmar's high IQ brain filter just got busted to pieces! Bowmar enquired, "What does not kicking a cow turd on a hot day have to do with this mission?"

Tater, using his heaviest Southern drawl, replied, "Well there, Bowmar, for being as smart as all get out, I guess I gotcha on that one. You are in my country now, Braniac Boy, and you need to listen up! It means: Don't go asking for trouble. Let's just run this here little time-travel reconnaissance mission nice and smooth, in my beloved home state of Georgia. Got it?"

Bowmar pointed at Tater with a half-scowl, half-smirk on his face as we all laughed. That was especially therapeutic for Bucky, who was soon to bring us face to face with President Franklin Delano Roosevelt (FDR). Bucky, having previously met with Roosevelt, had a deep personal respect and admiration for America's only four-term president, and was concerned about the dynamics of the upcoming interaction. We all knew something everyone else present in Warm Springs that day did not: that FDR was living his last few hours on Earth, and we were going to speak with him on this very fateful day, one way or another. Waldo, as usual, brought us all back into focus and reminded us to "pull it together," and "get our asses moving" towards the Little White House. We picked ourselves up, rehearsed the outline of our planned meeting with President Roosevelt one last time, and then got underway on foot.

Roosevelt, stricken in 1921 and recovering from the effects of polio (or what may have actually been Guillain-Barre syndrome) had come to Warm Springs, Georgia for the first time in October 1924. The attraction was the warm water of the natural spring located there, near Pine Mountain, with an average temperature of 88 degrees. The water was rich in minerals, including sodium, magnesium, iron, silica, sulfur, fluoride, and several others, giving the water a certain silky feeling. After first swimming in this particular spring water, Roosevelt said that he had never felt water so pleasant—and he was able to stand unassisted in four feet of water. In 1932, while serving as the governor of New York, FDR had a white clapboard cottage built on the slopes of Pine Mountain. The cost of the construction at that time was $8,738, including the landscaping work. During FDR's four elected terms as the 32nd president, the cottage became known as the Little White House. Roosevelt became quite attached to the local people of Warm Springs, and they inspired him in developing practical solutions to many of the nation's problems during his presidency.

The plan this morning was for us to meet face to face with President Roosevelt at close to 10:30 AM in his bedroom at the Little White House, while most of his personal staff were scheduled to briefly be off-site enjoying a swim in the pool or warm springs. We needed to be finished no later than 11:30 AM. Roosevelt was scheduled to sit at noon for artist Madame Shoumatoff, who was there to paint his portrait on this day. Bucky was personally acquainted with the president, having first met him on October 1, 1942, when he dined at the White House with FDR and his most-trusted scientific advisor,

Vannevar Bush. Bucky gave them his eyewitness account of the alien spacecraft crash at Indian Springs Airfield, or Groom Dry Lake (Area 51), on June 17, 1942 and the discovery of exotic matter that night. Roosevelt immediately liked Bucky's genuine and unassuming personality and personally chose him as the first test pilot for the White Hole Project time travel machine. Bucky had launched on March 14, 1945 (nearly one month prior to the date of this mission); he was lost and presumed dead on the inaugural time travel test flight. Roosevelt had written many letters to grieving parents of fallen soldiers, but felt personally responsible for the loss of Bucky. He had done his best to console Bucky's heartbroken parents, who lived in Denver, Colorado. A formal military memorial service, complete with a 21-gun salute, was held in Denver in Bucky's honor. Roosevelt would be shocked to hear from and then actually see Bucky alive. For his part, Bucky hoped to bring FDR some hope, joy, and wonder in the waning moments of his amazing and historic life here on earth.

Bucky, Bowmar, Waldo and I would try to visit directly with FDR under the veil of "classified military business," but our mission was to find out who else knew about the fate of the White Hole Project time travel machine and take the necessary steps to protect the integrity, secrecy, and future of the White Hole time machine, avoiding destruction, uncertainty, or maleficence. Our group had planned in advance to provide irrefutable evidence to Roosevelt that we were in control of the White Hole Project. In addition, Bowmar and I had prepared a letter that we hoped Roosevelt would sign, giving Bucky, Waldo and their designees the presidential authority to take whatever steps they deemed necessary to accomplish this directive.

As the five of us arrived at the Marine Corps sentry post at the entrance to the Little White House, it was 10:20 AM. The president had been enjoying the company of his cousins, friends, and close advisors, most of whom were indeed enjoying a morning swim at the pool or warm springs. The president was in his bedroom, quietly working at his desk, editing his Jefferson Day Address—which was scheduled to be delivered by radio broadcast the following day, April 13, 1945. The Marine Corps sentry on duty, Sergeant David Carter, saluted us and immediately enquired as to the purpose of our presence and business there, indicating that he had not been told to expect a group of four Air Force officers and a Marine officer. Waldo introduced himself as General Paul Thompson and introduced Captain Jack "Bucky" Smith, indicating that we were there with top-secret, highly-classified, military information for the president and that our very presence and delivery of this information could only be verified by Captain Smith speaking directly to the president. Sergeant Carter was polite and cooperative, but understandably appeared a bit uncertain about the validity of our request. He asked us to wait, and made a call directly to the President's desk phone. "Mr. President, I am sorry to bother you, but there are several officers here who say they have classified military information for you. One of these officers says he knows you personally, and to tell you his name is Captain Jack 'Bucky' Smith."

On the other end of the line, President Roosevelt stopped writing, leaned back in his chair in rapid thought and disbelief, and muttered, "Oh, my God!" There was a lengthy pause before Sergeant Carter finally asked, "What should I tell them, Mr. President?"

FDR responded, "Ask Captain Smith exactly where he was the night of June 17, 1942. I will hold on the line for his answer."

Sergeant Carter leaned out the door of his white, hexagonal guard post enclosure and asked Bucky of his whereabouts on the night of June 17, 1942. He then relayed Bucky's prompt answer to FDR.

"Mr. President, he says that he is a native of Denver, Colorado, a West Point graduate, and a special ops B-17 pilot. He was at the Indian

Springs Airfield, also called Groom Dry Lake, in the remote Nevada desert that night. He stated that he was the ranking officer present there that evening. He didn't pause for a second, sir."

"Put Captain Smith on the phone with me now. Let him shut the door while we talk, and keep an eye on the party that came with him," FDR responded.

"Yes sir, Mr. President!" Sergeant Carter promptly replied.

Sergeant Carter then held the guard post door open for Bucky and said, "The president wishes to speak with you privately, sir." He handed the phone to Bucky and then joined me, Bowmar, Waldo, and Tater for small talk just outside the guard post.

Inside the guard post with the door shut, Bucky took the phone. "Mr. President, it's really me, Bucky, and I am alive. There was a problem with the inaugural White Hole Project test launch; I was temporarily lost in time. The brave men who are here with me now used the White Hole Project time travel machine to rescue not only me, but also a small group of Jews and gypsies in Poland from certain death at the hands of the Nazis. The very day they rescued me, I went back with them to the year 1974, and I am now here to speak with you from the year 1975."

Roosevelt, not known to be too emotional, was overcome with wonder and other feelings as he listened to Bucky's voice and thought about the implications. He knew this voice, and it was like hearing from and speaking to someone from beyond the grave. FDR replied, "Bucky, I know it is you, I know your voice. Put Sergeant Carter back on the phone and bring who you must from your group with you. We will have about thirty minutes to talk, and we can meet in total privacy here in my bedroom. I don't want anyone to know about this meeting; this is quite literally off the record."

FDR gave specific instructions to Sergeant Carter, then hung up. We left Tater there to schmooze with Carter and any other Marine guards on duty, just in case we needed any "favors" as we departed. Bucky, Waldo, Bowmar, and I were then escorted down to the Little White House under a separate, two-Marine guard detail.

The Little White House cottage entrance was flanked by four white columns. A cozy, six-room, Colonial Revival structure, it was constructed of Georgia pine—clearly evident in the wall and ceiling paneling inside. Three of the rooms were bedrooms: one for President Roosevelt, one for his wife, Eleanor—located to the left of the entryway and sharing the connecting bathroom with the president—and one for his personal secretary. The other rooms were an entrance hall, a kitchen to the right of the entryway, and a living room/dining room combination straight ahead, with an attached back deck having a panoramic view of the beautiful wooded surroundings. We were all struck by the fact that FDR's Little White House was comfortable, inviting and nice, but by no means extravagant or overstated in any way, as you might expect with someone as historically important and powerful as President Roosevelt.

The president had been resting and recuperating at the Little White House since arriving in Warm Springs on March 30, 1945, following a demanding and rigorous negotiating trip to the Yalta conference in February, a meeting that was designed to help navigate the world through the end of World War II. Also present during this specific presidential trip to Warm Springs in April 1945 were FDR's cousins Margaret "Daisy" Suckley and Laura "Polly" Delano, his secretary Grace Tully, various military aides, his personal doctor Dr. Howard Bruenn, and FDR's beloved mistress, Lucy Mercer Rutherfurd.

It was Lucy who had arranged to bring along her friend and Ukrainian-born artist Madame Elizabeth Shoumatoff, who was working on a "new" presidential portrait at the time. Eleanor Roosevelt did not come to Warm Springs, Georgia this trip; she was in Washington,

D.C. on this day in 1945. As we approached the front door, FDR's rather famous Scottish Terrier, named Fala, and his cousin Polly's Irish Setter, Sister, both watched us approach through the paned glass windows flanking the door. We were escorted through the front door and made an immediate left turn through Eleanor's bedroom, then turned right around the corner through the connecting bathroom and into Roosevelt's private bedroom. Really, no one watched us coming into the Little White House other than the Marine escort and the two dogs; Fala and Sister happily tagged along with us into our private, secret meeting with the President.

The two Marine guards stood at attention as we entered the President's bedroom. FDR was sitting next to his private desk in his "comfortable" wheelchair with his back to the door that opened to the rear outside deck. There we were: Bucky, Waldo, Bowmar, and me, standing face-to-face with Roosevelt. It was 10:35 AM. The president stared hard at Bucky for a brief moment, then saluted the two Marines who led us inside. FDR told them they were dismissed, and to return at 11:15 AM.

CHAPTER FOUR:

POOF IS PROOF

"Magic is the sole science not accepted by scientists,
because they can't understand it."
—Harry Houdini

April 12, 1945 at 10:35 AM local time,
President Franklin D. Roosevelt's bedroom at
the Little White House in Warm Springs, Georgia

As the Marine guard detail turned and departed, the two dogs, Fala and Sister, eagerly walked right over to FDR and sat at his side. Bucky, thinking that FDR had aged beyond his years and looked frail compared to their last face-to-face meeting, walked up to President Roosevelt, leaned over, and gave him a warm bear hug. He said, "It's good to see you again, sir. We have a lot of ground to cover with you in a short time frame! Please accept our apologies for the unannounced, surprise visit, but this discussion is certainly of national and potentially global security. But before we get started, I have to know: How are my parents doing, and what do they know about what happened to me?"

Roosevelt, who now seemed invigorated and fully engaged with our presence, started what was perhaps the most amazing discussion that any of us could have ever imagined. "Bucky, it is utterly miraculous to see you here in the flesh! I want to meet your associates and discuss the fate of the White Hole Project, but let me tell you about my phone call to your parents. I remember the time frame precisely, because my fortieth wedding anniversary fell on St. Patrick's Day, which was Saturday, March seventeenth. That morning I received a classified and detailed briefing that despite all efforts to recall you from the initial White Hole Project time-travel launch, you were not coming back and therefore presumed dead or lost-in-action. This was a huge setback for our scientists, and especially for Albert Einstein and me. I was impressed with you and took a liking to you from the evening that we first met. I personally selected you as our initial White Hole Project test pilot, and felt personally responsible for your loss. I instructed my staff to contact your parents in Denver and arrange for a private phone call between us that afternoon.

"After having lunch with Eleanor and the family that day, I spoke directly to Jim and Elizabeth in the early afternoon. They were incredibly gracious and understanding in the face of news that no parents of our military service members ever want to receive. I explained to them that you were lost in action on a mission of utmost national secrecy, and that you were missing in action and presumed dead. I told them that we did not have your physical body or any remains, that you did not return from your mission and were therefore presumed dead. I offered to provide assistance for your memorial service, which they accepted. One week later, on Saturday, March 24th, you were laid to rest with full military honors in Denver. Before we parted ways on the phone call, your father made it very clear to me that you had gone 'missing' several times growing up while hunting and fishing in the mountains of Colorado, only to show up later. He even said you went missing one day in your uncle's plane, but did finally return and land after the sun had set and darkness was falling. I have to tell you, he said that you were 'one tough son-of-a-bitch and tough to kill' to which I wholeheartedly agreed! He acknowledged my statement that you were presumed dead and accepted my condolences, but he let me know that neither he nor your mom would ever fully accept your death without seeing your body or proof of your remains."

Bucky was smiling ear-to-ear and quietly chuckling to himself. He looked around at FDR and all of us and said, "Sometime, I'll have to tell you the story about why I was late with Uncle Barney's plane that day. I was 'in action,' but certainly not 'lost in action!' Mr. President, you truly helped ease my mind a little bit about my parents. Thank you for the way that you personally reached out to them. That was awesome!"

Roosevelt smiled warmly and said that he wanted to hear the story about Uncle Barney's plane someday. He looked around, gazing carefully at Waldo, Bowmar, and me as if he was studying us to make sense of a mystery. He then commented, "I cannot help but feel as if I have met you all before! It's the strangest feeling: a bit like déjà vu. Bucky, go ahead and introduce me to your associates here, and explain to me what on earth happened with you and the White Hole Project."

Bucky, with an infectious smile on his face, answered, "Well, Mr. President, it all started on March 14th, the day of the inaugural White Hole Project time-travel mission. That's when I got stung in the ass going through that White Hole time tunnel!"

We all found ourselves giggling a bit, and then the President said, "I hate getting stung in the ass! It happens to me nearly every day in this damn world of politics, and I've been President for over twelve years! How would you like to be stung in the ass every day for twelve straight years?" That made us all laugh even more, and we began to bond a bit as a group. I already liked this president as a person, for his wit and sense of humor.

Bucky continued, "I was struck in the ass by this quiet white lightning in the time tunnel, and it left me with a lightning bolt scar on my right butt cheek—exactly where my Global Cosmic Positioning Device had been implanted. However, I safely landed at the airfield in East Anglia, England on November 14, 1944 exactly as planned. I had been told that I would be brought back in one day, or a crew would join me within three days with further instructions for our top-secret, classified mission. By secret protocol, that was all that I knew."

Roosevelt interjected, "We actually tried to recall you on March 15th and 16th, making numerous attempts; despite our very best efforts, the mission was aborted. By executive order, I stopped any further launch attempts until a thorough investigation could be undertaken to determine what went wrong. That investigation is still ongoing as we speak—until, of course, you showed up here today. So, keep going."

"Well, sir, it is mind-boggling and confusing, but to me I thought that I was there at the East Anglia airbase waiting for a week until November 21, 1944. That morning of the twenty-first, we were scheduled to bomb the Merseburg oil targets deep inside the Third Reich, including the Leuna synthetic oil refinery. Immediately after the morning's mission briefing, my navigator and I were the first of our crew to drive out to the plane. When we arrived at our B-17 flying fortress, these two men, General Paul Thompson and Colonel Kevin Schafer, were there to meet us." Bucky then formally introduced the three of us. He smiled and said, "Sir, you can call General Thompson 'Waldo,' and you can call Colonel Schafer 'Bubble Butt, or BB'. The mastermind actually operating the White Hole Project time travel machine that sent the two of them and their crew there that morning is Lieutenant Nathan Williams here, and you can call him 'Bowmar.'" The three of us then all shook hands with the 32nd President of the United States.

FDR looked intently at Bowmar and enquired, "So, young man, you know how to run that White Hole Project time machine and make it work properly?"

Bowmar somewhat nervously responded, "Yes sir, no pun intended, but I know how to run it forwards and backwards. I have a little demonstration to show you, in about ten minutes."

Bucky resumed his story. "Waldo and BB showed me their mission orders, but I was troubled because technically they were four to six days late. I pulled them aside and asked what the hell took them so long, and if there was trouble with the White Hole Project."

Waldo briefly interrupted, "Bucky's demeanor had me worried enough, sir, that my Smith and Wesson was ready for action. But he came around a bit as we talked it all through." *There's that John Wayne thing again*, I thought.

Bucky then continued, "We were all shocked as we compared notes, but BB here quickly solved the puzzle. It was then that I learned that I had been 'lost in time' and stuck there because the Global Cosmic Positioning Device implanted in my right butt cheek had been struck by the white lightning—as I said, 'stung in the ass'—in the white hole time tunnel and rendered at least partially inoperable. That's why I could not be recalled by our scientific team and was presumed lost or killed in action. BB explained to me that they had launched from thirty years in the future, on November 21, 1974. Apparently, as history has unfolded, we weren't the only ones who thought of using the Phantom Fortress for a time-travel mission.

"My navigator, a guy named Darby 'Pumpkin' Nelson, and I then flew the mission that day on November 21, 1944 with Waldo, Bubble Butt, and their crew. We solo bombed the Leuna synthetic oil refinery, taking out about a third of its capacity. We flew from there to Poland to rescue thirteen Holocaust victims, then flew to Belgium to keep the story of the Phantom Fortress intact. During our rescue mission in Poland, I did get grazed in the head and knocked unconscious by a Nazi bullet." Bucky pointed to the scar creasing his left temple area. "But BB and the rest of the crew got us the hell out of there. I guess I really did live up to my dad's assessment of being hard to kill that day. My navigator, Pumpkin, adopted an orphan Jewish boy we had rescued and the three of us went back to November 1974 Tennessee with the rest of BB and Waldo's team that day. We have been living there in the future since then. By the way, they call themselves—or we call ourselves—the Bad Love Gang, sir, and we came to see you here today from April 12, 1975."

Roosevelt looked at all of us with big eyes, rather astonished. He exclaimed, "Wow, that is a story for the ages! I like all your nicknames, but I'm not sure what to make of the name Bad Love Gang."

I quickly responded, "Mr. President, where we come from in 1975, the word *bad* actually means good, or awesome!"

FDR fired back, "I'm really pulling your leg a little bit here, BB, because I have some badass people working for me, and I am glad they are on my side! You all have created a significant element of danger for yourselves, and I have some ideas about how we go forward from here. But before we do that, and since you are here from 1974, I cannot help but want to ask a few questions before we discuss the ongoing fate of the White Hole Project."

We had anticipated that Roosevelt would be naturally curious about the future, and had rehearsed how to deal with this possibility during our meeting with him. We had nominated Bowmar to judiciously answer any questions about the future, since he is a certified genius who remembers virtually everything he reads, and is basically a walking and talking human encyclopedia! Knowing that we were talking to FDR during the last few hours of his life, we had planned to keep the answers about the future honest, but try to put them in a positive light.

Roosevelt started, "I know the war in Europe is now rapidly coming to a conclusion, based on all our military intelligence reports. So, what happens to that megalomaniac son of a bitch Adolf Hitler?"

Bowmar was more than ready for that one. "Well, sir, 16 days from now, Hitler, confined to his bunker in Berlin and with the Russians rapidly closing in, decides to marry his mistress, Eva Braun. They are married for about forty hours when on April 30, 1945, eighteen days from now, Hitler commits suicide by shooting himself in the head. Eva Braun commits suicide along with him, by taking cyanide. Their bodies are carried up the stairs and through the bunker's emergency exit to the garden behind the Reich Chancellery, where they are burned with gasoline. Eight days later, on May 8, 1945, Nazi Germany unconditionally surrenders its armed forces to the Allies."

FDR looked at us and commented, "Don't quote me publicly, but I feel a bit sorry for Eva Braun. That bastard Hitler earned every goddamned second of that honeymoon in hell, though! By the way, this is all coming up quick. May 8th is my vice president's birthday; that's a perfect day for the Nazi's to wave the white flag. Harry Truman's going to have a heck of a birthday bash this year! What about victory in the Pacific?"

Bowmar jumped on that one as well. "On August 15, 1945, the surrender of the Empire of Japan will be announced to the world. On September 2nd, a formal surrender ceremony occurs aboard the battleship USS Missouri in Tokyo Bay."

Roosevelt then mused aloud, "Oh God, Berlin and the Nazis will fall very soon without us needing to use the atomic bomb. That means I will have to make a decision about using it to hasten the surrender of Japan sometime this summer. Don't tell me what happens,

Bowmar. I absolutely dread the thought of making the decision to use that weapon. According to our most brilliant scientists, it will be like unleashing the very pit of hell here on earth. We'll talk about issues related to the Manhattan Project in a few minutes, when we talk about the fate of the White Hole Project and what I am going to recommend for you to do.

"I don't want to know when I die, but do tell me about my legacy as president, Bowmar."

"I feel that I am among the least in this world to tell you about your legacy," Bowmar humbly replied. "You are the only four-term US president, beloved by a grateful nation for having led us out of the Great Depression and for leading us to total victory in World War II, then emerging as the world's leading superpower, both economically and militarily. You have quite literally reshaped the American presidency, building a bond between yourself and the American public by using the new technology of radio to deliver your fireside chats. You gave our nation encouragement, inspiration, and new hope when we needed it the most! The hallmark of a great legacy is to make the country a better place during your time in office. You have done that in spades, Mr. President."

Roosevelt smiled from ear to ear and said, "I'm really beginning to like you, Bowmar!" We all laughed together and then FDR stated, "Despite our best intentions, we will always have enemies who despise our democracy, our success, and our way of life here in America. How does that look for us in the future, Bowmar?"

Bowmar gave him an honest assessment. "While we have been allies during this World War II that is coming to a close, the USA and Russia will become fierce, competing superpowers on the world stage; we will soon become engaged in what will eventually be called the Cold War. By our present time in 1975, this upcoming Cold War has yet to result in an overt, declared shooting war between us. Instead, it has manifested as espionage, political subversion, and proxy wars.

"In addition, during the aftermath of World War II, we will also witness the rise of the communist influence in Southeast Asia, specifically with the People's Republic of China. There will be a Chinese Civil War in 1949 and the Chinese Communist Party will emerge victorious on the Chinese mainland while the Chinese Nationalists will be forced to retreat to the island of Taiwan. Two other bloody wars will draw America to distant battlefields in Asia. First, we will be engaged in the Korean War from June 1950 until July 1953, dividing the Korean Peninsula into Communist North and Democratic South. Then the Vietnam War starts in November 1955, and it is not yet totally over as of this day in 1975—but Vietnam is definitely falling into the communist's hands." (Waldo was a Medal of Honor veteran from the Korean War.)

Roosevelt commented, "Knowing what I know, you all are leaving little to my imagination. I can see the political forces moving precisely in all the directions you describe—in particular, that Russian leader Stalin, who has been a source of continuing frustration, especially regarding the future of Europe. I believe that we are headed toward a divided Europe after this war is over. Listening to your description of the future, this discussion has made me much more comfortable with your role involving the White Hole Project and your claim to be here from the year 1975. Assuming that you are really in control of the White Hole Project in that year, then we need to make our plans for the future now!"

It was 10:58 AM, and I quickly scribbled a short note and handed it to Bowmar. He took the note from me, shoved it in his front pocket, and gave me a quick look of reassurance, as well as a wink that only our close and enduring friendship could mutually understand and acknowledge. Bowmar then looked at President Roosevelt and said, "Mr. President, as an African American from the year 1975, it has been the privilege and honor of a lifetime for me to be here with you this morning. We decided beforehand to prove to you beyond any shadow of a doubt that we are in complete control of the White Hole Project. In thirty seconds, when the clock strikes eleven, I am going back to April 12, 1975. Please take both my hands and hold them now, sir."

Roosevelt was too stunned to do anything but take Bowmar's extended hands and hold them firmly in his own. As their hands connected, my adrenalin started surging and time slowed down. I glanced at my watch and saw there were seven seconds remaining. Bowmar and FDR were literally holding each other's hands, looking each other squarely in the eyes. I counted down, "Five, four, three, two, one..." Between the count of two and one, Bowmar opened his mouth to say something," but all I heard was "Good—"

At exactly 11:00 AM, Bowmar vanished into thin air and FDR's empty hands dropped back into his lap. The two dogs, Fala and Sister, whimpered and looked afraid. Bucky, Waldo, and I watched in amazement as Bowmar instantaneously disappeared, just as we had planned, and President Roosevelt got to personally witness and experience the miracle of the White Hole Project time travel machine.

Roosevelt was the first to speak. "By God, I have been left empty handed before, but this experience takes the cake!" We all smiled with relief. "Bucky, your presence here this morning, the detailed accountings of yourself and your Bad Love Gang associates, have all convinced me that you are indeed in control of the White Hole Project. Whether it is by chance or by choice, but certainly by fate, you and the Bad Love Gang have assumed a role and responsibility of gigantic magnitude, and proportionate danger." FDR looked around, sniffing the air. "By the way, do you all smell something strange right now, or am I the only one here that smells that odor?"

I responded, "Sir, that is the smell of time travel!"

CHAPTER FIVE:

THE FATE OF THE WHITE HOLE PROJECT

"I ask you to judge me by the enemies I have made."
—Franklin D. Roosevelt

April 12, 1945 at 11:01 AM local time,
President Franklin D. Roosevelt's bedroom at
the Little White House in Warm Springs, Georgia

F ollowing Bowmar's planned disappearance, Roosevelt remained totally engaged with us and focused on the remainder of our meeting time: "Let me explain the situation with the security lapses of the Manhattan Project, and potentially by extension with the White Hole Project. I want us to part ways this morning with a rational plan of action for the defense of the White Hole.

"What we are about to discuss is all highly classified, top-secret information. I am sharing it with the three of you now because Bucky and his designees will have to carry the torch of protecting the White Hole Project and its secrets from this day forth. Just so you know how secret this all is, Harry Truman, my own vice president, does not yet know about the Manhattan Project and our tremendous progress to become the first nation with an atomic bomb. With that said, I have entrusted Colonel Carter Clarke to protect the secrets of the Manhattan Project. As you have just so accurately described Russia's future behavior toward the United States, Colonel Clarke was suspicious of the Russians and the Germans executing a separate peace deal independent of us. With my permission, Clarke and his US Army Signal Intelligence Service have started the Venona Project. Clark and his expert code-breaking team have been intercepting and trying to read all diplomatic traffic being sent from the United States to Moscow. We started the Venona Project over two years ago, in February 1943; during that first year, we estimate that we decrypted roughly fifteen percent of Russian diplomatic message traffic. We are getting better with our counterespionage, and last year we estimated that our decryption rate was closer to fifty percent. Unfortunately, what we have discovered is not anything related to a separate peace agreement between Russia and Germany. Instead, what we have uncovered is a massive Russian espionage operation at the highest levels of our government, directed in particular at uncovering the secrets of the Manhattan Project and the atomic bomb.

"The Manhattan Project has been top-secret since its inception and our general goal has been to keep the project secret from our two primary enemies, Germany and Japan. As best that I can tell, we have succeeded reasonably well in that realm—but what we are now discovering is that our so-called ally, Russia, is our biggest espionage problem, and it is definitely real. It seems that Russian spies have penetrated the Manhattan Project, specifically at Los Alamos, and probably a few other locations as well. We are actively investigating the leaks, but my fear is that the Russian scientists are getting vital information about the atomic bomb and they will not be far behind us with their own version. That is why your description about the future between us and Russia rings so true to me this morning!"

I briefly interrupted, confirming the president's fears, "Your suspicions are spot-on, Mr. President. The Russians are the next nation after us to get the atomic bomb. They will test their first atomic bomb in August of 1949, and the next three nations to get the atomic bomb will be Britain in October 1952, France in February 1960, and China in October 1964."

Roosevelt looked directly at me with a scowl on his face and exclaimed, "*Shit!* See what we started?! The whole world is going to have the bomb! How complicated does *that* make things?!"

I gently responded, "Sir, we did the right thing to be the first nation with the bomb. Atomic bomb development was inevitable, and it is better for the United States to lead in this regard than to follow. In 1968, a United Nations-sponsored organization based in Geneva, Switzerland, will have negotiated the Treaty on the Non-Proliferation of Nuclear Weapons, called the NPT. It is a landmark international treaty with the objective of preventing the spread of nuclear weapons. It opened for signatures in 1968, and went into force two years later."

Roosevelt replied, "You just brightened my day again, BB. I have been hoping that this new United Nations organization that we are working on could or would function as a mechanism to promote world peace and security after this World War II ends."

"It is headquartered in New York City, and in 1975 we call it the UN. It is very busy and active in world affairs—but as you can imagine, it is complicated and has its limitations," I responded.

Waldo, in his classic, no-nonsense macho fashion, then added, "I served in the Korean War, sir, and have a bit more experience under my belt than either Bucky or BB here. The United Nations is fine and good for trying to address complicated world politics and the concept of peace. But at the end of the day, you can't trust anyone and the biggest, best, and strongest military wins; that's just the way the world turns!"

That's Waldo in the span of three sentences, I thought. FDR smiled at Waldo and interjected, "My fifth cousin, President Theodore 'Teddy' Roosevelt, famously said: 'Speak softly and carry a big stick; you will go far.' So, after living through this horrific World War II, I suspect that our military strength will remain number one in the world for the foreseeable future while we try our best to avoid another global conflict. Two world wars is two too many!

"Our time is running short, and we have to address the fate of the White Hole Project," FDR continued. "Bucky, knowing that you were the first White Hole Project test pilot and that you have traveled back in time last month to November 1944, then forward to November 1974, and now back again from April 1975 to today, I can only assume that somehow the White Hole Project's integrity has been protected between now and 1975. I can only conclude that you and your Bad Love Gang have something to do with that process—but I want to warn you, I believe that there are sinister forces that want to get their hands on the White Hole Project technology. I also firmly believe that time travel would be far more dangerous to human history than atomic weaponry, if it ever fell into the wrong hands! I am therefore directly assigning you to protect and defend the integrity and future of the White Hole Project, against all enemies both foreign and domestic."

Bucky simply replied, "It would be my honor, sir!"

FDR continued, "The White Hole Project has been kept even more secretive than the Manhattan Project, for many reasons. First of all, very few people know the final purpose of the White Hole Project. I commissioned Albert Einstein and Vannevar Bush to work together, with only their smallest circle of trusted colleagues knowing the true purpose and intent of the project. Secondly, while the Manhattan

Project required multiple locations across the country—the largest at Oak Ridge, Tennessee and Los Alamos, New Mexico but also in Chicago, Illinois and Hanford, Washington—the White Hole Project was solely constructed adjacent to the K-25 plant for uranium enrichment at Oak Ridge. Everyone working there assumed that the White Hole Project was a necessary operational component of the K-25 construction. After all, when it was completed in 1944, the four-story K-25 plant became the world's largest building under one roof, comprising over 1.6 million square feet. Finally, the White Hole was built adjacent to K-25, but deep below ground. The only activity directly related to the White Hole Project outside of Oak Ridge has been at the ultra-top-secret Indian Springs Airfield, where the alien spaceship crashed the night you discovered the existence of exotic matter and earned your top-secret clearance. The technologies that our scientists have gleaned from the alien spacecraft and the use of its blue exotic matter have been central to the construction and 'successes' of the White Hole Project. That alien spaceship in Nevada remains as our nation's number-one top secret.

"Despite this secrecy, Colonel Clarke and the US Army Signal Intelligence Service running the Venona Project have intercepted and decrypted a few messages from the Russians indicating that they know something different may be occurring at Oak Ridge, and that it is connected somehow to our top-secret airbase in the remote southwestern Nevada desert. Colonel Clarke and his people do not know details about the actual existence of the White Hole Project, or the Alien spaceship in Nevada. The messages they have decrypted so far raise questions about the Oak Ridge and Nevada connection, but do not indicate that they know anything of substance about the technology or the purpose of that connection. But we do have genuine concerns that the Russians or others know that something big, apart from the Manhattan Project, is afoot here in the United States.

"The Russian transmissions refer to me using the code name 'Kapitan,' and 'Kaban' or 'Wild Boar' as the code name for Winston Churchill. The few messages related to the Oak Ridge White Hole Project were decrypted late last year, along with some human intelligence we gathered regarding possible Chinese and Indian national interest in our secrets at the Indian Springs Airfield. As Waldo correctly pointed out a few minutes ago, we literally cannot trust anyone—but especially not the Russians! I do trust the British and Winston Churchill, and find it a bit amusing that our code names are lumped together in transmissions by the Russians. I am truly not sure what to make of any Indian national or Chinese involvement, but those two continents are historic, vast, complicated and destined to grow in world prominence after World War II ends.

"So here is the deal, as I have said: Bucky, it will be up to you and your designees to protect and defend the future of the White Hole Project. Give me a code name for this defense project, as an alternative to the Venona Project. When the three of you depart here in a few minutes, I will contact both Vannevar Bush and Colonel Carter Clarke to give them the project code name, and tell them to cooperate fully with anything that you may require to fulfill your duty by my executive order. By the way, as you think about a code name for the defense of the White Hole Project, consider that the word *Venona* really has no meaning."

Bucky, who thinks fast on his feet, did not hesitate to respond. "Sir, we will call it the Denver Project, and no one is going to get past this Denver boy who refuses to die, despite getting stung in the ass by the White Hole time-travel white lightning, getting stuck in time, and then being shot in the left temple by a Nazi bullet in Poland!" At that moment, my music brain started playing **"Get Out of Denver,"** from the *Seven* album by American rock singer-songwriter Bob Seger. *Seven* was the seventh studio album by Bob Seger, released in 1974, and the first Seger album to feature the Silver Bullet Band, which Seger would steadily rely on for the rest of his career. The album didn't do great on *Billboard's* Top 200 albums chart, but the single track "Get Out of Denver" reached number 80 and was a regional hit in Colorado.

Roosevelt looked at Bucky like a proud father and said, "I do admire and trust you like a son, and know you will do your best. The forces that will inevitably come against you are the forces of international espionage and domestic treason. Listen to me now. We are not talking Germans in Nazi uniforms, or Russians wearing Red Stars, or Chinese dressed in khaki uniforms, or Indian nationals in traditional clothing. We are talking about domestic and international, well-educated, articulate, well-dressed, attractive, everyday-looking incognito men and women who you might least expect, and they will be well-trained to use whatever means necessary to get what they want. They might use deception and charm or brute or deadly force, but you and your team must be ready for anything at any time. Train well and learn how to expect the worst, because you will be called into action when you least expect it!"

President Roosevelt's warning about what we were facing sent shivers down my spine, thinking about our recent New Year's Eve surprise attack. I thought about the moment last June when Bowmar and I had discovered the secret tunnel leading to the entrance of the White Hole Project, and how I instinctively knew at that moment that my life would never be the same. Even more concerning was the fact that our entire Bad Love Gang was now part of a larger mission to defend and protect the future of the White Hole time travel machine, and potentially its connection to Area 51, against enemies both foreign and domestic. And here we were at this moment, talking to President Franklin Delano Roosevelt about world history and the fate of the White Hole. It was so surreal that I pinched myself *hard*, and the pain I felt was convincingly real.

While I was thinking about our circumstances and pinching myself, FDR was taking a couple of minutes to write a note at his desk. He then stuffed it into an envelope with his presidential seal and handed it to Bucky. "I want you to take this note directly to my trusted General Claire Chennault, who commands the Flying Tigers and is assigned to the China-Burma-India Theater. Use the White Hole Project to go and deliver this note to him in June of 1942. Do your research first to pick the exact time frame to go in June 1942, don't read my letter, and don't go alone. General Chennault has excellent practical and working relations with ranking military and political powers in China, Burma, and India. He may be of good service to you. Can you fly a P-40 Warhawk?"

"Mr. President, I can fly anything with wings and an engine! But I'll make sure that Bubble Butt here and one or two of our other colleagues who can be my wingmen are ready to fly P-40 Warhawks before we go. I hear what you are saying about us going to see General Chennault, but what about the Russians?"

Roosevelt handed Bucky two phone numbers in addition to the sealed envelope and said, "Call Vannevar Bush and Colonel Clarke at these numbers tonight. I will have spoken to both of them. Bush knows the most about the White Hole Project, and Clarke knows the most about the status of the Russians. They will give you whatever current information they have, pertinent to any espionage or threats potentially related or connected to the White Hole Project. Then it is up to you to lead the way. And remember, the fewer people who know what you are doing, the better."

Bucky replied, "I will make those two calls tonight, sir. When we leave this cottage, we need vehicles and current US road maps. We are headed to Oak Ridge, Tennessee first, to Illinois second, then on to Colorado and possibly Nevada, or where ever else this mission takes us."

As Bucky finished speaking, I interrupted and handed the president a typed letter. "Mr. President, Bowmar and I prepared a letter that is an executive directive from you that will give Bucky, Waldo, and their designees the authority to, as you would say, protect and defend the White Hole Project." FDR read the letter, signed it, and placed it another envelope with his presidential seal. He then picked up the phone and called both Sergeant Carter and the Marine commander on duty at the onsite Marine encampment. He instructed them to provide us with vehicles and whatever else we needed, making it clear that we were to be treated discreetly and with the highest priority, by his direct orders.

It was now 11:17 AM, and the two Marine guards had been waiting at the door to Eleanor's bedroom for two minutes, precisely as they had been told. It felt like we had been with FDR for a long while regarding the incredible substance and depth of our meeting, and also like a blink in time due to how engaging and spellbinding our discussion had been.

It was time to say goodbye. Bucky couldn't help himself and gave the president another bear hug; FDR embraced him, slapped him on the back, and said, "Godspeed, Bucky, make me proud!" Bucky replied, "Yes sir, no question about it!" Waldo, being the Korean War veteran, saluted the president and said, "It has been an honor to meet you today and I will have Bucky's back, sir." I then firmly shook Roosevelt's hand, looked him in the eyes and said, "Until we meet again, I will remember this day like no other. Thank you for your trust." FDR looked at the three of us and said, "Thanks for a memorable morning, gentlemen, I am sure we will be seeing each other in the future. Good luck, and get moving!"

CHAPTER SIX:

ROOSEVELT MAKES THE CALLS

"We have always held to the hope, the belief, the conviction that
there is a better life, a better world, beyond the horizon."
—Franklin D. Roosevelt

April 12, 1945 at 11:20 AM local time,
the Little White House in Warm Springs, Georgia

At 11:20 AM, Bucky, Waldo and I walked out the front door of
President Roosevelt's Little White House cottage escorted by the
two Marines, who had returned for us at 11:15 AM as ordered by the president. Exactly one hour had passed since we arrived. We walked directly
back to the Marine Corps sentry post, where Tater was standing outside
the white, hexagonal guard shelter waiting for us, and Sergeant David
Carter had just hung up the phone with the President. Roosevelt had
explained to Carter that Tuskegee Airman Lieutenant Nathan Williams
(Bowmar), had left the property "discreetly," and not to worry about the
fact that only three of us were returning to his post.

The Marine commander on duty, Captain Vernon Montgomery,
pulled up in what appeared to be a brand new Willys MB Jeep. He saluted
us, introduced himself, and said, "Hop aboard, gentlemen, and I'll personally see to it that you get everything you need." We thanked the guard
detail and Sergeant Carter, then the four of us climbed into Montgom-

ery's Jeep. Waldo took the front passenger seat, as our two-star major general. Sitting next to Tater and Bucky in the back seat as we started driving, I asked Tater if he had gotten along with Sergeant Carter while we were gone.

Tater replied, "I asked him if he was in any way related to the 'Carter's Little Pills' family fortune. You know, the famous laxative formulated by Samuel J. Carter in 1868? He said no, but told me I needed to take a big handful of those pills because I was the most full of shit person he had met in a long while! We got along famously after that little exchange." We all got a good laugh, and we needed it.

Meanwhile, FDR needed to make his two calls quickly because he was planning to leave his bedroom at noon in his gray suit and crimson tie to sit for his portrait painting by Madame Shoumatoff. At 11:25 AM, he reached Colonel Carter Clarke on a secure line at the US Army Signal Intelligence Service office; Clarke was in charge of running the Venona Project. Clarke's team had intercepted and decrypted a few messages since late 1944 from the Russians, indicating that they knew something different than its stated purpose might be occurring at Oak Ridge, and that it could be connected somehow to our top-secret airbase in the remote southwestern Nevada desert (Area 51). With Colonel Clarke on the other line, FDR made the call brief and to the point.

"Carter, I have given the authority to establish a top-secret sister project to the Venona Project. I need you to fully cooperate with USAAF Captain Jack 'Bucky' Smith, whom I just appointed to lead this effort. It is called the Denver Project, and it is of equal if not higher priority than the Venona Project. Captain Smith will call you tonight on your secure line and brief you. Don't let me down. I trust him implicitly, and so can you. Are we clear on that?"

Colonel Clarke replied, "Yes sir, Mr. President. I understand, and I will look forward to Smith's call and working with him. I hope that you are getting some well-deserved rest down there in Warm Springs!"

"Thank you, Carter. Yes, it has been a much-needed break since the Yalta Conference. I'm actually getting my picture painted this afternoon, so I need to get off the phone and go to work on my good looks! Keep up the great work, and we'll talk again soon. Goodbye."

FDR next had a phone call placed to Vannevar (pronounced so that it rhymes with the word *achiever*: a totally appropriate rhyme with this amazing man's life) Bush. Vannevar was trusted completely by FDR, and was the unseen civilian director or conductor of the vast Manhattan Project. By way of background, Hungarian physicist Leo Szilard and Albert Einstein had crafted a letter that was signed by Einstein and delivered directly to President Roosevelt on October 11, 1939, warning FDR that Germany was pursuing an atomic bomb. On October 9, 1941, it was Vannevar Bush who met with President Roosevelt to discuss the actual feasibility of a US atomic bomb project and the growing concerns regarding the status of the German nuclear energy ambitions. Roosevelt approved and expedited the atomic pilot program after that meeting. The Empire of Japan bombed Pearl Harbor on December 7, 1941, pulling the United States into World War II. On March 9, 1942 Bush sent a memo to FDR with a strong argument for the United States to proceed with building the atomic bomb. He estimated that the project could potentially be completed in late 1944, if every effort were made to expedite the project. Two days later, Bush received FDR's affirmative reply, giving him the green light to build the atomic bomb, and to build it as quickly as possible. To keep the project and its massive funding secret, Bush also requested that the project be turned over to the Army. Roosevelt agreed and the approved project was given to the Army on June 16, 1942 for the all-out effort to build the world's first atomic bomb. It became known as the Manhattan Project.

As the civilian Director of the Office of Scientific Research and Development (OSRD) during the WWII time frame, Vannevar Bush coordinated the activities of thousands of leading American scientists in the applications of science to warfare. Simultaneously, he also coordinated a top-secret project that went well beyond the science of warfare. On October 1, 1942, President Roosevelt had invited Albert Einstein and Vannevar Bush to a private dinner at the White House. FDR explained to both men that prudence would demand that America have a backup plan to the Manhattan Project, in the event that Germany won the race to get the atomic bomb first. That night, he commissioned Einstein to construct a usable time travel machine, code named the White Hole Project, which we would use to foil Hitler if he had been first to get the atomic bomb. Bush was instructed to use the money going to the Manhattan Project to construct the White Hole Project in Oak Ridge, Tennessee. There would be no financial fingerprints leading to or touching the White Hole. The secrecy of the White Hole Project was on par with the hidden alien spaceship at Area 51, which was the source of the otherworldly blue exotic matter required to make time travel possible. All those associated with the White Hole Project, including Einstein and Bush, were sworn to take its secrets to their graves. This level of secrecy, above and beyond the Manhattan Project, was exactly why the purpose of the White Hole Project was such a gigantic magnet for espionage activity and explained why Vannevar Bush's civilian home phone had been secretly wiretapped by both Russian and Chinese spies. These spies were listening in as FDR connected with Bush, who was home for an early lunch on this fateful day.

At 11:30 AM, Roosevelt spoke to Bush. "Good morning, Vanne-var! I have some interesting news for you. I also have a new directive that requires your full cooperation. I am in a bit of a hurry now, and want to make this quick. I know that this is your home line, so that is the other reason for keeping it brief."

Vannevar replied, "As always, it is great to hear from you Mr. Presi-dent! I'll keep it quick on my end, too. I'm intrigued to hear your news, so fire away."

FDR answered, "Captain Jack 'Bucky' Smith is alive, and he just left from visiting me here at the Little White House fifteen minutes ago. I have necessarily placed him in charge of a new project and given him a new mission. I gave him your secure office number to call tonight. You are to cooperate with him fully and without reservations."

"Yes sir, understood. That is interesting news, and I look forward to speaking with Captain Smith. Did he look well to you?"

"He looks quite well, just as you remember him—except for a bullet crease scar across his left temple," FDR stated. "I need to get moving now, but I so appreciate all your loyal service and leadership, Vanne-var! I'm sure that I'll see you soon when I get back to DC. Take care."

Vannevar said, "Thank you, Mr. President!" As he hung up the phone, he sat back and marveled at what he had just heard. He was already anxious to speak with Bucky and find out what actually hap-pened with the inaugural White Hole Project time travel mission, which was currently under a full failure analysis investigation. In addi-tion, the Chinese and Russian operatives who heard and recorded the conversation got busy fast, looking to find the records and potential whereabouts of a US serviceman named Captain Jack Smith.

As President Roosevelt hung up the phone with Vannevar Bush, he lit a cigarette (FDR smoked two packs of unfiltered Camels per day). The president leaned back in his chair and took a deep draw.

As he thoroughly enjoyed this first cigarette in over an hour's time, he could not help but muse to himself for a few minutes about the unexpected and amazing events of the morning, and what he had just learned about the future. It was Vannevar who had firmly believed and espoused in late 1941 and early 1942 that the atomic bomb could be completed in late 1944. His estimation was nearly correct; it was April 1945, the bomb was nearing completion, and the war against Germany was ending in a few weeks. FDR wondered if he would be willing to use it against Japan if necessary, then mentally cringed at the thought of multiple nations acquiring the atomic bomb, including Russia and China, and living in a world of ever-present "atomic threats." The world was already crazy enough!

He thought about his presidential legacy as described by Bowmar, a brilliant young African American man from 1975, and smiled to himself at that future. He had watched Bowmar disappear into thin air, and literally *felt* his hands vanish as well. He knew deep in his heart that the White Hole Project and time travel must never fall into the wrong hands. He then remembered how Bowmar had said that Germany's surrender and victory in Europe would happen on May 8th, Vice-President Harry Truman's birthday. He decided to do one more thing before getting dressed for his portrait painting by Madame Shoumatoff; he wrote a brief note.

Dear Harry,

In the event that anything ever happens to me and you become the thirty-third president, please give your full ongoing support to USAAF Captain Jack "Bucky" Smith, whose work is of our highest national security.

Very truly yours,

Franklin

He then put the note in an envelope with his presidential seal, labeled it to *Harry S. Truman,* and placed it in the top drawer of his desk. It was time to get dressed for the portrait session.

CHAPTER SEVEN:

ROAD TRIP PLANNING AND FAMOUS LAST WORDS

"Tomorrow, at sunrise, I shall no longer be here."
—Nostradamus

April 12, 1945 at noon local time in Warm Springs, Georgia

I t was only a few minutes ride with Marine Captain Vernon Mont-gomery from the Marine Corps sentry post to the onsite Marine encampment. The scenery was beautiful; I found myself mesmerized by the surrounding forest of Georgia pine trees, sprinkled with white and pink flowering dogwoods and azaleas. Not unexpectedly, my music brain kicked into motion and started playing **"A Beautiful Morning"** by The Rascals. The song was released in March 1968, and by late June 1968 it was certified as a million records hit and reached number three on the *Billboard* Hot 100 chart. April 12, 1945 was a gorgeous spring morning, and history was changing big on this day.

As we parked at the Marine encampment, Captain Montgomery half turned in the driver's seat of the Jeep. With a bit of a southern accent, he said, "You men must be pretty damn important! The presi-dent called me, ordered me to come and get you and then to give you a vehicle and whatever supplies you need. I believe this is a first on my watch, but your wish is my command! Either your timing is impeccable or you are just plain lucky, because last month we took delivery on four new Willys MB Jeeps, giving us a couple extra Jeeps in our stable right now. So, what can I do for y'all to get you on your way?" As he finished, he was mainly looking at Waldo in the passenger seat, AKA USAAF two-star Major General Paul Thompson.

Waldo, who never really mixed his words with many niceties, responded plainly. "Captain Montgomery, we need a Jeep with a spare wheel, an extra gas tank, and a covered top, along with current road maps and some beefier guns." We were all armed with Colt .45 M1911 pistols.

I interrupted, "We need to make that request for two Jeeps, Captain, and we will take two of the brand-new ones that were just delivered."

Captain Montgomery looked at me a little sternly and said, "You look a bit young to be a colonel there, son."

Bucky jumped into the conversation then. "He took out a third of the Reich's most heavily-defended Leuna synthetic oil refinery deep in Nazi Germany, using a single B-17 bomber, then shot the hell out of Nazi ground troops in Poland while we rescued Holocaust victims, saving my life in the process, and then got us the hell out of there! What exactly have *you* done in the line of fire? And by the way, what did the commander in chief just say to you, Captain?"

Montgomery, who had an excellent and distinguished non-combat career with the Marines, and loved his current post at the Little White House, turned just a little bit red and said, "Please ignore my last comment entirely. Two new Jeeps it is, and what guns can I get for you men?"

Waldo, smiling after Bucky's quick defenses of me, replied, "We want a couple of M-1 Garands, with lots of extra clips. We could also use a couple of Thompson submachine guns, with several thirty-round box magazines."

I interrupted, "Make it four M-1s and four Thompson machine guns, to be exact." This time Waldo looked at me with a mix of curiosity and his own sternness. I tilted my head to the right, shrugged my shoulders a bit, and smiled. Looking him straight in the eyes, I said,

"We have company coming, General, that's why we need two Jeeps and extra guns." I then looked back at Montgomery and said, "Let's round this armament request off with a crate of Mk 2 grenades." (There were 25 grenades to a crate.)

Tater chimed in, "As we say on the Fourth of July, 'Holler in the hole' there, Captain Montgomery! If we're taking this much firepower, then I'm requesting a bazooka for this road trip! Can you oblige us with that one?"

Montgomery, who was now willing to play the game along with us, answered, "You bet your sweet ass I can, and I have an M1A1 bazooka with plenty of rocket ammo that I can add to your party! Does that cover it, gentlemen?" We acknowledged that it did, and Montgomery put his men to work. At noon, we pulled away from the Marine encampment in two brand-new Willys MB Jeeps filled with all our guns, weapons of destruction, and supplies and headed into the town of Warm Springs to get some lunch before starting our road trip to Oak Ridge, Tennessee. It took us less than ten minutes to drive to the Warm Springs Hotel, where we stopped for lunch.

Built in 1907, the hotel was busy during the Roosevelt era hosting foreign dignitaries, Hollywood stars, FDR's secret service men, the press, and many other important visitors. The four of us were all "starved" as we sat down to eat in the dining room, and requested a late breakfast despite the fact that it was noon. The staff gladly granted the "brunch" request from ranking military officers in uniform, and served up a delicious homestyle Southern brunch feast. Our meal included scrambled eggs, cheese grits, bacon, sausage, hot fresh biscuits with an assortment of jams and jellies, coffee and orange juice. Looking at all the awesome food served, Tater just beamed with Southern pride. "We're living in high cotton now, baby! Nothing warms the heart like Southern cooking. I think I'm gonna pop when I get done eatin' all this!" We all whole-heartedly agreed.

We used our time together at brunch to regroup and to begin planning our 1945 road trip. Waldo got the conversation going by asking, "So, Bubble Butt, what was that note that you handed to Bowmar to stuff in his pocket before he got zapped back home to 1975? And what did you mean by saying that we have company coming?"

I was mentally busting at the seams and eager to talk through our plans and trade notes with Bucky, whose brain had also been busy plotting and planning during our time with FDR: "From the moment we entered President Roosevelt's bedroom, I could see his face light up when he saw that Bucky was alive. It was obvious that our discussion was moving in a positive direction with regards to our continuing role with the White Hole Project. Knowing that Bowmar was getting zapped back to 1975 at precisely 11 AM as part of this morning's plan, I needed to give him some quick instructions about moving forward. I only had a minute to scribble a note, so I gave him some instructions. First, send reinforcements; we're going on road trip. Zap group number one to Oak Ridge High School on April 13, 1945, at 7 PM, in military attire. Then, start the Black Box Protocol."

It was the last statement that got everyone's attention. Waldo responded, "OK, that explains why you requested two Jeeps and more weapons, but what the hell is the 'Black Box Protocol'?"

I answered, "As Bowmar and I were planning this second time travel mission, we were concerned about how to communicate with each other across time and space. I joked that we needed a 'carrier pigeon'. Bowmar looked at me and said, 'That's an easy problem to solve.' He went to work and designed a 'black box' using fiberglass and Kevlar, which is really cutting-edge! Kevlar bulletproof vests just came onto the market in 1974, and somehow Bowmar got his hands on enough of it to build our black box, which has a Global Cosmic Positioning Device soundly incorporated into the design. When he sends the first Bad Love Gang group to us at 7 PM tomorrow night at Oak Ridge High School, he will send the black box along with them. He will then recall the black box twelve hours later, and I will send him a message in the box with instructions about what or whom we need next, and exactly where and when to send it or them. Alternatively, I might give him instructions to recall one or more of us at such-and-such a time. The black box will go back and forth so that we are communicating across time and space." I started humming the theme song from James Bond and smiled at everyone.

Waldo was the first to react to this Black Box Protocol revelation, with a big grin. "BB, you and Bowmar are a dangerous combination, but I like it! Maybe I can send a note in that box to Mary once in a while and tell her 'all our 'children' are behaving themselves—even though she knows that's never the case!" We all chuckled at that, and Waldo asked, "Why did you request even more firepower and grenades?"

"FDR surprised me a little when he said that our team 'must be ready for anything at any time' to train well and learn how to expect the worst, because we will be called into action when we least expect it. He knows that we are going to face some serious adversity in various forms. That's what happened to us on New Year's Eve. We were not expecting to be ambushed by Boris. We can't let that happen again, and we certainly don't want to be outgunned by anyone."

"Amen to that, brother. Now you understand my world view a little better." Waldo replied.

I rolled my eyes and shook my head. "Waldo, you are not going to be appointed as peace ambassador to anything anytime soon!"

"Bubble Butt, my ambassador is resting in my holster! You just let me know when you need some firm negotiating, OK?"

We all laughed and Tater chimed in, "My Aunt Jane from South Georgia always says, 'Whoever said diamonds are a girl's best friend has clearly never owned a dog or a gun.' I can't wait to tell her that I got a World War II bazooka to play with!" People were starting to stare at our table as we laughed, volume rising in our excitement.

I tried to get us refocused. "OK, boys, let's get back to business here. Bucky, Bowmar, and I discussed what steps we should take if President Roosevelt supported us as the defenders of the White Hole Project. Bucky, I heard you say that 'we are headed first to Oak Ridge, Tennessee, second to Illinois, then on to Colorado and possibly to Nevada, or wherever else this mission takes us.' Why don't you enlighten us about your thoughts there, and also give us your reaction about the envelope that FDR handed you to take to General Claire Chennault of the Flying Tigers. That one has me a bit puzzled."

Bucky was ready, as always. "As you, Bowmar and I already discussed, we are heading to Oak Ridge today and tomorrow morning we are going to seal it off from the K-25 plant. The tunnel connecting the K-25 plant to the White Hole Project is going down! We cannot take the chance of anyone else getting in there, security clearance or not. I will talk to Vannevar Bush tonight as I promised the president, and tell him that we are blowing that tunnel tomorrow. While we are there, we will try to observe for any suspicious activity.

"After we pick up the Bad Love Gang reinforcements that Bowmar sends to us tomorrow night and the black box, we will head to the Naval Reserve Training Command, Naval Air Station in Glenview, Illinois, which is north of downtown Chicago. We are going there to try and meet with Lieutenant Gerald R. Ford. Ford became the thirty-eighth president of the United States in August 1974, and is the current president in 1975. We may need his help disposing of foreign or domestic spies as we defend the White Hole Project, especially in light of our recent run-in with the Russian we are calling Boris. Having FDR as our friend has been a guiding light and a godsend. We want our current president in 1975 to trust us and be on our side as well."

Tater exclaimed, "Holy Sugar-Honey-Iced-*Tea*, we're gonna meet *another* president on this trip?!" This was his favorite way to avoid actually saying the word *shit*.

"Yes, Tater, and when we tell him that we are in charge of an ultra-top-secret government agency called the Denver Project, and tell him that someday he is going to be president, he will remember us if and when we come calling during his presidency."

Bucky then continued, "After leaving Illinois, we are headed for Colorado. Initially I was planning this part of the trip to see my parents in Denver, and let them know that I'm actually alive. However, now our trip to Colorado is even more important—and that gets to the heart of BB's last question. FDR handed me the envelope with a message for General Claire Chennault of the Flying Tigers and told us to go see him in June 1942. I could tell something was up by the look in FDR's eyes, and I have a suspicion about his request. The alien spaceship crashed at Area 51 in the southwest Nevada desert on June 17, 1942. That was the night that I boarded their ship, witnessed the aliens being transported away, and discovered exotic matter. Roosevelt said there was human intelligence regarding Chinese and Indian interest in Area 51. I have heard through my US Army Air Force connections that Roosevelt and Chennault have a close relationship. What if the aliens also landed ships in China and/or India? Maybe Chennault has information about that, and maybe that is why those two countries are so curious about Area 51 here in the United States. Finally, FDR wants us to go see Chennault in June 1942, the same month as the alien crash in Nevada. I sense a connection in all this."

I interrupted, "Bucky, I think you are on to something there and I see the potential Nevada connection, but you have us going to Colorado for some reason in addition to seeing your parents."

Bucky replied, "Oh yeah, I forgot to finish that thought! The 72nd Fighter Wing is headquartered at Peterson Army Air Base in Colorado Springs south of Denver. They train fighter pilots there using P-40 Warhawks and oversee operations at six other fighter training bases in the Southwest. When I was young, my parents would take us to the world-famous Broadmoor Hotel in Colorado Springs for vacations. That place is awesome! We are going to Colorado Springs and the Bad Love Gang is going to stay at the Broadmoor while I train you, Willy, and Pumpkin how to fly and fight in P-40 Warhawks at Peterson Air Base. The president specifically asked if I could fly a P-40 Warhawk. When we go to see Chennault in June 1942, the four of us will be ready to use his P-40s for whatever mission is outlined in this secret letter from FDR to Chennault."

Bucky then finished his thoughts about our road trip, "I did mention the possibility of going to Nevada which of course means Area 51. I may have to go it alone there because of the super-tight security around the alien spaceship. I may want to spend some time getting to know that spaceship a little better. If I can get Vannevar Bush's blessings, then the pilots in our group including BB, Willy, and Pumpkin, will go with me to Area 51."

Waldo looked at his watch and said, "Gentlemen, it is 1:15, and I suggest that we get on the road. I briefly looked at the 1945 maps that Captain Montgomery gave us. We will head to Atlanta and from there to Chattanooga, then on to the Knoxville/Oak Ridge area. This is going to be a little different than what we are used to in 1975, because there are no interstate highways. Depending on our progress, we can stay in either Chattanooga or Knoxville tonight and be at the White

Hole Project tomorrow morning to do our work. Bucky, remember that you have two important phone calls to make tonight, to Colonel Carter Clarke and Vannevar Bush, so we don't want to check into a hotel too late."

We paid for brunch, walked out of the Warm Springs Hotel and got into our two brand-new Willys MB Jeeps, with me and Bucky in one Jeep and Waldo and Tater in the other. Waldo, who always had a great sense of direction for our road trips, led the way out of town and we followed him, with me driving our Jeep. I looked at my watch and saw that it was nearly 1:25 PM. I then looked at Bucky and said, "I know how you feel about President Roosevelt. Just a few minutes ago, the president said his last words."

A short distance away at the Little White House, President Roosevelt had been sitting in his favorite chair in the living room accompanied by his mistress Lucy Mercer (whose visits with FDR had been arranged by his daughter, Anna Roosevelt Boettiger); two close cousins, Daisy Suckley and Polly Delano; and his dog Fala. Polly and Daisy had positioned FDR in his chair at the best angle for light to shine on him while Mercer's friend, the artist Madame Elizabeth Shoumatoff, painted his portrait. At roughly 1:15 PM, Daisy noticed that FDR seemed to be bent over and thought he might have dropped his cigarette. She moved to help him and looked at him. Their eyes connected for the last time as he put his hand on the back of his neck. He then spoke his last words in this life: "I have a terrific pain in the back of my head!" In the next moment, the president slumped unconscious in his chair, never to regain consciousness again. Despite a rapid response and the best efforts of his doctors, he was declared dead at 3:35 PM on April 12, 1945, having died of a sudden and massive stroke. Franklin Delano Roosevelt, the nation's longest serving president, died 83 days into his fourth presidential term, at the age of sixty-three.

As I was driving the Jeep and thinking about FDR's final moments from the dual vantage points of time traveling from 1975 to 1945, my music brain played a traditional American gospel song attributed to Claude Ely, called "There Ain't No Grave Gonna Hold This Body Down." The version that I knew from my upbringing was sung by Sister Rosetta Tharpe in 1956, on the Mercury label album entitled *Gospel Train*. Her version was called **"Can't No Grave Hold My Body Down."** Tharpe was a true American original who gained popularity in the 1930s and 1940s as a recording star of gospel music whose style and methods attracted and influenced early rhythm-and-blues and rock-and-roll aficionados and musicians. As the song played in my head, I looked over at Bucky (who had gotten a bit teary-eyed thinking about the President's fate) and he said, "I've been thinking, BB, about Roosevelt's initials, 'FDR.'"

"OK, what did you come up with?"

Bucky answered, "Finest Damn Ringmaster...Finest Damn Ringmaster."

CHAPTER EIGHT:

BUCKY'S LATE ON THE ROAD TO ATLANTA

"How did it get so late so soon?"
—Dr. Seuss

April 12, 1945 at 2:00 PM local time,
on the road from Warm Springs to Atlanta, Georgia

A s the four of us started the first leg of our 1945 road trip from
Warm Springs, Georgia, headed to the White Hole Project in Oak
Ridge, Tennessee, the sinister forces that FDR had alluded to in our
meeting were already in motion. Roosevelt's call to Vannevar Bush's
home phone had been intercepted by both Russian and Chinese spies.
The Russian master spy Leonid Kvasnikov, working in New York for
the KGB, received immediate notification of FDR's call to Bush. Kvasnikov was focused on stealing America's atomic bomb secrets from
the Manhattan Project, but had become intrigued by a possible connection between America's mysterious, remote and well-protected air
base (Area 51) in the southwestern Nevada desert and the Manhattan
Project in Oak Ridge, Tennessee. It was Kvasnikov who had personally
trained Borya Krovopuskov (Russ Krovo, or Boris,) and sent him to
Oak Ridge in late 1944. Kvasnikov acted on very limited information,
other than an intercepted message: *Captain Jack "'Bucky" Smith was*
alive, and had just left from visiting FDR in person at the Little White House

71

in Warm Springs, Georgia. He was put in charge of a new project, with a new mission. He put out a highest priority bulletin to the KGB network in the Southeastern US to try and identify, intercept, and establish surveillance of Captain Jack Smith. The bulletin went to Russ Krovo in Oak Ridge as part of that KGB network communication.

Simultaneously, the Chinese spies who intercepted Roosevelt's call to Bush were working for the Central Department of Social Affairs (CDSA), which was the precursor of the modern MSS Ministry of State Security, the Chinese secret service. The CDSA was headquartered in northern China during the 1937-1945 Second Sino-Japanese War, the war between China and Japan during WWII, but CDSA Chinese agents were working in the United States in the 1940's. They were also interested in anything related to America's atomic weapons Manhattan Project. However, starting in June 1942, they also had a particular focus on Area 51—and by early 1944, its potential connection to the Oak Ridge, Tennessee site of the Manhattan Project.

Stationed at the University of Tennessee in Knoxville was Chinese agent Li-Ming Sun, whose first name meant "beautiful and bright" and last name meant "grandchild, descendant." Li-Ming came to America in late 1943, under the guise of being a stellar graduate student in chemistry and physics. She spoke perfect English and was known by her local friends at school as "Ming." She was both brilliant and beautiful with straight, jet-black hair, piercing eyes, striking features, and a warm, inviting smile. She was 30 years old, but her documents said she was 24. Trained in martial arts and pistol marksmanship, she was a hidden danger if the circumstances pushed her into action. The Chinese CDSA agents in the Southeastern US received a secret high-level notification to try and identify "Captain Jack 'Bucky' Smith," find him, follow him and await further instructions. After receiving the covert message, Ming felt a chill go down her spine; this might be the break she had spent nearly the last three years waiting, watching, and hoping for.

Subconsciously trying to push some of the morning's stressful thoughts aside, I was daydreaming as I drove the Willys MB Jeep, following Waldo on the road to Atlanta. I was thinking how cool it was to be driving a brand-new World War II Jeep, and my mind started to wander a bit. I had just officially turned 16 years old on December 17, 1974 (four months earlier); I took and passed my driver's license exam on my sixteenth birthday, which fell on a Tuesday that year. I took the test in my dad's 1968 Ford Mustang, which I loved driving. As I *legally* (I learned to drive when I was 14) drove away from the Tennessee state testing site for the first time, I was on "cloud-nine". I remember turning the Mustang's AM radio on and the super-popular 1974 hit song **"Rock Your Baby"** by George McCrae was playing. It was George McCrae's debut number one single, an astronomical hit song that sold north of 11 million copies. That put it in an elite group of single records that sold more than ten million copies worldwide. This song was a perfect example of the cool, soothing, mellow, warm music of the '70s, with easy lyrics that made you happy to be behind the wheel of your favorite car. I was in a trance, half humming, half singing the song, while my head and shoulders were "dancing" with the music in my brain. Then I heard Bucky ask loudly, "Bubble Butt, what the *hell* are you thinking about?"

My mind snapped into focus and as I came back to reality, I started to really sing the words of the song. I kept my head and shoulders dancing as I stared at Bucky with an infectious grin on my face. It even helped Bucky to laugh. He looked back at me and said, "You and your music brain are just crazy, BB. But I like the way it makes you happy."

As the music faded in my brain, I was reminded of something that was mentioned while we were with President Roosevelt earlier that morning, and might actually match the music I was just singing, in some way. So, I quizzed Bucky.

"After talking to your Dad, FDR shared the story that you had gone missing one day in your uncle's plane, but did finally return and land as it was getting dark. You then said that someday you'd have to tell us the story about why you were late with your Uncle Barney's plane that day, saying you were 'in action' but certainly not 'lost in action!' Why don't you enlighten me about your tardiness that day, Bucky Boy?"

Bucky was clearly happy to share this youthful story of adventure with me. "My Uncle Barney had business connections and close friends at the Stearman Aircraft Corporation in Wichita, Kansas. In the late spring of 1934, shortly before the Stearman Corporation was made into a subsidiary of Boeing, he was given a pre-production Boeing-Stearman Model 75 biplane, which was called a Model 75 'Kaydet' at that time. Uncle Barney had a great reputation as a practical test pilot, and living in the Denver area, it was an easy flight to and from Wichita. The Kaydet was built tough—or maybe over-built, with a welded-steel fuselage. It had fabric-covered wooden wings, single-leg landing gear, and a dependable radial engine. Barney loved that plane and flew the heck out of it, testing it for his friends at Stearman. Barney literally helped write the manual for aerobatics using the Stearman biplane. Knowing that it was being pitched to the military as a trainer plane, Barney decided to make me his military wannabe, teenage test pilot to document teaching a rookie new pilot how to fly from scratch. Just as I was turning sixteen years old, in June of 1934, he started teaching me how to fly. I didn't know it at the time, but this particular model biplane did become the famous standard trainer plane for pilots in the US Army and Navy. I was way ahead of my time learning how to fly the Stearman at Barney's insistence, with his expert direction—and I learned fast and fearless! Barney taught me how to perform wing-overs, spins, inverted spins, loops, cartwheels, snap rolls, slow rolls, Immel-manns, the split-S—you name it! By early August of that year he had started to let me fly solo, as long as I stayed on a tight schedule. And he kept *close* track of me and that schedule."

Bucky was happily in his element. I was glad that he was getting his mind cleared with the story. He continued, "So I was learning how to fly during the summer of 1934, after my sophomore year, and I was heading into my junior year at West Denver High School. I had a crush on a girl named Peggy Sue Harding, who was a senior cheerleader and a year older than me. It was late August, school was starting the following week, and I decided that I would go for it and take Peggy Sue on a Sunday date that she would never forget! Her Dad was a Denver banker and well-to-do—so from my young dating perspective at that time, she was pretty, rich, and way above my 'pay grade'! I was sure she would only fall for me if I was a bit of a rebel or a bad boy! Whenever I got a chance to see her or speak to her that summer, I would tell her the stories of my Uncle Barney training me to fly a new 'experimental' airplane that was built to teach military pilots how to fly in combat and war. That got her attention big time! Then I would really ham it up by showing her with my hands and arms how the plane could do loops, and rolls, and literally fly upside down as I made sound effects of the engine gunning and running! It didn't take too long for her to be telling me that she wanted to go flying."

"How did she know that you weren't just making all stuff this up?" I enquired, smiling at Bucky. I chuckled a little bit as I visualized him making plane engine sounds to try and impress a girl. "After all, you were just sixteen years old and getting ready to start your junior year in high school."

Bucky continued, "Well, Bubble Butt, I was a young stud high school football player, going both ways as a defensive linebacker *and* offensive running back! But if that wasn't enough to convince her, I did show her the Stearman flight manual that Barney had given me to study and learn, along with a picture of the plane. Air travel was new and exciting, advancing in the Denver area at that time. Denver Municipal Airport had opened in 1929, and the local Denver Post newspaper complained that it was too far from the city, and claimed its location had been chosen to benefit the mayor's rich financial backers. Peggy Sue's dad was one of those financial backers, and she had heard a lot about the Denver airport politics at home growing up. When it opened, Denver Municipal Airport was used mainly for mail service and private pilots like my Uncle Barney. However, with four runways, a large covered hangar, and a terminal, it was also said to be the West's best airport. When I told her that I was learning to fly out of that airport, she knew a lot about it because of her dad's involvement there."

"All right, enough of the background details! You have tweaked my curiosity. I want to know what happened, and why you were late getting back with the plane!"

"When you're out training and flying for hours, that doesn't stop the call of nature. I mean, when you gotta go, you gotta go! That summer I learned where all the suitable farmer's fields were to land the plane, take a leak, and get back in the air again. One of those fields was located west of Denver West High School, and that farm was owned by my Aunt Edith. We called her "Edy;" her husband's name was Fred; they had no children of their own. Both of them were very laid back, and never asked many questions. I gave Peggy Sue directions to their farm, telling her to take the second right gravel road until it dead ended at one of Aunt Edy's fields and park there. Edy and Fred were accustomed to me landing in their fields from time to time and wouldn't think twice about it. I told her to meet me there at 2 PM on

Sunday afternoon, and to look up in the sky 'for a date she would never forget!'"

"Why didn't you just leave together from the Denver Municipal Airport?" I asked.

"Her dad knew a lot of people there, and I was reasonably certain that no parent was going to let their precious daughter go on a first date with some sixteen-year-old boy bursting with testosterone, flying aerobatics in a Stearman biplane. I told her to make up a lame excuse to borrow the car to go meet with some of the cheerleaders for practice or whatever. Since this was going to be the 'date of the decade,' I told her we would avoid asking for permission and instead ask for forgiveness later, if anyone found out. It was great; I was building on my 'bad boy' persona with her by using this approach, and a secret rendezvous location only added to it!"

"OK, now you've got me hooked, Bucky! What happened? Did you pull it off?"

"We almost got busted before we got started. I told Peggy Sue to bring a warm coat to fly in; even though it was sunny and hot in late August, it can be cold at thirteen thousand feet. Her mother saw her walking out the door to get in the car with a winter coat tucked under her arm. Completely baffled, her mother ran outside and stopped her, asking her why she was taking a winter coat to cheerleading practice in August. Already nervous about our secret rendezvous, Peggy Sue nearly froze up. She blankly stared at her mom for a few seconds that seemed like an eternity before she recovered and said, 'I was looking for a blanket to sit on in the field. I couldn't find one so I grabbed my coat. It will be OK, Mom; it's my old coat!' Her mom responded with a warm smile, 'OK, honey, but try to ignore those horny football players who are always hounding you beautiful cheerleaders!'

"I told my Uncle Barney that I was taking the plane out solo that Sunday afternoon, and that I would be gone until 6 PM. As per our flight training agreement, I was to stop at his house after I landed, and was on my way home to give him a report of the day's flight activities. I discreetly packed a picnic lunch for us, and told my parents that I might be a few minutes late for dinner. I drove to the airport and got the Stearman in the air on time to be circling over Aunt Edy's farm field at 2 PM. Peggy Sue was only a few minutes late; I saw her coming in the distance in a convertible coupe! I circled around behind her as she was taking the dead-end gravel road, and made a slow roll pass over her and out in front of her. Then I circled back and landed, pulling the plane near to where she had parked.

"She was driving her dad's new 1934 Lincoln Model KB Convertible Roadster by LeBaron. I'm not sure what was more awesome, her dad's car or the Stearman biplane. That V-12 Lincoln convertible roadster was a cream color with red leather interior, and Peggy Sue looked like an absolute goddess getting out of that thing! She was wearing a long pleated red and black plaid skirt with a white blouse that had puffy shoulders, and she had bright red lipstick on; it was just too much for this young man's imagination! Nevertheless, I contained myself, keeping my cowboy demeanor as I strolled over to her and the car. I pulled off my leather flight cap and goggles and said, 'Looks like a nice day to go conquer the sky, don't you think?' To the delight of my fantasies, she came right up and hugged me, tickled my cheek with her auburn hair held in her hand, and teased me in a flirty voice. 'I have a special mission for my secret military pilot! Do you think you are up for the job, big boy?'"

This story was getting better than watching TV at home in 1975! We were on the main two-lane highway heading north into Atlanta, following Waldo closely. I was sure that Tater was talking up a storm with Waldo, but I was feeling totally entertained by Bucky's story. "OK, you big stud-muffin, what was this special mission?"

Bucky ran his right hand through his hair, leaned his head back, and smiled. "I held her hand as we walked over to the Stearman, while I told her that I was 'Captain Denver', ready for battle, and to lay it on me!

"She responded, 'I'm actually the co-captain of the varsity cheerleading squad. To make today's story more factual with my parents, I scheduled a practice session at 2:30 this afternoon, with both the varsity and junior varsity squads, out on the auxiliary field.'

"As she was speaking, I grabbed the spare leather flight cap and goggles and started to pull the flight cap over her beautiful auburn hair. She never missed a beat, but our eyes fully connected as I fastened her helmet under her chin. She continued with her mission plans.

"'Since I am trying to tell the truth that I went to practice today, your mission is to fly close enough to that practice session for me to say I was there. I'm sure a couple hundred feet is close enough for me to be a truthful co-captain! Is that a mission that Captain Denver can accomplish?' she purred.

"Captain Denver at your service, madam! Let's get you on board and make this mission count!"

I interjected at this point, "Bucky, don't tell me that you buzzed the high school with the Stearman biplane in 1934! There went your secret rendezvous! Oh yes, and by the way, I don't think I can help myself: I'm going to call you 'Captain Denver' at some point in the future. You just can't make this stuff up!"

Bucky went on, "Barney's Stearman Kaydet biplane was painted yellow with a red stripe around the fuselage. Peggy Sue's long, red and black plaid, pleated skirt made it look like she had dressed for the part that day! It had a typical tandem biplane seating arrangement with open cockpits, only the pilot sat in the rear and the passenger in front. With Peggy Sue in the front cockpit wearing her coat, leather cap, and goggles, we took off from Aunt Edy's field and headed east toward the Denver West High School auxiliary field, where cheerleading practice was already underway. Peggy Sue had let her best friend and co-captain, Mary Evans, know to expect something highly unusual at practice that day. She was correct, we were high and we were unusual! We came over the practice field at three thousand feet, and from there I executed a loop directly over the heads of the cheerleaders. This was Peggy Sue's first plane ride and within a few minutes in the air, she found herself in a full loop over the cheerleading squad! She was screaming the whole way through the loop. Co-captain Mary Evans and the squad below were mesmerized, gasping at our yellow Stearman biplane giving them a stunt show.

"After the full loop, I decided to give them a little scare with a spin maneuver, this time starting at about thirty-three hundred feet. When you do a spin, the airplane is completely stalled; you're falling toward the ground nose first, following a corkscrew path through the air. It looks like you're going to crash. To recover from the spin, you apply full rudder opposite to the direction of the corkscrew rotation, and follow with positive forward stick. When the rotation stops and you are in a straight dive, you neutralize the rudder and then smoothly pull the stick back to pull out of the dive. I definitely got her within a few hundred feet of her practice session as I pulled out of that dive! Peggy Sue was again screaming at the top of her lungs, but laughing at the same time.

"I told Peggy Sue to make sure that her safety belt was still completely tight and her goggles were securely over her eyes. I took us over the field in a slow roll so that we were perfectly upside down just as we flew over the cheerleading squad's position. I am sure that her friend Mary and the squad below could hear Peggy's screams as we flew by inverted, and then rolled back upright after going by. I finished the 'show' with an Immelmann maneuver: a half loop followed by a half slow roll at the top of the loop. By that time, I think there was a small crowd gathering around the school, and Peggy Sue seemed a bit dizzy and disoriented as to what was up and what was down. I yelled up to her and asked, 'Was that close enough, madam cheerleader?' She loudly responded, 'Yes Captain Denver, mission accomplished!' I then made one last pass over the practice field at a lower altitude, waving our wings at the group below as I headed west toward the foothills and then turned north. I believe we got a standing ovation from the cheerleading squad, and gave them all a memorable Sunday afternoon!

"For the next thirty minutes, we cruised up the front range along the Colorado foothills like two birds, gliding in the blue sky on a gorgeous summer afternoon. It was just a perfect day to be in the plane. I let her take the control stick in the front cockpit and taught her how to do gentle turns and go up and down. We were flying up in the Boulder, Colorado area, where the pioneer women had said they thought the mountain rocks there looked like the irons they used to press their clothes. That whole Front Range mountain formation then became known as the 'Flatirons;' it is quite scenic and beautiful there. It was past time for lunch by then, so I brought us in to land in a flat valley field below the Flatirons, just south of Boulder. It was there that we made our spread on the ground and had our late afternoon picnic lunch together. We ate lunch while we giggled and laughed about our aerial stunt show, and how shocked everyone must have been at the cheerleading practice! After eating, we took a long walk up to the base of the closest mountain and held hands all the way. We hit it off big time, talking about all our friends, the upcoming school year, football, cheerleading, and of course, flying! Then we walked back near the plane where we had our picnic lunch, lay down on our blanket, and started making out. She was a great kisser; I could have stayed with that action indefinitely!"

"Did you have sex?" I enquired without hesitation.

"Bubble Butt, get your mind out of the gutter, boy!" He shoved me on the shoulder. "It was our first date!" He tilted his head, smiled and said, "We waited a couple of months to have sex! Anyway, we did overstay our time on that valley field by the Flatirons, enjoying each other's company. Time flew by and I didn't notice the sun was getting so low until the Flatirons cast a long shadow over us, with the sun setting in the West. I thought, *Oh, shit! Bucky, you are* really *late–and that's not good!* It was already almost 7 PM, and I had to get Peggy to her car and me and the plane to Denver Municipal Airport before sunset. We gathered ourselves up, got in the Stearman, took off, and headed directly to Aunt Edy's field. Even though I was nervous about being late, the flight to Aunt Edy's was magical. It was a magnificently clear evening, with no wind, and I was crazy in love for the first time. It felt like Peggy Sue and I were floating home on a magic carpet!"

As soon as he said that my music brain started playing **"Magic Carpet Ride"** by Steppenwolf. The song was initially released in 1968 as the lead single from their album called *The Second*. The song peaked at number three in the US, but its popularity lasted for 16 weeks— which was a longer chart run than any other single Steppenwolf song. I enquired, "So how does this story end there, stud boy?"

Bucky laughed at me and continued, "When we landed at Aunt Edy's field, I walked Peggy Sue over to her dad's V-12 Lincoln Convertible Roadster, and we kissed some more as we leaned against that beautiful car! I was mesmerized by her. She finally said, 'Time for you to go Captain Denver, but I'll never forget this day so long as I live. We'll have to do this again sometime!' I regained my bad boy composure and told her that she better haul ass in that V-12 to get home quick, and think of a good story to tell her parents. With that exchange, we parted ways and I ran to the plane. I took off and circled for a few minutes, watching Peggy Sue get off the gravel road and start heading east back toward Denver. Once she was back on pavement I flew down and buzzed her, then pulled up in a climb in front of her, waving my wings as I flew toward Denver Municipal Airport.

"By the time I got to the airport, the sun was down and it was nearly dark. I have to say that I was getting a little afraid, but was determined to get the plane safely on the ground before it was pitch dark. I hit the ground a little hard and bounced as I landed, but kept the plane on course and on the runway. Those Stearman biplanes have sturdy landing gear! As I taxied to the hangar, my dad, Jim, and Uncle Barney were standing there with their arms folded, looking *super* pissed. I didn't know whether to tell the truth or make up a lie. So, I did what every teenager on earth does: I took my best first shot with a lie."

I interjected, "Bucky, this is already the greatest teenage adventure story ever told, and it happened in August of 1934. I can totally visualize the whole thing, and I'm shaking in my knickers thinking about your dad and your uncle ganging up to beat the crap out of you for scaring them to death—thinking that you had crashed and died that day!"

"You got that right, BB. My dad was the first to speak. He said that Barney drove to our house to tell him and my mom that I was late, and he was worried because I was never late with the plane. Mom freaked out, got all teary-eyed; she sent Dad and Barney to the airport, and told them not to come home without me. They snooped around a bit at the airport, but no one there had seen me since about 1:30 that afternoon. They decided to wait at the hangar and hope for the best. It was almost dark and they were just about to leave and report me as missing to the Denver police department when they heard the drone of Stearman radial engine in the distance, and watched me bounce as

I landed the plane nearly in the dark and rolled up to the hangar. Dad looked at me sternly and asked, 'What happened, Bucky?'

"Well, I took off this afternoon to practice all my stunts, and it was a beautiful day for flying. I got out west and north of town and didn't pay close enough attention to my fuel level. I must have burned more fuel than usual because of all the stunts I was running. By the time I noticed how low I was on fuel, I knew that I couldn't make it back. I landed in a field over by Boulder and had to walk at least a mile to a gas station, making several trips back and forth. Then I had to walk the gas can back after I had enough fuel on board. I'm so sorry; I knew you would be worried and think that something bad had happened."

I looked over at Bucky and said, "That sounds like a pretty logical story, plus walking back and forth like that would take quite a bit of time. Did your Dad and Barney buy it?"

Bucky, smiling with his lips pursed, shook his head. Looking rather guilty, he replied, "Not exactly, BB."

"Well, what happened?" I anxiously asked.

"Barney was staring at me with a smirk on his face, shaking his head widely. He blurted out, 'I guess some girl at the gas station must have given you a big kiss on the neck there, Bucky. I don't think those red lip marks came flying through the air and landed perfectly on your neck like that while you were doing a loop or a spin?"

Bucky went on, "I turned beet red, and knew my goose was cooked! I had wiped Peggy Sue's lipstick off my lips earlier, but didn't think to check my neck. Both Dad and Barney were standing there with their hands on their hips, staring at me, I think with a mixture of anger, relief, and curiosity. I had to come clean and tell them the truth about what happened that day. I got grounded for a few weeks, but when I brought Peggy Sue over to meet my parents and Uncle Barney, they all really liked her. The momentary terror of me gone missing in the plane became a faded memory for everyone."

"What happened to you and Peggy Sue?"

"We dated steady all through her senior year and the following summer. In the fall of 1935, her dad—who was a devout Catholic and had moved to Denver from his home town of Chicago—sent her to Mundelein College, a private Roman Catholic women's college in Chicago. We wrote letters to each other for a while, but gradually drifted apart. After I went to West Point in the fall of 1936, I never heard from her again. I do think about her from time to time; after all, she was my first love."

As Bucky finished his story, we were coming into Atlanta, still following right behind Waldo and Tater. The high priority bulletins that had gone out to the Russian and Chinese spy networks in the Southeastern US had indicated that an American officer known as "Captain Jack 'Bucky' Smith" was alive, had just left from visiting FDR in person at the Little White House in Warm Springs, Georgia, and was put in charge of a new project with a new mission. The orders were to identify, intercept, and establish surveillance of Captain Jack Smith. Surveillance was set up primarily to the north and south of Warm Springs, Georgia—and on the southern fringes of Atlanta in particular—looking for military vehicles carrying an American military officer or officers. Two brand new Willys MB Jeeps driven by officers and following each other into Atlanta on a Thursday afternoon was as good a bet as any for those trying to find us. Unbeknownst to us, as we drove through Atlanta, we were being followed by spies from both Russia and China.

CHAPTER NINE:

THE ROAD TO TENNESSEE

"Because the greatest part of a road trip isn't arriving at your destination. It's all the wild stuff that happens along the way."
—Emma Chase

April 12, 1945 at 3:05 PM local time, Atlanta, Georgia

As we drove through the middle of Atlanta, Waldo took an exit and pulled into a Gulf gas station. When we pulled up to the gas pumps, the gas attendants quickly came out to service our Jeeps, washing the windshields and filling the tanks. I asked Waldo, "Is your big prostate feeling the call of nature again?"

He smartly answered, "As a matter of fact, Bubble Butt, I *am* ready to tap my bladder and get myself a nice cold bottle of Coca-Cola. Maybe you should drain that tiny lizard of yours before we get back on the road to Tennessee."

I responded, "You mean my Tyrannosaurus rex?"

We all used the restroom and got cold bottles of Coca-Cola to take on the road. We huddled and talked at the gas pump about the next leg of the journey. Waldo had made the executive decision that we would drive from Atlanta to Chattanooga, Tennessee and stay the night at the famous Read House Hotel. The Read House had modern amenities for 1945, and Bucky could make his two phone calls to

Colonel Carter Clarke and Vannevar Bush there, as he had been instructed by FDR. We would then get an early start to Oak Ridge in the morning, and begin to execute our plan to secure the future of the White Hole Project. As we were talking, we were being spied upon and photographed by the Russian and Chinese spies who were watching our every move.

With our Jeeps full of gas again, our bladders empty, and some caffeine to consume in the form of cold, original Coca-Cola, we got back on the road again and headed to Chattanooga, Tennessee. We were oblivious to the fact that we were being followed by both Russian and Chinese spies. The spies were oblivious to each other, thinking they were "alone" in their surveillance. Also oblivious to just about everything at this moment was yours truly, Bubble Butt. As we got back on the road, I was briefly in my own world, thinking about what was going on in 1975. I loved rock and roll, and one of my favorite popular bands at that time was the Canadian group Bachman-Turner Overdrive, also known as BTO. They had released their third album (which I proudly owned), called *Not Fragile*, in September 1974; their huge number-one hit single from that album was called "You Ain't Seen Nothing Yet." In January 1975, BTO released another single from the *Not Fragile* album, called **"Roll on Down the Highway,"** which had just peaked at number fourteen in the United States and number four in Canada in March of 1975. It was rumored that they had written the song for a Ford Motor Company commercial, but Ford never used it. So what? BTO used it, and made millions! The song was banging in my brain; I was tapping my left foot on the floor and bobbing my head, my right hand on the steering wheel.

I was holding my bottle of Coca-Cola between my legs and reflexively took a sip, which somehow snapped me back to reality. I looked at Bucky, who was also enjoying a sip of his Coke. "Hey Bucky, did you know that Coca-Cola does not have a patent on this beverage we're drinking?"

"I never really thought about it, BB. I would think they would want a patent on this delicious and famous drink so no one could copy them," Bucky replied.

"That's the problem, my 'aerobatic, romance in the sky, pilot friend'!"

"Cut the crap, BB. What do you mean, 'that's the problem?'"

I continued, "Having a patent on this beverage would be a big problem for the Coca-Cola Company. When you write up and get the office to issue a patent, you tell the world exactly how you make your product. Then your secret is out, and everyone can see it. Sure, no one is *supposed* to infringe on your patent rights, but how do you prove that infringement on a beverage, which is a liquid product with some blended ingredients? The Coca-Cola people were very smart. They trademarked their product brand name, made their name and lettering world-famous, and kept their Coke formula secret in a vault somewhere all these years. Try as they might, no one else knows exactly how to blend Coca-Cola—and they have an unbeatable brand name, recognized everywhere on planet Earth! They did patent their uniquely shaped bottles. Maybe you and I can come up with an idea like that someday!"

Bucky responded with a grin, "I like pork and beans with my barbecue. Maybe we should try to trademark 'Bucky's Beans?'"

"That's not catchy enough," I responded. "Why don't we try 'Bubble Butt Beans?' The commercial could tout it as 'the triple-B to move your bowels!'"

"For sure that would help you, BB, because you are so full of shit!" Bucky concluded.

"I want to take this new Willys MB Jeep back home with us to 1975," I said, changing the subject. "This thing is awesome; everybody wants one, and it also has quite a storied history!"

"Since you are on such a history roll right now, why don't you go ahead and enlighten me, Colonel Butt Beans!" Bucky retorted.

"OK, Captain Denver, sovereign protector of the White Hole Project, here we go... Before World War II started, the US Army had an aging fleet of military vehicles consisting of some Ford Model T's, motorcycles and antiquated trucks. In the summer of 1940, concerned about the growing prospect of another war, the Army requested bids from US auto companies for a new quarter-ton, four-wheel drive truck or vehicle that could adapt to demanding battlefield conditions, and serve for reconnaissance as well. Leave it to the military to be in slow motion until they want something bad; they gave the auto makers a time frame of about four months to design and deliver the first test vehicles. Given that time frame, only three companies entered the competition: American Bantam Car Company, Willys-Overland, and Ford. Interestingly, Bantam actually won the initial contest and got the first prototype built, but they lacked the production capacity to fill the Army's orders. By the fall of 1940, both Willys and Ford got in the game and submitted their own prototypes. This Jeep we are driving was originally called the Willys 'MA,' for 'military model A.' Despite the initial short 'schedule' requested by the Army, it took them until the summer of 1941 to make a final decision."

"That's typical of the Army, BB. No matter what happens in the outside world, they move at their own pace. It's called the 'chain of command,' and every link has to make their opinion known. A lot of hands would be in on the decision-making process to acquire a new vehicle like the Jeep. Don't forget, I graduated from West Point," Bucky added.

I smiled and saluted Bucky. "Yes sir, I will always remember that! In the summer of 1941, the Army selected Willys-Overland as the winner of the competition. They needed standardization of the Jeep. Willys had the best price, at about seven hundred fifty dollars per Jeep—and the best engine, with their torquey sixty-horsepower, four-cylinder, 'Go-Devil' engine."

"Maybe Ford should have come up with a better name for their engine!" Bucky quipped.

"Well as a matter of fact, some of the Ford and Bantam design features got incorporated into the final Willys' Army Jeep version, and it was then designated as the *Willys MB*, which is what we are driving now. In late 1941, the Army needed so many Jeeps that Willys could not keep up with production demand. Ford got to join the party after all; they just had to produce Jeeps using Willys' blueprints, so that all the parts were precisely interchangeable. Ford stamped every part, including nuts and bolts, with the letter *F* and designated their Jeeps as *GPW*, after their own original competition model designation of GP, with the *W* added to reference the Willys' licensed design. More than six hundred and sixty thousand Jeeps were built for use in World War II, with Willys building the most. And here we are, driving one of those famous vehicles right now! Enzo Ferrari famously said that the Jeep was 'America's only real sports car,' and General Eisenhower said the Jeep was 'one of the tools that won the war.'"

Bucky commented, "I've seen some modern Jeeps driving around Oak Ridge since I went back to the future with you."

"That's right," I replied. "After World War II was over, Willys trademarked the *Jeep* brand name and started producing public versions of the Jeep called the CJ, which stood for civilian Jeep. The American Motors Corporation now owns the Jeep name brand, and you could buy a CJ-5 Jeep in 1975 Oak Ridge! I suspect the Jeep name brand will go on forever, just like Coca-Cola."

Bucky exclaimed, "Here's a toast to that!" We clinked our Coke bottles together and drank what was left.

We took US Route 41 north to Chattanooga, averaging 40-45 mph in our Willys Jeeps. This route took us straight through the center of the small town of Calhoun, Georgia, where Waldo decided to pull over and stop to stretch and get a snack at the local pharmacy, which in 1945, was the place to get just about anything you needed. We all gathered around stretching for a minute on the sidewalk, and Bucky told the group that when I wasn't singing some song to myself, I was talking up a storm about the history of Coca-Cola and Jeeps. I told everyone that Bucky was also known as "Captain Denver, the Romeo of the skies!" Waldo said that Tater had talked nonstop since Warm Springs, and he needed to get out of the Jeep to stretch his legs and rest his ears, not being sure which was in greater need! He mentioned that we had another 50 miles to drive to get to Chattanooga. I looked at Tater and caught him staring at something down the street, then asked what he had to say for himself.

Tater looked around at all of us and in his thick southern accent said, "I'm sure glad to see all of you wearing your sidearms. I mentioned my Aunt Jane from South Georgia to all of you earlier... Well, her husband, my Uncle Mike, always says, 'If you want good Social Security, invest in lead.' I'll explain more when we get inside."

I thought that was a bit of an odd comment, if even coming from Tater. We all walked into the Calhoun Pharmacy and before we could take a look around inside, Tater called us back together. He explained, "There is a black 1940 Chevy coupe parked down the street, same side as us. I noticed that very car behind us on the highway a few times, while I was yakking away at Waldo. There are two men sitting in that car watching us. I'm from Georgia, and no one in a small Georgia town like this one dresses as nice as those guys are dressed. If those guys are spying on us, we might have to go cancel their birth certificates!"

Waldo, who had taken FDR's direct warnings to us to heart that morning, asked the pharmacist to show us the back door and said, "Follow me, boys! Let's go check these guys out!"

Sitting parked in a 1940 black Chevy Coupe down the street from the pharmacy were two Russian spies: Viktor Bykov, known in Atlanta as Vic Bison, and Stefan Petrov known in Atlanta as Steve Rock. They had been tailing us from Atlanta, with instructions to identify and follow an American military officer named Captain Jack "Bucky" Smith.

Viktor, who was the driver, looked at Stefan and said, "Lucky for us, these Americans sure have to stop and piss a lot!" Stefan chuckled at that comment. He snapped a few more pictures of the Jeeps to go along with those he had taken of us standing on the sidewalk in front of the pharmacy, using his Leica camera. After we walked into the pharmacy, they had apparently waited for a minute or two before taking a break to light up a couple of Lucky Strikes. Stefan was smoking with his right hand and was halfway through his cigarette. He dropped his hand outside the door, still holding his half-smoked Lucky Strike. At that moment, I grabbed his right hand and yanked it back hard; Bucky put his Colt .45 to Stefan's head. Simultaneously, Waldo put his pistol to Viktor's head. If that was not enough, Tater popped up in front of the car with his pistol pointed at both of them through the front windshield.

Waldo, whose left shoulder was still sore from the bullet wound on New Year's Eve, was in no mood to play games or mince words—not this time. "Give me your ID's and your guns now, or I'm putting the first bullet in your crotch and ending your manhood forever. Do you understand?"

They both promptly complied, and Viktor said that they worked for the government. Their ID's identified them by their American names, Vic Bison and Steve Rock. Their English was perfect; we did not detect any obvious accents. However, Bucky did see Stefan's Leica camera on the car floor.

We took their guns and Bucky demanded possession of Stefan's camera. Waldo asked, "What branch of government is assigned to follow American military officers?"

Viktor replied, "We work for a secret branch of government and I cannot divulge our purpose."

Waldo didn't buy it for one second. "Bucky, show Steve that we mean business." With no hesitation whatsoever, Bucky summarily cold-cocked Stefan, nearly knocking him unconscious. Waldo continued to address Viktor. "Listen to me, Vic; turn this car around and head south, straight back to Atlanta, right now. I will watch you drive away. Tell your superiors that we will find you, kill you, and send you back to Russia, or wherever the hell you came from, in a plywood box. If we see your ugly faces or this car again, we will not hesitate to make you beg for mercy at the pearly gates, or burn in hell—your choice. Now *go!*"

We all continued to point our weapons at them as Viktor started the car and drove off. As he drove away, Viktor must have realized their man had been identified, that it was Bucky who had hit Stefan. At least part of their mission had been accomplished.

After the black Chevy coupe was out of sight, Waldo congratulated Tater for being so observant. "Now let's get the hell out of here, and head to Chattanooga for the night. Bucky has two important phone calls to make, and I'm ready to call it a day!"

The Chinese spies had been stealthier and more careful not to be detected; they had observed our whole encounter with the Russian spies. As we got back into our Jeeps to head to Chattanooga, we were still being followed. Viktor Bykov and Stefan Petrov drove south to Cartersville, Georgia and stopped there to place a phone call to their KGB station chief, telling him that they had positively identified and made initial contact with USAAF Captain Jack "Bucky" Smith in Calhoun, Georgia. They indicated that Captain Smith was headed north into Tennessee with three other officers, and they gave descriptions. They also mentioned that agent Petrov got pistol whipped alongside the head and this group was armed and dangerous. Another high priority bulletin went out minutes later to the KGB network in Tennessee, including Borya Krovopuskov (Russ Krovo) in Oak Ridge. The Chinese spies alerted agent Li-Ming Sun, stationed at the University of Tennessee in Knoxville.

CHAPTER TEN:

BUCKY MAKES THE CALLS

"You have to learn the rules of the game.
And then you have to play better than anyone else."
—Albert Einstein

April 12, 1945 at 7:09 PM local time at the Read House Hotel,
in Chattanooga, Tennessee

It took us about ninety minutes to finish our drive to the historic Read House Hotel, located in the heart of Chattanooga. The hotel dated back to 1847, when Thomas Crutchfield built the Crutchfield House Hotel across from the Western and Atlantic Railway Station; it was the center of social and political activity in old Chattanooga. In 1863, Crutchfield House became a hospital to serve both Confederate and Union troops, and many soldiers were treated and/or died there. It is said that this part of the grounds' history has been a source of haunting the Read House. The Crutchfield House caught fire and burned to the ground in 1867. After the fire, the Crutchfield family chose not to rebuild. John T. Read stepped in to build a new hotel in its place.

The new Read House Hotel opened in 1872 and several expansions were made in the 1880's. In 1904, Coca-Cola was introduced to the city of Chattanooga at the Read House drugstore. In 1926, the hotel was torn down and a brand new, modern, $2.5 million, ten-story hotel was built, with 400 rooms. In 1927, a woman named Annalisa Netherly arrived at Read House Hotel and occupied room 311 for some time. The stories about her real-life activities vary, but her life ended in the bathtub in that room; her throat had been slit, and she bled out in the tub. The room is famously haunted by her spirit, who is said to hate men who smoke. In 1932, Winston Churchill stayed at Read House while on a lecture tour. He made national headlines during his stay by declaring, "Prohibition is a bad thing!"

Somehow missing getting written into the history books, a contingent of the Bad Love Gang checked into the Read House Hotel in Chattanooga, Tennessee at precisely 7:09 PM Eastern War Time on April 12, 1945, while Harry Truman recited the oath of office as administered by Supreme Court Chief Justice Harlan Stone in the White House Oval Office. Truman became the 33rd President of the United States at that moment, following the unexpected death of Franklin Delano Roosevelt from a massive stroke earlier in the day at the Little White House in Warm Springs, Georgia.

After checking in, Bucky got to work making the two phone calls to Colonel Carter Clarke and Vannevar Bush, as instructed by FDR. We agreed that I would listen in and help if possible. Colonel Clarke and his US Army Signal Intelligence Service had been in charge of running the Venona Project since February 1943. Clark and his expert code-breaking team had discovered that Russian espionage efforts were active at the Manhattan Project in Los Alamos, New Mexico. Even more surprising, Clark's team had intercepted and decrypted a few messages from the Russians indicating they suspected something different was occurring at Oak Ridge, connected to our top-secret airbase in the Nevada desert (Area 51). Clarke himself did not know of any such connection, mainly because anything related to Area 51 was known by so few people. Clarke was therefore very anxious to speak with USAAF Captain Jack "Bucky" Smith about the "Denver Project" that FDR had alluded to. Bucky and I had decided to use my story about top-secret, weapons grade, plutonium production connecting Area 51 and Oak Ridge. Anything related to the existence of exotic matter or time travel was off-limits with Colonel Clarke and the Venona Project team. On the other hand, Vannevar Bush knew about the discovery of exotic matter, Area 51, the details of the White Hole Project, and Bucky's inaugural time travel mission. The two conversations would take separate tracks and Bucky would be careful to maintain that separation.

Bucky dialed Colonel Clarke first; he answered the phone on the first ring. "Good evening, Colonel Clarke, this is Captain Jack Smith, but please feel free to call me 'Bucky.' I am sorry to have to call you on this somber day. I was actually very close to President Roosevelt, and was with him a few hours before he died today. He instructed me to call you tonight so that we could coordinate our efforts with the Venona and Denver Projects."

Clarke responded, "The president called me just before noon today and said that you would be calling tonight. My orders are to cooperate fully with you, Bucky, and help you in any way possible. Like you, I admired the president immensely; losing him is difficult to measure or accept. Please let me know what I can do for you."

"A few hours ago, my team and I were intercepted by two Russian spies, who probably tailed us from Atlanta. They drove a 1940 black Chevy coupe, and their IDs said they were Vic Bison and Steve Rock. I recommend that you find those two men and learn what you can from them."

"Bison is on our watch list in the southeast. Steve Rock is a new name to my memory bank," Clarke replied.

Bucky continued, "We are headed to Oak Ridge early tomorrow morning to formally launch the Denver Project. I can tell you that there is a connection between our secret airbase in Nevada and the Manhattan Project in Oak Ridge, and it has to do with a new method to process weapons-grade plutonium better than any nation on earth. Anyone or any nation interested in developing atomic weapons would want to get their hands on this process. The Denver Project will protect this secret process at all costs, by direct order from the president—and he has put me in charge. My team and I will be in Oak Ridge tomorrow, and we will travel from there to Chicago. Then we are going to Denver, Colorado, followed by Colorado Springs, Colorado and finally to the base in Nevada. Do you have any advice regarding Russian espionage activity that I should be aware of, given this travel itinerary?"

"I'd say that you better keep your eyes sharply peeled all along the way, except I do not think that anyone will be foolish enough to follow you in the southwest Nevada desert; they would be too obvious. That said, we have seen some violent encounters in Chicago and in the Denver area, where we call the Russian spy cell there the Vodka Cowboys. It's a little bit like the snake bitten wild west out there, so don't be afraid to shoot first if you have to! We also know that there is espionage activity at Oak Ridge, but only because we have decrypted some messages that obviously came from that location. By the way, my main job is decryption of Russian communications; to some extent, you and your team are on your own as you travel across the country. However, I do have a lot of resources and valuable connections that I can call into play to help you as you go. It will be very useful for you and me to continue to trade notes as you develop and run the Denver Project."

Bucky replied, "Thank you Colonel Clarke. FDR said that you would have the most current information about the Russians, and I appreciate your insights tonight. Can I reach you at this phone number at any time?"

"Yes, this number rings directly to the US Army Signal Intelligence Service office. There is someone here at all times, and the line is secure."

"That is perfect," Bucky said, "and I am sure we will talk again sometime soon. If we have any more encounters with the Russians, I will be in touch right away. Thank you and good night, sir."

As Bucky hung up, I said, "That was pretty smooth going, and he did know something about that Vic Bison guy we ambushed today. It sounds like the rest of our road trip will not be boring! I am interested to hear what your friend Vannevar Bush has to say about us blowing the White Hole Project connecting tunnel tomorrow."

Bucky then placed the second call to Vannevar Bush's secure office phone line. Vannevar answered the phone in the middle of the first ring and immediately enquired, "Bucky, is that you?"

"Yes, Vannevar, it is certainly me. I am alive, and it is great to hear your voice! I am so sorry that we have to talk business on the very day that the president died, but this is what he wanted."

"I fully understand, Bucky, and I am so relieved to know that you are alive! Please give me the short version of what went wrong with the inaugural White Hole Project time-travel mission, how you got back, and how I can help you with what Franklin called the 'Denver Project.'"

"This is the short version, Vannevar. The White Hole Project time-travel machine works just fine. My Global Cosmic Positioning Device got damaged when I was struck by what we are calling 'white lightning' in the time tunnel on my way to East Anglia, England. You could not recall me because my GCPD was damaged, so I was stuck in time. A group of people—who are my heroes—from 1974 Oak Ridge found the White Hole Project, learned how to use it, and traveled to East Anglia to use the Phantom Fortress to rescue some Holocaust victims. They exchanged my GCPD for a good one, and I went back to the future with them. We were all celebrating New Year's Eve together at the White Hole Project in 1975 when we were ambushed by a Russian spy. Rather than tell the authorities, five of us returned to Warm Springs, Georgia this morning, to meet with the president. We wanted to see if it would make more sense for us to be in charge of protecting the security and integrity of the White Hole Project. The president actually agreed with that assessment and put me directly in charge of that security mission, which we are calling the 'Denver Project'. I am calling you from Chattanooga, Tennessee tonight, and we are headed to Oak Ridge early tomorrow morning to take our first steps to secure the integrity and future of the White Hole Project."

Vannevar replied, "I believe that I know what the president was thinking. You really are the only person who could connect the necessary dots to ensure the security of the White Hole Project, and his other main concern."

"What other 'concern' are you referring to, Vannevar?"

"What else did the President ask you to do, Bucky?"

"Wow, OK...he handed me an envelope addressed to General Claire Chennault of the Flying Tigers in China, with the presidential seal, and asked us to use the White Hole to deliver that envelope directly to Chennault in June of 1942."

Vannevar audibly exhaled. "Bucky, the two largest secrets in the entire history of the United States, and perhaps the world, are resting on your shoulders tonight. We are now calling Indian Springs Airfield in Nevada, where the alien spaceship crashed, 'Area 51'. You did not realize it until now, but I am telling you that the president has made you and your 'Denver Project' the security mission for both the White Hole Project and Area 51. That is why he is sending you to see General Chennault. Can you fly a P-40 Warhawk?"

Listening to this conversation, I had to check to make sure my pants weren't turning brown! My music brain, trying to make me cope with what was happening, started playing **"Paranoid,"** by Black Sabbath. The British heavy metal band released the song in 1970; it hit number four on the UK Singles Chart, and number 61 on the *Billboard* Hot 100. It was a bona-fide head-banger, and exactly what I needed at the moment! Bucky, a little red in the face said, "You're sounding a little bit like FDR right now. *Hell yes*, I can fly a P-40 Warhawk! Upside down, right side up, in a dive, in a spin, in a roll, you name it, I can do it! We are going to Peterson Army Air Base in Colorado Springs in a few days so that I can teach a couple of my heroes here how to fly the P-40 as well. As soon as we finish our first steps in securing the integrity and future of the White Hole Project in Oak Ridge tomorrow, we're taking a road trip to Chicago, and then on to Denver and Colorado Springs, to train in the P-40s. We will finish our road trip at Area 51. After all that, we will head to China in June 1942 to meet with General Chennault and give him this letter from Roosevelt."

"Are you going to Chicago to meet with the Met Lab scientists?" Vannevar enquired.

"Who and what are the Met Lab scientists?" Bucky questioned.

"The Chicago Metallurgical Laboratory scientists built and operated the first prototype atomic reactor called Chicago Pile One, in an abandoned squash court under the grandstands of Stagg Field at the University of Chicago in December 1942. CP-1 demonstrated the validity of the theories that have made the Manhattan Project, and the atomic bomb, possible. A physicist named Arthur Compton is the director of the Met Lab. Compton won the Nobel Prize in 1927 for demonstrating that electromagnetic radiation has a particle, as well as a wave, nature. He and the Met Lab have been the ones in charge of building the nuclear reactors in Oak Ridge and Hanford, Washington to produce weapons-grade plutonium from uranium, identifying ways to separate plutonium from uranium, and designing the atomic bomb," Vannevar replied.

Bucky responded, "Nope, we are going to the Chicago area to the Naval Air Station in Glenview, Illinois, to track down Navy Lieutenant Gerald R. Ford."

"Who the heck is Gerald R. Ford, and why do you need him?"

"Most recently, he has been assigned to coach football for the Athletic Department at the Navy Pre-Flight School at Saint Mary's College of California. This month he is being transferred to the Naval Reserve Training Command in Glenview, Illinois as the staff physical and military training officer. Twenty-nine plus years from now, on August 9, 1974, he will be sworn in as the thirty-eighth president of the United States, and we may need his help in 1975 to deal with a Russian sleeper cell spy network that is threatening the White Hole Project."

Vannevar replied, "All right, Bucky! You are already thinking way ahead, which is very good indeed! What do you need from me tonight or tomorrow to help secure the White Hole Project?"

"We need to permanently seal off the White Hole Project tomorrow so that no one has any access to it between now and June 1974, when it is discovered by the Bad Love Gang."

"Who the hell is the Bad Love Gang?" Vannevar immediately shot back.

"They are my heroes; they're the ones who accidently discovered the White Hole Project in 1974, learned how to use it, and rescued me in November 1944 on their way to rescue Jews and Gypsies from the Holocaust. Without them, I would still be stuck in time or dead. I am now a member of the Bad Love Gang, and one of the other members is here with me now. His name is Kevin Schafer, but you can call him by his nickname: Bubble Butt, or BB for short."

"Hi, Vannevar," I interjected with Bucky's introduction. "My friend Bowmar, who is a certified genius, and I were the first of our group to discover the White Hole Project in 1974. We learned how to use the machine, devised a time-travel mission to rescue a small group of Holocaust victims from Poland in November of 1944, and met Bucky along the way. It was me, Bucky, Bowmar, and one other Bad Love Gang member named Waldo who met with President Roosevelt this morning before he called you. We actually zapped Bowmar back to 1975 while he was holding FDR's hands this morning. That served as proof-positive that we are operating the White Hole Project. I have read all about you, your amazing life and your connection to President Roosevelt, convincing him to undertake the Manhattan Project."

"Someday, BB, people will be reading about you, Bucky, and the Bad Love Gang—and your roles in securing the White Hole Project and Area 51. But as top-secret as all this is, don't hold your breath; it will be a long, long time from now!" Vannevar replied.

I responded, "That's OK by me. I just want to get through tomorrow and make sure we succeed in sealing off the White Hole Project, so no one finds it before we do in 1974!"

Vannevar then continued, "For tomorrow, here is what you need to do. The Manhattan Project at Oak Ridge is called Clinton Laboratories, and a guy named Martin D. Whitaker is the director. I will call Martin just as soon as we hang up and give him instructions to admit you, Bucky, and Waldo to the K-25 plant tomorrow morning. On the southeast corner of the ground floor of the K-25 building, there is a heavily-guarded entrance tunnel to the White Hole Project."

"I know where it is, I have been through it before," Bucky interrupted.

"Excellent," Vannevar replied. "Other than the secret exit tunnel that led the Bad Love Gang to discover the White Hole Project, that heavily-guarded tunnel entrance is the only way in and out of the White Hole. When we built the White Hole, we had planned to eventually seal it off from the rest of the world. It was built deep below ground to keep it secret, and to shield its activities from ever being detected by any and all snooping devices or other espionage efforts, however sophisticated! Now, here are the secrets that you need for tomorrow. Under the control panel where you insert the GCPD's to send and recall time travelers, there is a cabinet with a false door in the back. You'll see a button to the right of the false door. Push that button seven consecutive times and the door will open. Inside, there is a detonator box with a red button. There are high energy explosives lining the second half of the connecting tunnel—the section of the tunnel closest to the White Hole—and that portion of the tunnel was specially built to collapse upon itself and seal off the tunnel permanently when those explosives detonate. Make certain that the inner entry hatchway door to the White Hole is sealed tight. Once you hit the red button, the White Hole is sealed for good, except for the emergency tunnel out, which you will have to use for your exit. In addition, have someone seal the guarded K-25 tunnel entrance. There is a panel on the massive entry hatch at the nine-o'clock position. Open the panel to access the lock, combination six, seventeen, nineteen, forty-two, two. That opens a small inner door with a red button. Hit the red button and that giant doorway welds itself shut forever."

Bucky then enquired, "Why do you think that the Denver Project includes maintaining the secrecy or integrity of Area 51 as well as the White Hole Project?"

Vannevar answered, "While I don't know all the details and I would have to make some guesses, I do know that FDR and General Chennault had a special relationship. Something big happened in China a while back, so Roosevelt is sending you there in June of 1942 for a reason. I will do some more investigating while you're on the road. I cannot help but believe there is a connection between China, Area 51, and the White Hole Project."

"We shall see...and no pun intended, but time will tell!" Bucky asserted.

Vannevar concluded, "I'll call Martin Whitaker now, and tell him to be expecting you at about 11 AM tomorrow in Oak Ridge at the K-25 building. That should give you plenty of time to drive there from Chattanooga in the morning. Call me anytime you need me. You and the Bad Love Gang have a lot on your proverbial plates. I always tell my colleagues, 'Fear cannot be banished, but it can be mitigated by reason and evaluation.' Bucky, you and your friends are headed into the arms of destiny. Be strong and know that you when you are faced with the impossible, you quite literally have time on your side. No one else can make that claim! Good night, and good luck!"

After hanging up, Bucky looked at me and said, "No one else can make that claim, except perhaps a few aliens that I watched disappear from plain sight in June of 1942."

A shiver ran down my spine as I pondered Bucky's statement, and all that had happened on this historic day of April 12, 1945.

CHAPTER ELEVEN:

SEAL THE DEAL IN OAK RIDGE

"Mankind invented the atomic bomb,
but no mouse would ever construct a mousetrap."
—Albert Einstein

Friday, April 13, 1945 at 6:30 AM local time,
Chattanooga, Tennessee

A s soon as the yellow warning flag went up, Bucky and I had rushed to our Flying Tigers' P-40B Tomahawks (the predecessor to the P-40 Warhawk). General Claire Chennault, leader and commander of the legendary Flying Tigers, had received the calls from his radio-man warning that the outlying watchers had reported a large formation of incoming Ki-48 Lily Japanese medium bombers. What was not reported were a dozen Japanese Nakajima Ki-43 Hayabusa fighter aircraft sent to protect the bombers (called Oscars, and also the Army Zero by American pilots, because it had a similar appearance to the famous and better-known Japanese Navy Mitsubishi A6M Zero).

We had met with Chennault the night before and handed him the envelope that we had been requested to personally deliver to him by President Franklin Roosevelt. After carefully examining the presidential seal and reading the letter, Chennault told us to get a good night's sleep, and to be ready to fly at sunrise. As we warmed up our

P40B Tomahawks on the gravel runway with the sun rising in the east, I noticed that we were the only two planes up and ready. I radioed Bucky to tell him that the two of us were the only active planes on the flight line. Bucky promptly responded, "I know that, BB. Don't worry; the rest will soon follow. Whatever you do, stay on my wing and follow my lead."

"Roger that," I replied, and at that moment, Chennault hoisted the red flag. Bucky and I thundered down the runway side by side and took off on a southerly heading. We climbed to 15,000 feet. Our P-40B Tomahawks were armed with two .30-caliber machine guns in each wing and two .50-caliber Colt machine guns mounted in the fuselage, which fired at a rate synchronized to the rotation of the constant-speed propeller. After less than 30 minutes flight time, we spotted the bombers in the distance, flying in a V-formation at about 12,000 feet in preparation for their bombing run. Bucky radioed me and told me to use the clouds for cover, following him to dive on the bombers and shoot as we came down on them.

A few minutes later, Bucky started his dive. I followed him off his left wing. We each picked a Ki-48 Japanese bomber to target. The Ki-48 was only defended by the equivalent of three .30-caliber machine guns, and our attack caught them by surprise. They barely got their first shots off before we dived by. We were both firing on the bombers with all six machine guns blazing, and Bucky's .50-caliber nearly sawed the wing off the first bomber. Its right wing folded upward at the fuselage, then it caught fire as it spiraled hopelessly toward the ground. My bullets tore through the left wing and fuselage of the bomber that I targeted, and its left engine started to smoke as I dived past. It was then that panic struck.

As I cleared the bomber formation and looked down and to the right to stay with Bucky, I saw two Japanese Nakajima Ki-43 fighter planes directly on his tail opening fire. I yelled over the radio, "Bucky! You have two fighters on your tail! Take evasive action! I am coming for you."

"BB, I am putting the plane into a hard dive and a roll; they can't keep up with a P-40 in a hard dive. *Shit!* I'm hit!"

"I'm almost there!" I yelled again, as I banked hard in a dive to the right to close on Bucky's tail. I began to fire on the lead plane, which was directly behind Bucky. I must have hit him, because he peeled off to the right and pulled up and away—but then the second plane began to fire on Bucky. Simultaneously, my plane began to take fire; I looked behind to see that I was also in the crosshairs, and two Oscars shooting at me too. "Bucky, I'm under fire now too!"

"BB, turn and dive with me, it's our best chance!" Bucky screamed back.

I nosed down, rolled right, and put the P-40 into a steep dive. It was too late. Several bullets tore into my engine compartment, ripping holes in the liquid coolant system and setting the engine on fire. As I peered through the smoke coming from my engine, I could see Bucky ahead of me in a terminal dive. I radioed, "Bucky, my engine is on fire and I need to bail out! What the hell are you doing?! Your dive speed is too fast!" The ground below us was coming at us like a speeding freight train.

He radioed back, "My flight controls must be shot to hell. They're not responding!"

I pulled my cockpit canopy back and got ready to bail out, fighting the thick black smoke and heat blowing back at me from the burning engine. Bucky was still fighting his controls. At the top of my lungs, I yelled one last time over the radio. "Bail out, Bucky! *Bail out!*" as I jumped.

I landed on the floor next to my bed at the Read House Hotel, waking up disoriented and covered in a cold sweat. I could not believe how vivid my dream/nightmare had just been. I had to pinch and slap myself several times to accept that it was actually Friday morning in Chattanooga, Tennessee and I was on the floor in a hotel room—not hurtling through the air from thousands of feet up, about to die.

I looked at my watch and saw it was time to get moving. We had all agreed to meet in the lobby at 7:15 AM for breakfast, then drive to the Manhattan Project (AKA Clinton Laboratories) in Oak Ridge. Our plan was to meet Martin D. Whitaker, the Director of the Clinton Laboratories, at the K-25 production facility at 11:00 AM. Martin would be expecting us, after receiving the call from Vannevar Bush the night before. Today was the day that we would blow the tunnel connecting K-25 to the White Hole Project and seal it off, securing it in secrecy until we would "discover it" in June of 1974, giving us the best shot at controlling its future destiny. At 7:00 PM tonight, Bowmar was sending us reinforcements from the Bad Love Gang, zapping them and the Black Box to the field behind Oak Ridge High School. We would all be staying at the historic Andrew Johnson Hotel in downtown Knoxville tonight, and begin our road trip to Chicago on Saturday morning.

April 13, 1945 at 11:07 AM local time, the K-25 Production Facility in Oak Ridge, Tennessee

Oak Ridge, Tennessee processed uranium into plutonium for the atomic bomb, and was one of the three so-called "secret cities" of the Manhattan Project, along with the Hanford Site in the state of Washington and Los Alamos, New Mexico. The world's first atomic bomb, called Trinity, was exploded at 5:29 AM on July 16, 1945 in the area near Los Alamos. That first atomic bomb test explosion was the equivalent of 22 kilotons of TNT; that's 22,000 metric tons, or in plain English, 48,501,640 pounds of TNT. The desert sand, largely made of silica, melted and became radioactive green glass called trinitite, lining a 30-foot-wide crater in the desert floor. The night became brighter than day, and the atmospheric colors changed from purple to green to bright white. The shock wave was felt over 100 miles away, and the mushroom cloud reached an altitude of nearly 40,000 feet. That dawning of the atomic age was made possible by the "City behind the fence" known as Oak Ridge, Tennessee, and was also known as the home of the Bad Love Gang when growing up in post-WWII Tennessee.

We had driven our Jeeps from Chattanooga to Oak Ridge, which was literally surrounded by security fences, and pulled up to the guard gate to gain access to the K-25 production facility. Before arriving at the gates, we had sent Tater in the other Jeep to meet us at the secret White Hole Project exit tunnel. The military guard on duty at the gated entrance to the Oak Ridge Manhattan Project was Army Private First Class Buford Buchanan. Since Bucky was our "point person" familiar with layout of the Oak Ridge Secret City, and the heavily-guarded K-25 secret entrance tunnel to the White Hole Project, he drove our Jeep. General Paul "Waldo" Thompson was in the passenger seat, and I sat in the back. Buford, respecting the ranks of three military officers pulling up in an army Jeep, saluted us. "I'm Private Buford Buchanan; what can I do for you gentlemen today?" I couldn't help but stare at Buford's prominent set of buck teeth. Bucky, having issues with that visual himself, smiled and replied, "I'm Captain Jack Smith, and along with General Paul Thompson and Colonel Kevin Schafer here, we are scheduled to meet Director Martin Whitaker this morning at K-25."

"Yes, sir. I'm covering this post for the first time today, and hanging in here like a hair in a biscuit!" Buford had used this Southern phrase before: it meant he felt out of place. "My mama told me that I was born at night, but I can tell you, it wasn't last night!" He said this with a big smile, which made his front teeth stick out even more. "Let me try to check that out. I'll make a quick phone call and see if I can get you on your way."

As Buford turned to make his call, Bucky laughed and looked at me. He said, "I love this Buford Buchanan's buck teeth! We're gonna have to nickname him 'BB-Two.' He can be your new sidekick there, BB-One."

I quickly replied, "No, he favors your looks and intelligence quotient a bit more than mine, so let's nickname him 'Bucky's Teeth,' and let you bite on that possibility for a while, you little shit!"

We all busted out laughing together as Bucky took a swing at me and missed. Buford finished his call and leaned a bit out of his guard post. He saluted us and said, "You men must be pretty dang important, because Director Whitaker himself has a hankerin' to meet with you. He's gonna personally meet you at the main entrance to K-25. I'll raise the gate, and y'all just follow the signs."

Martin Dewey Whitaker was the first director of the Manhattan Project, AKA Clinton Laboratories, in Oak Ridge, Tennessee from 1943 through early 1946. Whitaker earned his PhD in physics in 1935 at New York University (NYU), with a doctoral thesis regarding the absorption and scattering of neutrons. He then acted as chairman of NYU's department of physics until 1942, when he joined Arthur Compton with the Manhattan Project Met Lab (Metallurgical Laboratory) at the University of Chicago. It was Compton who appointed Whitaker to become the first director of the Clinton Laboratories in Oak Ridge, which later became the Oak Ridge National Laboratory (ORNL) after World War II ended.

We typically learn more from our mistakes than our successes. Such was the case regarding one of Whitaker's most significant contributions to the field of radiation safety. The X-10 Graphite Reactor at Oak Ridge, also known as the Clinton Pile and X-10 Pile, was the world's second artificial nuclear reactor, and it was the first in the world that was built for continuous operation. On one side there was a large opening through a 6-foot-thick concrete shield to the radioactive graphite-uranium pile. This opening was placed there in order to conduct tests of various materials, such as shielding samples. Materials were placed in the opening to test their ability to stop radiation. When the opening was not in use, water containing neutron-absorbing boron was pumped into a holding tank in the opening to prevent exposure to neutron and gamma radiation.

One day, Whitaker was leading some dignitaries from Washington, DC on a tour of the X-10 Graphite Reactor. Some experiments were being conducted and the boron solution shielding tank was empty. The group ignored the *No Admittance* signs and yellow ribbons warning of danger that had been placed in the area, and proceeded with the tour. The group, including Whitaker, was exposed to what could have been a potentially life-threatening beam of invisible radiation coming from the reactor operating pile through the unshielded opening. The group was not wearing film badges, so their radiation exposure could not be measured. It was estimated that they received a dose of up to 50 roentgens, but no one will ever know for sure. For a single exposure, around 400 roentgens is normally enough to kill 50% of exposed humans; 1,000 roentgens kills pretty much everybody. What really saved their lives was time. Radiation exposure is minimized by shielding, increased distance from the source, and time. The group spent only seconds in the area of the reactor opening; that was most likely their salvation.

This mistake became a valuable learning experience and arguably, Whitaker's best contribution to the Clinton Laboratories. Following that unfortunate event, anyone and everyone who might conceivably enter a radiation zone was required to wear a film badge. In addition, they risked being fired from their jobs if they ever ignored yellow danger ribbons and warning signs. Safety became the first priority at Oak Ridge forevermore.

We drove to the entrance of the gigantic K-25 building and met Martin Whitaker at the main entrance. We all introduced ourselves and not surprisingly, Whitaker immediately handed us all radiation badges to wear during our visit. Martin started the discussion by addressing Bucky directly. "I received a call from Vannevar Bush last night, instructing me to assist you and your colleagues with whatever you need. He told me that your activities were top secret, impacting national security. He did not say much more, other than you are here by presidential authority."

Bucky responded, "Thank you, and that is all correct, Martin. There is a guarded tunnel entrance at the southeast corner of this K-25 complex; we need you to take us there."

Whitaker replied, "Ever since I was appointed director here, that large entryway has been guarded around the clock. Very few people ever go through that door, and I am not privy to their names or business. It is strictly run by the military and Vannevar Bush has been the only person who has ever spoken to me about it. It's a little bit creepy, because the Manhattan Project here is very top secret—but whatever goes on behind those doors is even more secret, which seems impossible. I guess I would have to call it ultra-top secret!"

"Well sir, you will not have to deal with that entrance or the secrecy around it any longer. We are here today to permanently seal that tunnel, and terminate its related activities. It has served its purpose to the military to the fullest and we are very pleased with the outcome, as well as the time we have spent here in Oak Ridge. Please take us to the closest entry point to that guarded entrance," Bucky answered.

When Bucky said the phrase "time we have spent here," my music brain unexpectedly started to play the song **"A Hazy Shade of Winter"** by Simon and Garfunkel. The song was released as a stand-alone single in October 1966, and peaked at number 13 on the *Billboard* Hot 100. It later was included on the duo's fourth studio album, called *Bookends*, in 1968. The song references a change in direction or seasons of life, and I suppose my brain was pondering the changes here in Oak Ridge, with World War II ending soon and the White Hole Project being sealed off for a long season of hibernation.

The U-shaped K-25 structure was four stories high, a mile long, and covered 44 acres. At this moment in time, it was the largest building in the world under one roof. Martin Whitaker hopped in the Jeep with us and directed us to a parking area near the southeast side of the enormous building. He led us inside to the lower level. Bucky recognized the area. Once he had his bearings, Bucky bid farewell to Whitaker and indicated that he would communicate any future needs through Vannevar Bush, if necessary. We all thanked Martin and he headed back to his office.

After Whitaker departed, we huddled for a minute in a long hallway lined with 1940's computers, deciding that all three of us would take the secret K-25 tunnel to the White Hole Project, inspect its status, and make certain no one else was there. We would then prepare to detonate the explosives to collapse the tunnel and seal the White Hole Project away from K-25. Prior to blowing the tunnel, we would give Waldo ample time to backtrack through the tunnel and follow Bush's directions, which would permanently weld the large K-25 entryway hatch shut. Waldo would then take the Jeep and meet us at the White Hole secret exit tunnel entrance in the woods. Tater would rejoin us there as well.

We agreed on the plan and it was almost noon on April 13, 1945 as the three of us started walking down that long hallway toward the heavily-guarded entrance tunnel to the White Hole Project. By chance, the three of us happened to walk right by the younger version of Russ

Krovo, making his routine morning rounds to check on the K-25 equipment operations. Krovo, for his part, had never before seen this group of officers on the premises, and noticed that the officer leading the way was an Air Force captain, followed by a tough-looking general, and an Air Force colonel who looked a bit young for the part. As his intense espionage training had prepared him, Krovo found himself automatically trying to take mental pictures of our faces, despite the fairly rapid and uninterrupted pace of our progress down the hall. Simultaneously, Bucky, Waldo and I all took a quick look at Krovo. From a timeline perspective, it would be nearly another thirty years before Krovo would see the three of us together again, when he would ambush the Bad Love Gang at the White Hole Project on New Year's Eve 1975. However, from our perspective, all of us had seen his beady eyes through his black mask just three and a half months ago. I only glanced at him, but an emotional shockwave shot through my soul. I fought to contain it and keep moving forward, not looking at him as we walked toward the tunnel entrance.

Within a few minutes, the three of us arrived at the guarded K-25 tunnel entrance to the White Hole Project. Three regular Army guards, a sergeant, and two first-class privates stood in front of the large entrance doorway, which looked like an oversized bank vault door thick enough to literally withstand direct artillery fire. All three guards immediately saluted us. The sergeant introduced himself as Sergeant Sterling Sinclair, along with Privates Dixon and Bassett. Sinclair also had a heavy southern accent, keeping in line with our day so far. The three of us then introduced ourselves. Studying the massive entryway, I could see the panel on the left,' which Waldo would soon use to weld the doorway shut forever.

Bucky addressed Sergeant Sinclair as he handed him the letter of direct presidential authority. "Sergeant, we are here to permanently terminate all activities behind this door, and General Thompson will be back in a short while to seal this doorway shut. After that, your job is finished here."

Sergeant Sinclair responded, "I'm really glad to hear that, Captain Smith. For the past three-plus weeks, this has been the most boring job on earth for three people to stand here and do nothing all day and all night. There's no chewing gum made that will last long enough for this job. I mean, it is like we are going through a serious drought of not seeing any people. It's so dry the trees are bribing the dogs!"

That made us all laugh; I wondered if Tater might meet his match here. I asked if anyone had been admitted entrance recently, and Sinclair assured us that no one had come through on their current shift. Bucky then ordered Sinclair to open the massive door and let us through. He reminded them that General Thompson (Waldo) would be back soon to seal the door for good.

As we walked through the tunnel connecting K-25 to the White Hole Project, I noticed that we were walking on a downward slope. It felt just like the secret exit tunnel from the woods, only this tunnel had a few more curves to it for some reason. The tunnel was brightly lit, and there were narrow gauge rail tracks to our left for moving heavy equipment or supplies. I reminded Waldo about opening the panel and entering the combination (6-17-19-42-2) to expose the red button that would weld the giant doorway shut forever. Waldo wondered out loud about the combination. Bucky responded, "I thought about that one last night. It was June 17, 1942 that I boarded the alien ship in Nevada and discovered exotic matter. I'm not sure what the last 2 is about."

After walking down the tunnel for about ten minutes, I announced that I had an important comment to make. Both Waldo and Bucky looked at me with a mix of curiosity and worry, because that was an odd statement coming from me. I then said, "As we were walking down the long, computer-lined hall to this tunnel, we passed a guy who was checking on all the computers. We were walking fast, but my eyes caught his eyes for a brief second. In an instant, I experienced an emotional rush of fear and adrenaline. I think those eyes may belong to the guy we are calling Boris, who attacked us on New Year's Eve. I can't be sure, but I know what I felt. If it was him, then we may have our first lead to track down his identity."

Waldo commented, "You know what, Bubble Butt? I noticed him too." Waldo was smiling as he continued, "My senses are getting old and dull like my prostate, but that guy's eyes were beady and trained on the three of us. If I see him on the way out of here, I'll try to get his name. He isn't going to 'meet and greet us' for another thirty years, so we have the advantage here. I can't kill him now, because I'm not sure he's our guy—and that might be too big of a wrinkle in time, even if he is our guy!"

"That makes three of us, BB," Bucky added. "Now that you say that, I can't help but think you may be on to something there. I felt like he was trying to photograph me with his cold, piercing eyes. I was a bit preoccupied with making a beeline here. If we see him again, let's confront him. Otherwise, I'll request a list of K-25 workers from Vannevar and we can do a little real spy work ourselves."

We continued on, and soon realized that this tunnel from K-25 to the White Hole was longer than the tunnel from the woods. We knew we had walked for nearly a mile. The hatchway into the White Hole Project was just like the one in the other tunnel; we had to turn a wheel like a submarine hatch to open the door. As we came through the door, I saw the lights inside the White Hole were on—and as opposed to my first encounter with the White Hole Project, everything inside was spotlessly clean with no collected dust anywhere. It was so shiny and new, and I couldn't help but get goosebumps.

I timed our walk from the K-25 entrance to the White Hole, which took us 23 minutes. I told Waldo that I would give him 30 minutes to get out and seal the giant doorway at the K-25 entrance shut, then immediately went to the control panel and looked in the cabinet below. Indeed, as Vannevar had explained, there was a false door in the back. Using a flashlight, I could see the button to the right of the false door. I pushed that button seven consecutive times, and the door opened. The detonator box opened up and we were ready to rumble! I showed Bucky and Waldo the red detonator button and said, "Let's divide and conquer. We'll go floor by floor and room by room to make certain there is no one else here before we blow the tunnel."

We quickly proceeded to the fifth floor, then efficiently and systematically worked our way down floor by floor, room by room. Last but far from least was the exotic matter containment room, on the ground floor. There was an Albert Einstein quote above the door: "A new type of thinking is essential if mankind is to survive and move toward higher levels." This room was virtually soundproof; the entry was a huge steel door with a submarine airlock-type latch. As we entered the room, I immediately heard a thud from the back, as if a box had fallen. The three of us literally sprinted toward the sound, drawing our .45 caliber ACP pistols on the run. It took mere seconds for us to reach the back of the lab. There, standing directly in front of the small, heavy-duty crates labeled *Top Secret* that contained blue exotic matter, was a stunningly beautiful Indian woman. Her skin was light brown, framed by black hair. She had an oval-shaped face, almond-shaped nearly black eyes, and dark lips. She was wearing a black 1940's era dress, and had a name badge pinned to the front. She was not armed, and looked very surprised to see three US Army Air Force officers rapidly appear with pistols trained on her.

"Who are you? Do you work here? When did you come in here?" I demanded.

Somewhat nervously she replied, "Please don't shoot me." We realized that we still had our guns aimed at her and holstered our weapons. "My name is Nisha Singh. I do work here, and I've been the only one here since 5:00 AM. Who are you?"

I approached her and looked in front of her on the floor. The crate that she must have dropped was the last crate of blue exotic matter delivered with the date Tuesday, April 10, 1945 marked on it. I knew this room like the back of my hand—and she was in our space, as far as I was concerned. I answered her question as I carefully restacked the exotic matter crate in its proper place on the back wall behind her. "We are with the US military Special Forces, and our job is to shut this failed project down. That is happening today. We will need to verify your role here with Vannevar Bush, later today or tonight. Until then, you are staying with us. I am Colonel Schafer, and this is General Thompson and Captain Smith." Waldo and Bucky smiled and politely nodded their heads. The rear corner office door was right next to us, so I told her to wait in that office for a minute as I closed the door behind her.

In almost a whisper, Bucky spoke first. "As long as she's not on the wrong side, I want to take her home with me!"

I replied, "And you think *my* mind is in the gutter all the time? Straighten up, Captain Denver! Fly-boy, we've got work to do! Here's the plan: Waldo is gonna take Nisha with him, and she stays with us until we can verify her identity with Vannevar."

Smiling, Waldo said, "Yes sir, Colonel Bubble Buttocks, it will be my pleasure to escort Nisha safely away from the blast zone—and keep her around for a little while!"

I responded, "You guys can't see straight; we find a beautiful woman, and all our plans are shot to hell! God help us now! Waldo, take Nisha, and we will give you thirty minutes to clear the tunnel and seal the K-25 entrance door. Don't take Nisha to the secret tunnel exit in the woods. Wait for us in your Jeep at the end of the dirt road, out of the woods. Bucky and I will blow the tunnel, then head out the exit tunnel and ride with Tater to meet you. We will have time to go check into the Andrew Johnson Hotel in downtown Knoxville before we come back to pick up the Bad Love Gang reinforcements and black box that Bowmar is zapping to us tonight at seven."

We all agreed with that plan. Waldo took Nisha with him, and reached the massive K-25 entrance at about 2:00 PM. He had Sergeant Sterling Sinclair, along with Privates Dixon and Bassett, watch Nisha while he quickly followed the protocol to seal the massive entry door shut forever. He then dismissed the guards, took Nisha to the Jeep, and drove away to meet us. Although he was watching carefully, he did not see any sign of Boris on the way out. At 2:07 PM, I punched the red detonator button and the entry tunnel blew like a perfectly planned building demolition event. The portion of the tunnel closest to the White Hole collapsed just as planned by the engineers, with the ground far above it not moving at all. However, a small tremor was felt at the K-25 plant and in the general vicinity. Bucky and I left the White Hole through the secret exit tunnel and met Tater, who had been waiting for us in the woods. We rendezvoused with Waldo and Nisha, then headed to Knoxville, 25 miles away, to check into the well-known Andrew Johnson Hotel.

Our day was far from over.

CHAPTER TWELVE:

BAD LOVE REINFORCEMENTS ARRIVE

"Alone we can do little; together we can do so much."
—Helen Keller

Friday, April 13, 1945 at 7:00 PM local time,
Oak Ridge High School

B ucky, Waldo, Tater, and I had been sitting in the bleachers in the field behind Oak Ridge High School, relaxing and chewing the fat for the last 15 minutes while we finished off a round of bottled Coca-Cola that we brought with us from Knoxville. We had checked into the historic Andrew Johnson Hotel, with the beautiful Nisha Singh in tow. Bucky was able to reach Vannevar Bush on his secure private office phone line. First, Bucky asked him to work with Martin Whitaker to try and identify the man at the K-25 plant that we suspected could be Boris. Bucky was able to give Vannevar a pretty accurate description, blending the features he noticed with those that stood out to Waldo and me. Vannevar assured him that he would conduct a comprehensive investigation, promising not to do anything with his findings without first discussing it with Bucky.

Second, Bucky enquired about Nisha Singh. Vannevar confirmed that she was very new to the limited White Hole Project staff; Singh had formally started at the time of the failure analysis, when Bucky could not be recalled and was lost in time-travel. She was certified brilliant, from a very wealthy, well-connected Indian family. Nisha had been allowed to train in nuclear physics at the prestigious Indian Institute of Science, under the renowned physicists C. V. Raman and Homi J. Bhabha. She had made a stop in Chicago with Compton's team and was being transferred to work in Oak Ridge when she was diverted from joining Martin Whitaker's Manhattan Project team to helping with the White Hole Project failure analysis. Her credentials were impeccable, but what Vannevar and his small team did not know was that she also worked for the Indian Intelligence Bureau: the precursor to the modern Research and Analysis Wing (RAW), the Indian's foreign intelligence agency established in 1968. Bucky was enraptured first by her beauty, then by her intelligence. He was relieved that Vannevar had vouched for her. We had dropped her off at her apartment in Knoxville on our way back to Oak Ridge.

Covertly spying on our activities and witnessing Nisha Singh with us was Chinese agent Li-Ming Sun (locally called "Ming") who was stationed at the University of Tennessee in Knoxville. Ming could not follow us through the security gates surrounding the "Secret City" of Oak Ridge, but she was lying in wait for our return to the Andrew Johnson Hotel in Knoxville. She was not alone lying in wait for us in Knoxville.

We had watched members of our Bad Love Gang being zapped away in time travel from the White Hole Project. However, none of us had actually witnessed any of our gang being zapped to a specific location by the White Hole. Tater and I launched a plan to welcome the Bad Love Gang reinforcements as they arrived in the field behind our beloved Oak Ridge High School. We enlisted Waldo and Bucky to join in our fun. We bought a bag of balloons in Knoxville, filled them with water at the hotel, and gently put them in a box to take with us. I had wanted to make them ice cold, but the portable ice chest had not yet been invented in 1945. It was invented by Richard C. Laramy of Joliet, Illinois in 1951 and patented in December 1953. The Coleman Company popularized the portable cooler with a galvanized version in 1954, and developed plastic versions about three years later. In 1975, our Bad Love Gang used virtually everything made by Coleman for our various camping trips and canoe floats: camping stoves, coolers, tents, sleeping bags, and lanterns. Sitting in the bleachers at 6:58 PM, I announced, "Load the cannons and prepare to unleash the floods of heaven on my command!" All of us grabbed water balloons. Tater blurted, "These guys are gonna be about as confused as a fart in a fan factory when they get this wet welcome to 1945!" We were all laughing our asses off as the clock hit 7:00 PM.

At 7:00 sharp in the field directly in front of us, the Bad Love Gang reinforcements and the black box "magically" appeared out of thin air. The moment they appeared, we could tell there was a mental pause as their brains came to the realization that the time travel trip had ended. Cleopatra and Crisco, dressed as Women's Army Corps sergeants, were sitting together facing us; the Runt and Meatball were back to back behind them, and Goondoggy, Crazy Ike, Spaghetti Head, the Pud, and Bowmar were scattered around them. All the guys were dressed in military attire as well.

We gave them an ever-so-brief moment to mentally adjust, then I yelled, *Fire all cannons!* The four of us got at least eight water balloons in the air just as Cleopatra and Crisco were the first to actually see and recognize us on the bleachers. My music brain was already playing **"Summer Rain,"** by Johnny Rivers. Released in November 1967, the song reached number 14 on the US *Billboard* Hot 100. I loved this song! Rivers was a brilliant musician, and probably a bit underrated at the time. The song was a big hit among our troops in Vietnam, and a favorite rainy-day song to play while having romantic daydreams. The first wave of water balloons hit Cleopatra squarely in the chest, and Crisco in the legs. They both screamed as they simultaneously saw the four of us, and yelled, "You *bastards!*"

Water balloons landed on and around the guys as well, but not all of them exploded. They quickly came to their senses as the next wave of balloons was launched, and the fight was on. Goondoggy, the Runt, and Crazy Ike quickly grabbed the unexploded water balloons. Goondoggy yelled "CHARGE!" As they were beginning their charge, the Pud tried to catch an incoming water balloon face high, but it exploded in his hands. Water soaked his face and head, and I could hardly stand up, I was laughing so hard! Waldo, Bucky, Tater, and I reloaded as Goondoggy, Crazy Ike, and the Runt charged us. I commanded them, "Wait until you see the whites of their eyes, men!" We stood as they approached across the field. I kept commanding, "Wait... steady, men...wait, not yet...waait..." When they were 10–15 feet in front of us, I finally yelled, "NOW! *FIRE!*" Seven water balloons arced through the air: three coming at us, four headed at them. I put my head down and my hands over my crotch, knowing Crazy Ike would be aiming to make one of us a queen for the night!

They were pissed, and their aim was good. I took a hit in the shoulder, which soaked me and also partially drenched Waldo next to me. Tater took a balloon directly to his crotch. He yelled at Crazy Ike, his voice high-pitched as he bent over in pain, "Ike, you're going to Hell on a scholarship for that one!" Bucky turned away and got hit in the back of the neck, drenching the back of his head and upper back. Two of our four balloons landed as well: Crazy Ike took one to the solar plexus, and one to his groin. He dropped to the ground, cursing in perfect German.

The battle was over at that point, so we all licked our wounds and gathered together, hugging, laughing, and high-fiving. As I turned around during our group welcome, Crisco was right there behind me and gave me a full-on frontal hug, wrapping her arms around me—while secretly holding the last intact water balloon in her right hand. She chirped, "So good to see you, BB!" Then she squeezed the water balloon against the back of my neck, popping it to send water running down my back. I cringed a bit, hugged her back, smiled, and replied, "Thanks Sergeant Crisco. My back was feeling a bit dry today, and I know that you always have my back!" She looked into my eyes and warmly responded, "You got that right, BB."

We gathered on the bleachers and marveled at the back side of our very own Oak Ridge High School as it stood there at its original location in eastern Oak Ridge, on a hill above the community's first commercial center at Jackson Square. In April 1945, it was basically brand new, having been established in 1943 by the US Army to educate the children of the workers and families building and operating Manhattan Project facilities in Oak Ridge. Bowmar had already explained to the group what had happened in our meeting with President Roosevelt the day before, up until the moment Bowmar got zapped back to 1975. I proceeded to tell the Bad Love Gang reinforcements the "short version" of what happened after Bowmar's departure to bring them up to speed, and let them know the plan going forward from here.

"Bowmar was holding hands with FDR when he disappeared into thin air, leaving that odd smell of time travel. The president's hands fell into his lap, then he looked at us and exclaimed, 'By God, I have been left empty-handed before, but this experience takes the cake!' After that, he signed an executive order to put Bucky—and all of us—in charge of defending the White Hole Project. Bucky coined a code name for our defense of the White Hole, calling it the Denver Project.

Roosevelt gave us two key contact points for our work: Colonel Carter Clarke and Vannevar Bush. Colonel Clarke and his US Army Signal Intelligence Service are spying on the Russians, using something called the Venona Project, and he is helping us to monitor and deal with the Russians. Vannevar Bush was in charge of implementing and building the White Hole Project. He is our contact for everything related to our work with the White Hole Project. There is concern that the Chinese and India nationals may also be after the secrets of the White Hole, but we have no definite intel regarding their whereabouts or motivations. Vannevar also thinks that we are simultaneously defending the secrets of Area 51 and the White Hole Project."

Bowmar, who rarely cusses, interjected, "Holy shit, BB! I don't want to interrupt your train of thought, but having us defend the secrets of Area 51 is totally out of bounds!"

I continued, "Oddly, before we departed ways with FDR, he handed Bucky an envelope embossed with the presidential seal, containing orders for a group of us to use the White Hole Project and hand deliver it to General Claire Chennault of the famed Flying Tigers, in China, in June of 1942. We are hypothesizing that this may be somehow connected to the alien spaceship crash in Nevada in June 1942, and perhaps could explain the potential Chinese and Indian interest in Area 51 and the White Hole.

"We left Warm Springs yesterday in two Willys Jeeps and drove to Chattanooga last night. We encountered two Russians named Vic Bison and Steve Rock, following us and spying on us when we stopped in Calhoun, Georgia yesterday on the way to Chattanooga. Colonel Clarke confirmed last night that Bison is on their watch list in the southeast. Steve Rock was a new name to Clarke. We 'gently persuaded' them to turn around and head back to the hole they crawled out of."

Waldo smiled at the group, pulled out his .45 ACP pistol, held it up so we could see it, and sarcastically said, "It was this 'gentle persuasion' that convinced our Russian friends to return to their comrades. It's like magic; it works every time!" We all laughed; it was classic Waldo!

"Today we drove here to Oak Ridge and met with Martin Whitaker, the first director of the Manhattan Project, at the K-25 plant. That building is *enormous*! He escorted us to the hallway leading to the tunnel entrance to the White Hole Project. Using Vannevar's directions, we imploded the tunnel connecting K-25 to the White Hole, and sealed that entry point to the White Hole Project forever. Two interesting things occurred while we were there to blow the connecting tunnel. First, we may have seen the Russian we are calling Boris in the K-25 hallway. Second, we found and nabbed an Indian national named Nisha Singh, working alone in the White Hole Project exotic matter containment room. Vannevar did verify that Singh was working for him, so we let her go. He is trying to track down the name of the guy we thought could be Boris. Nisha Singh is brilliant, and stunningly beautiful. I am not so sure that she is 'one of the good guys,' but Bucky is hoping otherwise." Bucky scowled at me, and Crisco frowned at Bucky.

"After we blew the K-25 connecting tunnel earlier this afternoon, we secured the White Hole, left through the exit tunnel to the woods, and secured the hatch. We checked into the Andrew Johnson Hotel in Knoxville, where we are all staying tonight. Tomorrow, we leave on a cross-country road trip with our first mission stop at the Naval Reserve Training Command, Naval Air Station, Glenview, Illinois, where we plan to catch up with a young Navy lieutenant named Gerald R. Ford. As you all know, he is President Ford in 1975, and we want to enlist his future cooperation to help us dispose of Boris and his entire Russian spy cell—and any other future espionage threats to the White Hole.

"We will then leave the Chicago area and head west to colorful Colorado! It sounds like all fun and games, but Colonel Clarke warned us they have seen some violent encounters with Russian spies in Chicago and in the Denver area, where they call them Vodka Cowboys. Clarke went so far as to say, 'Don't be afraid to shoot first if you have to!'"

Waldo, of course, smiled as he raised his pistol above his head with his finger on the trigger, rocking the gun back and forth with some wrist action. "The Vodka Cowboys meet the Bad Love Gang at the OK Corral in Colorado! I'm changing my name from Waldo to Wyatt Earp for this shootout, boys and girls! Bring it on!" We all just laughed at Waldo's extreme bravado.

I continued, "We are going to Denver so Bucky can show his parents that he is still alive, and did not die in the failed first White Hole Project launch. Then we are headed to Colorado Springs, where Bucky will train me, Willy, and Pumpkin to fly and fight using P-40 Warhawks at Peterson Army Air Base. I'm hoping that the Runt and Meatball can learn some of the mechanics of the P-40 while we are there, and figure out how to juice our planes a bit. We expect to be using P-40s when we time travel to China in June 1942 to hand-deliver FDR's presidential sealed envelope to General Chennault. Roosevelt specifically asked Bucky if he could fly a P-40 Warhawk. Of course, Bucky answered that he could fly anything with wings and a big motor." Bucky held both his hands in the air palms up, and nodded. "There will be a very special treat for us during our time in Colorado Springs!"

The Runt briefly interrupted and said, "There's that glint in BB's eyes again! I know we're heading for trouble now!"

"It will be quite the contrary this time, Runt." I replied. "The treat is that we will all be staying at the world-famous Broadmoor Resort and Hotel in Colorado Springs while we train on the P-40 Warhawks at the nearby Peterson Army Air Base. Bucky has been there before, with his family, and says it is amazing: a beautiful taste of the finest European hotels, right there in Colorado Springs! When we finish our training in the Springs, most of us will go back to 1975; the four of us flying the P-40 Warhawks will go to Area 51. Soon thereafter, this particular mission will end in China, when we go to see General Chennault and the Flying Tigers, and find out what is in store for us there. I think I'm done with the 'short version' of the story now."

Goondoggy spoke up, "Good luck, BB, getting Willy to go to China with you to fly a P-40 in any kind of combat! That sounds a bit too risky for his sense of adventure."

I replied, "Good point there, Goondoggy. I think he will come to learn how to fly P-40s in Colorado Springs because he likes flying. We'll work on him then."

Cleopatra jumped in and commented, "Finally you got something right here with this time travel stuff, BB. I can't wait to go to a world-class resort in Colorado Springs! Crisco and I are gonna light that place up, big time! We're going to show you amateurs how to relax in style. We might have to stay a little extra longer to rejuvenate our weary bodies!"

The Pud then said what most of us were feeling, "My body is *weary* right now! If I heard this story right, you guys have just two Army Jeeps that you drove up here from Georgia. By my count there are thirteen of us sitting here, along with our backpacks full of equipment and Bowmar's black box. How the hell are we going to get all of that *and* all of us back to the hotel in Knoxville tonight, using two Jeeps?"

"Oh, Pud, ye of such little faith! We brought roller skates for you, and we're gonna throw you a rope and pull your ass behind us as we drive back to Knoxville. I hope you brought some good knee pads in that backpack of yours." The Pud smiled and flipped me off. "When we called Vannevar Bush earlier today to verify the identity of Nisha

Singh, we requested an Army truck to complement our two Willys MB Jeeps. He managed to send us a 1944 Chevrolet G-506, one and a half ton, four by four truck with a front wench and a canvas-covered rear cargo area. We have plenty of room for everyone and our equipment with our three vehicles. Let's get everyone loaded up and make our way to Knoxville for some good shut-eye! We are headed to Illinois in the morning."

April 13, 1945 at 9:30 PM local time, the Andrew Johnson Hotel, Knoxville, Tennessee

Located at 912 South Gay Street, the Andrew Johnson Hotel, named for President Andrew Johnson, was Knoxville's premier hotel from the time of its completion in 1929 through the 1960s. In the early years, the hotel was popular with foreign dignitaries visiting Knoxville to inquire about the newly created Tennessee Valley Authority. The studios of radio station WNOX, which played a role in the early Tennessee-centric development of country music, were located in the Andrew Johnson in the late 1930s. In April of 1945, the hotel was the city's tallest structure at 203 feet, and was the cornerstone of the downtown skyline. A large neon sign reading *Hotel Andrew Johnson* stood atop the building and glowed in the night. The hotel staff was all super-accommodating to all of us dressed as US military members during this waning time of World War II. As everyone got tucked away in their rooms, Bucky and I went down to make sure that the truck and two Jeeps were empty of valuables and weapons, and secure. We had parked the vehicles in tandem on the side of the hotel, with the two Jeeps in front and the truck in the rear.

It had been a warm, sunny, spring day in eastern Tennessee with a high of 84 degrees, putting us in the mood for the water balloon welcoming. The temperature had fallen to 64 degrees, and there was a slim sliver of a moon in the sky above on this Friday the thirteenth, 1945. The night was clear, but the side street was not lit as well as the front entrance. We had flashlights and I told Bucky to check the truck while I inspected the two Jeeps, starting with the one in the very front. As Bucky was focused on checking the back cargo hold of the truck using his flashlight, a medium built man dressed in black was quickly and quietly sneaking up behind him with pistol drawn. Another slightly built man dressed in black came around the corner of the building with pistol drawn also pointed at Bucky. Both Bucky and I had our service pistols holstered; neither of us was expecting any trouble. In retrospect, we should have been more vigilant and inspected each vehicle together, rather than separating. I was about 20 feet away from Bucky when the trouble started.

The medium built man dressed in black reached Bucky and tapped on his shoulder. Bucky, bent over looking inside the back of the truck, thought it was me. He straightened and said, "What do you want, BB?" The man pistol whipped Bucky and he slumped to the ground, briefly losing consciousness as he went down. The smaller man dressed in black moved closer, with gun trained on the encounter at the back of the truck. I clearly heard Bucky say "BB," and I quickly headed to the back of the truck, but had no reason to think to draw my pistol. I came from the street side to the back of the truck, and will never forget the scene that rapidly unfolded. As I realized what was happening, my adrenaline surged and time slowed down.

Bucky was on his back, moaning, starting to regain consciousness. Standing over him, dressed in black, with his pistol pointed down at Bucky, was the man I immediately recognized as the Russian agent Steve Rock, who Bucky had cold cocked the day before in Calhoun, Georgia. Simultaneously, I saw the second agent was also wearing a black mask; he stood about fifteen feet behind us. That agent's gun seemed to be trained directly on me, in case I made a move. Rock looked at Bucky, pointed his pistol squarely at his chest, and with rage in his voice said, "You will never live to harm me or another Russian comrade again!" He squeezed the trigger, and a loud shot rang out. I instinctively lunged toward Rock as soon as I sensed he was going to shoot Bucky point blank. Rock fell into my arms dead, the back of his head bleeding. I looked behind him and saw the other agent disappearing around the corner of the building. I dropped Rock on the street, and despite the fact that he was already dead, I soccer kicked him and said, "You bastard, nice try!" I then tended to Bucky, who was coming to, and said, "Hey buddy, we have to seriously quit meeting like this! It's a good thing you're so damn hard-headed, or you might really get hurt one of these days!

Bucky's first groggy words to me as he could speak again were, "I'm hard to kill, BB, hard to kill."

CHAPTER THIRTEEN:

THE ARCHITECT OF THE NUCLEAR AGE

"Before I came here, I was confused about this subject.
Having listened to your lecture I am still confused.
But on a higher level."
—Enrico Fermi

Saturday, April 14, 1945 at 6:00 AM local time,
Knoxville, Tennessee

I woke up in my room on Saturday morning at the Andrew Johnson Hotel in Knoxville, looking at the black box sitting on the floor as I wiped the night's sand from my eyes. Bowmar was sleeping in the connecting room with Bucky so I could get some good sleep—and in case Bucky had any issues recovering from being pistol whipped. With a dead Russian agent in the street the night before, we had called Colonel Carter Clarke at his US Army Signal Intelligence Service number to tell him what had happened; he would take care of the details of the dead Steve Rock with the local Knoxville police. Waldo had gotten a room directly across the hall from us, and lay there with his pistol on his chest all night long, ready to shoot anyone suspicious who unexpectedly approached our doors during the night. Waldo was super pissed after hearing the details of our harrowing close call. He did not like the thought of any of us Bad Love Gang members getting ambushed, injured, or killed in action. It brought back bad memories from his Korean War battlefield experience. Coupled with his fatherly love for us, the incident made him feel a bit hypervigilant, if not downright paranoid. While sitting on my bedside sorting out my waking thoughts, I wondered if the other agent's bullet was meant for me, and had accidentally hit Rock in the back of the head—or if that bullet had found its intended target. Whatever the case, my thoughts eventually came into morning focus and I was curious as hell about what was in the black box!

The black box, invented by Bowmar, had a Global Cosmic Positioning Device (GCPD) incorporated into its design. The box was the size of a large circa 1975 Coleman Cooler, but built with Kevlar shielding and a combination lock. The black box was scheduled to be zapped back to 1975 at exactly 7:00 AM, with Willy at the controls of the White Hole Project. I entered the combination and opened the lid of the black box for the first time in the history of our time-travel adventures. At this early morning hour, I wasn't quite ready for the next encounter.

As I raised the lid, I found myself staring into the eyes of Rasputin, and he stared right back at me. Sitting upright in his cage, he was about to consume a sunflower seed held in his tiny hands. His little nose and whiskers quivered as we looked at each other. I exclaimed, "Holy shit, it's Rasputin!" The Bad Love Gang had decided to buy a group pet for the White Hole Project, and we settled on a Golden Hamster. We bought the hamster in January of 1975 after Boris ambushed us at the White Hole Project, and we kept the adorable Rasputin there. We decided a Russian name for him would be fitting, and called him Rasputin after Grigori Rasputin, born January 21, 1869 and dying December 30, 1916.

Grigori Rasputin's life and death had been, if anything, controversial and mysterious, becoming mythological after death. He was born to a peasant family and had some type of a religious conversion experience after attending a monastery in 1897. In 1903, he went to St. Petersburg, Russia, where his charisma caught the attention of influential church and society members; although, he never held any position with the Russian Orthodox Church. In October 1912, Rasputin purportedly healed the only son (Alexei) of the last Russian Emperor, Tsar Nicholas II. Alexei, suffering from hemophilia, had been injured jumping into a rowboat in September 1912, hitting his thigh or groin on a protruding oarlock, causing a large hematoma. In early October, the boy was reinjured in the same location, causing his hematoma to rupture and bleed again. Alexei's mother, the Tsarina Alexandra, called Rasputin's reported healing powers into action after her son, Alexei, had received his last sacrament. Alexei was healed nearly overnight, and Rasputin's influence and mystic healing powers were cemented in Russian lore and history. In 1915, Nicholas II departed St. Petersburg to command the Russian forces in World War I and Rasputin's influence with Alexandra reached its high point. When Russian defeats in World War I mounted in late 1916, Rasputin was poisoned and then shot by a group of Russian noblemen who opposed his influence over Alexandra and the Tsar, on December 30, 1916. Even in death, Rasputin's reputation became the subject of Russian mythology: a story circulated that his poisoned and shot body was thrown into a local ice-cold river, but he was later pulled out and he was found to be still alive.

Bowmar had decided to "experiment" with his newly-invented black box technology and sent our hamster along for the first ride. Fortunately for Bowmar, Rasputin seemed perfectly healthy. Otherwise, I suspect Bowmar would have been "drawn and quartered" by our animal-loving Bad Love Gang!

After getting over the visual shock of seeing Rasputin sitting in his cage inside the black box, I was thrilled to see my new 1974 Marantz Superscope CRS-152 boom box was in there as well, along with a shoe box filled with my cassette music collection. Bowmar had redeemed himself. We had music for the rest of our 1945 road trip, and I was stoked! I immediately pulled the boom box out, rifled through the cassettes and plugged one in to play to get psyched for the day's start of our road trip to Illinois. The Marantz Superscope had survived the time-travel trip along with Rasputin and worked perfectly. The Eagles song **"Already Gone"** started to play; released in April 1974, the song was ubiquitously popular on the radio, but only peaked at number 32 on the *Billboard* Hot 100. The song was totally empowering for anyone getting dumped in a relationship and trying to get over it. But for the start of today's journey, there were no chains holding us back; we were going for it! Bowmar, in the connecting room, heard the music playing and got out of bed to check out the scene. I was standing on my bed playing my air guitar and lip syncing as Bowmar walked in, wearing just his boxer shorts. Despite the fact that he was a certified genius, I took credit for influencing his love of rock and roll and contemporary music since we had grown up together as best friends. Without a word spoken, Bowmar joined in the lip syncing, using his fake microphone with me as I jumped off the bed. We started dancing and pretending that we were the Eagles! Bucky woke up to this commotion. He came into the room holding his head and sat on the bed, watching us and shaking his sore head. Waldo knocked on the door, and we let him in as well. He was still holding his pistol in his hand, shaking his head at our teenage antics. Our day was off to a fairly "normal" start.

When the music faded, I hit the hit the off button on the boom box and said, "Good morning, boys—and you too, you old fart!" Waldo responded to being referred to this way by waving his index finger at me like I was a naughty child and giving me a fake frown. I then continued to look in the black box, and there was Crisco's awesome camera. She was artistic growing up and her family had made the financial sacrifice to buy her a Canon F-1 High Speed model. The F-1 was Canon's first truly professional-grade SLR system; equipped with a motor drive, the camera could shoot up to nine frames per second—the highest speed of any motor driven camera at the time. Nicknamed the "heavy tank" by its adoring users, the F-1 Canon camera was widely known for its durability and reliability. Bowmar and Crisco had packed the camera with a variety of lenses and 35mm film in the Black Box. They had set up a film-developing lab at the White Hole Project so no one else would be privy to our time-travel pictures. Knowing Crisco like I did, she would be taking snapshots of all of us along the way across America during the rest of this road trip.

Last but not least, there was a folder that held two letters: one addressed to Waldo from his beloved Mary (our surrogate Mom), and one from Willy addressed to me. I handed Waldo his letter and "insisted" he share its contents with us. Waldo opened and read the letter silently while we sat there in suspense. He then neatly folded the letter and put it in his pocket. His face beamed with joy as he said, "Some of this is for my eyes only, you nosey bastards, but she did say that I better bring all of you home safely, if I want my fantasies to be fulfilled!" That got us all laughing big time for it being so early in the morning.

The second letter from Willy to me was simple; he asked me to write down the time and place to send the black box back to us, which I announced to the group. I needed to act fast, because the black box would be zapped back at 7:00 AM sharp. I was starting to feel a bit anxious, but Bowmar was prepared and told me how to respond. Bowmar stated, "I have already calculated our route to Chicago over the next two days. We are spending tonight in Indianapolis, and will arrive in Chicago on Sunday. Tell Willy to send the black box back to Stagg Field at the University of Chicago, at 7:00 PM on Sunday, April 15, 1945." I wrote that down, then Bowmar added the coordinates of Stagg Field—latitude, longitude, and elevation—to my note, and told Willy to double check everything. I also told Willy that we were going to need him and Pumpkin in few days, and that at a minimum, Bowmar would be returning to run the White Hole. While we wrote the note to Willy, Waldo wrote a return note to Mary. We put our letters in the black box, and pulled Rasputin and his cage out to take with us. I wanted to play a joke on Willy, like sending a fake rattlesnake back in his place, but we were about out of time. Bucky quickly grabbed some leftover pecan pie from his room, which he said was some of the best he'd ever tasted. We put that in the black box with a note:

> To Willy, Pumpkin, and Ben—
> Here is a taste of 1945, by time-travel special delivery!

We sealed the black box just in time. The four of us sat back and watched our synchronized American A-11 military watches, counting down the time to 7:00 AM. At precisely 7:00 AM, the black box vanished into thin air and a small whiff of the unique time-travel scent was briefly present, then gone. I looked at everyone and said, "It's time to take this magic show on the road. Let's get moving."

The thirteen of us, all dressed in military attire, ate breakfast together in the hotel dining room. While we ate, we discussed what had happened the night before and the need to stay obsessively vigilant at all times. What normally would have been a one-day drive from Knoxville to Chicago on modern 1975 interstate highways was going to be a two-day drive in our 1945 Willys Jeeps and 1944 Chevrolet

G-506 military truck on the roads of April 1945. Before leaving the Andrew Johnson Hotel, Bucky called and shared our plans with both Vannevar Bush and Colonel Carter Clarke, just in case more trouble followed us and to keep them aware of our movements. We planned drive to Indianapolis and stay the night at the Hotel Severin. Built in 1913 by Henry Severin Jr. with the financial support of the renowned founders of the Indianapolis Motor Speedway, Carl Fisher and James Allison, the Hotel Severin was strategically built across from the Indianapolis Union Station. In its heyday near the turn of the century, the Indianapolis Union Station serviced an average of 120 trains per day carrying 25,000 passengers. The Hotel Severin thrived as a result and hosted US presidents, foreign dignitaries and royalty, Hollywood celebrities, and legends of the music industry. It would soon be hosting the Bad Love Gang and their pet golden hamster, Rasputin!

At 8:15 AM the Bad Love Gang departed our home state of Tennessee from Knoxville, en route to Indianapolis. Waldo, Bucky, the Runt, and Spaghetti Head were in the lead Willys Jeep. Bowmar, Crisco, Cleopatra, and I were in the second Willys Jeep, followed by Crazy Ike and Goondoggy driving the military truck with the Pud, Meatball, and Tater riding in the back with most of our equipment, guns, and grenades. We did not detect it, but once again we were being covertly followed.

I had the boom box in our Jeep. As we got underway, I asked Cleopatra and Crisco to pick out a song for us to sing and chair-dance to. Crisco, already delighted to have her Canon F-1 in her hands and ready to snap pictures, was on it big time! She hunted through the shoe box of cassettes and handed me one to play. I had Bowmar plug the cassette in and hit the *play* button as I cranked up the volume. It was Paul Simon singing **"Kodachrome,"** and we all went crazy, singing at the top of our lungs in our pretend microphones and bringing our heads together as we rolled down the highway, leaving the home of our Oak Ridge High School in the rearview mirror. I was surprised that I didn't run off the road from the rampant distraction in our Jeep! Released in May 1973, "Kodachrome" peaked at number two on the *Billboard* Hot 100. It was an amazing melody, and so easy to sing! In my brain, I could hear Casey Kasem announcing this song on the weekend radio top forty show while driving my dad's Mustang. Crisco started taking pictures of us all singing together. Despite the fact that we were on a time-travel mission in April 1945, I felt like I was home, singing with my best friends! Crisco told us that photography was the only non-crap course in high school.

We listened to more music for a while, and then I asked Bowmar to explain to us why he chose Stagg Field at the University of Chicago as the place for us to pick up the black box on Sunday night. I mentioned that Vannevar Bush had told Bucky and me about the Chicago Metallurgical Laboratory (Met Lab) scientists, who had built and operated the first prototype atomic reactor, Chicago Pile-1. Vannevar had indicated that the director of the Met Lab, physicist Arthur Compton, and his team were in charge of building the nuclear reactors in Oak Ridge and Hanford, Washington to produce weapons-grade plutonium for the atomic bomb. I figured that our genius, Bowmar, could fill in a few gaps, since he had us heading to Stagg Field on Sunday night.

Bowmar explained, "You listened well to Vannevar, BB, but there is more to the story of the dawn of the atomic age. As early as May 1941, Arthur Compton, appointed by Vannevar Bush, visualized the future prospects of developing nuclear propulsion for ships and nuclear weapons using uranium-235 and/or plutonium. By November that year, Compton submitted a report that the atomic bomb was feasible. Compton was placed in charge of the Chicago Metallurgical Laboratory (Met Lab) in February 1942. He hoped to achieve a controlled nuclear chain reaction by January 1943, and to have an atomic bomb by January 1945. In June 1942, the United States Army Corps of Engineers took control of the US nuclear weapons program, and Compton's Met Lab became part of the Manhattan Project. In June 1942, it was Compton who gave the physicist Robert Oppenheimer the responsibility for designing the world's first atomic bomb. Compton had to decide which of the different types of reactor designs should be pursued. He had groups working on plutonium and nuclear reactor design at Columbia University, Princeton University, and the University of California, Berkeley—all contributing research to the Metallurgical Laboratory in Chicago."

Hearing all this, I still couldn't grasp how Bowmar's brain worked like an encyclopedia, but I was sure glad that he was on our side! As Bowmar drew his next breath, his sister Cleopatra brought him down to earth a bit. "Listen here, little brother; you may know a lot about all this atomic bomb shit, but you can't keep your bedroom straight or pick out matching clothes without your big sister!"

We all laughed with Cleo while Bowmar ignored her and continued, "There is another guy in this story who is one of my heroes of physics. His name is Enrico Fermi, a brilliant Italian physicist who was awarded the Nobel Prize in Physics in 1938 for his work on man-made radioactivity induced by neutron bombardment, and for the discovery of transuranium elements. He left Italy in that year to escape the dictator Mussolini, Italian Fascism, and Italian racial laws that affected his Jewish wife, Laura Capon. After immigrating to the United States, he joined Compton's team at the Met Lab in Chicago, then created and designed the world's first nuclear reactor called Chicago Pile-One, which went critical on December second, 1942. That beat Compton's timetable by one month! It was the first human-created, self-sustaining nuclear chain reaction; for his work on that, Fermi has been called the 'architect of the nuclear age'. He was personally present when the world's second nuclear reactor, known as the Clinton Pile and X-10 Graphite Reactor, went critical in 1943 in our hometown of Oak Ridge, Tennessee. He was there when the B Reactor at the Hanford Site in Washington State, the first large-scale nuclear reactor ever built, went critical in 1944. He was also present at the world's first atomic bomb explosion in New Mexico, the Trinity test on July sixteenth, 1945, where he used his Fermi method to estimate the bomb's yield.

"With all this history focused around the activities originating with the Met Lab at the University of Chicago, I thought it would only be appropriate for the equally amazing but unknown White Hole Project to become a part of that history by sending the black box to the 'hallowed grounds' of Stagg Field."

Cleopatra, still a bit annoyed with her brother's show of intelligence, blurted out, "Maybe they should rename that field 'Bowmar's Big Pile.' Or if we put Rasputin out to pasture there, they could call it 'Rasputin's Range.' He'd have a great time, walking all around there with all those smart people!" She then gave Bowmar's head a good "Dutch rub," and we all had a good laugh together.

We stopped for a late lunch in downtown Louisville, Kentucky, where we ate at the Blue Boar Cafeteria on Fourth Avenue. They had excellent food there. The cafeteria style worked great for our group of thirteen hungry souls. Bucky's head was feeling a bit better, as he had somehow managed to sleep a bit during the day's drive. The Pud, Tater, and Meatball studied the M1A1 bazooka during their ride in the back of the truck, and were very confident they could use it if needed. We were all feeling somewhat more relaxed and discussed that we now had "strength in numbers" with thirteen of us, which might thwart any maleficence directed toward us—unless we were split up in some fashion. That said, we had been covertly followed all day with strict orders for surveillance only. Those orders would change, but for now, no one was noticeably watching or following us, as best we could tell.

It was a relatively short drive from Louisville, Kentucky to the Hotel Severin in Indianapolis, Indiana. We checked in at 6:45 PM and ate dinner together at the superb hotel restaurant. At dinner, the group discussion focused on a tug of war about who was going to get to keep Rasputin for the night, and the choice of our hotel in Chicago the next day. When we initially discovered the White Hole Project, the wardrobe warehouse came replete with a collection of world-wide monies, as well as everything else needed to dress and play the part of the global 1942–1945 timeframe. As a group, we had decided not to be shy about using that money during our time travels, expanding our "cultural horizons and historic perspectives" as we went! Chicago had an incredible collection of historic hotels; we debated about staying at the InterContinental Chicago, the Staypineapple Chicago, the Blackstone, the Drake Hotel, or the Palmer House. Bowmar carefully described each one in detail, and we made it fun by writing our votes on secret ballots. The Drake Hotel won by secret ballot popular vote. The drive to Chicago on Sunday would be shorter, but I reminded everyone that Colonel Clarke had warned Bucky and me that they had seen some violent encounters in Chicago and the Denver area. The more dangerous phase of our road trip could start soon.

CHAPTER FOURTEEN:

FINDING A FORD IN THE LAND OF LINCOLN

"Things are more like today than they have ever been before."
—Gerald R. Ford

Sunday, April 15, 1945 at 12:30 PM local time,
Naval Air Station in Glenview, Illinois

We left Indianapolis at 7:30 Sunday morning and drove a little more than 200 miles to Glenview, Illinois, stopping twice along the way for gas and lunch. We arrived at the headquarters of the Naval Reserve Training Command, Naval Air Station, Glenview, Illinois at 12:30 PM. This is where we planned to catch up with a young Navy Lieutenant named Gerald R. Ford, who was in the midst of transferring to Glenview from the Navy Pre-Flight School at Saint Mary's College in Moraga, California. We hoped to indelibly impress Lieutenant Ford with our knowledge of the future in order to enlist his future cooperation to help us dispose of Boris, his Russian spy cell, and any other future espionage threats to the White Hole in 1975.

Gerald Rudolph Ford, who would become the 38th President of the United States on August 9, 1974, was given the name Leslie Lynch King, Jr., at birth on July 14, 1913, in Omaha, Nebraska. A mere two weeks after his birth, his parents separated and his mother took her new baby boy to Grand Rapids, Michigan to live with her parents. In February 1916, his mother, Dorothy King, married Gerald R. Ford, a Grand Rapids paint salesman. Raised by his mom and stepfather, his name was legally changed to Gerald R. Ford, Jr. Ford attended South High School in Grand Rapids, where he was an excellent scholar as well as an athlete, being named to the honor society and the All-City and All-State football teams. He was also active in scouting growing up, achieving the rank of Eagle Scout in November 1927 at the age of 14. He was our nation's first Eagle Scout to be named president.

Following high school, Ford received a scholarship to the University of Michigan, which he attended from 1931 to 1935. He distinguished himself playing football for the Michigan Wolverines and he was also a college frat boy as a member of the Delta Kappa Epsilon fraternity. He earned spending money at the DKE frat house by working in the kitchen, washing dishes. Ford was a star at college football, playing both sides of the ball as center and linebacker. He helped the team to two undefeated seasons and national titles in 1932 and 1933, and as a senior in 1934, he was named the team's most valuable player. Later in life, his political opponents would sometimes refer to Ford's athletic past, including a memorable quote from the opposing political party president, Lyndon B. Johnson, who said Ford had "played too much football without a helmet."

Upon graduation from the University of Michigan, Ford had the opportunity to play professional football. The Green Bay Packers and the Detroit Lions both made offers, but he turned them down and headed off to Yale University in New Haven, Connecticut, taking a position as head boxing coach and assistant football coach. His plan was to attend Yale Law School, but they liked him too much as a coach; they initially turned down his law school application. In 1938, Ford applied again to Yale Law School and was accepted. In the summer of 1940 as a law student, he got his first taste of Washington politics when he worked with the Wendell Willkie presidential campaign. He earned his law degree in 1941, graduating in the top 25% of his class. Ford passed the bar exam and returned to Grand Rapids, Michigan to practice law.

Ford's law career was very short-lived. Less than a year went by before Pearl Harbor was attacked on December 7, 1941. Like most young, patriotic men of his day, he sought military duty and enlisted in the US Navy as an ensign. He was initially assigned as a physical training officer of naval recruits in North Carolina. Unsatisfied working stateside, Ford requested combat sea duty. He got his wish; from the ship's commissioning on June 17, 1943, until the end of December 1944, Ford was assigned to the Pacific battle theater aboard the USS Monterey, a light aircraft carrier.

On the Monterey, Ford was first assigned as athletic director and antiaircraft battery officer, then as assistant navigator. The Monterey took part in most of the major operations in the South Pacific battle theater, and Ford would earn ten battle stars by the time his combat duty ended. His closest call with death during combat duty was not from enemy fire, but during a massive storm called Typhoon Cobra in the Philippine Sea on December 18, 1944. That particular storm sank three US destroyers, damaging numerous other ships; more than 800 sailors lost their lives. The future president came within inches of losing his life when he was almost swept off the topside deck during the typhoon. As he was going to his battle station on the bridge of the ship early that morning, the ship rolled 25 degrees. Ford lost his footing and slid toward the edge of the deck, and the unforgiving, raging sea below. A two-inch steel ridge around the edge of the carrier slowed him down and saved him from going overboard. Ford used his athletic ability to twist and swing onto the catwalk below the deck.

During Typhoon Cobra, several of the ship's aircraft broke loose from their cables, crashed against the deck and each other, and caught fire. The fire damage crippled the Monterey, and the ship was taken out of service. On Christmas Eve of 1944, Ford left the Monterey and his combat career behind. He was sent to the Navy Pre-Flight School at Saint Mary's College in Moraga, California, where he was assigned to the Athletic Department for a short time (supposedly with a role to coach football), until April 1945. He was transferring to the Naval Reserve Training Command, Naval Air Station, Glenview, Illinois, in April 1945 as the staff physical and military training officer, where we would intercept him and experience another major surprise.

Our Bad Love Gang "convoy" entered the Naval Air Station at Glenview with Bucky, Waldo, and me leading the way in our Willys Jeep, passing the entrance guard station using our rank and direct presidential orders, which no one questioned. We pulled up to the commanding officer's building, the front door bearing the signage *CDR W. J. Staples*. We told the rest of the Bad Love Gang to sit tight while we went inside to enquire as to the status and whereabouts of a new transfer to the Naval Reserve Training Command at Glenview, Navy Lieutenant Gerald R. Ford. As we entered Commander Staples' front office, we saw a Navy WAVE (WAVES: Women Accepted for Volunteer Emergency Service) with striking auburn hair. She stood with her back to us behind the office desk, half bending over as she filed something in a cabinet. It was impossible not to notice her feminine hourglass shape in her Navy uniform. The WAVES' uniforms had been designed by a New York fashion house through the efforts of a former fashion editor at *Vogue* Magazine (whose subscriptions had surged during WWII) named Josephine Forrestal. Josephine had married the assistant secretary of the US Navy, and it was she who secured the fashion designer Mainbocher's voluntary wartime services.

The WAVES winter uniform was made from navy blue wool, worn with a white, button-down shirt and dark blue tie. The jacket was single breasted and went along with an unbelted, six-gored skirt. The uniform's accessories included black Oxford shoes and plain black pumps, a cap and brimmed hat, black gloves, black leather purse, and rain and winter coats.

The enlisted WAVE, keeping her back to us as she was filing, was the first to speak. "Commander Staples is off base today, and won't be back until tomorrow afternoon."

I looked at Bucky, and his face first froze and turned white like a ghost before turning an alarming shade of beet red. Waldo was quietly enjoying the scenery, but I was baffled by Bucky's facial fireworks. There was a pause while Bucky's facial color returned to normal and his mind came into focus. He was next to speak, "Captain Denver at your service, madam. It looks like a nice day to go conquer the sky, don't you think?"

The shapely WAVE let out a scream as she dropped her files and turned to face us. She looked at Bucky and exclaimed, "Oh my God! Bucky, is that you?! How on earth—what are you *doing* here?!" She was gorgeous, and I immediately recognized her as Peggy Sue Harding, Bucky's first love from Denver West High School. As she raced around the desk and into Bucky's arms, my music brain clicked into action and started playing Buddy Holly's classic hit **"Peggy Sue."** The song went to number three on the *Billboard* Top 100 chart in 1957, and many baby boomer girls were probably named after this song. As my brain played the guitar solo, my head bobbed and I unconsciously played my air guitar—until Waldo nudged me back to reality.

After a huge hug and kiss with Peggy Sue, Bucky introduced us and answered, "We are here to track down a new transfer to this base,

Lieutenant Gerald Ford coming in from California. What are you doing here?" Bucky asked.

Peggy Sue responded, "I'm sure you remember that my dad sent me from Denver in the fall of 1935 to Mundelein College, here in Chicago. I graduated in thirty-nine, and stayed in Chicago working for a large law firm. I tried marriage to a lawyer I met, but failed at having children and he divorced me three years ago. In 1943, I decided to try something different, so I enlisted with the WAVES. I requested to stay in the Chicago area, since I have friends and family here. I was assigned with the first contingency of WAVES to work here at NAS Glenview in 1943, and now I work for Commander Staples."

Waldo interrupted, and unknowingly gave a tiny hint about the future. "I have a bumper sticker on my car that says 'I don't brake for lawyers!' Don't you worry about that shithead lawyer; my wife Mary and I can't have children of our own, but we found a way to make it work." He looked at me and winked.

Peggy Sue smiled as she replied, "I'm not sure exactly what a bumper sticker is, but that ex of mine would look good with tire tracks or skid marks across his big, fat, lying ass!"

We all laughed together and Peggy Sue then continued while keeping her eyes glued to Bucky, "You guys are lucky for more than one reason," she said as she winked at Bucky. "I just took Lieutenant Ford over to the officers' barracks to check out where he will be living. He is on leave from California, on his way to visit family in Grand Rapids, Michigan. He starts here at the end of this month as our staff physical and military training officer. I read his file; he was a lawyer before the war broke out, and he has served with distinction in the Pacific theater. Besides that, he strikes me as a genuinely nice guy, with an infectious smile and a nice sense of humor."

With a devilish smirk on his face, Waldo conceded, "Well, maybe not *all* lawyers deserve to be run over." We all laughed again.

Bucky asked Peggy Sue, "Do you think you could go get Lieutenant Ford and bring him back here for us to meet with him here, privately in the commander's office?"

"I can accomplish that mission under one condition, Captain Denver," she somewhat seductively replied.

"I'm afraid to ask, but what is that?" Bucky enquired.

"You take me flying to see the Chicago skyline before the sun sets tonight. We have a Stearman Kaydet here on base with your name on it!"

Bucky looked at me and Waldo, bright-eyed and hopeful. We both shrugged, and I sarcastically said, "You can take that secret mission, you big stud muffin! We'll come back here to get you after we pick up our special delivery at seven tonight."

We introduced Peggy Sue to the rest of the Bad Love Gang parked outside, and I could tell that Crisco seemed a bit annoyed; maybe she was jealous, learning that Peggy Sue was Bucky's high school sweetheart. I reassured the group that this would not take too much longer, then Bucky, Waldo, and I went into Commander Staples' office to wait. Peggy Sue took a Jeep to retrieve Lieutenant Gerald R. Ford, bringing him to us in the span of ten minutes. Peggy Sue escorted the young Lieutenant Ford directly into the commander's office, then introduced us by name and rank as Ford stood saluting us. When Peggy Sue closed the door behind her, Waldo (as the ranking officer in the room, a US Army Air Force two-star major general) spoke. "At ease, Lieutenant. You need to listen to us very carefully, because we are part of a top-secret military program known as the Denver Project. We are going to tell you a true story about your future, and when you hear from us or see us again thirty years from now in 1975, we will look and sound exactly like we do at this moment. We will need your cooperation and help on a matter of national security, and want you to remember this meeting when we contact you in 1975. Colonel Schafer will brief you now. Try to ignore his youthful appearance; he earned his wings in an unconventional way." Waldo winked at me again.

Known as the "Accidental President," Ford was elected by the US Senate to replace President Richard Nixon's vice president, Spiro Agnew, in December 1973 after Agnew resigned his office in a tax evasion scandal. Eight months later, Richard Nixon resigned the presidency in the heat of the Watergate debacle. On August 9, 1974, Gerald R. Ford was sworn in as the 38th president of the United States. As a result of these events, he was the only US President never elected by the voting public to either the vice presidency or the presidency. However, as a Republican congressman from Michigan serving in the US House of Representatives from January 1949 to December 1973, he was undefeated through 13 elections, always winning with more than 60 percent of the vote during his entire tenure in Congress.

Ford, age 31 at this moment in time, enquired, "Permission to speak, sir?" Waldo nodded. "I am scheduled to start here at the end of this month as the staff physical and military training officer. I'm relatively fresh off combat duty in the Pacific with the USS carrier Monterey, but I have never been part of any kind of special or top-secret operation. I am drawing a blank about why I am standing here now with a general, a captain, and a young-looking colonel involved in a top-secret military program." He gave me a warm smile and I smiled back, shrugging.

"Lieutenant Ford, I am going to tell you some important key events of your future life—not to, in any way, spoil the fun of your amazing future, but to make certain that you know that we are the 'good guys' when we call upon you in the future, and that you can trust us," I explained. Ford continued to look puzzled, understandably. "You will run for Congress in 1948, get married during your first campaign, and spend your honeymoon attending Republican Party rallies. A future American president will be assassinated, and you will serve on a congressional committee investigating that assassination. You will represent your district in Michigan in Congress for twenty-five years. You will never be elected as vice president or president, but you will serve as president of the United States. You will face a difficult decision to use your power to pardon as the president."

Ford looked at us totally bewildered and said, "I'll remember everything you said, Colonel Schafer, but I have more romantic aspirations than to spend my future honeymoon at political rallies—and I am way too nice a guy to ever be the president of the United States."

We all shared a good laugh, as we found the young Gerald Ford to be totally affable and likeable. I had one more critically important thing to share with Lieutenant Ford. "We will have to contact you through the White House switchboard in 1975, and that will be tricky. You will know that it is us because the message will say, 'The Denver Project needs you,' and there will be a phone number for you to call us. When you hear or see the phrase *Denver Project*, that is your cue to respond. Just in case you have a really good memory, when we call upon you in the future, I'm known as Bubble Butt or BB, General Thompson here is known as Waldo, and Captain Smith is known as Bucky. We are all members of the Bad Love Gang."

Ford responded, "So long as you don't call me Leslie Lynch King, Jr. I'll be waiting for you in the future; you can count on me!"

We all shook Ford's hand, thanking him for his time, and he left the commander's office. Peggy Sue then took him back to the officer's barracks. The three of us joined the rest of the Bad Love Gang convoy in the parking lot, and I told them "Mission accomplished, and it's time to go check in at the famous Drake Hotel." Waldo and I got back into the lead Jeep while Bucky stood in the parking area and watched us. I told Bucky that we would be back for him at about 9:00 PM, and recommended that he and Peggy Sue stay on the base when not flying, since he was going to be separated from us for the next several hours and he was still nursing a sore head. Peggy Sue returned in five minutes to pick up Bucky. As we pulled away and headed for the base exit gate, Peggy Sue and Bucky drove towards one of the large base hangars. They had a plane to catch!

CHAPTER FIFTEEN:
SHOTS AT STAGG

"There are no secrets about the world of nature.
There are secrets about the thoughts and intentions of men."
—J. Robert Oppenheimer (the "Father" of the atomic bomb)

*Sunday, April 15, 1945 at 7:00 PM local time, Stagg Field,
University of Chicago*

After we left the Naval Air Station at Glenview, we made a beeline to check into the Drake Hotel in downtown Chicago. Bucky and Peggy Sue took a Sunday tour of the giant NAS Glenview military base in Peggy Sue's Jeep while they reconnected after not seeing each other for nearly ten years. The sun would set at 7:31 PM in Chicago on this day in history, and Bucky would make good on his promise to take Peggy Sue for a romantic sunset flight to view the Chicago skyline in one of the base's Stearman Kaydet biplanes. They reminisced about how much fun they'd had the day they buzzed the cheerleading squad at West High School in Denver together, in Uncle Barney's Stearman Kaydet, then resolved that they would buzz the Bad Love Gang at Stagg Field just south of downtown Chicago at about 7:00 PM. As they toured NAS Glenview, Bucky was impressed with the expansive Navy base and the beautiful WAVE sitting next to him, who was so genuinely glad to see him again.

Naval Reserve Air Base (NRAB) Chicago was officially dedicated in August 1937. In early 1942, with the outbreak of World War II, NRAB Chicago rapidly became a focal point for the Navy to train carrier pilots. Nearly 570 acres of additional land was purchased adjacent to the base, and a massive construction project was launched. Once construction contracts were awarded in April 1942, one of the largest and fastest concrete paving jobs ever untaken in the Midwestern United States took place at NRAB Chicago. In a record 121 working days, 1.3 million yards of concrete were poured for runways and landing mats. Included in this amazing story of US wartime construction were military barracks, dining facilities, a recreation hall, a gymnasium (with a large training pool), a firehouse, a hospital, shops, theater, paved streets, sidewalks, streetlights, chapel... Everything needed to make a self-contained military community. The longest runway was 6,600 feet long and 200 feet wide; there were 26 refueling pits along the apron of the main runway.

The Navy's goal was to efficiently train aircraft carrier pilots and flight deck personnel, getting them into battle as quickly as possible. They came up with a novel solution to get this accomplished. The Navy purchased two, large coal-burning Great Lakes paddlewheel excursion ships, originally named the *Greater Buffalo* and the *Seeandbee*. These two ships were subsequently converted into flattops to simulate aircraft carrier conditions on nearby Lake Michigan. The *Seeandbee* was retrofitted with a wooden flight deck and renamed the USS *Wolverine*, entering service in August 1942. The *Greater Buffalo* was retrofitted with a steel flight deck and renamed the USS *Sable*, entering service in May 1943. They were the only inland "aircraft carriers" ever commissioned by the US Navy, and became part of the Navy fleet known as the "Corn Belt Fleet." These two carriers on Lake Michigan trained pilots and flight deck personnel 24/7/365 during WWII, logging over

135,000 carrier-based landings and training over 15,000 pilots. In January 1943, NRAB Chicago was re-designated as Naval Air Station (NAS) Chicago, and in 1944, the base was renamed Naval Air Station (NAS) Glenview.

Bucky and Peggy Sue took off in their Stearman Kaydet biplane from NAS Glenview at 5:45 PM and headed southeast along the shoreline of Lake Michigan to take in the downtown lights of the Chicago skyline on a beautiful spring evening. From there, they would fly south of the downtown loop to the University of Chicago and Stagg Field, where the Bad Love Gang was retrieving the black box, which would be zapped there by Willy, at the controls of the White Hole Project, at 7:00 PM local time. Bucky was not expecting trouble while flying with Peggy Sue, but he did have his loaded Colt .45 M1911 holstered at his side, especially in light of all that had happened in the past two days. Their flight in the Stearman was all that Peggy Sue had hoped for, and more. Bucky swooped down along the shores of Lake Michigan, did a few gentle rolls, and even flew a wide loop as they passed the downtown Chicago skyline. It was like a giant, gentle rollercoaster in the sky in front of Chicago; Bucky was born to fly, and Peggy Sue loved every minute of it.

In the meantime, the Bad Love Gang arrived at the University of Chicago and Stagg Field at 6:30 PM. Bowmar was super excited to be there, and led the group to the west stands of Stagg Field. We all sat in the stands, with an excellent view of the football field, where we could watch for the black box to appear at 7:00 PM. Waldo had reminded us to carry weapons in case Colonel Carter Clarke's warnings about violent encounters in Chicago materialized. Goondoggy, Crazy Ike, Meatball, and the Pud were all carrying Thompson machine guns. The rest of us had M1 Garand rifles, along with our Colt .45 M1911 pistols. As we sat down in the west stands, two bulky, muscular Russian spies, Kolya Lukin and Nikolai Markoff, covertly made their way to the top of the north and south towers respectively, and were watching us from above. In addition, a smaller-framed spy dressed in black entered the east stands and was secretly watching us from across the field.

Bowmar was anxious to give the rest of the group a little history lesson about why he chose this particular site to receive the second black box launch. We all humored him while we waited for 7:00 PM to arrive.

"The Atomic Age began at 3:25 PM on December 2, 1942, in a squash court underneath these football stands, exactly where you all are sitting at this moment. The famous Italian physicist Enrico Fermi and his colleagues engineered the first controlled, self-sustaining nuclear chain reaction with the world's first crude nuclear reactor, called Chicago Pile-1, at this very site. When Chicago Pile-1 reactor went critical that initial chain reaction was too weak to power even a single light bulb, with an output of only half a watt. But ultimately, it operated at two hundred watts maximum. Fermi's reactor design was the basis for the X-10 Graphite Reactor in Oak Ridge, as well as the first full-scale B Reactor, at Hanford in Washington State. Their experiment here was a key step in the Manhattan Project development of the atomic bomb during World War II."

Cleopatra playfully interrupted her brother's history lesson. "Listen, little brother, I don't think two hundred watts can keep my bathroom lights and hair dryer running at the same time, so those guys better go back to the drawing board real quick!"

We all laughed and Tater jumped in, "I don't know, Cleo; my ass was starting to feel hotter than two rabbits screwin' in a wool sock from sitting on these stands!"

Crisco joined in the fun. "I have a radioactive cat at home!"

We all responded, "How do you know?"

"It has eighteen half-lives!" Crisco replied.

The Runt reacted to Crisco, "Can I jump in your lap, Crisco? I'm sure your big butt would shield my gonads from the radiation and making alien babies in the future!"

Crazy Ike chipped in with his most annoying smirky smile, "I don't know about the rest of you, but I think this radioactivity seeping up from below is making all my freckles glow—just like my wonderful personality!"

I couldn't help but try to put Crazy Ike back in his place. "I think you *meant* to say it's making your turds glow, just like your shitty personality!"

"This radioactivity is making me feel like *The Six Million Dollar Man!*" the Pud exclaimed, referring to the TV series of that name that we all started watching in 1973. It was the story about a USAF astronaut, Colonel Steve Austin, played by actor Lee Majors. Rebuilt after a terrible accident, he had superhuman strength from bionic implants and could run at speeds exceeding 60 mph. He had the strength of a tank, and his bionic eye was like a telescope. "You all won't be calling me the Pud anymore!"

Goondoggy put the nix on the Pud's aspirations. "You mean *The Six Dollar Man*: capable of working at the Quick Shop, while chewing gum at the same time. Remarkable!"

Bowmar, appearing a bit frustrated and deflated, loudly interrupted. "All right, you idiots, *we are not getting exposed to radiation sitting here* in this historic spot! The Chicago Pile-1 nuclear reactor beneath these stands was terminated in February 1942; the experimental reactor was dismantled and moved to the Argonne Forest to be safely away from any dense population area. On July 1, 1946, the Chicago 'Metallurgical Laboratory' at this site was formally re-chartered as the

Argonne National Laboratory, to build nuclear reactors for peacetime purposes."

Meatball teased Bowmar, perfectly using the tone of a mother speaking to her baby child for appearing to be upset over nothing. "Aw Bowmar, does it have a temp-poo-tour?" We all died laughing.

I had planned for this moment to lighten up on Bowmar's history lesson by using some music as a preamble to watching the black box "magically appear" at 7:00 PM on the field in front of us. I moved to the front of the group with my boom box and invited the group to dance and sing with me as I hit the *play* button. I cranked up the volume and on came Edwin Starr, singing **"War,"** which was released in June 1970 to protest the Vietnam War. It rapidly became a smash hit, holding the top position on the *Billboard* Pop Singles chart for three full weeks, during August and September 1970. Everyone stood up in the stands and started to swing back and forth, dancing and lip syncing the words with me, almost as if we had choreographed it. Of course, Waldo stood up with all of us, but was mainly watching us and laughing at our antics. There we were, all dressed in WWII American military uniforms, dancing to early 1970's music in the west stands of Stagg Field, on an April Sunday night in 1945!

Russian agent Nikolai Markoff, spying from the top of the south tower, radioed the other spy, Kolya Lukin, who was watching from the top of the north tower. "Kolya, do you think these could be aliens dressed as American soldiers?"

Kolya responded, "I don't know, Nikolai, I have never seen or heard anything like this, even when I am drunk with motherland vodka! Soon we shall see if they bleed like earthlings!" The other agent, watching from the east stands, found himself bobbing his head with the music just a bit.

As the music stopped, it was almost 7:00 PM. I heard a plane approaching from the southeast. Looking up, I saw that it was a biplane and immediately knew it was Bucky and Peggy Sue, taking their sunset plane ride together and coming our way to check us out. I exclaimed to the group as I pointed to the plane, "Here comes Captain Denver of the US Army Air Force!"

Bucky and Peggy Sue had flown south of the University of Chicago from the downtown skyline of the Chicago Loop, along the south shore of Lake Michigan. They then turned west until they could see Stagg Field, and turned north to come in and buzz us. He had timed it to arrive at our position at 7:00 PM, then land back at NAS Glenview at 7:30 PM—right at sunset. As Bucky came in low from the south, he saw the two Russian snipers positioned on top of the south and north towers, spying on the Bad Love Gang. Bucky yelled back at Peggy Sue as he pointed below, then drew his Colt .45. "Peggy Sue, there is trouble brewing below! Pull your seatbelt tight, we are going into battle!" He held his pistol up so she could see it and she acknowledged that she understood. Bucky did not have radio contact with the Bad Love Gang below. He knew full well that any shots he could fire would not be accurate, but he also knew it would serve to warn the Bad Love Gang that they were under attack, and to respond with force.

Bucky pushed the throttle to full power and pulled the Stearman into a rolling dive, lining up his trajectory from south to north along the stadium's west wall. Peggy Sue pulled her seat belt as tight as she could and wanted to scream, but she knew that Bucky meant business. The spy dressed in black watching from the east stands heard and saw the biplane approaching and readied his rifle. At the moment, I thought that Bucky was getting ready to display his aerobatic skills and give us all a little sunset show.

As Bucky approached the south tower and Nikolai Markoff's position, he half-completed his roll and came over the south tower fully inverted (upside down), flying at an airspeed of 120 mph. He was flying with the stick in his left hand and his Colt .45 M1911 pistol in his right, knowing he had to time his shots ahead of what he was sensing as his ground position. He had no time to experience the emotions of anger or fear; he was determined to do his best to warn his friends below.

Nikolai heard the noise of the plane, but had been focused on the Bad Love Gang in the west stands and talking to Kolya on the walkie talkie as the music died. By the time the Stearman's engine was loud enough; Nikolai was just looking up and behind his position on top of the south tower to see what was happening. Bucky, flying inverted with his left hand and shooting with his right, let loose with a barrage of seven .45 caliber bullets. He took four quick shots approaching the south tower, paused briefly, then fired the last three shots to time them with passing over the north tower. One of the first four shots ricocheted off the ledge of the south tower, startling Nikolai, and one of the last three shots hit the north tower wall, directly below Kolya's position. Nikolai stood up and started firing at the Stearman, while Kolya stood up to watch the Stearman fly by. He then paused ever-so-briefly before turning to open fire on the Bad Love Gang below. That unplanned pause would be his final mistake on earth.

Watching all this rapidly unfold from the west stands, some of the Bad Love Gang hit the ground upon hearing shots fired, but several of us were all eyes and ears as the action unfolded. We pulled our guns off our shoulders, preparing to fully defend ourselves. Watching from the east stands, the spy dressed in black was the first to see Nikolai Markoff raise his rifle to fire shots at the Stearman, then start to lower his aim to shoot at us. The spy aimed and fired at Nikolai, hitting his right shoulder, which forced him to drop his rifle and hit the ground, startled that he had been targeted. He then promptly and wisely made his escape from the south tower.

We heard the shot fired from the east stands, and looked there to see the spy in black swing his rifle around to point at the north tower, which then had us looking squarely at big, bulky-chested Kolya Lukin, who was turning to shoot at us. Rather than risk engaging us any further, the spy in black quickly made his escape out of the east side of the stadium. None of Nikolai's shots hit the Stearman; Bucky had enough airspeed to pull a reverse loop and then begin a return dive toward the north tower.

As we turned our attention toward the north tower, we saw the bulky, big-chested Kolya Lukin make his slightly-delayed turn to face us with his assault rifle. I could hear Crazy Ike cursing like a sailor, ranting about how he was fed up with getting shot at, and how this "son of a bitch was gonna pay big!" Simultaneously, I watched as Crazy Ike, Goondoggy, the Pud, and Meatball all pulled their Thompson machine guns off their shoulder slings and pointed their guns directly at Kolya Lukin, who was lowering his assault rifle toward us as he approached the edge of the north tower. His large, hard-to-miss chest faced us; perhaps Kolya did not realize how well we were armed. In the next millisecond, it sounded like the scene from a 1920's era gangster movie when Crazy Ike, Goondoggy, the Pud, and Meatball all let loose with their Thompson Machine guns, each with 30-round box magazines. The guns could fire at a rate of 1,500 rounds per minute, which meant that it took less than two seconds for a total of 120 rounds to be hurtling toward Kolya's big-chested target. The force of the impact shredded Kolya's chest, and blew him backwards right off the tower. He was dead before his body landed and thumped on the ground below. Crazy Ike, in keeping with his nickname, lowered his gun, blew the smoke off the tip of the barrel, and said, "Take *that*, you Russian bastard!"

Bucky and Peggy Sue were in a dive back towards the north tower when he saw the flashing lights of our unleashed Thompson machine guns, and Kolya's large body get blown off the top of the tower. Bucky buzzed us and then waved his wings as he pulled up and away headed back to NAS Glenview to land by sundown. As soon as we all took our eyes away from Bucky and Peggy Sue, flying off into the sunset, we looked to the middle of Stagg Field. There sat the black box, having arrived from 1975 while we were busy. We went down to the field to get the black box, then made haste to depart before drawing any more attention. Waldo and I took one of the Willys Jeeps to go get Bucky, and the rest of the Bad Love Gang headed back to the Drake Hotel.

Waldo and I met up with Bucky and Peggy Sue at Commander Staple's office at NAS Glenview after dark, at about 8:45 PM. As we came through the door, I noticed Bucky was wiping off his lips with his forearm. I walked up to him and started inspecting his neck. "What the hell are you doing, BB?!"

I replied, "I wanted to see if any red lip marks came flying through the air and landed perfectly on your neck while you were doing that loop earlier tonight!" Peggy Sue busted out laughing and Bucky shoved me away, calling me a little smart ass. I said, "This little smart ass wants to thank you for giving us a fair warning just in the nick of time tonight. You saved our lives. I want you to call Colonel Clarke right now and tell him about that big, dead Russian spy back at Stagg Field, so he knows what happened there."

Bucky answered, "Yes, that's a good idea, BB. But first, I have a request of you and Waldo, before we leave here."

Waldo and I simultaneously asked, "What's that?"

"As BB knows, Peggy Sue's parents live in Denver, where we both grew up and went to high school together. Since we have successfully completed our mission here and are starting our drive to Denver tomorrow, Peggy Sue would like to go with us—and I would like for us to have some more time together. What do you think?"

Waldo and I looked at each other. Waldo said, "You already put Peggy Sue in danger tonight, Bucky. We have good intel that we are going to face additional unknown dangers in Colorado."

Peggy Sue passionately spoke up. "This is the most excitement that I have had in nearly ten years! You don't know how mundane it is to sit behind this desk, day after day. What are the chances that I would see Bucky again, especially like what happened here today? The chances are *infinitesimal*, and you both know it. I may be an enlisted WAVE, but I am ordering you to take me with you!"

"*Holy shit, this is a strong woman who knows what she wants!*" I thought. Waldo was silenced by the force of Peggy Sue's comments, so looking at Bucky, I spoke next, "So long as you accept and take responsibility for Peggy Sue's safety, we will be glad to have her come with us. I have a feeling that she can hold her own pretty well."

Peggy Sue gave me a huge hug and kiss on the cheek. Waldo looked at me and said, "Why can't I ever seem to say the right words?" We all laughed together, then Bucky called Colonel Clarke with a report about the evening's events. Clarke again warned Bucky about the potential for more trouble in Colorado, and the four of us climbed in the Jeep and drove to the Drake Hotel to spend the night.

CHAPTER SIXTEEN:

GO WEST, YOUNG MAN, GO WEST

"Courage is being scared to death but saddling up anyway."
—John Wayne

Monday, April 16, 1945 at 7:00 AM local time, the Drake Hotel in Chicago

The historic and world-famous Drake Hotel was designed in the Italian Renaissance style, built on the cornerstone of the Magnificent Mile and Lake Shore Drive in Chicago, and founded in 1920. It rapidly became one of Chicago's landmark hotels. During the roaring '20s, The Drake became high-society's place to be seen and top choice in opulence. In 1940, The Drake's pink neon sign was illuminated, prominently cementing the hotel's landmark image in one of world's most-recognized skylines. The walls of the Drake have seen many famous American politicians, heads of state, Hollywood and sports celebrities, and international personalities. Notable Drake guests have included Winston Churchill, Eleanor Roosevelt, and Presidents Herbert Hoover, Dwight Eisenhower, and Gerald Ford. Other famous icons who stayed there include Hugh Hefner, Walt Disney, Elizabeth Taylor, Judy Garland, Frank Sinatra, Dean Martin, and Charles Lindbergh. Joe DiMaggio and Marilyn Monroe carved their initials into the wooden bar of the Cape Cod Room. In April 1945, dressed as WWII

American military officers and personnel, the Bad Love Gang spent the night at the Drake.

Bowmar and I spent the night in a room connected to Cleopatra and Crisco's room. Waldo was directly across the hall. Bucky and Peggy Sue got a room with a view of Lake Michigan, and the rest of the Bad Love Gang was clustered in nearby rooms on our floor. Before calling it a night, Bowmar, Waldo, and I had reviewed our road trip route from Chicago to Denver and checked out the incoming contents of the black box, getting it ready to be zapped back to the future at precisely 7:00 this morning. At least this time, Willy did not send us another live pet to handle! We opened the black box and to our delight, Willy had sent some 1975 snacks for our continuing road trip. He had packed the box with several boxes of Hostess Twinkies and Ding Dongs, Snyder's of Hanover pretzels, a case of canned Dr. Pepper, a dozen canisters of Pringles Newfangled Potato Crisps, and every flavor of the brand-new Pop Rocks. Originally offered to the American public by General Foods in 1975, Pop Rocks was new to us, and very different from typical hard candy. Pressurized carbon dioxide gas bubbles were embedded inside the candy, and this created a popping reaction as the candy was dissolving in the mouth. There were mythical stories of children nearly "blowing up" after consuming this candy, which made it even more desirable and in demand. In addition to the awesome snacks, there was the mail file with another letter from Mary to Waldo. Willy had sent my dad's WWII army dog tags as well, which he had found hanging in the back office of the exotic matter containment room. He also sent a few more cassettes from my music collection!

Our return message to Willy and Pumpkin had a lot of information for them to process as the next segment of our 1945 road trip unfolded. We were leaving the Drake Hotel and Chicago, and would take US Route 45 South to US Route 40 West and stay in St. Louis, Missouri at the Mayfair Hotel that night. On Tuesday, April 17, 1945, we would drive to Kansas City and stay at the Muehlebach Hotel. On Wednesday, April 18, 1945, we would drive to Wilson, Kansas and stay at the Midland Hotel. On Thursday, April 19, 1945, we would drive to Denver and stay at the Brown Palace Hotel. The road trip to Denver would take us four full days, given our mode of transportation and the 1945 road conditions. On Thursday, April 19th, we requested that Willy zap both Bowmar and Spaghetti Head back to 1975 Oak Ridge. That would give Bowmar one day to bring Willy and Pumpkin up to speed about the status of our trip. Bowmar would then operate the White Hole Project to send Willy, Pumpkin, and the black box to us on Friday, April 20th at 7:00 PM with the coordinates for Bucky's alma mater at the West Denver High School football field. We requested that Bowmar and Willy also send the Pud's VHF radio equipment to use with the P-40 Warhawks. After scooping up Willy, Pumpkin, and the black box on Friday night, we would drive to Colorado Springs.

We needed Willy and Pumpkin (who both knew how to fly) to train with me and Bucky to fly the P-40 Warhawks at Peterson Army Air Base in Colorado Springs, starting on Saturday, April 21, 1945. The entire group would be staying at the world-famous Broadmoor Hotel and Resort in Colorado Springs while the four of us trained together, under Bucky's expert direction and leadership, to fly and fight using the P-40s. We planned to conclude this overall mission with a time-travel trip to temporarily volunteer for General Claire Chennault's Flying Tigers in June of 1942, at the direct request of President Roosevelt. Spaghetti Head had asked to return with Bowmar on Thursday to attend the weekend christening of his older sister's newborn baby girl: his very first niece, named Izabella Russo. Spaghetti Head had been talking about it constantly, trying to decide whether he was going to call her Bella or Izzy.

Waldo wrote a return letter to Mary, and Meatball wrote a note to Ben; we placed those, along with our long message about the upcoming segment of the road trip, in the black box mail file. A few minutes before 7:00 AM, a small contingent of Bad Love Gang members came to our room to watch the black box disappear. I tried to sell admission tickets but no one was buying! Crisco, Cleopatra, Waldo, Bowmar, Meatball, Tater and I were all there. I picked out a song to play on the boom box, and asked Crisco to sit on the black box beside me. I knew that Crisco had a crush on Bucky; she was taking this Bucky/Peggy Sue reconnection "coincidence" a bit hard, and personally. Crisco and I had a thing for each other that went back to the onset of puberty, and I had always had a heart for her (as did the rest of the Bad Love Gang). She and I had covertly connected on and off again as teenagers, with no real strings attached; it worked for both of us. I decided I would do what I could to mitigate her bruised aspirations for Bucky and make this particular road trip more interesting. Crisco looked at me with a raised eyebrow and said, "I'm not in the mood to be abused this morning, Bubble Butt."

"This is a medical and physics experiment, and I need your scientific help to prove my theory." I pushed the *play* button on the Marantz boom box, put my arm around her shoulders, and we sat down on the black box together.

The song **"Superstition"** by singer-songwriter Stevie Wonder filled the room as Crisco and I sat down on top of the black box at 6:59 AM. "Superstition" was released in October 1972, and the lyrics described multiple popular superstitions and their negative effects. The song hit number one on the US *Billboard* Hot 100, as well as the US *Billboard* R & B chart. We were all rocking out to the music as Crisco and I lip synched the song to each other. The clock hit 7:00 AM, the black box disappeared from beneath us, and Crisco and I thumped straight to floor and fell backwards together. The others were laughing at us and the music was still playing as she looked in my eyes and enquired, "What did that medical and physics experiment prove, Doctor Bubble Butt?"

"Well, two things, Nurse Crisco," I replied. "From a medical perspective, the fall just bruised our egos; and from a physics perspective, you can't help but fall for me."

She warmly smiled as she continued to look into my eyes and responded, "Nice try, Colonel. Keep it up; you might get lucky someday."

Monday, April 16, 1945 at 8:15 AM local time, the Drake Hotel in Chicago

At breakfast in the hotel dining room, Bowmar and I reviewed the plans for the entire road trip with the group. Everyone was psyched to get on the road for the first leg of the trip to St. Louis, Missouri. We again reviewed our need to be ever-vigilant in light of the constant stream of new threats that had come our way. We checked out of the Drake Hotel and our Bad Love Gang convoy departed at 8:15 AM. On this day, we would drive south from Chicago on US Route 45 for about 210 miles to Effingham, Illinois, then turn west on US Route 40 for another 100+ miles to St. Louis. We divided the trip to Denver over the next four days, with daily drives in the range of 225 to 390 miles, mostly along US Route 40, all the way to Denver. During its heyday, US Route 40 (created in 1926) was known as the Main Street of America, traversing the midsection of the United States and stretching 3,157 miles from Atlantic City to San Francisco.

Waldo, Bucky, and Peggy Sue were riding in the lead Willys Jeep. Bowmar, Crisco, Cleopatra, and I followed in the second Jeep, and the rest of the Bad Love Gang were in the truck, bringing up the rear. We had split up the yummy snacks and Dr. Peppers that Willy sent, and we were ready to ride! As had been the case since we had departed our hometown of Oak Ridge, Tennessee, the agent that we now referred to as the "spy in black" was covertly following us, undetected. The Russians had also set up a network to map our progress, despite having lost two good agents in the last three days. Our "convoy" was bigger than it appeared.

As we drove away with Chicago fading in the rearview mirror and Crisco taking intermittent pictures with her Canon F-1, my music brain wasn't letting go quite yet. I grabbed one of the fresh cassettes that Willy had sent in the latest black box and plugged it into the boom box. I cranked up the volume as it was my all-time favorite song from the American rock band named Chicago, **"25 or 6 to 4."** The band originated in Chicago, Illinois in 1967, blending elements of jazz, R & B, classical music, and pop rock. They originally called themselves the Chicago Transit Authority, but subsequently shortened their name to Chicago in 1969. The song, released as a single in June 1970, reached number four on the US *Billboard* Hot 100 chart and number seven on the UK Singles Chart. It was banned in Singapore in 1970, due to "alleged allusions to drugs," which probably helped propel its popularity elsewhere. Crisco, Cleopatra, Bowmar, and I rocked out to this five-minute-long tune, singing along and playing our fake horns and air guitars all the way!

As we settled into our drive south on US Route 45, Cleopatra, sitting with Crisco in the back seat, brought up a rather serious topic of discussion. She grabbed Bowmar's shoulder from behind, shook him a little bit, and said, "Hey little brother, have you been getting some looks from all the white people, like we don't belong in our military uniforms—or at all?" Cleo and Crisco were both dressed as a Women's Army Corps (WAC) sergeants, and Bowmar was dressed as a USAAF Tuskegee airman first lieutenant.

All of us Bad Love Gang members had grown up in Oak Ridge, Tennessee, which as a city and community, had been a leader in the post-World War II desegregation movement in the South. Oak Ridge High School was the first high school in the southern United States to integrate after the US Supreme Court's 1954 *Brown v. Board of Education of Topeka* decision, which prohibited state-sponsored school segregation, declaring it unconstitutional. On September 6, 1955, a total of 42 African American students attended the first day of school at Oak Ridge High School and were photographed by Life Magazine. Nearly 20 years had passed since then; integration was "normal" for us in 1975, at the Home of the Wildcats. Bowmar was my best friend, and Cleopatra was like a sister to me. The color of their skin was never an issue at all. The only issue was the fact that Bowmar was a certified genius, and I was always looking for ways to bring him down to earth!

Bowmar answered, "At President Roosevelt's Little White House in Warm Springs, Georgia, I certainly didn't feel out of place. Roosevelt himself made me feel welcome and at peace in his presence. That WAC uniform you are wearing came with its share of challenges for black women in World War II. The efforts to include African Americans in the WAC were made by black journalists and activists like Mary McLeod Bethune, a member of President Roosevelt's 'Black Cabinet,' and her good friend First Lady Eleanor Roosevelt. Through their efforts, a quota was set for ten percent of the total WAC to be African Americans. But with all that said, yes, I have felt some piercing eyes since we left Oak Ridge on this road trip. It's not like we haven't watched and experienced racism in our lives in 1975 America, it's just that we are a bit spoiled by the way we have grown up, compared to many black Americans—especially in big cities and the Deep South. We have our parents and the Bad Love Gang to thank for that. Besides... knowing you, big sis, I really doubt that you'll ever take shit from *anybody*, at any time, in your whole life. That's just not in your DNA."

I broke in with something I had thought about since I was a little boy. "Racism never really made any sense to me, since I can remember. Think about it; white people love their dogs like their own children. They own black Labradors, black Scottish terriers, black Great Danes, black toy poodles, black Belgian sheepdogs, along with dogs of all different colors, shapes and sizes and even downright ugly dogs like English bull terriers and Mexican hairless dogs. They would walk on thin ice on the pond in the winter to save their dog in distress. But then they see a black person—not a dog, but another human being with a heart and a soul—and they don't like them because of the color of their skin? That just defies explanation. It's some special kind of wicked evil, if you ask me. There is no excuse for it and no place for it, ever!"

I continued, "What happens when we meet aliens from another planet? What if they aren't white or black, but some other color—or multiple colors? What if they have six fingers, three toes, and we can't tell if they are male, female, both, or neither? Are we going to automatically hate them because they don't look like us? Maybe that is why aliens avoid us earthlings: They know the human race won't accept them, maybe even shoot first and ask questions later!"

Crisco tapped me on the back. "Hey, Colonel Bubble Butt, do you know something the rest of us don't? Why are you bringing up aliens, all of a sudden?" She looked at Bowmar. "How do you cope with those 'piercing eyes,' or being the victim of prejudice or racism, Bowmar?"

I answered first. "Only the Bad Love Gang, Vannevar Bush, Albert Einstein, a few high security clearance workers at Area 51, and the soldiers present at Area 51 on June 17, 1942 know with certainty that aliens have already visited our planet. Bucky is the only known Earth eyewitness to the aliens being zapped back to their own planet from their spaceship the night it crashed in Area 51. Bucky described their clothing as being skin tight and having a reflective sheen. There were six of them in the eye of the racetrack, and one of the little ones, possibly an alien child, waved at Bucky at the moment they were zapped away. Who knows what they really look like underneath those shiny outfits? If we Earthlings ever get to visit with them, we have to go in with an open mind. It's the exact opposite of prejudging based on appearance."

Bowmar spoke next. "Our parents have quite a story, with Dad being a black nuclear physicist and Mom being a black attorney. They were both raised in Virginia, which was a so-called 'border state' between the Confederate South and the Union North during the Civil War. Virginia did not declare secession from the Union or join the Confederacy. Mom and Dad grew up with the Jim Crow laws, state and local laws that mandated 'separate but equal' status for black Americans. In reality, this led to treatment and public accommodations that were almost always 'separate and unequal,' inferior to those provided to white Americans. For example, public parks were forbidden for African Americans to enter, and theaters and restaurants were segregated. Waiting rooms in bus and train stations were required to be segregated. Things in common public areas, such as water fountains, restrooms, building entrances, elevators, and even cemeteries, were segregated under Jim Crow laws. That is the world that our parents came from. Fortunately, both our parents were smart, gifted, excellent students growing up and they both attended Howard University in Washington DC, which is where they first met.

"From the time that Cleo and I were little, we talked as a family at the dinner table every night. Our parents taught us about how they were raised in the days of segregation. Both parents told us probably hundreds of times, 'Don't you ever in your life act like or feel like you are a victim of prejudice, or you're gonna face our wrath! You don't ever win by playing the victim; you win by being the best, setting an example and keeping your head held high!' They told us to steer clear of small-minded people as much as possible, to focus on school and learning and being good at everything we put our minds to. I took them quite literally, while Cleo took their advice a step further: meaning she should be the queen of society. We are in big trouble if she ever gets into politics!"

"Shut up, little brother!" Cleopatra loudly exclaimed. She slapped him alongside the head from her backseat position. "I will make a fine queen someday, you little shit!" We all laughed at their sibling banter.

"The whole prejudice and racial thing probably makes me more sad than angry," Bowmar added.

Cleopatra exclaimed, "Not me; I get pissed off!" We laughed, but knew she was telling the truth.

"Whether sad or angry, I just smile and keep moving forward. That's how I cope, Crisco."

My music brain kicked in again after Bowmar's last comment, and I decided to end this serious discussion on a positive note. I grabbed a different cassette, plugged it into the Marantz and told Bowmar to crank it up. **"The Tears of a Clown,"** by Smokey Robinson and the Miracles, came blasting out and got the four of us moving in our seats. Stevie Wonder and his producer actually wrote the music, but couldn't come up with lyrics to fit. Stevie gave the track to Smokey Robinson at a Motown Christmas party in 1966 to see what he would do with it. In the song, the male character is sad because a woman has dumped him. He compares himself to clowns who hide their hurt and anger behind empty smiles; the song has a distinctive circus-like rhythm to it, with a piccolo playing in the background. The song was a number one hit in both the US and the UK, and was the band's first and only number one hit while Smokey Robinson was the lead singer of the Miracles.

We stopped in the town of Tuscola, Illinois for lunch, and Bowmar told us all an interesting story about Tuscola. You would never know it for being such a small town, but for many years it had been known as the home of radio station WDZ. Radio station WDZ was the third dedicated broadcasting facility in the nation; it had been started at the request of a local grain broker named James L. Bush, who wanted to broadcast market grain quotations to local grain elevator operators. Curtis Marsh, an errand boy age 14, would put a record on the radio to signal an upcoming market report. When he was handed the report, he would go to the microphone, stop the record, strike a gong, and then read the report. That is how WDZ got started. Only KDKA of Cleveland and KMOX of St. Louis predated radio station WDZ.

After lunch, our Bad Love Gang convoy got back on Route 45 South. I couldn't get my music brain off Curtis Marsh, striking a gong on radio station WDZ back in the day. I had to get this off my mind and get us rocking on the road trip again, so I plugged in a new cassette tape and cranked the volume. Our Jeep was filled with the song **"Bang a Gong (Get It On),"** by the British rock group T. Rex. Released in July 1971, this song actually spent four weeks at the top of the UK charts. It was by far the group's biggest hit overall; it peaked on the US *Billboard* Hot 100 chart at number ten. We were all lip syncing and rocking out to the music. When I looked in the rearview mirror, I could see Crisco's blonde hair blowing back in the breeze. She was taking pictures of the 1945 road signs, billboards, and countryside as the music blared. She looked totally cute-tacular! I hatched a mental plan for us to potentially have a little rendezvous later that night, while putting the ball in Crisco's court. We continued south to Effingham, Illinois, which is where we made our turn west on US Route 40. That would take us to St. Louis today, and then all the way to Denver over the next few days. We were officially headed west on our epic 1945 road trip!

CHAPTER SEVENTEEN:

ST. LOUIS—THE GATEWAY TO THE WEST

"Have you ever thrown a ball 100 miles an hour?
Everything hurts. Even your ass hurts."
—Cardinal Baseball Hall of Fame Pitcher, Bob Gibson

Monday, April 16, 1945 at 7:00 PM local time,
the Mayfair Hotel in St. Louis

T he Bad Love Gang checked into the Mayfair Hotel at 6:30 PM, and agreed to meet in the dining room for dinner at 7:00 PM. The historic Mayfair Hotel in St. Louis was built in 1924–1925 by Charles Heiss, a German immigrant to the US. The structure was designed in the Italian Renaissance style, similar to the Drake Hotel that we had just visited in Chicago. The hotel was built of concrete, and faced with red brick and a terra cotta trim that was carried into the main lobby, which was adorned with beautiful hand-painted ceilings and crystal chandeliers. There were three high-speed elevators servicing the 18-floor, 400-room hotel, and the elevators were manually operated by uniformed elevator operators. Each room had its own private bath, somewhat unusual at the time. The hotel's massive water pumps had the capacity to service a small 1945 city; they were able to pump up to 500,000 gallons of water per day. The hotel also featured a nine-chair barbershop and a six-booth beauty parlor in mezzanine level rather than the hotel basement, as was typical in those days.

World-famous KMOX Radio, known as the "Voice of St. Louis," got its start on the mezzanine level of Mayfair Hotel in 1925. KMOX purchased and installed a cutting-edge Kilgen and Son organ in its Mayfair Hotel studio; Kilgen and Son was the largest and most well-known organ company in St. Louis. Organ recitals were played every evening from 6:00–7:00 PM, broadcast to the listening radio audience in St. Louis and the surrounding areas. In 1927, KMOX became one of the first 16 CBS Radio Network stations; in 1929, CBS purchased KMOX Radio outright. They moved the studio out of the Mayfair Hotel in 1931, and built one of the earliest 50,000-watt radio transmitters. When completed, KMOX was a pioneer clear channel station, with a signal that could be heard at night throughout much of the US. Broadcasts could sometimes be heard as far away as Scotland, New Zealand, South Africa, and the Arctic Circle. KMOX was big into sports radio from its earliest days, and aired the Cardinals-Yankees World Series in 1926. Starting the next season, the station began airing St. Louis Cardinals' games. My parents, Larry and Gloria, were both born in St. Louis; and despite growing up in Oak Ridge, Tennessee, I had been a fan of St. Louis Cardinals' baseball since my early childhood, and knew about KMOX sports radio. I was planning to share a bit of St. Louis Cardinal Sport's trivia from my childhood with the Bad Love Gang at dinner this evening.

We all met at the hotel restaurant, the Mayfair Room at 7:00 PM and requested a table for fourteen guests. The maître d' was away from his post when we arrived, so a busboy took our group to a large corner table that could accommodate all fourteen of us. Bowmar, Cleopatra, Crisco, and I had been talking about Jim Crow laws in the post-civil war "border" states during our drive earlier in the day. None of us had thought to consider that Missouri was a border state with active Jim Crow laws in 1945. Under these laws, Missouri prohibited interracial marriage between whites and blacks. Separate schools had been built for blacks, making it illegal for them to attend white schools.

By way of perspective, excluding Bucky and Peggy Sue, the rest of us sitting at the dinner table were time travelers from 1975 who had grown up in Oak Ridge, Tennessee. By 1975, the Jim Crow laws had been completely abolished. In 1948, President Harry Truman ordered full integration of the US military. Well known to us at Oak Ridge High School, the Supreme Court had ruled in 1954 that educational segregation was unconstitutional, in *Brown v Board of Education of Topeka*. That brought the end of the era of "separate-but-equal" education. Ten years later, in 1964, President Lyndon B. Johnson signed the Civil Rights Act. The Civil Rights Act legally ended the segregation that had been institutionalized by the Jim Crow laws. The following year, the Voting Rights Act halted efforts to keep minorities from voting. In 1968, the Fair Housing Act ended discrimination in renting and selling homes. Passed by Congress on January 31, 1865, and ratified on December 6, 1865, the 13th amendment had abolished slavery in the United States. It took more than another hundred years to enact further meaningful legislation to improve the playing field for blacks in America.

Returning to his post after we had been seated, the Mayfair Room maître d', Hans Klein, noticed that there were two black soldiers seated with our group of fourteen. Hans made his way to the head of our table, where Waldo (dressed as two-star General Paul Thompson) was sitting. Hans stood at the head of table and politely and matter-of-factly announced to us, "This is a segregated dining area; negroes must sit in a separate area to dine with us." My brain immediately kicked into high gear, and I thought *Oh, God help us! The shit is about to hit the fan!*

Waldo's face and the top of his bald head turned a bright shade of red. He stood up and faced Hans, then said, "This *entire* military group is on a mission under the direct orders of the president of the United States, and you think we're going to separate our group because two of our distinguished members are black?!"

Hans politely replied, "Yes, sir. The rule applies to military and civilian negroes alike."

Crazy Ike, sitting a little further away, detected that Hans was of German descent. He immediately stood up and approached Hans, speaking in perfect German. (None of us understood, but he gave us a translation after he calmed down.) "You stupid, pea-brained, piece of lowly snail shit! I'm going to take you outside and beat the living crap out of you, right now! No one is going to recognize you when I am done!"

I got up to slow Crazy Ike down, knowing full well this was going to get out of hand fast. As I got up, Cleopatra spoke to Hans—*loudly*. "Listen *here*, white boy! You can take your Jim Crow laws, and stick them so far up your ass that you *choke!*"

The head waiter, Peter Stewart, rapidly approached our table and exclaimed, "Excuse me, everyone, *please!*" We all momentarily stopped in our mental and physical tracks, and there was brief moment of quiet. Peter then enquired, "Is there a Captain Jack Smith here at this table?"

Bucky stood up. "I am Captain Jack Smith. Why do you ask?"

Peter replied, "Sir, this is highly unusual, but the president of the United States, Harry S. Truman, is on the phone and asking to speak with you. He says it is important and cannot wait."

As Peter made his announcement, Hans turned white as a ghost; I think he started to hyperventilate just a bit! My brain was now in hyper-drive. I was running a zillion different scenarios about how and why President Truman, the 33rd president of the United States, was calling for Bucky. On Thursday, April 12, 1945 (the day our present time travel mission had started, and the day FDR died from a sudden, massive stroke), Truman had just adjourned a session of the United States Senate when he was summoned to the White House. He initially thought that President Roosevelt had unexpectedly returned early from Warm Springs, Georgia and was summoning him to the White House. Truman was met at the White House by First Lady Eleanor Roosevelt, who informed him that President Roosevelt was dead. Shocked and dismayed, Truman asked Mrs. Roosevelt, "Is there anything I can do for you?" Eleanor famously replied, "Is there anything we can do for you? For you are the one in trouble now." At 7:09 PM Eastern War Time, two hours and 24 minutes after FDR's death, Truman recited the oath of office as administered by Supreme Court Chief Justice Harlan Stone. Four days later, almost to the minute, President Truman was asking to speak to Captain Jack "Bucky" Smith.

Bucky, Waldo, and I followed Peter to the phone. Waldo told Hans to follow us as well, and Hans complied without speaking a word. Bucky picked up the phone and said, "Hello, Mr. President. This is US Army Air Force Captain Jack Smith speaking."

President Truman responded, "It took a little effort to track you down, Captain Smith, but I am glad to have you on the phone with me now. As you know, our beloved President Franklin Roosevelt died of a sudden and massive stroke last Thursday afternoon."

"Yes, Mr. President, I first met FDR and Vannevar Bush in late October of 1942, at the White House. I was close to President Roosevelt; I am working for him now, and I was with him briefly the morning that he died last week," Bucky replied.

President Truman continued, "We found a handwritten letter with FDR's presidential seal, addressed to me, in Franklin's private desk drawer at the Little White House in Warm Springs. The letter was brief, but important. I am going to read it to you now. It says, 'Dear Harry, In the event that anything ever happens to me and you become the thirty-third president, please give your full ongoing support to USAAF Captain Jack 'Bucky' Smith, whose work is of our highest national security. Very truly yours, Franklin.' After I was sworn in as president last Thursday night, I was informed by FDR's secretary of war, Harry Stimson, of a new and terrible weapon being developed by physicists in Los Alamos, New Mexico. I am scheduled to meet with Stimson and the Army general in charge of this project, Leslie Groves, on April 24th to be fully briefed on this new, destructive weapon. Is this the project related to your mission?"

Bucky answered, "No, Mr. President, my mission is called the Denver Project, and it is more secretive than the destructive nuclear weapons project that you are referring to."

Truman exclaimed, "Jesus Christ and General Jackson! How can that be?! I did not even know about this new bomb while I served as Franklin's vice president. Who else knows about the Denver Project?"

"Well, sir, it's a tight circle. I am in charge of the Denver Project and have a team pulled together, all of whom are with me now. They are code named "The Bad Love Gang." Other than us, the only other two people in the know are Vannevar Bush, who knows virtually everything, and Colonel Carter Clarke of the US Army Signal Intelligence Service, who runs the Venona Project. Clarke does not know the full extent of our mission, but he has been extremely helpful to us."

"I don't know how the hell your team got the code name Bad Love Gang, but it sounds like something one of our bomber crews would paint on the side of their planes! When I get time, I'll talk to Vannevar and Clarke and let them both know that you have my full support. I will look forward to meeting you one of these days, Captain Smith.

Is there anything that I can do to help you with your present mission before we hang up?" Truman asked.

"Yes sir," Bucky replied. "Mr. President, FDR called me by my nickname, Bucky. I would like for you to do the same. I have a prepared letter from FDR that is a presidential directive, giving me and my designees the authority to execute our Denver Project secret mission, in case anyone questions us. Could you provide me with a similar letter with your signature, and get it to the Broadmoor Hotel in Colorado Springs, Colorado, where I can pick it up in a few days? Our team will be staying there starting on Friday night, if all goes well this week. Four of us from the Bad Love Gang will be doing some special fighter pilot training in P-40 Warhawks at Peterson Army Air Base. Oh, and one more thing, two of the officers on our team are negroes, and it seems these folks here in Missouri want to separate us in the dining room. Do you think you could take care of that for us?"

"Consider it done, Bucky. You know that I am from the 'Show-Me State' of Missouri: I was born in Independence, Missouri. I'll have your letter waiting for you at the Broadmoor when you get there. Put the guy in charge there on the phone, and good luck, son. By the way, where are you staying tomorrow night, as you make your way out to Colorado?"

"Thank you, Mr. President. Tomorrow night we are staying at the Hotel Muehlebach in Kansas City."

Truman responded, "Great choice in accommodations, Bucky!"

"I was quite fond of President Roosevelt, and I know that you have a lot of work to do following in his footsteps. Thank you, sir, and good luck to you as well!" Bucky said. He handed the phone to Hans, saying, "The president would like to speak with you."

Hans timidly took the phone. As we walked away, we could hear the president yelling while Hans again turned whiter than his bleached and overly starched shirt.

Back at the table, Bucky filled the rest of the group in on the story, starting with the fact that FDR had left a private letter for Truman to read in the event that FDR died and Truman became president. We discussed that Roosevelt must have been having some premonitions of his own death, to have written the note immediately after we left the Little White House on Thursday morning, April 12, 1945. Even though we hadn't thought much about our continuing presidential authority since FDR had died four days prior, we were relieved to know that we still had the full support of the office of the president of the United States, in the pursuit of our mission to protect and defend the integrity of the White Hole Project. Roosevelt had thought about this potential contingency before we had, making our respect and admiration for him even greater than before.

We all ordered dinner and had the famous Mayfair dressing served on our salads. The Mayfair salad dressing was believed to have been created around 1935, at this restaurant; it was made from vegetable oil (such as corn or canola) and a whole egg base, seasoned with anchovies, garlic, prepared mustard, celery, onion, champagne, and black peppercorns. It was amazing, and I just wanted to keep eating salad! Tater exclaimed, "If you put that salad dressing on top of your head, your tongue would beat your brains out just trying to get to it!" We all had a good laugh together at that one.

As we ate our delicious salads, the maître d' returned to our table carrying a bouquet of a dozen fresh red roses. Hans handed them directly to Cleopatra, saying, "I apologize for our insensitivity, and thank you for your service to our country. Your dinner tonight is on the hotel. If there is anything that we can do to make your stay here better, please let us know."

Crazy Ike grinned at this turn of events. In perfect German, he said, "Good work, Hans. Now I won't have to rearrange your face after dinner. I want you to shake the hand of the black male soldier sitting here, who is her brother, and tell him you're sorry and that you respect him."

We didn't understand what Ike was saying, but when he was done, Hans went to Bowmar, shook his hand and said, "Thank you for your service, sir. I apologize for my comments earlier, and I respect what you are doing." Hans then walked away as we all sat there, amazed.

Bucky commented, "It's nice having friends in high places. I guess the president set him straight in a hurry!"

Bowmar, in his typical Brainiac fashion added, "During the 1948 presidential election campaign, Truman delivered a speech attacking the Republicans. During the speech, a supporter yelled out, 'Give 'em Hell, Harry!' Truman immediately said, 'I don't give them Hell. I just tell the truth about them, and they think it's Hell.' After that encounter, the phrase 'Give 'em Hell, Harry!' became a lifetime slogan for Truman supporters. I'd say our friend Hans caught a little Hell from Harry tonight!"

I had wanted to share a little St. Louis Cardinals sports trivia with the gang tonight. While they were talking about "Harry," it reminded me of Harry Caray, the famous Cardinals baseball announcer. As dinner was served, I told the group about Harry Caray, who was born in St. Louis and was the baseball radio announcer for the Cardinals for 25 years, through the end of the 1969 baseball season. I had listened to Harry Caray on the radio whenever I could catch a KMOX Cardinal's broadcast growing up, and when we visited my parents' relatives in St. Louis. Harry Caray was famous for popularizing the singing of "Take

Me Out to the Ballgame" during the seventh-inning stretch of baseball games. As I told the story, I cajoled the Bad Love Gang to sing "Take Me Out to the Ballgame" along with me, acting as the music conductor while the rest of the Mayfair Room restaurant patrons stared at us. A few actually joined in and sang with us! Then I told them how whenever a Cardinal player would smash a ball headed for a home run, Harry Caray would keep the radio listeners in suspense. The ball would be hit and Caray would announce, "That ball was hit *hard*! It's waaayyy back... it might be...it could be...it *is* a home run!" The batter had rounded the bases and was probably crossing home plate by the time you knew it was actually a home run, but the suspense made it all the more fun.

I told them about my favorite Cardinals baseball pitcher growing up, future hall of fame pitcher Bob Gibson. Born in Omaha Nebraska, he excelled at both baseball and basketball in high school, and was a star basketball player at Creighton University. He even played with the Harlem Globetrotters from 1957–1958. In 1957, he signed with the Cardinals, and made his major-league baseball debut in 1959. In the 1964 World Series against the Yankees, he went 2–1, winning Game Five at Yankee Stadium, then won Game Seven at home in St. Louis on only two days' rest. He was named the 1964 World Series MVP. Three years later, the Cardinals faced the Boston Red Sox in the 1967 World Series. Bob Gibson memorialized his reputation as the unstoppable playoff pitcher in this series, allowing only three total runs over three complete games and being named World Series MVP for a second time. In 1968, Gibson went 22–9 with an unearthly low ERA of 1.12, to go along with 15 consecutive wins, 13 shutouts, 268 strikeouts and a stretch of 92 innings in which he gave up just two runs. That year he went 2–1 in the World Series, beating the Detroit Tigers in Games One and Four before going the distance in a Game Seven loss. He brought home both the 1968 Cy Young Award and the National League Most

Valuable Player Award. Following the 1968 season, professional baseball actually lowered the height of the pitcher's mound because pitchers, led by Gibson, were dominating hitters and games were historically low-scoring. Bob Gibson in his prime years may have been the most intimidating pitcher in history.

We talked about our planned drive to Kansas City the next day as we finished dinner. Everyone was feeling pretty played out from the long day on the road. When dinner ended and we were making our way to our rooms, I asked Crisco to stop and talk with me for a minute. I said, "You know, Crisco, it has been quite a while since we spent some serious time together. Maybe we should catch up on that a bit tonight. Do you remember that song by Tony Orlando and Dawn, **"Knock Three Times?"** That song was released in late 1970 and hit number one on the US *Billboard* Hot 100 in January 1971, eventually selling six million copies. It also peaked at number one in Canada, England, Australia, New Zealand, and South Africa.

Smiling and staring into my eyes she answered, "Yes, of course; I loved that song when it first came out. Why do you bring that up now, BB?"

I gave her my room number and said, "Knock three times tonight, and I'll know it's you."

She replied, "Nice try again, Colonel Schafer. You never cease to surprise me with your sense of timing. Have a good night—and thanks for the interesting dinner stories."

"Anytime, Sergeant O'Sullivan," I said as we parted ways to our respective rooms. At about 10:30 PM, I was nearly asleep when I was startled by three discreet knocks on my hotel room door...

CHAPTER EIGHTEEN:

MIZZOU TIGERS AND THE CITY OF FOUNTAINS

"If I were ever stranded on a desert island, there would
be three things I'd need: food, shelter, and a grip."
—George C. Scott

Tuesday, April 17, 1945 at 8:30 AM local time,
the Mayfair Hotel in St. Louis

W e all gathered for breakfast in the Mayfair Room and discussed
the next leg of our road trip, traveling west on US Route 40
from St. Louis to Kansas City. We would stop for lunch at the halfway
point, in Columbia, Missouri: the home of the University of Missouri,
Columbia, AKA Mizzou, and the Missouri Tigers. Crazy Ike was floating around on cloud nine about this leg of the journey, because he
had been recently accepted to the world-famous University of Missouri
School of Journalism, with the plan to start there as a freshman in
August 1975. The Missouri School of Journalism (known on campus
as the J-school) was founded in Columbia in 1908, claiming to be the
first of its kind internationally—a claim disputed by the French, an
assertion which fell on deaf ears at Mizzou. Of particular interest to
our Bad Love Gang Women's Army Corps' sergeants, Cleopatra and
Crisco, a Mizzou J-school graduate, Marie Hansen, was one of the first
female photojournalists employed by *Life* magazine. She joined the

magazine in 1941; within a month of her appointment as staff photographer, she produced a photographic essay on the training of the first women officers in the Women's Army Corps. Crazy Ike was so excited to see the college as it stood in real life in April 1945. It was an accomplishment that he was going to Mizzou's J-School; nevertheless, I teased him that despite this real-time lesson in campus history today, it would do nothing to help with his grades, and he would actually have to learn how to study for once in his life! With a shit-eating grin on his freckled face, Ike fired back, "Listen BB; just like I managed to get into Mizzou's J-School, I have my ways to succeed, too! Don't you worry your petty little bubble butt about me, I can take care of myself!"

Crazy Ike named a list of famous people who had graduated from Mizzou's J-School prior to 1975. Other than Marie Hansen, I recognized two names: newsman Jim Lehrer and actor George C. Scott. I had recently seen Jim Lehrer on live TV, covering the revelation of the incriminating Nixon Watergate Tapes and the subsequent Senate Watergate hearings for PBS. I liked the way Jim presented the news: as a straight shooter. When Ike mentioned George C. Scott, my brain went wild because I was a huge fan of two of his movies. Scott played the role of General Buck Turgidson in the 1964 movie *Dr. Strangelove: or How I Learned to Stop Worrying and Love the Bomb*, directed by Stanley Kubrick. I loved this crazy satirical comedy about the Cold War paranoia of a nuclear conflict between the Soviet Union and the United States. Scott played the role of a United States Air Force general gone crazy who orders a surprise first-strike nuclear attack on the Soviet Union. The president of the United States and his team try to prevent the crew of an American B-52 bomber—piloted by a hilarious Slim Pickens, playing the role of a determined USAF B-52 pilot Major T. J. "King" Kong—from nuking the Soviets and starting an atomic holocaust. Slim Pickens straddles the atomic bomb like a cowboy riding a prize bull in the end. The film has been considered one of the best comedies ever made.

I also loved George C. Scott in the 1970 epic war movie *Patton*, about US General George S. Patton during World War II. The beginning of the movie was really different; it opened with a monologue delivered by Scott, playing the role of General Patton with an enormous American flag draped behind him as he spoke to the American Third Army. As I recall, Patton said, "You don't win a war by dying for your country; you win war by making some poor bastard die for *his* country!" There was another line about ripping the guts out of our enemies and "greasing our tanks with them," showing Patton's ruthlessness in the heat of war and battle to win at all cost. *Patton* won a total of seven Academy Awards, including Best Original Screenplay, Best Director, and the most-coveted Best Picture. Scott won the Academy Award for Best Actor for his portrayal of General Patton, but declined to accept the award, stating in a letter to the Academy that he did not feel that he was in competition with the other nominated actors. I was beyond excited to see the University of Missouri J-School in person!

Our Bad Love Gang convoy got underway at 8:30 AM, and I asked Bowmar to give us a morning tidbit of knowledge about this particular day in history. Our walking, talking encyclopedia of fun facts did not disappoint: "Across 'the pond' earlier today, in the British House of Commons, Sir Winston Churchill paid tribute to Franklin Roosevelt, saying, 'President Roosevelt's physical affliction lay heavily upon him. It was a marvel that he bore up against it through all the many years of tumult and storm. For us, it remains only to say that in Franklin Roosevelt there died the greatest American friend we have ever known, and the greatest champion of freedom who has ever brought help and comfort from the new world to the old.'"

Crisco was busy snapping pictures of 1945 St. Louis as we made our way onto US Route 40 West. Cleopatra said, "Little brother, I just don't know what you are going to do, with all those brain cells firing away all the time! I hope you never blow a fuse! Is that a puff of smoke I see coming out of your left ear?" She started tugging on and fanning his left ear.

Bowmar shooed away Cleopatra's annoying hand and said, "You know that Winston Churchill was a brilliant guy who never wasted an opportunity to give a smart answer. Lady Nancy Astor was an American-born British politician who was the second female member of British Parliament, and she had a few famous exchanges with him. One time, Churchill told Lady Astor that having a woman in Parliament was like having a woman intrude on him in the bathroom, to which she responded, 'You're not handsome enough to have such fears.' He got her back good later when she said to Churchill, 'If you were my husband, I'd poison your tea,' to which he responded, 'Madam, if you were my wife, I'd drink it!'"

We all laughed at Bowmar's cleverness, and once again I found myself looking in the rearview mirror. As St. Louis, Missouri grew smaller in the distance behind us, my music brain kicked in. I pulled a cassette out of the shoe box and plugged it into the Marantz, then looked at Crisco in the rearview mirror. Thinking about our secret rendezvous the night before, I teasingly said, "I bet you'll enjoy singing this song, Crisco."

"Lay it on me, BB; let's see what you got!"

The music boomed, **"Rescue Me"** from Fontella Bass. Bass was born in St. Louis, Missouri and began singing R&B songs at local St. Louis contests and fairs while attending St. Louis Soldan High School. At age 17, she started her professional career working at the Showboat Club near the Chain of Rocks, Missouri. Released in 1965, "Rescue

Me" became the biggest single hit of Bass's career, reaching number one on the R&B charts for four weeks, hitting number four on the *Billboard* Hot 100, and peaking at number eleven on the UK Singles Chart. Crisco punched me in the back, saying "Very funny!" and we laughed out loud at each other.

Cleopatra, who was privy to most, if not all, Crisco's secrets, pushed at Crisco's right shoulder and blurted, "Oh, no! You two did *not* hook up again!"

Crisco denied it. "No way, Jose!" Cleopatra rolled her eyes, and the four of us rocked out to this classic '60's tune.

The drive to Columbia, Missouri took us over three hours, with one restroom pit stop in Warrenton, Missouri. As we approached Columbia at about noon, we could see the *TIGER* sign on the roof of the historic Tiger Hotel. In 1945, the eight-foot-tall red neon letters could be seen for miles in daytime, but even farther away when glowing red at night! Built in 1928, the ten-story Tiger Hotel was the most lavish hotel in Columbia in its heyday; it was the first skyscraper between Kansas City and St. Louis. Built with more than 100 guest rooms, elevators, and a "modern" circulating ice-water cooling system, the Tiger Hotel set high standards in Columbia, Missouri. On seeing the neon sign atop the Tiger Hotel, I passed Waldo and Bucky's Jeep, motioning them and the truck to follow me. Since we were on our way to Colorado Springs to learn to fly and fight in P-40 Warhawks and ultimately time travel to volunteer for the Flying Tigers in China at the request of FDR, I wanted to eat lunch and get our group picture in front of the Tiger Hotel. Crazy Ike was driving the truck, and I could see him giving me the "thumbs up" with his arm out the driver's side window.

We had a great lunch and took several group pictures in front of the Tiger Hotel. Then Crazy Ike took us for a walking tour of the college campus as it stood in 1945. The fourteen of us, all in military attire, did stand out a bit amongst the college students walking to and from class on a Tuesday afternoon. Ike had been to the campus twice to investigate the J-School in 1974-1975, and he was curious to see how it looked and felt in April 1945. By way of Mizzou history, Academic Hall, completed in 1843, was the first building of the University of Missouri, and the first public university building west of the Mississippi River. The hall's six iconic columns were made from limestone drums quarried from the bluffs of the Hinkson Creek area, just south of the campus. Rising 43 feet tall, the columns stood at the original portico of Academic Hall; they were all that remained standing when it burned to the ground in 1892. After that devastating fire, the university was rebuilt; that rebuilding process shaped the "modern" institution. The columns were preserved, and became the most recognized landmark of the University of Missouri, standing in the middle of the Francis Quadrangle, the historic center of the Mizzou campus.

Crazy Ike was acting like a proud dad showing off his first baby as he led us to the quad. We got another group picture in front of the columns, with the famous Jesse Hall behind us. Jesse Hall, built in 1895 after the fire, had a beautiful, capital-like gold dome towering 180 feet above the south end of the quad, making it the tallest building in Columbia. It had become the main administration building for the University of Missouri. I thought we should caption that picture *Bad Love Tigers from Mizzou,* in line with our upcoming time travel mission to volunteer for the famous WWII Flying Tigers.

Crazy Ike continued the tour, pointing out the residence on the quad that was the home of the chancellor, and the oldest building on campus. He then showed us the Missouri School of Journalism, located at the northeast corner of the quad. He pointed out that the campus was divided into the Red Campus and the White Campus. The Red Campus consisted of the historic core of mostly red brick academic buildings around the Francis Quadrangle. In the early 20th century, the University began a period of expansion to accommodate growing academic programs and the burgeoning student body. The new buildings, constructed in Neo-Gothic style from native Missouri limestone, formed the White Campus. The most notable White Campus building was the Memorial Union, which was an impressive, ornate Gothic tower completed in 1926. The tower was planned to be flanked by two wings, one for men and one for women.

We walked from the quad to Memorial Union, and Crazy Ike pointed out that in 1975, the Memorial Union Tower was flanked by two wings that were not there, in our present time frame of 1945. He asked Crisco to get photographs and I suspected that he was going to somehow use these pictures for a "history essay," as one of his ways to score brownie points in his freshman year of J-School. As Crisco was taking the pictures, I happened to notice two well-dressed men, wearing hats and looking a bit out of place, who were watching us. We faced east, staring at the Memorial Union tower. One of the men stood next to a tree north of us; the other was slightly behind and to the south of us, standing on the steps of the Ellis library. I playfully put my arms around the shoulders of Goondoggy and the Runt like nothing was wrong and discreetly nudged Waldo, who was standing next to Bucky and Peggy Sue. I softly said, "I think we are being watched by two men. Don't look yet, but one is to our north, leaning against a tree. The other is on the library steps, behind us and to the south. I doubt they're gonna try to engage us with firearms with all these students walking around, but what do you say we try to find out who the hell they are?"

Goondoggy replied, "We just can't seem to shake these clones of Boris, can we? I say we go beat the crap out of them right now!"

The Runt agreed. "I know I can catch 'em in a short sprint, but I want some backup—just in case they know some sort of 'Joe Jitzu' martial arts shit. I only know brass knuckles."

Bucky added, "To be quite honest, I'm getting real tired of being wacked in the head nearly every day."

Waldo, our senior voice of reason responded, "The last thing we want is any gunfire whatsoever in the midst of campus. There are too many innocent people who could get hurt or die, and we can't let that happen. Even if we split up into two or more groups, what if they're decoys or bait? What if there are more where they came from, and they pop out once our force is divided? Don't get me wrong, I just want to kill them—but Mary would kill me if anything happens to her 'children.'"

We all chuckled at Waldo's assessment. I said, "Waldo's right. Let's stick together, and keep a close eye on Moe and Larry to see if Curly and Shemp show up along the way back to our vehicles." We were all fans of *The Three Stooges*. "Besides, we need to get to Muehlebach Hotel in Kansas City, preferably before dark. If these guys follow us on the highway, Tater can blast them with his bazooka."

Tater, standing next to us, was eavesdropping. "I hear what you guys are talking about... How about I go kick one of those guys so hard that he sees tomorrow today? What about that, ol' sunshine Waldo?"

We laughed again at Tater's wit and saw that Crisco had just finished taking photos of the Memorial Union tower from all the angles and perspectives that Crazy Ike wanted. They were both oblivious to our discussion during their photo session. I told the group that it was time to get back on the road to Kansas City. As we walked back to our vehicles, we kept an eye on Moe and Larry; I covertly circulated amongst the group, informing them that we were being watched. What we didn't see was the agent in black watching the watchers. Moe and Larry faded away as we got close to the Tiger Hotel, ready to make our exit from Columbia, Missouri and Mizzou.

The Bad Love Gang convoy got back on US Route 40 West, en route to Kansas City and the Muehlebach Hotel. Officially nicknamed the "City of Fountains" on its corporate seal, Kansas City got this name from having tons of both public and private fountains claiming to have the second-greatest number of fountains in the world—just behind Rome, Italy. Apparently, the city's love affair with water was somehow connected to the city's roots at the confluence of the Missouri and Kansas Rivers. In addition, the city had more boulevards than any other city in the world except for Paris, France. As a result, it was also called "Paris on the Plains." I started singing, "Kansas City, here we come!" as I hit the *play* button on my boom box. **"Kansas City"** by Wilbert Harrison was perfect for the moment. I loved the record label for this 45 RPM single, because it was released by "Fury Records;" what a great name for a recording company! I wanted to sing for some company named "Fury!" In the spring of 1959, there were at least five different versions of the song "Kansas City" circulating on the charts—probably a record phenomenon in and of itself—but Wilbert Harrison's version on the Fury label rose to the top, and was a smash number one hit on both the *Billboard* Hot 100 and R&B charts, and became one of the top selling records of 1959.

As we came up to speed on Route 40 West, Cleopatra enthusiastically asked for the shoe box containing all the cassettes. She rummaged through them quickly, reading all the titles until she found what she was looking for. I knew she was planning to tease me and Crisco over her suspicions that we had hooked up on this road trip. As she grabbed the boom box and plugged in the tape, she announced, "Everyone close their eyes—except you, BB. You keep your eyes on the road. Imagine BB singing this song." The music came on loud and it was **"Goin' Out of My Head,"** by Little Anthony and the Imperials. Released in November 1964, this hit single reached number six on the *Billboard* Hot 100, and number one on the Canadian RPM list in 1965. We were all giggles as we listened to the words. This time, Crisco shoved Cleopatra to the side. For some reason, I was having a bit of a brain fart about who was singing this song. "That can't be me, or any man, singing. That's gotta be a woman singing that song." We then had a spirited discussion about who was singing, and I couldn't believe the words were coming from a man's vocal cords. I said, "Close your eyes again and listen; that *has* to be a woman singing!"

We kept an eye out for vehicles tailing us on the road to Kansas City, but did not detect anything suspicious. At 6:30 PM, we arrived at the historic, 12-story high, brown brick Hotel Muehlebach in downtown Kansas City. Built at the previous site of a Baptist Church, the hotel opened 30 years prior to our arrival in May 1915. The Muehlebach was visited by every president from Theodore Roosevelt to our 1975 US president and newfound friend, Gerald R. Ford. In addition, President Harry S. Truman— whom Bucky had just spoken to the night before, and who was now supporting our mission—stayed in the Hotel Muehlebach's Presidential Suite so frequently that the hotel became known as "White House West" during his tenure. This explained why President Truman had so enthusiastically endorsed our plan to stay there, when he spoke to Bucky on Monday night. Through the years, the hotel also hosted such luminaries as Babe Ruth, Frank Sinatra, Bob Hope, Elvis Presley, and The Beatles.

As the Bad Love Gang entered the Hotel Muehlebach front lobby to check in, everything about the place screamed absolute elegance. The lobby had a peculiar blend of English Colonial mixed with a Southern flair. Very fancy furniture with an Elizabethan motif was everywhere. When we checked in at the front desk, the receptionist looked a little nervous. She leaned over and whispered, "Are you the Bad Love Gang?"

"Yes ma'am, that's us."

She responded, "Stand by, we have been expecting you," and made a phone call.

A minute later, the hotel manager, Mr. Barney Allis, a short but serious looking man—who had taken over the hotel management in 1931, and whose demanding expectations of employees had become something of a local legend—approached our group. His stern look morphed into a broad smile as he firmly shook our hands and declared, "I got a call from President Harry Truman himself this morning, telling me to be on the lookout for you and to make your stay here special. You must be very important! That's a first for me, to get a personal call from the president of the United States about incoming guests! I've prepared the Presidential Suite for Captain Jack "Bucky" Smith, and have the rest of your group staying in our best rooms and suites."

Goondoggy declared, "Hot damn! I'm already feeling special!"

We all chuckled as Waldo nudged Goondoggy and said, "Behave yourself; that's an order."

Peggy Sue whispered to Bucky, "I agree with Goondoggy. I can't wait to see where we're sleeping tonight!"

I could see Crisco trying to read Peggy Sue's lips and I caught her eye, shaking my head and mouthing the word *no* while winking at her.

Mr. Allis enquired, "Is there anything else that I can possibly do to make your stay more comfortable?"

I answered, "Yes sir, there is. Could we have dinner together in your dining room in an hour, and sample some of that famous Kansas City barbecue? We especially want to try some of those burnt ends!" Kansas City barbecued meats are rubbed well with blended spices, cooked slowly over a variety of flavorful smoking woods, and served with a thick, molasses-infused, tomato-based barbecue sauce. Burnt ends refer to the crusty, fatty, flavorful meat cut from the point of a smoked beef brisket.

Smiling ear to ear, he replied, "We can certainly make that happen. All you have to do is bring your appetites! Make sure to wear the special bibs we give you at the table; we wouldn't want those fine uniforms to suffer any tragic spills!"

We all chuckled and I looked at the Pud, dressed as USAAF Lieutenant Gary Jacobson. "Lieutenant Jacobson, it is your duty to make sure that all dinner bibs are worn properly and fastened securely."

The Pud saluted me and replied, "Yes sir, Colonel Schafer, will do—but I'm afraid there's not a bib big enough to protect Lieutenant Eichenmuller." In the same breath, not giving Crazy Ike a chance to defend himself, the Pud addressed Mr. Allis. "Do you have any extra-large body bags that might work for Lieutenant Eichenmuller at dinner tonight?!"

Crazy Ike responded, "Listen here, 'Private Pud,' I'm gonna court-martial your ass in barbecue sauce, and turn those weight-lifting pectoralis muscles you're working on into burnt tits!"

We all laughed so hard we had trouble breathing. The Kansas City barbecue was spectacular, and we teased and laughed all through dinner. Our accommodations were amazing as well. At about 10:00 PM, just after I had turned the lights out, there were three distinct but familiar knocks on my door...

CHAPTER NINETEEN:

THE CZECH CAPITAL OF KANSAS

"Hurry up, Doctor. This baby gots to go winky tinky."
—Madeline Kahn, as Trixie Delight in the movie *Paper Moon*

Wednesday, April 18, 1945 at 8:45 AM local time,
Hotel Muehlebach, Kansas City

W e all mutually decided to sleep in a little later on this day of the
road trip, for two reasons. First, the accommodations at the
Muehlebach were wonderful, since President Truman had personally
called the hotel manager on our behalf. Secondly, our planned drive
would be 240 miles to Wilson, Kansas, where we would spend the
night at the small but historic Midland Hotel. The following day, on
Thursday, we would get an earlier start to drive the last 380 miles to
Denver, Colorado. In general, given our two Willys MB Jeeps, our
1944 Chevrolet G-506 one-and-a-half ton truck, 1945 road conditions,
14 travelers with variable bladder capacities, and a lunch stop each day,
we averaged about 35-45 mph, divided into whatever distance we were
traveling to get our total drive time for the day. There was no way that
we were going to drive 600+ miles from Kansas City to Denver in one
day, so we had decided to spend the night in Wilson, Kansas.

Bucky had called both Colonel Carter Clarke and Vannevar Bush
the night before from his fancy Muehlebach Presidential Suite to give

them a progress report, make a few special requests, and let them know that we had received the continuing support of President Harry Truman the day before. Clarke was relieved that we hadn't left any more dead Russian bodies strewn on the ground anywhere in the last 24 hours. He warned us there had been a significant spike in Russian telephone and radio traffic in the eastern Colorado area over the past two days. He suspected they knew we were coming, and that we would be using US Route 40 as we made our way west to Denver. Bucky informed Clarke about the Russian agents spying on us earlier that day in Columbia, Missouri. He also described the movements of the agent in black who seemed to be shadowing us and watching our backs rather than moving against us. Clarke did not have any clues about the identity of the agent in black or his potential motivations, and told Bucky that no American agent was covertly assigned to watch our backs, insofar as he and his agency knew. As they neared the end of the call, Clarke enquired if Bucky or the Bad Love Gang needed anything that he could provide.

Bucky took Clarke up on his offer. "Yes sir, you can help. Knowing that we may be facing a higher level of opposition in Colorado, we may want to beef up our defensive firepower a bit. Where can we get some additional weaponry on our way to Wilson, Kansas tomorrow?"

"I have friends at the Topeka Army Airfield in Topeka, Kansas. That place is amazing; they are currently processing new B-29 Super-fortress bomber crews for duty in the Pacific. It is right on your way down US Route 40 tomorrow, and you can stop there for lunch and ammo! Ask for gunnery Sergeant Al Davidson, and he will fix you up with whatever you want or need. I will contact him in the morning so that he will be expecting you and your crew," said Clarke.

Bucky responded, "That's perfect, Carter! We have a shorter drive tomorrow from Kansas City to Wilson, Kansas and have plenty of time to stop there in Topeka and load up! Tell Sergeant Davidson to expect us at or before noon. I want you to know, if those Colorado Vodka Cowboys try to seriously engage us between here and Denver, you can expect some more dead Russian bodies to clean up out there on the prairie."

"I'm kind of getting used to that as I vicariously follow you and the Bad Love Gang across the country, Bucky. Just make sure we're cleaning up dead enemies and not dead Americans!"

"Yes sir!" Bucky firmly answered. "I haven't told you this yet, but I am hard to kill. Thanks for all your help. I'll call you again when we get to the Brown Palace Hotel in Denver Thursday night."

The second call, to Vannevar Bush on his secure office phone was even more interesting. Bush had been trying to research the potential Chinese connection to Area 51 and the White Hole Project, and had news for us. He had discovered that General Claire Chennault of the Flying Tigers had privately communicated with President Roosevelt in late June 1942 about a report of a strange airship (or possibly spaceship) that had crash landed east of Kunming, China. Chennault was concerned about the origin of this airship and was receiving intelligence that it was being pursued by both Chinese and Japanese forces, who were still at war with each other. The day he had first heard of this supposed crash site, he sent a single P-40 Warhawk there from his airbase in Kunming on a reconnaissance mission; it was never heard from again. That was Thursday afternoon on June 18, 1942. One week later, on Wednesday, June 25, 1942, there were multiple reports of a Japanese air force bombing raid in the vicinity of the reported crash site. Sometime around sunset that evening, bright lights and sightings of what sounded like a flying saucer were reported in the sky east of Kunming. Chennault felt it best to report this unexplained and strange phenomenon directly to the president.

Before they parted ways on the phone, Bucky told Vannevar that he was planning to make a stop at Area 51 to review his familiarity with the alien spaceship before making the time-travel trip to deliver Roosevelt's letter to General Chennault in June 1942. Vannevar agreed that this was an excellent idea, in light of what he had just discovered and relayed to Bucky. Bucky had a special favor to ask of Vannevar as well. "I know that Area 51 holds our nation's highest-level, top-secret designation, but so does the White Hole Project. I want Colonel Kevin 'Bubble Butt' Schafer, Lieutenant Billy 'Willy' Blanchert and Sergeant Darby 'Pumpkin' Nelson to accompany me when I go to Area 51. The three of them will be on the mission with me to China; they need to see and experience the reality of what we are expecting. Besides, the Bad Love Gang has been charged with protecting the secrets of Area 51, in addition to our primary role of protecting and defending the integrity of the White Hole Project."

"After the four of you finish your training in the P-40 Warhawks at Peterson Army Air Base in Colorado Springs, call me and let me know what day you will arrive at Area 51. You personally have permanent security clearance there. I will arrange for at least temporary clearance for the other three men. In addition, there will be a surprise waiting for you there. You'll understand when you see it," Vannevar said.

Bucky replied, "Thank you, Vannevar, I'm getting pretty used to surprises these days!" They laughed together.

Vannevar enquired, "Why is that one guy called 'Pumpkin?'"

Bucky explained, "His face turns a funny shade of orange when he gets embarrassed." They chuckled again. "I really appreciate all of your help, Vannevar. Please continue to find out whatever you can about the China connection, and the circumstances there in June 1942. We'll talk again soon." As they hung up, Bucky's mind was racing about the upcoming mission to China.

We all ate breakfast together in the Muehlebach dining room, and Bucky briefed us about his calls with Colonel Clarke and Vannevar Bush. He emphasized the spike in Russian radio traffic in Colorado, challenging the group. "I want you to think about whatever weapons we might want to arm ourselves with, in addition to what we already have with us. I'd rather us be armed to the teeth and not have to use it than face trouble and be less than fully prepared. We'll take Clarke up on his offer, and meet with gunnery Sergeant Al Davidson for lunch at Topeka Army Air Field. We'll load up!"

Using his deepest southern drawl, Tater announced, "I'm teaching Crisco and Cleopatra right now to be our World War II country-girl WACS, and Peggy Sue to be our country girl WAVE. Country girls don't retreat, they just reload—and, you never piss off a country woman holding a gun! I already know what guns I'm recommending for them: a couple of military Ithaca Model thirty-seven pump action, twelve-gauge shotguns, with magnum shells. You just hold the trigger down and pump the fires of hell out of the barrel. It'll kick back a bit, but these are strong women we got here!"

Cleopatra said, "Listen here, my little country bumpkin; don't you forget that Crisco and I manned the fifty-caliber waist gunner positions on our recent B-17 mission over Germany and Poland. I bet that crazy Nazi I shot riding his motorcycle is still recovering! I think we'll handle those shotguns just fine!"

Peggy Sue added, "I'll just pretend that the bad guys are clones of my high-class lawyer ex-husband, who dumped me for not bearing children. I think I can hold that gun steady and pump hell out of the barrel!"

Goondoggy, who liked building and setting fires when we were kids, sarcastically added, "I know you all will find this highly unusual, but I've always wanted to try out one of those World War II M2 flamethrowers."

Developed by the United States for the Marine Corps and Army, the M2 flamethrower was capable of shooting for seven seconds straight at a range of over 20 meters; it was a weapon that instilled fear into the hearts of the enemy. However, it was heavy: weighing 43 pounds empty, propellant and fuel added 25 additional pounds. Soldiers carrying this weapon became targets for the enemy, because it had a tendency to explode if shot. I pointed this fact out to Goondoggy.

Goondoggy quipped, "I've never let fear of explosions worry me before; why should I start now?"

We all cackled at that comment, and Spaghetti Head added, "I'm with you, Goondoggy. I'd like to shoot one of those flamethrowers too."

Crisco joked, "Yeah Spaghetti Head, if you don't get to use it on some Russian spies, you can treat us all to a big batch of that flaming Italian cherries jubilee you're always talking about your family making."

"Nothing beats those fifty-caliber machine guns that we used to decimate the incoming Nazi forces when we had to get the hell out of Poland in the B-17!" I exclaimed. "I'm thinking about that sixties TV show called *The Rat Patrol*. The unit's commander, Sergeant Sam Troy—played by actor Christopher George—always wore that cool Australian Army slouch hat. Whenever they had to get moving, he would declare, 'Let's shake it!' They had Browning M2 fifty-caliber machine guns mounted in their Willys Jeeps. I say we trade in our two Willys for two with fifty-caliber machine guns."

Meatball and the Runt were all over that idea. They simultaneously declared, "I'm good with that! I'll man a fifty-caliber any day!"

Bowmar, who really did not like the idea of a possible gun battle but understood the concept of self-defense, commented, "Just give me a good rifle with a scope; I'll play the sniper role if absolutely necessary."

"I'm proud of you, bro," Cleopatra said. "I hope you're not needed."

Crazy Ike and the Pud said they would stick with their Thompson machine guns, along with some grenades. Tater was determined to us his M1A1 bazooka if duty called. Waldo, our Korean War medal-of-honor veteran said, "Nothing fancy for me: just an M1 rifle, a pistol, and nerves of steel. God help anyone foolish enough to come against us."

To lighten up the discussion, I switched the topic to describe our venue for the day. After leaving Topeka Army Air Field, we were headed to Wilson, Kansas, which affectionately called itself the "Czech Capital of Kansas" due to a high number of Czech immigrant settlers in its early history. We had planned to stay at the historic Midland Hotel in Wilson. The hotel, built in 1899 and originally named the Power Hotel, was gutted by fire in 1902, then rebuilt and opened under the new name, the Midland Hotel. The three-story hotel was constructed of beautiful native limestone; the third floor had a mansard roof profile. The mansard roof (also called a French roof or curb roof) is a bi-sloped roofline punctured by dormer windows. At one time, the hotel was known as the greatest hotel between Kansas City and Denver, and was a famous stop on the Union Pacific Railroad for those traveling between Kansas City and Denver. Businessmen would frequent the hotel to try and sell their goods and wares to other travelers, making the Midland a hot spot for commerce. One of the hotel's most notable moments came in 1973, when it was used as a shooting location for the movie *Paper Moon*, starring the father-daughter duo Ryan and Tatum O'Neal.

When Crisco heard that the movie *Paper Moon* was partially shot there, she exclaimed, "I loved that movie! Tatum O'Neal won an Academy Award at age ten for her role as Addie, making her the youngest winner in the history of the Academy Awards! She and her real-life dad Ryan teamed up, playing the roles of two unrelated Kansas con-artists, named Moses and Addie, in the thirties. After the death of Addie's mother, Moses tried to swindle Addie out of her money—but it backfired, and he had to take Addie on as a partner. As they conned their way through Kansas farm country, they were nearly done in by an angry bootlegger—and also by Madeline Kahn, who played the role of a burlesque dancer. In the end, Addie and Moses decided to stay together. Madeline Kahn, who cracks me up, was also nominated for an Academy Award for that movie."

We finished breakfast and at 9:45 AM, the Bad Love Gang Convoy departed the Hotel Muehlebach on US Route 40 West. We arrived at Topeka Army Air Field (TAAF) at 11:45 AM. We were met at the gate by gunnery Sergeant Al Davidson, who had us follow him in his Jeep to the base supply depot. TAAF was a bustling, interesting air base. We could see the impressive new 1945 B-29 Superfortresses coming and going. Congress had authorized the building of TAAF within two weeks after the attack on Pearl Harbor. The completed air base, along with three 7,000-foot long by 150-foot wide paved runways, was finished in the span of merely eight months. In August 1942, the first military personnel arrived; by September 1942, the field was the home of the 333rd Bombardment Group. By the time we arrived in April 1945, TAAF was one of three air force centers where newly trained air crews claimed their new B-29 Superfortresses and took off, destined for the Pacific war theater. The B-29 superseded the famous B-17G, which we had used for our first Bad Love Gang rescue mission. The B-29 had a pressurized cabin, could carry a 20,000-bomb load, and had a range of 3,700 miles—making it ideal for long-range Pacific theater bombing missions against the Empire of Japan. It was used to drop the world's first atomic bombs on Hiroshima and Nagasaki. Interestingly, the $3 billion cost of designing and producing the B-29 bomber far exceeded the total $1.9 billion cost of the Manhattan Project, making the B-29 bomber program the most expensive US wartime program of World War II.

As Sergeant Davidson fulfilled our order, he commented, "It looks like you all are headed into heavy duty battle somewhere—but this is Kansas, ladies and gentlemen! You guys must be pretty damn important, considering the orders I received to accommodate your needs to the Nth degree!"

Bucky replied, "Yep. We get that comment a lot these days."

We ate a light lunch on the base while Davidson got us locked and loaded. At 1:15 PM, we departed TAAF in two 1945 Willys Jeeps with Browning M2 .50-caliber machine guns mounted in the back; our truck was filled to the gills with weapons and ammunition. The 160-mile drive to the Midland Hotel in Wilson, Kansas took us just under five hours. Arriving at 6:00 PM, we checked into the hotel; the Bad Love Gang filled half of the 28 rooms! We had an excellent steak dinner in the hotel dining room, along with a nice pie selection for dessert. We determined to get to bed a little early and meet for breakfast at 7:00 AM, since it would be a longer drive to Denver the following day, coupled with our growing concern about potential trouble ahead. As we all split up to go to our rooms, Crisco softly whispered, "I think I'll stay in my own room tonight, BB."

I replied, "No problem either way, if you change your mind."

I turned out the lights at nine PM and was a bit startled at 10:30 PM when I awoke to three knocks on my door. I was groggy as I opened the door, saying, "Crisco, I thought—" And I was kicked squarely in the chest, sending me flying backwards onto the bed. Before I could yell, the person we had been calling the Agent in Black was on top of me, his hand pressed against my mouth. I noticed that he was a small person, and did not weigh as much as I would expect. The agent took his black mask off, and he was a she! She was Asian, with beautiful jet-black, pin-straight hair, piercing eyes, and striking facial features. She spoke perfect English with only a slight accent. She whispered, "My name is Li-Ming Sun, but you can call me 'Ming.' Please remain quiet. I am not going to hurt you; you would already be dead, if I had wanted to kill you." She lifted her hand from my mouth.

As soon as I could speak, I softly said, "You can get off me now. I won't yell, and we can talk. We have noticed you following us. It has been pretty impressive, to say the least. What do you want?"

"I would have gone straight to Bucky tonight, but he is not alone; he is with a woman," she explained.

I replied, "So, you know Bucky? Well, that is his high school sweetheart. They hadn't seen each other for about ten years, and they are getting reacquainted. How do you know Bucky? And why are you tailing us so methodically?"

"I met Bucky almost three years ago in China, at a crash site east of the city of Kunming. He saved my life; I owe my life to him! I work for the Chinese Central Department of Social Affairs, and I am supposed to be spying for my government on America—even though we are allies in the war against Japan."

I was rapidly connecting dots, but did not want to give her too much information. "OK, I get that you are connected to Bucky for saving your life, but what do you want?"

Ming passionately explained, "Bucky's life—all of your lives—are in grave danger! The Russians want Bucky alive; they don't care if he is hurt or injured, as long as he is alive. All of you who are traveling with him are expendable, and they will kill you if necessary. I am here to warn you and try to return the favor, saving Bucky's life like he saved mine. You all need to turn around now and avoid going into Colorado. That is what I want."

We could hear someone coming down the hallway, and movement in the room next door. Ming promptly headed for the window. "Listen to me, Bubble Butt; don't put your lives in jeopardy tomorrow!" she implored. And with that, she was gone. As she fled out the window, I thought, "*She even knows my nickname?*"

CHAPTER TWENTY:

THE VODKA COWBOYS FROM COLORADO

"Life is tough; it's even tougher if you're stupid."
—John Wayne

Thursday, April 19, 1945 at 7:00 AM local time,
Midland Hotel, Wilson, Kansas

W e all gathered for breakfast in the hotel dining room at 7:00 AM as planned. I started the conversation by telling the group about my encounter with the Agent in Black the night before. "I shared how Ming had passionately told me that all our lives were in grave danger and that the Russians wanted Bucky alive—but the rest of us traveling with him were expendable. I also disclosed how she told us to turn around and avoid going into Colorado. The Bad Love Gang was pretty shocked by this revelation; our ensuing breakfast discussion was mostly on a serious tone about the day ahead of us.

Before Bucky could ask any questions, I said, "So, Bucky... When you talked to Vannevar Tuesday night, you said he related a story about General Claire Chennault of the Flying Tigers, privately communicating with President Roosevelt in June 1942 about a spaceship that crashed east of Kunming, China. Chennault sent a single P-40 Warhawk from his airbase in Kunming on a reconnaissance mission to the crash site, and it was never heard from again. Remind me, when exactly did he say that happened?"

Bucky answered, "He said it was Thursday afternoon, June 18, 1942."

Bowmar quickly interjected, "Kunming, China is fifteen hours ahead of Area 51 in Nevada. The spaceship that crashed east of Kunming, China early Thursday afternoon June 18th crashed at the exact same time as the one that crashed in Area 51 at 10:00 PM on June 17, 1942, when Bucky discovered it. That must be why Roosevelt is sending us on a time-travel mission to General Claire Chennault and the Flying Tigers in June 1942. We are being sent to keep the secret of blue exotic matter, along with the secrets of time and space travel, out of anyone else's hands. President Roosevelt knew that our mission to protect and defend the integrity of the White Hole Project meant that we would be protecting the secrets of Area 51 at the same time. Knowing what he knew about how slowly government reacts to changing circumstances, he probably figured we were as good a bet as anyone to accomplish this mission and get it done!"

I had rarely seen such a light bulb turn on in Bowmar's head as in that moment. He was always two or three steps ahead of everyone and everything, but this came as a revelation to even his amazing brain! I asked Bucky, "What else did Vannevar say about the China crash site?"

Bucky replied, "Vannevar said that a week later, on Wednesday, June 24 of 1942, there were multiple reports of a late afternoon Japanese air force bombing raid in the vicinity of the reported crash site. Sometime after sunset that evening, bright lights and eyewitness sightings of what sounded like a flying saucer were reported in the sky east of Kunming, China. That is the extent of what Vannevar has been able to uncover so far."

The proverbial puzzle pieces were all starting to come together. I continued, "Ming told me that she met Bucky almost three years ago, in China, at a crash site east of the city of Kunming. That correlates nicely with timing of the simultaneous UFO crashes in both Nevada and China. She then went on to say that Bucky saved her, and that she owes her life to him. Before she departed, she said, and I quote, 'I am here to warn you, and to return the favor and save Bucky's life, like he saved mine.'"

Bucky retorted, "I don't know this woman Li-Ming Sun, and I did not save her life in June of 1942 in China. I was in Nevada in June 1942, as you all know."

"Actually...she knows you, but you do not know her just yet," Bowmar interposed. "You are going to be taking a time-travel mission to China in June of 1942, and you are going to save her life. It has already happened to her or for her; you are the one in the dark at this moment."

Meatball, Goondoggy, and the Pud all started humming the theme song to the *Twightlight Zone* TV show. That brought some needed levity to our discussion!

I reminded the group about what FDR had said after Bowmar had been zapped away during our April 12, 1942 morning meeting. "FDR told us to use the White Hole Project to deliver his letter to General Chennault in June of 1942. He said, 'Do your research first to pick the exact time frame to go in June 1942.' I think we have come closer to establishing that time frame in this morning's brainstorming session."

Waldo interrupted, "Boys and girls, I hate to spoil your science project here, but agent Ming did say that the Russians wanted Bucky alive, but the rest of us traveling with him were 'expendable.' Actually, all of us are irreplaceable—at least according to my lovely wife Mary, even though she and I don't agree one hundred percent of the time." He had a smirky smile on his face when he said that, and we all laughed a bit. "Since I am the seasoned war veteran here, I want to prepare all of us for what I see coming as we drive west into Colorado today. Bucky, you're a West Point Grad, so feel free to shoot holes in anything that I have to say."

"You're the Medal of Honor guy here, General Waldo. Lay it on us, and I'll throw in my two cents." Bucky agreed.

Waldo proceeded, "Our convoy is going to drive into an ambush today." That statement sent a chill down everyone's spine. "An ambush is a long-established military tactic; the Russkies will try to take advantage of concealment and the element of surprise to attack us from hidden positions, such as among dense underbrush, from concealed ditches or ravines, or behind surrounding tree groves or hilltops. We are headed west on US Route 40, straight into Colorado, and the Russians know it. The land is pretty flat, but there are some gentle hillsides and several groves of trees. My best guess, looking at the map, is that they will strike somewhere between Kit Carson, Colorado and Limon, Colorado. I think they'll hit us somewhere along the Union Railroad tracks and Big Sandy Creek, which is a long tributary of the Arkansas River: both parallel Route 40 along that stretch. Somewhere along that route, they will establish a kill zone for their ambush. They will undoubtedly set up intersecting crossfire, from multiple locations or angles. The execution of their plan depends on close proximity to us, because we will be on the move; it is tougher to accurately hit moving targets. Don't be surprised if they block the road to try and stop our convoy. They have the element of surprise, which is to their advantage, but they want to take Bucky alive at all costs—and that is our big advantage. Plus, they have no clue how well we are armed, or that we have been tipped off by Ming. The minute we cross the border into Colorado, I want everyone armed and ready. Bucky, how many changes of uniforms did you bring?"

"I brought three uniforms. Why do you ask?"

Waldo continued, "Like I said, them wanting to take you alive is our biggest advantage today. They know that you are the only USAAF Captain in this crowd. We are going to have Captain Jack 'Bucky' Smith seen driving all three vehicles to confuse the enemy. They won't know who the real Captain Smith is as they study our convoy through their binoculars or scopes."

"Brilliant strategy, General," Bucky conceded. "How do you propose we engage them once fired upon?"

"First of all, *we are not going to run*. That would only separate and weaken us. We are going to fight, and win decisively. What happens today will send a very stern message to the rest of the Russian espionage community; we are dangerous, and deadly. They will stand off more after today."

Goondoggy commented, "I'm glad my brother Willy, isn't here. His white pants would be totally brown by now!"

We couldn't help but laugh, no matter how inappropriate or ill-timed the comment was at the moment!

Waldo continued, "I want the three drivers to all have their walkie talkies activated so we can communicate with each other. Once we are fired upon and we identify their positions, then I want the two Jeeps with Meatball and the Runt manning the 50-caliber machine guns, aggressively attacking each of their positions. The crazier we drive the Jeeps, the harder targets we become for them to avoid killing 'Bucky.' We are taking the fight to them, not standing back for one second. I want Goondoggy and Spaghetti Head in the passenger seats of the two Jeeps, with their flame throwers ready. As the Jeeps' 50-caliber machine guns hold the enemy off or mow them down, we will try to get within sixty feet of their positions and cook them down—a little Russian barbecue! Once any of them see those M2 flamethrowers in action, they'll have fear in their hearts. And that is exactly what we want; we want them to scatter and run, back to whatever holes they crawled out of!

"I want Tater and the Pud working the bazooka together with a walkie talkie. Tater, you fire the bazooka. Pud, you reload it and operate the walkie talkie. You two are responsible for taking out any vehicles or guns that the two Jeeps aren't addressing. We will try to radio you with anything we see that you don't."

Tater drawled, "Any of those Russkies that get in my bazooka sights better give their hearts to Jesus, 'cause their asses are *mine!*"

Waldo wasn't done. "I am driving the lead Jeep, BB is following me, and Bucky, you are driving the truck. Crazy Ike, you are in the passenger seat of the truck with Bucky. Crisco, Cleo, and Peggy Sue are in the back of the truck with their shotguns. If anyone tries to get into the back of the truck, you three unleash the fires of hell on them! Bowmar, you try to find a good spot to use your sniper rifle. Just remember, they are trying to get Bucky alive, and all three drivers are going to be dressed as 'Bucky.' Can any of you think of anything I missed?"

I had one semi-related concern, which I had thought about the night before. "When we sent the black box back to Willy Monday morning, we told him to zap Bowmar and Spaghetti Head back to 1975 on 'Thursday,' which is today. Bowmar is going back to brief Willy and Pumpkin, and then operate the White Hole to zap them to us on Friday night. Spaghetti Head is going back with Bowmar to attend the weekend christening of his older sister's newborn baby girl, his very first niece. The problem is that I don't remember giving Willy a specific time of day to zap Bowmar and Spaghetti Head. I think I screwed up a bit on that one detail."

Listening carefully, Bowmar agreed, "Now that you mention it, BB, we didn't give Willy a specific time. Unfortunately, we just said

'Thursday.' Spaghetti Head and I are both still sitting here, and it is Thursday morning. Sometime today, Willy is going to zap the two of us back to 1975 Oak Ridge, Tennessee."

Waldo said, "We don't have either of you driving today. However, knowing this, Spaghetti Head can't strap the M2 flamethrower fuel tanks to his back, and be zapped back in time with those attached to his body. Spaghetti Head, you will have to put those tanks on the floor of the Jeep and hold them still with your legs and feet. If you and Bowmar both get zapped away in the heat of battle, we will all just have to adjust accordingly. If the two of you disappear before the battle starts, I'll try to make adjustments to everyone's assignments. Did I miss anything that you can think of, Bucky?"

Bucky thought for a few seconds, then added, "At West Point, I was trained in US Army tactics and how to be an Army officer. I joined the US Army Air Force after I graduated from West Point, and my focus shifted to air battle tactics after that. I've never been in a bona-fide, live-fire Army ground battle like Waldo has in the Korean War. Waldo is a battle-hardened Army guy, and covered our strategy here pretty well. I would just add that Colonel Clarke told me that these Russian KGB assets from Colorado act like bad cowboys, and that we might have to shoot first and ask questions later to save our own lives. As I square that with my training, I'd have to say that in the heat of battle, whether on the ground or in the air, you cannot hesitate nor have second thoughts about vanquishing the enemy. A moment of hesitation can mean the difference between life and death, between victory and defeat."

Waldo then added some final perspective. "I saw some crazy shit on the battlefield in Korea. Everyone in this group is smart, and has a good head on their shoulders. We even have an authentic genius in our midst." He winked at Bowmar. "In Korea, the enemy had an officer in charge who was usually pretty smart. But the soldiers under him weren't so smart. In fact, some were downright dimwits, who would just put themselves in harm's way; I guess they confused that with bravery! That approach got them killed. If we do get ambushed today, I know for a fact that we'll face some stupid people out there. They are in for a big surprise, and they better run like hell!"

Thursday, April 19, 1945 at 1:30 PM local time, just west of Kit Carson, Colorado

Timur Volkov, whose Russian first name meant Iron Man and last name meant Wolf, was in charge of the Colorado KGB spy cell. Locally, in Denver, he was known as Tim Volk. He had joined the salesforce of the brand new Rickenbaugh Cadillac car dealership in downtown Denver in January 1945. The dealership also functioned as the new regional distributor for the Cadillac Motor Car Division. Tim had received instructions to intercept and apprehend USAAF Captain Jack "Bucky" Smith, using any and all means necessary. Allegedly, Captain Smith held secrets more important than the new American atomic bomb program. Volk was under strict orders to take Captain Smith alive. He was to assemble a team, then engage Smith and his group as they traveled in a small American military convoy, consisting of two Willys Jeeps and a single military truck. The targets would be heading from Kansas into Colorado along US Route 40, on their way to Denver. The convoy's occupants were billed as being "lightly armed officers" with standard US Army pistols, rifles, and a couple of Thompson machine guns. From Tim's perspective, he had received this communique with little time to prepare, but he had managed to put a plan in place to stop this convoy and use overwhelming numbers to apprehend Captain Smith.

Tim was a Russian spy, fully trained by the NKGB (the forerunner of the KGB). He had been working in Denver, Colorado for close to five years and had successfully recruited a spy cell of nearly 40 agents, many of whom were communist sympathizers living in and around the Denver area. His "team" all loved guns; they regularly met under the guise of a local "gun club" to shoot guns and vodka. They would get drunk and swear loyalty to "the "Party and the Motherland." While he and his recruits knew that the American intelligence agencies referred to their Colorado spy cell as the Vodka Cowboys, they took false pride in their drinking prowess: the bond that held them together and made them tough. Tim himself was big, strong, smart, and tough; he was not an alcoholic. Tim effectively commanded respect from his team. Inwardly, he was concerned about how well they could execute an effective ambush as a team, but he would be right there with 28 of his men as they executed their plan to apprehend Bucky.

Just west of Kit Carson, Colorado, paralleling the Big Sandy Creek tributary of the Arkansas River along US Route 40, Tim and his team laid their ambush. Seven individual groups of four men each were strategically placed in an "inverted U pattern" along Route 40. Once they got advance word that our convoy was approaching, they took an old pickup truck and flipped it on its side in the middle of Route 40 to make it look like a wreck had just occurred. One man gave the appearance that he was trying to climb out the window; three others hid behind the truck with their guns ready. Two groups of four men each flanked the truck, hidden behind trees, rocks, and small berms along the side of the road. In the middle of their planned "kill zone," east of the blockade, there were two groups of four men hidden in ditches and covered with brush. Tim was embedded with this group on the south side of US Route 40. Bringing up the rear were two black 1942 Cadillac Series 62 four-door sedans, which Tim had "borrowed" from

Rickenbaugh Cadillac. Each car carried four agents, each one armed with a shotgun or machine gun. The Cadillacs were parked off the road, to the east of the two groups hiding in the ditches. They would complete the ambush by coming at our convoy from behind, effectively boxing us in from all four sides. All of Tim's men were armed with pistols, rifles, shotguns, and a few machine guns. Many of the men were drinking, challenging each other to afternoon shots of vodka as they waited for us to appear on the scene, and boasted about taking us with little or no resistance. All of the seven groups had field binoculars and a walkie talkie so they could communicate with each other. They were under strict instructions to identify "Captain Smith" and avoid shooting him. There were a total of 29 NKGB "agents" lying in wait for us. We were outnumbered by two to one.

The Bad Love Gang convoy had been on the road for almost six hours, having crossed the Colorado border 45 minutes earlier. Waldo was driving the lead Willys Jeep, with Goondoggy and his M2 flame-thrower in the passenger seat and the Runt manning the Browning .50-caliber machine gun. I was driving the second Jeep, with Spaghetti Head in the passenger seat. His M2 flamethrower tank actually stood on the floor so that he could point and shoot, given the short length of the connecting hose. Meatball was manning the .50-caliber Brown-ing in our Jeep. Bucky drove the truck behind us, with Crazy Ike in the passenger seat armed with his Thompson machine gun and some Mk 2 grenades. Locked and loaded in the back of the truck were Tater and the Pud, ready to go with the M1A1 bazooka. They had mock-practiced their teamwork to load and fire the bazooka during the drive to the Colorado border. They figured they could at least get off five rounds per minute with their adrenalin flowing. Cleopatra, Crisco, and Peggy Sue had practiced the pump action mechanism of their mili-tary Ithaca Model 37 12-gauge shotguns during the drive, unloaded;

their guns had been loaded with magnum shells and were ready to go. Bowmar was armed with an M1 Garand configured with a sniper scope. Waldo and I were dressed in Bucky's two spare Captain's uniforms and both he and I had M1 Garand rifles next to us, along with our pistols and several grenades.

I knew we were driving into danger and battle, but I couldn't help myself. I wanted to calm my fears of battle with some music, and try to confuse the enemy a bit in the process. I had the Marantz boom box loaded and ready with "(I Can't Get No) Satisfaction," written by Mick Jagger and Keith Richards. Released by the Rolling Stones in June 1965, the song went to number one in the US, UK, South Africa, Norway, West Germany, Ireland, the Netherlands, and Austria. Both Meatball and Spaghetti Head were fine with the idea; I didn't dare ask for Waldo's blessings!

Li-Ming "Ming" Sun was distressed that we had not heeded her warning, and that Bucky and the Bad Love Gang were continuing west to Colorado. Driving a green 1940 Chrysler Windsor Coupe, she kept her distance behind our convoy at first, but grew more anxious after we crossed the Colorado border and drew closer. She would be the first to see the two black Cadillacs, carrying four men each, come onto the highway behind us after our convoy went by. Ming was trained as a marksman and carried a Colt M1911 pistol on the seat next to her, and a smaller Colt M1903 tucked behind her back.

Shortly after passing the tiny town of Kit Carson, Colorado, Waldo was the first to spot the overturned truck in the distance. He was immediately suspicious; there was no smoke, fire, or commotion, and through his binoculars he could not even see any skid marks on the road. Simultaneously, Tim Volk's groups were radioing in that there were "Captain Smiths" driving both Jeeps and the truck, enquiring which one was their target. Tim told them to stay in place and hold their fire until the scenario played out somewhat.

Waldo radioed us on his walkie talkie and calmly said, "Ladies and gentlemen, this is it. We are driving into their trap, but they don't know how well prepared we are for this. Right now, they are trying to figure out which 'captain' is Bucky; the element of surprise is ours, for the moment. I am slowing down and stopping a hundred and fifty yards in front of their fake wreck. I suspect that we are already surrounded, so watch both sides of the highway and behind us for surprises. As soon as we roll to a stop, we are taking the canvas covers off our fifty-caliber machine guns. I want Tater and the Pud out on the right side of the truck, wasting no time to take the first shot with the bazooka, aimed directly at the fake wreck. Crazy Ike, you cover Tater and the Pud's asses on the north side of the road. If any vehicles come onto the road in front or behind us, alert Tater and the Pud to try and take them out. Bucky, you watch the south side of the road; the women will protect the back of the truck. Tell Bowmar to try and find a place to use his sniper rifle, but to not take any chances. Once the first rocket is fired, I'm charging the truck wreck ahead and looking for the enemy to declare their positions. Bubble Butt, you follow me. As we approach the soon to be blown-up wreck ahead, I'll break to the right, and you break to the left. We'll sweep the area ahead. Once the coast is clear, we are all getting the hell out of here."

By the time Waldo finished the last of his instructions, he had come to a stop about 150 yards away from the fake truck wreck ahead. Bucky and I stopped as well. Tim Volk was on his walkie talkie talking to his men while looking through his binoculars, studying the three captains who were driving our vehicles. As the convoy came to a stop, Volk's eyes were on the two Jeeps in front. In that brief moment, he probably thought this was all unfolding nicely, with the convoy stopping in the middle of his planned kill zone. In the next instant, the Runt and Meatball forcefully yanked the canvas coverings off their mounted Browning .50-caliber machine guns, assuming firing stances. Volk's eyes widened, and he said, "Oh, shit; there are fifty calibers mounted in those Jeeps!" He didn't see Tater and the Pud getting out of the back of the truck with the bazooka. Tater quickly assumed a firing position, kneeling on the north side of the truck. He was not in Volk's field of vision, from his position on the south side of the road. Crazy Ike came out of the passenger side with his Thompson pointed north, his eyes scanning the road, to provide cover for Tater and the Pud.

As the next few seconds ticked by, Tim Volk heard his walkie talkie squawk, "That's a *bazooka!*"

"Where?!" Volk demanded. "I don't see it!" At that moment, Tater, living up to his military family heritage and dressed as a US Marine Corps first lieutenant, fired the first rocket at the fake wreck. The bazooka's rockets had an effective range of 300 meters (328 yards). It was an interesting sight to behold; Tater's shot was right down the middle, but just a tad low. Rather than exploding early, the rocket skimmed off the pavement in front of the truck, creating some bright sparks, and then hit the truck directly. The detonation decimated the truck and the four men associated with it in a large, fiery explosion. The fight was on!

Vodka Cowboys on the north side of US Route 40, who had first seen Tater and the Pud with the bazooka, were eager to get into the battle. They came up shooting, popping out of the ditch on the north side of the road. Crazy Ike saw them rise up and swept their position with his Thompson, bullets blazing. One of the four was fatally shot; the other three ducked back down into their protective ditch while Tater and the Pud sought cover behind the truck and quickly reloaded the bazooka. When not reloading Tater's bazooka, the Pud had an M1 Garand rifle that he used to scan for targets.

Bowmar, scared to death but not wanting run from battle, exited the back of the truck and was scanning the south side of the road through his rifle scope when real fear struck his heart. The cross hairs of Bowmar's scope came upon a magnified Tim Volk, who was lying low and had his rifle pointed directly at Bowmar. The last thing that Bowmar saw through his scope was Volk's muzzle flash. The world turned white; Bowmar thought he was dead. He wasn't dead, but in the midst of the White Hole time tunnel going back to 1975 Oak Ridge, along with Spaghetti Head. Bowmar found himself screaming as he and Spaghetti Head landed on the padded circular eye of the White Hole Project time machine's ground floor racetrack. Willy ran onto the lower racetrack, hugged the screaming Bowmar, and greeted Spaghetti Head, who appeared totally disoriented. Tim Volk, who thought he had just shot a black American officer in the chest, witnessed Bowmar vanishing into thin air. Tim had to rub his eyes and look twice, but to no avail; the man he thought he shot was gone!

When the "wrecked" truck in front of us blew to smithereens, Waldo turned back toward me and was waving for me to follow him. Waldo had witnessed Spaghetti Head's disappearance, and frantically pointed to my passenger seat. I saw the seat was empty, realizing Spaghetti Head was gone. Meatball, manning the .50-caliber behind me, acknowledged that he knew what had happened as well. My adrenaline was pumping big time, and I had an idea what to do with the flame thrower. The M2 weighed 68 pounds fully loaded, but I yanked it off the floor and positioned the entire unit on the passenger seat so I could strategically shove it out of the Jeep. I yelled at Meatball that we were going to use the M2 flamethrower as a "bomb," and that he would have to shoot it when we did. In the next moment, I declared, "Let's shake it!" as I started following Waldo and punched the Marantz' *play* button. The Rolling Stones blasted out **"(I Can't Get No) Satisfaction,"** and we headed into battle.

The two groups of four agents in the woods, flanking the charred, burning truck, had witnessed their four comrades in the middle of the road meeting their Maker. Half of them were drunk on vodka; fear, anger, and confusion were setting in. All eight of them saw our Jeeps rapidly advancing to attack, which was totally unexpected. Two men from the right flank and one man from the left foolishly decided to charge our Jeeps with their guns blazing. It was just like Waldo had talked about that morning, a stupid way to end their lives! The Runt opened fire on the two men on the right with his Browning, and Meatball did the same on the left. All three men went down, and the .50-caliber rounds tore into the woods behind them. The other five men got down fast as the bullets tore through the trees like a hot knife through butter.

We approached the two flanking positions and I'm sure the three men on the left could hear the Rolling Stones blasting as Meatball and I turned a hard left and swung by. Meatball could see no targets and had momentarily stopped shooting. I shoved the M2 out of the Jeep in front of the wooded area flanking the south side of the destroyed roadblock. At the same moment, Waldo had banked right and then turned hard left, slowing to a crawl. Driving with one hand and holding his pistol pointed toward the woods with the other hand, his maneuver allowed Goondoggy to drench the right flank with his M2 from the passenger seat, setting one of the men hiding behind the trees on fire. The other man, hiding behind the berm, could feel the intense heat. The guy on fire rolled on the ground frantically to extinguish the flames, and they both high tailed it out of there. The Vodka Cowboy with the walkie talkie to the south screamed "flame thrower!" then turned and ran. As Meatball and I pointed back east, I yelled, "Light up the M2!" Meatball fired on the M2 canisters, which promptly exploded in flames with a satisfying concussion of sound.

While we were clearing the way up front, the truck was under siege. The two black Cadillac sedans were approaching fast, with men hanging out of the windows to fire their guns. Tater and the Pud had seen them coming from a ways out, and Tater's first bazooka rocket had missed. When they were about 50 yards out, Tater's second shot hit the Cadillac on the left, stopping it in flames and mortally injuring the two front passengers. Tater and the Pud sought cover under the truck as the remaining Cadillac approached. The Pud started emptying rounds from his M1 Garand into the Cadillac. Still on the north side of the truck, Crazy Ike was firing like a madman, emptying another 30-round clip from his Thompson machine gun across the ditch, where he last saw the enemy. When his second clip was empty, he rapidly threw two grenades as far as he could in that direction, then drew his service pistol and got under the truck with the Pud and Tater.

The Pud saw a green Chrysler Windsor coupe with only a driver following the remaining black Cadillac. The Cadillac stopped 30 feet behind the truck as the Pud emptied his Garand's clip and was reaching to grab another. It was looking bleak from the Pud's perspective as the Cadillac came to a stop behind the truck. Three things happened in that moment, as the four men in the remaining Cadillac opened fire. First, Cleopatra, Crisco, and Peggy Sue unleashed the fires of hell, returning fire from the back of the truck. Each woman pumped seven, 12-gauge Magnum shells through their Ithaca Model 37 shotgun into the remaining Cadillac. Ming had swooped in perpendicular to the back of the Cadillac, targeting the agents inside in crossfire with her pistol. Third, Tim Volk had the remaining men on the south side of the road cover him as he rushed the driver's side of the truck. Bucky was pinned down by gunfire; Volk effectively made it to Bucky's position and got the draw on Bucky, telling him to drop his pistol and get out of the truck, or take a bullet in the head. Volk was a big strong man, determined to take Bucky with him. As Bucky got out of the truck, Volk grabbed him from behind, pushing his pistol firmly into the side of Bucky's head. Neither Bucky nor Volk really knew the true status of the battlefield at that moment.

The second black Cadillac was neutralized in the horrendous cross-fire—but not without consequences. Peggy Sue had taken a bullet in the right side of her chest and was badly, if not mortally, wounded. Crisco and Cleopatra were tending to her, applying direct pressure to Peggy Sue's chest wound as she lay in the back of the truck. Ming, keeping her eye out for Bucky, saw Volk grab Bucky from behind and put his pistol to Bucky's head, dragging him across the road to join his remaining men. Ming put a new clip in her Colt M1911, which had a bullet in the chamber. She quickly exited the Chrysler and ran towards Volk and Bucky, completely focused and determined. She was an award-winning marksman with a pistol, and knew her time had come.

Meatball and I had rounded the corner ahead in our Jeep and were headed back. I had turned the music off. Waldo, Goondoggy, and the Runt had also turned back east. After Crazy Ike's two grenades had exploded and he had sought cover under the truck, the remaining three men hiding in the ditch on the north side of the road popped up from their position. The Runt saw this from the distance, and opened fire in their direction with his .50-caliber machine gun. Those three men had apparently seen and experienced enough; they started running away. Headed back down the south side of the road, I could see Volk holding Bucky—and the gun pressed against Bucky's head. Volk's three remaining men came out from hiding on the south side of the road, covering Volk's retreat as he backed towards them with Bucky in tow. For a moment, it looked like we were headed for a Mexican standoff. We certainly did not want to put Bucky's life in any more jeopardy as this battle was winding down.

Just as I was running mental scenarios about a Mexican standoff, I saw the Agent in Black, Ming, rushing Volk's and Bucky's position from behind the truck. While I wasn't certain of Ming's intentions, I knew she was a well-trained Chinese agent who had followed us across the country to return a favor for Bucky saving her life in June of 1942. I had heard that the Chinese value loyalty very highly, enough that loyalty would often trump all other considerations when a Chinese person is making a decision. I was about to watch that principle in action.

I told Meatball to train the .50-caliber on the three men covering Volk as we came to a stop in our Jeep, trying to see and hear what would happen next. Waldo also slowly pulled around the back of the truck, stopping his Jeep when he saw Bucky in Volk's possession and Ming on the scene, confronting them.

All the shooting had stopped. Volk was only about 25 feet shy of rejoining his remaining men. Ming was still dressed all in black, but was not wearing a mask any longer. She yelled, "Stop, Timur Volkov!" She raised her pistol and faced him squarely. Volk, not a respecter of women, stopped when she addressed him by his Russian name.

"How do you know my name, woman?!" Volk loudly exclaimed.

"Let him go, right now, and you won't get hurt. I won't ask twice."

Volk was bigger and stronger than Bucky. He had his large, muscular, left arm clamped around Bucky's chest. His right hand shoved the gun firmly into the right side of Bucky's head. His broad shoulders were partially exposed.

"Go back to China, woman! You're done here!" he barked.

As Volk's lips curled in a contemptuous sneer, two shots rang out. Ming put a .45 caliber round in each of Volk's shoulders, dropping him backwards to lie on the ground. Volk dropped his gun and lost his grip on Bucky at the same time. Meatball immediately fired a burst of .50-caliber rounds at the feet of Volk's three remaining men, which tore the ground up in front of them with such force as to make them fall backwards as well. "The next time you hear this fifty-caliber will be your last!" Meatball threatened.

With Bucky free and the enemies vanquished, Ming walked straight up to Bucky, put her arms around his neck, and kissed him on the lips. "Now we are even! I hope to see you again, Captain." Bucky just stood there, dumbfounded and speechless. She ran to her green Chrysler and drove away, headed back east on Route 40.

As the Pud, Tater, and Crazy Ike crawled out from under the truck, I asked them to pressure tape the injured Russian's shoulders, then duct tape him and his fellow surviving agents in a restraining fashion at the side of the road. We would call Colonel Clarke to send someone to clean this mess up and take these last four survivors into custody. Cleopatra emerged from the back of truck, bawling loudly. "Peggy Sue has been shot in the chest! I don't know if she's going to make it!" she wailed.

Bucky and I rushed to the back of the truck. The front of Peggy Sue's shirt was covered in blood, and Crisco was holding pressure directly on the entrance wound. For the first time, I saw Bucky in panic mode. He hugged her, caressed her hair, and started to cry out loud. Quietly sobbing, he said, "I should have never let you come along with us. I'm sorry; I am so sorry!"

"I'm not dead yet, Captain. Get me to Denver General Hospital; that's an order," Peggy Sue said, clearly short of breath. Hearing Peggy Sue say that, and knowing that she was a Denver native with family there, I told everyone to load up and drive like hell to Denver while Crisco, Cleopatra, Bucky and I stayed in the back of the truck with Peggy Sue. It would be the longest three hours of the entire Bad Love Gang 1945 road trip.

CHAPTER TWENTY-ONE:

THE MILE-HIGH CITY

"I think the biggest problem in the world is that we
have a generation of young people, and maybe two,
who don't think it's going to get any better."
—John Denver

Thursday, April 19, 1945 at 5:00 PM local time,
Denver General Hospital

W e had briefly stopped in Limon, Colorado to refuel, and for
Bucky to place a quick call to Colonel Clarke on his secure line
at the US Army Signal Intelligence Service office. The Bad Love Gang
took no chances; everyone not attending Peggy Sue had guns drawn
and ready. We had just fought our way out of our first ambush, outnumbered two to one, and any remaining fear in our group had been
transformed into fierce determination. We looked like we were at war;
anyone watching us would sense that we meant business. Bucky told
Clarke that the Bad Love Gang had decimated the Russian NKGB
Vodka Cowboys west of Kit Carson, Colorado, and left four survivors restrained on the south side of US Route 40. One of them was a
bona-fide Russian spy, named Timur Volkov. Clarke reacted strongly
to hearing that name. "Wow, we have been trying to identify that guy
for a long time. Good work, Bucky!"

Bucky explained to Clarke that Navy WAVE Peggy Sue Harding, a native of Denver and stationed at NAS Glenview in Chicago, was traveling with us and had taken a bullet to the chest in the battle with the Russian spy cell. She was hanging on for dear life, and the Bad Love Gang Convoy was en route to Denver General Hospital. Clarke was quick to respond. "Listen to me, Bucky; we are not going to let a Navy WAVE die on us. I have connections in Denver, and as soon as we hang up, I will have a Packard 180 Henney ambulance with a surgeon and nursing team headed east on Route 40 out of Denver to meet your convoy. That Packard can fly! When they intercept you, get that WAVE in the ambulance and they will do the rest."

"One of WAC's attending to our injured WAVE has some nursing knowledge and thinks that the bullet wound to the chest has caused a 'pneumothorax.' Please tell the medical team to be prepared to deal with the possibility of a collapsed lung, sir."

Clarke replied, "Trust me on this, she will get the best-of-the-best care. I will make it happen. I got a call from our new president earlier this morning. Truman enquired about you and the Denver Project. I briefed him about our actions to date, and he told me about Roosevelt's private letter to him regarding you and his phone call with you when you were in St. Louis. Truman said that he thinks that letter was the last letter ever penned by FDR before his untimely death. He told me to give you whatever you needed, whenever you needed it. Somehow, Bucky, you have managed to endear yourself to two presidents in a row!"

"Thank you, Carter. I am glad to hear that. We are leaving now, and not wasting any time! Get that ambulance headed our way; we will be watching for it. Thanks again." Bucky hung up, and our convoy pushed the limits of our vehicles: 50 mph.

Roughly 45 minutes later, a white Packard 180 Henney Ambulance coming out of Denver intercepted us. The surgeon on board the ambulance introduced himself as Dr. Andrew Stockman. He was a stocky, jovial guy who quickly and expertly assessed Peggy Sue's acute status, confirming that she indeed did have life-threatening pneumothorax. He mentioned it was "under tension." His team put Peggy Sue on a stretcher, quickly transferring her from our truck to the ambulance. His nurse went to work immediately; starting an IV she had prepped on the way. As they were about to shut the ambulance door, I saw Stockman take a glass syringe with a large bore needle and stick it between two of Peggy Sue's upper right ribs after pulling out the plunger. I could hear the air rushing out of that needle! Stockman smiled and said to Peggy Sue, "We are off to a good start! Now we need to know how much blood you have lost." With that, the door shut and the Packard headed to Denver General Hospital at high speed.

Denver General Hospital was established in 1860 and was originally founded near 11th and Wazee Street in Denver. However, in 1873, a new Denver General Medical Center was built at the corner of 6th Avenue and Cherokee, which is where our Bad Love Gang Convoy drove to, arriving at 5:00 PM. The hospital was well known for founding the first nursing school west of the Mississippi, and for being one of the earliest facilities for treating tuberculosis.

Bucky led the way into the hospital. They were expecting us, having been contacted by Colonel Carter Clarke and his team using the authority of President Truman. Peggy Sue was already in surgery. We waited anxiously until 6:30 PM, when Dr. Stockman came out of the operating room to brief us as a group. He had such a kind and reassuring manner about him as he said, "Peggy Sue lost a lot of blood, had a collapsed lung and a broken rib from the forty-five-caliber bullet that we retrieved. Fortunately, the bullet missed her major blood vessels. Having us meet you halfway in the ambulance surely saved her life. It will take her about two weeks to recover here in the hospital, and a month or so after that to recuperate at home. Before we went into surgery, she requested that Bucky speak to her parents and let them know that she is here at the hospital. She is one tough lady, I can tell you that!"

We all hugged and thanked Dr. Stockman, and Bucky reassured him that he was on his way to see Peggy Sue's parents. As we left the hospital, Bucky asked me to go with him to the Hardings to visit with Peggy Sue's parents. Waldo and the rest of the group went to check into the famous Brown Palace Hotel in downtown Denver. We would join them there as soon as we finished at the Harding's home.

Since we were in Bucky's hometown of Denver, he swung by his high school alma mater. Denver West High School was only about two blocks north of Denver General Hospital. Bucky pointed out the football field that Pumpkin and Willy would be zapped to at 7:00 PM the following night, Friday. West High School's roots began when it was organized in 1883. The school joined the Denver Public School system in 1901, to become the city's second high school—East High School being the first. In 1926, West High School became involved in the City Beautiful project and was moved to Sunken Garden Park at 9th and Elati Streets. It was Mayor Robert Speer's vision to have each of the four directional high schools (East, West, North, and South) associated with a major park in one of Denver's four quadrants. West was a beautiful high school building designed in the English gothic style and executed in light brick, with buff terra cotta trimmings. I was impressed, and told Bucky as much.

"What is your high school mascot?" I asked.

Bucky answered, "It's the home of the Cowboys. Only we are the Good Cowboys, not the Vodka Cowboys!" We had a laugh about that, and it was a relief to laugh again.

As we drove to the Harding's home, Bucky, reached across and put his right arm across my shoulders. "BB, I was so scared that Peggy Sue was going to die." His eyes were welling up again, and he made me want to cry too. "I just don't know how I could ever forgive myself if she died because I let her come with us... It would just be too much!"

I reached across the back of his shoulders with my left arm and said, "I know Bucky. We were all scared to lose her; you were not alone. If there was ever a time for the Bad Love Gang to be praying, I can tell you it was on the road to Denver after the ambush. Hearing Dr. Stockman tell us that Peggy Sue was going to make it was one of the first times I felt like real prayers got answered. It all felt so surreal."

"Thanks, BB. I'm not sure why or how fate brought us together, but you have become the best friend I've ever had, and I mean that. You're like a younger brother to me now."

We both had tears dripping down our cheeks. I said, "I feel the same way, Bucky. And I'm glad you said 'younger brother,' rather than 'little brother.' Otherwise, I would have punched you!" We laughed with tears still in our eyes as I concluded, "Live dangerously, have fun, don't die. You and I have some real adventures out ahead of us!"

We relaxed, wrung out from everything that had happened in the past 24 hours. Bucky enquired, "How do you think I should handle the situation with Peggy Sue's parents?"

"Well... First of all, you have to remember that John and Sue Harding think you are dead. Your parents had a bodiless military funeral for you last month on Saturday, March twenty-fourth. You were laid to rest with full military honors here in Denver."

"Oh, shit. I'm glad we're talking about this. In the crossfire of all that happened today, that fact totally slipped my mind—even though the primary reason I wanted to come to Denver is to show my parents that I'm alive."

"Here's how I suggest that you handle the discussion with John and Sue Harding: Tell them that you work for a secret military project and to keep your cover, the military wanted you presumed dead. Introduce me as part of your team, then explain that we met up with Peggy Sue at NAS Glenview by chance, and that you and she 'instantly' reconnected. Tell them that she wanted to travel with you to Denver and visit them in the process. Then you'll have to let them know that we were ambushed by hostile forces on the way to Denver—and that Peggy Sue got shot. That part will be tough, but at least you can tell them that she will survive, and that she will need to be convalescing at home with them after she leaves the hospital," I explained.

"Shit, BB; can't you just tell that story for me?!" Bucky exclaimed as we turned off Sixth Avenue onto Franklin Street and drove into the Denver Country Club's neighborhood. Founded in 1887, Denver Country Club was the oldest country club west of the Mississippi, and one of the oldest in the United States. It originally centered on horse racing, but expanded to tennis, polo, golf, and a myriad of other sports. The homes in the neighborhood were all stunningly beautiful in both architecture and land-scaping, and no two houses were alike. We pulled up to a brown brick Tudor-style mansion and parked. Bucky looked at me and said, "I told you she was way above my 'pay grade'."

I replied, "You got that right, Captain Denver. Now keep your story straight in there."

We walked to the front door and knocked. Peggy Sue's mother, Sue Harding, answered the door and gaped at Bucky. She half-screamed, "I think I'm seeing a ghost! Bucky?! Is that you, or am I seeing a ghost?!" John Harding, Peggy Sue's father, quickly ran up behind Sue when he heard her scream.

Bucky calmly replied, "Yes, it is really me, Bucky, in the flesh and alive. This is my associate and friend, Colonel Kevin 'BB' Schafer. Can we come inside?"

We went inside and Bucky recounted the story about what had hap-pened with Peggy Sue to John and Sue Harding. When Bucky got to the

NAS Glenview part of the tale, Sue interrupted him to say, "Peggy Sue married that shit-for-brains lawyer in Chicago, and that jerk screwed her big time!"

John Harding looked at his wife and enquired, "Honey, how do you really feel about it?"

Sue shoved her husband's shoulder and replied, "Shut up, John." Then she looked at Bucky and said, "Before Peggy Sue married that butthead, she used to write me letters telling me how you were 'the one that got away.' I'm certain that when she saw you, it reignited all her old feelings for you."

John interjected, "Bucky, I know my daughter; she is as strong-willed as they come, and there is no way that she would let you talk her out of going with you. Don't you feel guilty about that. You didn't have a chance of keeping her from coming to Denver with you and your team."

Sue wept as Bucky told them about the bullet wound to Peggy Sue's chest, and John held Sue tightly as the story unfolded. John knew about Dr. Stockman's reputation in Denver, and softly reassured Sue that Peggy Sue was in great hands. John told us he and Sue would go directly to Denver General Hospital and asked us where we were headed. Bucky told him that he was going to see his parents in the morning, and our group was going to Peterson Army Air Base for some special training after that. John commented, "That Peterson Air Base is really something. They trained a lot of B-24 Liberator bomber crews there until last summer; then they switched to training fighter pilots. It's a busy place!"

We all hugged and as we were parting ways, Sue held Bucky squarely at arm's length as she looked into his eyes and told him, "Please make sure that we see you again, Bucky."

Bucky replied, "Yes, ma'am. You can count on it. Take care of Peggy Sue while I'm away."

Thursday, April 19, 1945 at 8:00 PM local time,
the Brown Palace Hotel, downtown Denver

Built on a triangular plot between 17th Street, Tremont Place, and Broadway in 1888—just 12 years after Colorado became a state—the Brown Palace Hotel was a classic Colorado landmark. Using Colorado red granite and Arizona red sandstone for the building's exterior, the historic Brown Palace Hotel was built in the Italian Renaissance style. For a unique finishing touch, there were 26 medallions carved in stone, each one depicting Colorado animals, between the seventh-floor windows on the hotel's exterior. The impressive atrium lobby was surrounded by balconies with cast iron railings, and ornate grillwork panels extended eight floors above ground. Its center was topped by a stained-glass ceiling and skylight. The lobby had 12,000 square feet of Mexican onyx paneling. No wood was used in the construction of the floors and walls; they were made of hollow blocks of porous terracotta fireproofing, making the Brown Palace the second fire-proof building in America. When it opened in 1888, the hotel had elevators, steam heat, a private electric plant, and its own private artesian well, dug 750 feet into the ground beneath the hotel. The Brown Palace was known for its daily proper high teas contrasting with the annual showings of the National Western Stock Show's Grand Champion Steer, brought into the same lobby. Famous past guests gracing the walls and halls of the Brown Palace Hotel included the "Unsinkable" Molly Brown—who stayed at the hotel only a week after the Titanic disaster—the Beatles, the Rolling Stones, and Presidents William Taft, Warren Harding,

Harry S. Truman, and Dwight D. Eisenhower. On Thursday, April 19, 1945, the Bad Love Gang spent the night at the Brown Palace Hotel.

Bucky and I arrived and checked in at the front desk. Colonel Clarke had pulled some more strings, using his ties and presidential authority; the Bad Love Gang were all staying in the "best rooms and suites available," while Bucky had been given the key to the Presidential Suite. The front desk clerk let us know that the rest of our group was eating dinner in the Ship Tavern, a wood-paneled hotel restaurant and pub opened in 1934 that had model sea-going clippers on display. We joined the Bad Love Gang and brought them up to speed on our visit with Peggy Sue's parents. Everyone was completely exhausted from a day that would go down in Bad Love Gang lore for the remainder of our lives. As we all finished dinner and retreated to our rooms, I told the group that we would meet in Bucky's Presidential Suite at 8:30 AM. I had planned a little surprise to get us all psyched for a new day, and our continuing time-travel trip in 1945 Colorado.

CHAPTER TWENTY-TWO:

BROADMOOR BOUND FOR FIGHTER PILOT TRAINING

"I am one of the richest men in America and
I can't buy that which I want the most—time."
—Spencer Penrose

Friday, April 20, 1945 at 8:30 AM local time in the
Presidential Suite of the Brown Palace Hotel,
Denver, Colorado

T he entire Bad Love Gang straggled into Bucky's Brown Palace Hotel
Presidential Suite at 8:30 AM still rubbing sleep from their eyes,
having slept long and soundly the night before. Everyone was oohing
and aahing about the sheer size of the room, the palatial furnishings,
and the luxe finishes. I had moved a few pieces of furniture to create a
decent-sized dance floor, and placed the Marantz boom box on an end
table in the middle. After they had a chance to tour the suite, I asked
everyone to gather around me and the boom box. Tater commented
that I was "Grinnin' like a possum eatin' a sweet tater!"

I announced, "Ladies and gentlemen, we all had one helluva day
yesterday, putting those Colorado Vodka Cowboys down and almost
losing Peggy Sue in the fight. But we made it here to Colorado, and
I thought we should get today and the rest of our trip off to a brand
new start! So when this music starts playing, you just let your feet do

the dancing. Let's get this little Colorado hoedown started!" I pushed the *play* button and the song **"Thank God I'm a Country Boy,"** by John Denver, blasted us with sound. The song was literally brand new to us, having been released in March 1975; in April 1975 (our current, modern time frame) it was steadily rising on the charts. The song was a live version 45 rpm single when released; it went to number one on both the *Billboard* magazine Hot Country chart, in May 1975, and the *Billboard* Hot 100 chart, in June 1975. It also went to number one in Canada and Yugoslavia! The song was a typical two-step that just made you want to start dancing, hooting, hollering, and singing—and that is exactly what we did!

The Bad Love Gang loved it, and we immediately started moving in a circle dance, alternating arm to arm and person to person while singing along. Goondoggy, Meatball, the Runt, Crazy Ike, and Tater then all broke away to do their own creative solo jigging, with crazy shuffles, leaps, and heel clicking. Crisco and Cleopatra were dancing together, both slapping their hips with one hand and twirling imaginary rodeo ropes with the other. Even Waldo got into the act, pretending he was riding a horse with the reigns in one hand and his crop in the other. It was great fun, and soon the Bad Love Gang was back: true to form and ready to go!

We all went to our rooms to get ready, and met for breakfast at 9:15 AM. We had three objectives that day, for which Bucky, Waldo, and I had developed a strategy to accomplish. First, we needed to get the entire group checked into the world-renowned Broadmoor Hotel and Resort in Colorado Springs, 75 miles to our south. Second, Bucky would meet with his parents to let them know he was alive and well. Third, Willy, Pumpkin, and the black box would all be zapped to the Denver West High School football field at 7:00 PM sharp.

Bucky had not been to the Broadmoor since the summer of 1936, with his family. He was fired up to go there; he kept telling us how absolutely wonderful it was! It would be a long day, with a lot of driving for some of us. Our convoy would drive to the Broadmoor first, to check in and get settled. Then a smaller group would return to Denver, for Bucky to see his parents and to pick up Willy, Pumpkin, and the black box. Bucky's parents lived just blocks from Denver West High School; we would go to see them before scooping up our time travelers. As was the norm for us now, we would be continually well-armed and vigilant for any potential trouble.

When Bucky called Colonel Carter Clarke late the night before with a status report, Clarke had made it a point to say that any Russian or other foreign communication traffic had gone virtually dead silent after our decisive crushing of the Vodka Cowboys yesterday. Clarke figured that we had bought ourselves some respect and breathing room from any more immediate trouble, other than the ever-present possibility of "spying eyes."

The Bad Love Gang convoy departed the Brown Palace Hotel at 10:30 AM and took US Route 87 South, which connected Denver to Colorado Springs. This highway would take us nearly straight to the Broadmoor. Waldo led the way in his Jeep with the Pud and Tater. We followed next; I drove our Jeep and Bucky rode shotgun, with Crisco and Cleopatra in the back. Crazy Ike drove the truck with the rest of the crew. Crisco was constantly snapping pictures of 1945 Denver as we drove out of town. As we started moving faster on Route 87, I tried to pick out one of my favorite road songs for this leg of the journey, shuffling through the shoe box containing all of the cassettes. I plugged a new cassette into the boom box, and warned Bucky that this was pretty heavy, modern rock and roll. Crisco commented, "What else is new,

Bubble Butt? Just lay it on us, and let's rock!" I was glad to know that Crisco was coming around after such a traumatic day on Thursday.

Cleopatra added, "When you say rock and roll like that, I always know we're in for heavy guitars, thumping drums, and some head-banging. So go for it, BB!" I hit the *play* button and **"Radar Love,"** by the Dutch rock band Golden Earring, filled the air with classic rock and roll.

"Radar Love" reached number 13 on the *Billboard* chart in the United States. It also hit the top ten in many countries, including Canada, the United Kingdom, Australia, Germany, and Spain. Listening to this great road trip song, I imagined myself as a driver having a psychic relationship with my hot girlfriend; I had to get to her by going fast! This epic rock song made you want to crush the accelerator pedal and keep it floored until you hit light speed. A generation of 1970's teenagers were pulled over by the police for excessive speeding who explained, "I'm sorry officer; I was listening to 'Radar Love.'" To which the officer would often reply, "Sorry to pull you over; have a good night!" I looked over at my "big brother" Bucky, and saw that he was getting into it big time! It tickled me, seeing a guy from the 1940s becoming a 1970's music convert!

The drive to the world-renowned Broadmoor Hotel and Resort was easy and quite scenic, with the front range of the Colorado Rockies in view to our right in the west. Pike's Peak was straight ahead as we headed south on US Route 87, on this beautiful spring day in 1945. We approached the front entrance of the impressive Broadmoor Hotel on its circular drive and were awestruck by the nine-story central hotel tower. The Broadmoor's main building was crowned by an open cupola and flanked by four wings. Officially opened on June 29, 1918, the Broadmoor was the culmination of the new world hotel and resort vision of founder Spencer Penrose and his wife, Julie Penrose. Their goal was to partially mimic but improve upon the very best that Europe had to offer, and to make that happen at the foot of the Rocky Mountains in Colorado Springs. The hotel's stepped asymmetrical architecture resembled the clustered, angled rooflines seen in a classic Italian countryside or Mediterranean seaside village. The design appeared to "float" amongst the layered silhouette of foothills and mountains, rising directly behind the building to the west. The striking red-tiled roofline and rich, cream-and-pink stucco façade furthered the appeal of Italian Renaissance style architecture. Guests with rooms on the west side of the resort could look across Cheyenne Lake as they gazed at the beauty of the mountains immediately to the west of the hotel.

Spencer "Spec" Penrose, the founder of the Broadmoor, was born on November 2, 1865, to a prominent Philadelphia family. His father, Richard Alexander Fullerton Penrose, was an obstetrician and gynecologist, considered one of Philadelphia's finest doctors. The Penrose family sent their sons to Harvard University. Graduating at the bottom of his class at Harvard—which may have predicted his future worldly success—Spencer "Spec" Penrose had no desire to become a doctor or politician, but he did have the wanderlust to travel west in search of success and the American dream.

After leaving Harvard, Spec traveled first to Las Cruces, New Mexico, where his mercantile, produce, and hay businesses failed to succeed. Failure is often a learning laboratory to future success; such was Spec's story and destiny. Charles L. Tutt Sr., Spec's close childhood friend from Philadelphia, was a successful real estate developer and geologist in the midst of the gold rush in Cripple Creek, Colorado. Spec moved to Colorado in 1892 and joined Tutt in what would become a highly successful and lasting business partnership. They started with the Cripple Creek real estate business, which included the Cash on Delivery (C.O.D.) Mine: one of the most successful mines in

Cripple Creek. They sold the C.O.D. mine in 1895 for $250,000 and used that money to purchase the Colorado-Philadelphia Reduction Company, an ore processing facility. Spec and Tutt needed someone with expertise in ore processing, so they added Charles Mather Mac-Neill, a tenured miner and miller, to their partnership. By 1899, the Colorado-Philadelphia Reduction Company and its plant were processing over $3 million of Cripple Creek ore annually. The three men would create a mining, milling, and real estate empire in the years that followed. This incredible success story propelled Spencer Penrose to lasting greatness, and enabled building one of the most storied hotels in America (which we were about to enter).

Spencer Penrose had died in December 1939, but his widow, Julie Penrose—who was the hotel's vice president in 1945—lived on the sixth floor when we went to check in. Coming through the front entrance doors into the main lobby, we were quick to appreciate the spectacular detailing, including a curved marble staircase, dramatic chandeliers, and Della Robbia-style artwork, along with the hand-painted beams and ceilings. There was a fancy drugstore with a soda fountain in the lobby, and a 100,000-gallon indoor swimming pool and spa located off the main lobby. This early spa included facilities for both men and women, with steam rooms, hot and cold plunge pools, tonic baths, massages, and salt glows. Seeing this, Cleopatra nudged Crisco. "Yeah, baby! Look at that! You and I are going for that action, big time! My weary body is ready for some re-ju-ve-*na*-tion and bea-u-ti-fi-*ca*-tion!"

Penrose had created a culture of service from the opening days of the Broadmoor, having tasked each and every employee with providing the level of service and hospitality that was expected in European hotels—but not often found in the US in those days. All Broadmoor employees, from executives to bellhops, received comprehensive training that enabled them to provide meticulous service, as well as sustaining a high level of employee loyalty. As we entered the lobby, the doors were held open for us. Approaching the front desk to check in, we were flanked by several bellhops who asked if they could assist us in any way. In addition, with all of us dressed in full military attire, the staff seemed even more respectful.

Bucky stepped up to the front desk and the clerk behind the desk enquired, "Sir, may I have your name?" Bucky answered, and the clerk responded, "Captain Smith, we have been expecting you. Welcome to the Broadmoor!" He immediately dialed a number on his phone and said, "The Captain Smith party has arrived at the front desk. Yes sir, I will bring them to you." When he hung up, he asked our entire group to follow him to an office located behind the front desk. Once inside that office, we were greeted by the Broadmoor Hotel's president, Charles L. Tutt, Jr. He was the son of Spencer Penrose's business partner, Charles L. Tutt, Sr., who died in 1909. Also present was the hotel manager, Charles R. Drake, who had managed the hotel since May of 1942.

Charles Tutt, Jr. had thinning hair, wire-rim glasses, and wore an expensive-looking gray wool suit and tie. He had a nice smile, I noticed, as he introduced Charles Drake. They warmly welcomed our entire group, both shaking all of our hands. Tutt initially looked directly at Bucky, then gazed around at all of us before focusing on Bucky again as he spoke. "I was a captain in the Army in World War I, and I have a great deal of respect for all that you are doing to defend our great nation. I received a personal phone call from our new president, Harry Truman, on Tuesday. He told me that he had sent a special delivery letter regarding national security here, for me to directly hand to Captain Jack 'Bucky' Smith." He handed Bucky an official envelope from the White House. "Then I received a *second* call from President Truman last night. That's two calls in the span of three days, from the commander in chief of the United States of America! In his second call last night, he said, and I quote, 'Charlie, this Captain Jack 'Bucky' Smith and his military team that he calls the Bad Love Gang who are coming to the Broadmoor are a bunch of goddamned national heroes! They just single handedly took out nearly the entire Russian spy network in Colorado. You treat these folks like they are pure gold coming out of your beloved dad's Cripple Creek gold mine!' He went on to say that a few of you would be doing some special fighter pilot training in P-40 Warhawks at Peterson Army Air Base. The Broadmoor has had a special relationship with Peterson since it was activated in May 1942 and underwent construction. Many of their personnel have stayed with us.

"If you all don't want to drive those military Jeeps or that truck during your time here with us, we have the largest and best-equipped fleet of Cadillac and Pierce Arrow tourist cars in Colorado, which are yours to use. We can take you on a tour to the summit of Pikes Peak, weather and roads permitting. Hedy Stenuf, a young woman who started skating in Vienna Austria at age six and electrified the skating world by winning the Austrian senior championship at age fourteen, is currently appearing in our 'Fantasy on Ice' show at the Broadmoor Ice Palace. I have arranged for front row seats for all of you, tomorrow night! Our Broadmoor Golf Club Manager, James Baird, took over the golf club back in 1932, and he knows *everyone*. He will personally take care of any of your group wanting to play golf during your stay with us. Mr. Bullock is our stable manager; many of our guests love to go horseback riding on the trails around Cheyenne Lake. You can take the Cheyenne Mountain Cog Railway to our Cheyenne Mountain Zoo, where we have over three hundred animals in beautiful surroundings. We have canoeing and water cycling boats on Cheyenne Lake out back. The food here is world-class; we have both a lovely dining room and our famous Tavern Restaurant, which is a local favorite, where you can dine at your leisure any time. Adolf Stoltz runs our barbershop, if any of you want a shave or haircut. Mr. Caldwell runs our hotel laundry service; he can clean your uniforms, if needed. I have arranged for your group to stay in our very best rooms and suites, all with awesome views of Cheyenne Lake and the mountains."

Tutt turned to Drake and asked, "Is there anything that I missed?"

Drake replied, "No sir, but if any of you need anything at all, call me directly and I will make it happen! I will have a team of our bellmen show you all to your rooms now."

We all stood there for a moment, stunned by what we had just heard and feeling downright giddy about our present situation. Cleopatra was the first to speak. "BB, you, Bucky, Pumpkin, and Willy need to extend your P-40 Warhawk training right on through the end of the year! One week will definitely not be long enough!" We all giggled at Cleo's comment.

Crazy Ike chimed in, "You all know how super spiritual I am; all I have to say is amen, sister... A-men!"

Waldo added, "If Crazy Ike is spiritual, then you all can start calling me Pope Waldo!"

"Let's meet for lunch in the Tavern Restaurant at one thirty," I suggested. "We'll have both Crazy Ike and Pope Waldo bless our first meal here!" We all thanked Tutt and Drake, then we were taken to our rooms.

Friday, April 20, 1945 at 1:30 PM local time,
the Broadmoor Hotel Tavern Restaurant,
Colorado Springs, Colorado

Lunch at the Tavern was superb. We were all talking excitedly about how amazing our rooms were, and how incredibly magnificent and breathtaking the overall Broadmoor property was to behold! We did have some business to conduct, though, so I led the way. "I spoke to Drake and arranged to use one of the hotel's limousines for a group of us to drive back to Denver and visit Bucky's parents, then pick up Willy, Pumpkin, and the black box at Denver West High School at seven. Who wants to go with me and Bucky?" No one volunteered. Tater said, "I'm as happy as a tick on a fat dog! Why would anyone want to ever leave this place?"

I knew I was fighting an uphill battle, so I added that the Cadillac we were taking was a 1942 Cadillac Series 75 Imperial Limousine, all decked out and powered by a smooth, 346-cubic-inch V-8, making it totally luxurious yet sporty! The Runt responded to the Cadillac's siren song and said, "I'll go—if I can drive that sucker!" Waldo also agreed to go, noting that we shouldn't assume all the trouble was totally in our rearview mirror. He added, "That Caddy will be well armed, just in case."

I reiterated that beginning the next day, Saturday, Bucky, Willy, Pumpkin, and I would start training in the P-40 Warhawk fighter planes at Peterson Army Air Base. I wanted the Runt and Meatball checking out the mechanics of the P-40 while we were training to see if there was any way to boost the engine or fuel mixture, something to give us an edge in China for our time travel mission to fly for General Claire Chennault and the Flying Tigers. I wanted the Pud to ensure that we had good VHF radio communications between the P-40s and the ground. In general, the rest of the crew was at liberty to enjoy all that the Broadmoor Hotel and resort had to offer until our flight training was completed.

Friday, April 20, 1945 at 5:30 PM local time at the home of
Jim and Elizabeth Smith, Denver, Colorado

Jim and Elizabeth "Liz" Smith, both in their early 50s, lived in a two-story craftsman-style home at the corner of 9th and Lipan Streets in Denver, just eight blocks west of Bucky's alma mater, Denver West High School. We arrived in front of their home in the black Cadillac limousine provided by the Broadmoor Hotel. Bucky was more excited than nervous to see his parents. We all agreed that he would go first, alone, and then invite us in to meet his parents after the reality settled in that Bucky was indeed alive, not dead as they had been told.

Bucky went to the front door and knocked. His dad opened the door. Jim Smith stood face to face with his only child, biting hard on his lower lip as he shook his head in joyful amazement, with tears flowing down his cheeks. He then grabbed Bucky, wrapping his arms tightly around his son. Jim wept as he said, "I have been counting the days, son, believing you couldn't be dead! They couldn't find your body. It has been twenty-seven days since your memorial service, and your twenty-seventh birthday is coming up in June. My heart and soul were ripped out of my body when Roosevelt called us with the news of your death! I refused to believe it, but I didn't know if that was just my own denial and wishful thinking—or if you could somehow, someway, still be alive!"

Bucky's mom then came to the door behind Jim. Liz froze when she saw Bucky in Jim's arms. She held her hands over her mouth and started crying like a baby, rocking as the tears freely flowed down her cheeks. Jim wasn't letting go of Bucky, so Liz came around and hugged him as tightly as she could from behind, Bucky sandwiched between them.

Bucky was crying, too. He said, "I am so, *so* sorry Mom and Dad! I was part of a top-secret mission, appointed directly by President

Roosevelt. I've lost count of how many times I thought I was dead or going to die. Dad's right; I *am* hard to kill. I'm not sure why that is, but it must have something to do with the two of you. You must be praying for me non-stop—or have a direct line to God."

Liz conceded, "I am always praying for you, Bucky, that God would surround and protect you with His mighty angels!"

Bucky tried to smile through his tears as he replied, "Yeah, Mom, the latest angel was a Chinese woman named 'Ming'. I have no idea where that woman came from. There are three other guardian angels out in the car that I want you two to meet. How about we all sit down together and visit for a short while? We have to leave here at six forty-five to continue our mission."

Bucky walked back to the Caddy and invited me, Waldo and the Runt inside to visit with his parents for a while. We had a wonderful visit, and could see why Bucky was such a solid guy; his parents were open, honest, straightforward, and obviously happily married to each other. They did not enquire too much about Bucky's mission, but Bucky did share that it involved the highest national security interests, and he did not have a good feel for how often he would be able to come home. At this moment, all that Jim and Liz cared about was that Bucky was alive—they were good with that fact. Bucky told them about Peggy Sue Harding, and that her parents also knew he was alive. He asked Jim and Liz to go visit John, Sue, and Peggy Sue at Denver General Hospital, giving them their support, and keep the fact that Bucky was alive between them. Before we departed, Liz Smith went to her bedroom and returned with a large envelope. She handed it to Bucky and said, "I put this together after I thought that you had died. You keep it, and look at from time to time, sweetheart." We all hugged both of them and headed out the door at 6:45 PM.

Friday, April 20, 1945 at 7:00 PM local time,
Denver West High School football field, Denver, Colorado

It only took us five minutes to drive to the Denver West High School football field from the Smiths' home. We made it to the bleachers with five minutes to spare, looking out onto the field in anticipation of Willy, Pumpkin, and the black box's arrival. We decided not to try any practical jokes this time. We would not abuse or disorient them in any way, although I had been pondering different ways to have fun with that in the future! At 7:00 PM sharp, Willy, Pumpkin, and the black box magically appeared in the middle of the football field. Both of them sat cross-legged on the ground, with their arms folded across their chests: a landing style they had rehearsed for this arrival. Pumpkin was nursing his right ankle; sure enough, he had been stung by the silent white lightning during the time travel trip, and had a jagged lightning-bolt scar forming on his ankle. Pumpkin declared, "I was utterly *knackered* before I left Oak Ridge, but that lightening pepped me up a bit!" His posh English accent made everything he said sound so much better than it actually was.

Willy looked around with wide eyes, taking in his first sights of 1945 Denver. He was impressed with the size and architecture of Bucky's high school alma mater, and said as much. The black box felt a little heavy; Bowmar and Willy had thought to send extra VHF radio gear from the Pud's stash for the P-40s. The six of us walked off the field and got into the limousine, with the Runt acting as our chauffeur. "Where to, sir?" he enquired.

I said, "Take us home, James. Take us home, and step on it!"

On the way back to Colorado Springs, we brought Willy and Pumpkin up to speed about our encounter with the Colorado Vodka Cowboys and the great support that we had received from President

Harry Truman. Bucky started to brief us on the handling characteristics of the P-40 Warhawks in preparation for our training the following day. As we neared the Broadmoor Hotel, Willy, who had been briefed by Bowmar about our planned mission, commented, "I'm really excited to fly the P-40 Warhawk, but going to China is another thing!" I decided to let that comment go without a response. We needed to get flying the next day, and that was all I cared about at the moment.

CHAPTER TWENTY-THREE:
THE PETERSON PANDA BEARS

"Boy, if the Chinese only had 100 good pursuit planes
and 100 fair pilots, they'd exterminate the Jap air force!"
—General Claire Chennault of the Flying Tigers

Saturday, April 21, 1945 at 8:00 AM local time,
the Broadmoor Hotel Dining Room,
Colorado Springs, Colorado

A t 7:00 AM Saturday morning, Bowmar recalled the black box as per protocol. We sent our group pet hamster, Rasputin, back to Bowmar with instructions to recall everyone except Bucky, Pumpkin, Willy and me in one week, on Saturday, April 28, 1945 at 8:00 AM. On the 28th, after the rest of the Bad Love Gang were zapped back to 1975 Oak Ridge, Tennessee, the four of us would take our P-40 Warhawks from Peterson Army Air Base and fly directly to Indian Springs Airfield (Area 51), in the remote southwest Nevada desert. We would be finishing this phase of the mission by going to Area 51 to familiarize ourselves with the alien spaceship hidden in a giant hangar there before taking our time travel mission to meet with General Clair Chennault in June 1942, hand delivering President Roosevelt's sealed message to him. We also directed Bowmar to zap the four of us back at 5:00 PM Pacific time that same day.

Vannevar Bush discovered and revealed to Bucky that Chennault had privately communicated with President Roosevelt in late June 1942 about a report of a possible alien spacecraft that had crash landed near Kunming, China. Chennault had received intelligence that the crash site was being simultaneously pursued by both Chinese and Japanese forces, who were at war with each other. Chennault mysteriously lost a single P-40 Warhawk from his airbase in Kunming on a reconnaissance mission to the crash site late Thursday afternoon on June 18, 1942. One week later, on Wednesday, June 24, there were multiple reports of a late afternoon Japanese Army Air Force bombing raid in the vicinity of the reported crash site. Later that same evening, there were reports of a UFO leaving Earth. Our working assumption was that the alien spaceship crash in China had occurred simultaneously with the crash in the Nevada desert at Area 51. That night, Bucky had witnessed six aliens being zapped away; the technology had been reverse engineered to build the White Hole Project. Somehow these events were interconnected, and we were being sent on a time travel mission to ensure that the secrets of Area 51 and the White Hole Project remained America's secrets.

Bucky, Pumpkin, Willy, the Runt, Meatball, the Pud, and I met for breakfast in the Broadmoor dining room prior to heading out to Peterson Army Air Base to get our P-40 Warhawk fighter pilot training underway. We had decided to give ourselves one full week of intensive, non-stop flight training, with Bucky teaching Pumpkin, Willy, and me to fly and fight in the P-40s. We all knew how to fly, but we needed this time to learn as much as we could about the P-40 Warhawk and General Chennault's Flying Tigers' aerial tactics.

With Bowmar's help, as well as on their own, Pumpkin and Willy had thoroughly researched General Claire Chennault and the Flying Tigers before they were zapped to Denver West High School. This was important, since we were all about to get some serious airtime in the P-40 Warhawks and then go to China to complete our mission by volunteering for the Flying Tigers. Bucky was also somewhat familiar with Chennault's story through his various USAAF intelligence channels. The three of them shared their thoughts and research on the topic as we had breakfast together at 8:00 AM.

The Second Sino-Japanese War was a military conflict waged between China and the Empire of Japan from July 1937 to September 1945. In other words, Japan was fully at war with China before they attacked the United States by bombing Pearl Harbor on December 7, 1941. The Flying Tigers, known originally as the American Volunteer Group (AVG), was the brainchild of Claire L. Chennault. In August 1937, Chennault was a retired US Army Air Corps officer when he began working in China, one month after war broke out between Japan and China. Chennault first worked as a military aviation advisor to Generalissimo Chiang Kai-shek in the early months of the Sino-Japanese War. He later became a director of the Chinese Air Force flight school in Kunming, China. Chennault spent the winter of 1940–1941 in Washington DC, lobbying and arranging for the purchase of 100 Curtiss P-40B Warhawk fighter planes for China's Air Force and air defense. He went about recruiting 100 pilots as well as some 200 ground crew and administrative personnel who would constitute the creation of the Flying Tigers. Sixty of the original Flying Tigers volunteer pilots came from the Navy and Marine Corps, and forty came from the Army Air Corps. The group had contracts with the Chinese government, drawing salaries ranging from $250 a month for a mechanic to $750 for a squadron flight commander—earning roughly three times what they could make in the US Army Air Force. The AVG Flying Tiger fighter pilots were also eligible for a $500 bonus for every confirmed Japanese aircraft they shot down or destroyed.

Basically, the initial AVG pilots were mercenaries, originating from the US military and paid by China. The AVG had no ranks, or division between officers and enlisted soldiers. It was Chennault who brought them all together for one of the greatest and inspiring adventure stories of WWII.

The Flying Tigers were divided into three squadrons. The first squadron was called the Adam & Eves, and the second squadron was called the Panda Bears. Those two squadrons were initially based out of Kunming, China. The third squadron called themselves the Hell's Angels. On December 20, 1941, only 13 days after the Empire of Japan bombed Pearl Harbor, the AVG Flying Tigers, under Chennault's command, intercepted ten unescorted Japanese Kawasaki Ki-48 Lily bombers that had been sent to attack Kunming, China. It represented the first American aerial combat mission against the Japanese Air Force in WWII, excluding the documented aerial attempts to defend against the attack on Pearl Harbor on December 7, 1941. Trying to evade Chennault's attacking P-40B Warhawks, the Japanese bombers were forced to harmlessly drop their bomb loads before reaching Kunming. The battle lasted 30 minutes; the Japanese bombers were outmatched and outgunned by the Flying Tigers. Initially, it was reported that four of the Japanese bombers were shot down; Chinese intelligence later intercepted Japanese communications indicating that only one of the ten bombers returned to their base. Whatever the true count, the Japanese discontinued their raids on Kunming, China while the Flying Tigers were based there. However, the most significant consequence of this first air victory encounter in China was the giant morale boost that it gave both the Chinese fighting forces and America. On Monday, December 29, 1941, *Time* Magazine ran an article entitled "BATTLE OF CHINA: Blood for the Tigers" detailing the AVG's victory over the Imperial Japanese Army Air Force and cementing their name in history forevermore as the Flying Tigers.

On April 7, 1942, Chennault (who had been officially retired from the US military) was restored to active USAAF duty as a major. On April 22, 1942, he was promoted to brigadier general in command of the First American Volunteer Group; he held that post until the First AVG was dissolved on July 4, 1942. On that day, called Dissolve Day by the original Flying Tiger volunteer force, the US Army Air Force took over the Flying Tigers; Chennault's command was thereafter called the China Air Task Force (CATF). We would be catching General Chennault in June 1942, as the original AVG Flying Tigers were approaching Dissolve Day.

After listening to the initial phase of this discussion, and knowing that I needed to get Willy more engaged to overcome his innate fear of risk taking, I asked him, "Which one of the three Flying Tiger squadrons do we want to join when we go to China? Should we be Adam and Eves, Panda Bears, or Hell's Angels?"

Willy thought for a minute, then gave a more detailed answer than I was expecting. "The Chinese people see the Panda Bears as warriors because of their strong, independent qualities. Pandas are able to find food for themselves, climb trees, and withstand extremely cold temperatures while being as strong as tigers. They are tough and strong like warriors, but they also symbolize peace and friendship because they have a gentle temperament and aren't known for attacking others. Their black and white color is seen as representing the yin and yang, and how proper balance brings about harmony and peace."

"Shit, Willy, after listening to that dissertation, I want you to tell me about how Adam and Eve worked together with the Hells Angels!" I exclaimed.

Willy laughed and said, "Well BB, I kinda cheated on that one. I was the one who did the research on the three AVG Flying Tiger squadrons. Anyway, to answer your question, I say we call ourselves Panda Bears while we are training here at Peterson Army Air Base. When we meet 'Old Leatherface,'" he referred to General Claire Chennault with a smile, "we tell him we're volunteering for the Panda Bear squadron."

"Sounds good to me," I replied. "Bucky, how about we call you Panda Leader One, and we call Pumpkin Panda Paw Two as your wingman? I'll be Panda Yin Three, and Willy will be Panda Yang Four as my wingman."

The Pud interjected, "I gotta write this down, if I'm gonna be keeping track of the four of you on the radio!"

I laughed and replied, "You got it, Panda Pud Five! That goes for you too, Panda Runt Six and Panda Meatball Seven!" We all cackled together at our newfound Flying Tiger handles.

Bucky then took over the discussion, "Let's talk about the P-40 Warhawks for a bit, and what we need to practice. The Warhawk has a very tough frame, self-sealing fuel tanks, a semi-modular design, and a very strong five-spar wing. The plane can pull high-G turns, and can even survive some midair collisions. Don't get any ideas, but P-40s have intentionally rammed enemy aircraft and recorded victories that way. The point is that P-40s are able to take a tremendous amount of punishment; they can conduct violent aerobatics, sustain damage, and still get you home. Dive acceleration and speed are excellent, with one of the fastest maximum dive speeds of any fighter. The maximum permissible diving speed is an 'indicated' speed of 475 miles per hour; that equates to a true airspeed of 658 miles per hour. Beyond that, your controls will be useless. Why? Because at that speed, you are well into compressibility as you start to approach the speed of sound, 767 miles per hour. Compressibility causes a change in the density of the air around the plane, and you lose control. There is no recovery at a higher dive speed, so keep your maximum indicated dive speed at 475 miles per hour or less."

Meatball exclaimed, "This is awesome shit, Bucky! I'm getting tingles down my spine just listening to you! I wanna fly one of those birds!"

"We are flying P-40Ns this week, but we will fly Chennault's recently delivered P-40Es when we arrive in China in June 1942. The P-40Es have an eleven hundred fifty horsepower Allison, liquid-cooled power plant. You don't want to take a bullet to the engine, lose coolant, and start an engine fire. You are shit out of luck if that happens," Bucky stated flatly.

I said, "That's what happened in my nightmare last week on Friday the thirteenth, when I woke up on the floor in Chattanooga after bailing out of my plane and falling out of bed at 6:30 AM. You were going down, Bucky; I think you were diving into compressibility, and couldn't pull out. I'm having déjà vu. This is so weird."

Bucky reassured me as he continued. "That is why we are here to practice this week: so we fly smart, and fly with confidence. It was just a dream, BB; that's not going to happen. Anyway, the P-40E has a landing speed of 85 miles per hour and a maximum speed of 354 miles per hour. Cruising speed is 258 miles per hour, and the service ceiling is 29,000 feet. The plane has a pretty good range: 1,150 miles, with the auxiliary fuel tank. The plane is armed with six Browning fifty-caliber machine guns, three in each wing. The P-40Ns we're flying this week are only eight miles per hour faster, with a service ceiling of 30,000 feet and a range of 850 miles. So, there isn't that much difference. Maybe the Runt and Meatball can figure out how to give us a little extra punch while they're tinkering around with the plane's mechanics this week."

The Runt smiled slyly and said, "We'll find a way to make the Panda Bears 'float like a butterfly and sting like a bee.'" The famous quote from Muhammad Ali fit our mission perfectly.

Meatball added, "I like this Mario Andretti quote, too: 'If everything seems under control, you're not going fast enough!' We'll figure out how to give you guys an extra edge."

"That brings us to battle tactics," Bucky said. "Chennault drilled his pilots relentlessly and insisted upon two-plane teams at all times, just as BB has suggested. He wanted to make certain that his men took advantage of the P-40's strengths, especially its ruggedness and superior diving ability. Chennault's approach to air combat was different in that dogfighting with the Japanese fighter planes was to be strictly avoided. The Japanese fighters were faster and more maneuverable, but relatively 'flimsy and more vulnerable to damage' in battle, compared to the durable P-40's pilot and engine shielding. In fact, some of the Japanese fighters could not stay in a high-speed dive with a P-40 without coming apart mid-air. Given the P-40's strong dive characteristics, Chennault's doctrine called for his pilots to take on enemy aircraft in teams from an altitude advantage, telling them to identify the enemy while flying high above and then execute a diving or slashing attack, continuing to dive away to set up for the next attack. This 'dive-and-zoom' technique was contrary to what most US pilots had been trained to do.

"You three will have a significant advantage, because we are going to train this week to perform diving attacks and head-on attacks. We will also train for strafing, which means to attack ground targets using your fifty-caliber machine guns while flying low. Strafing sounds easy, but there is an art and science to it. We will practice landing and taking off in rural fields because I anticipate that we will have to find a suitable flat place to land near that suspected alien spaceship crash site when we go to China. We will also thoroughly test the aerobatic abilities of the P-40 Warhawk. When we are done here, the four of us will be able to predict each other's moves and fly together as an effective and lethal team."

The seven of us at the breakfast table all cried out, "Hell *yes!*" as we high-fived each other. We got up from the table and took a short walk behind the hotel to stretch our legs, wanting a closer look at Cheyenne Lake and the gorgeous mountains immediately to the west. The setting was so peaceful and beautiful on this spring morning. On the sidewalk paralleling the scenic lake, a fashionably dressed lady approached us, taking her two poodles for a morning walk. Willy had grown up with poodles and stooped down to pet the two dogs, asking the lady their names. She replied, "Pitty Pat and Yala." As Willy petted the canines, he shared his love for dogs and particularly poodles, then thanked her for stopping for a moment. He stood up and introduced himself as Lieutenant Billy Blanchert, and she introduced herself as Julie Penrose. She smiled kindly at our group and commented, "I bet you all are members of the Bad Love Gang that Mr. Tutt told me about yesterday. I sure can't forget *that* name! Thank you all for your service to our country, and the best of luck to you." We took our hats off and thanked and complimented her for the marvelous Broadmoor property and hospitality. As she walked away, I thought, *That is history walking away from us. What an amazing American story!*

Saturday, April 21, 1945 at 10:00 AM local time,
Peterson Army Air Base, Colorado Springs, Colorado

Bucky, Pumpkin, Willy, the Runt, Meatball, the Pud, and I took the Cadillac limousine from the Broadmoor Hotel to Peterson Army Air Base. Described as a home for sagebrush, jack rabbits, and rattlesnakes at the time construction started, Colorado Springs Army Air

Base got its military activation orders on April 28, 1942. Construction started within a week of base activation. The first troops arrived May 13, 1942, and by August 1942, construction crews had completed the first new runways. On August 8, 1942, Lt. Edward J. Peterson, Operations Officer for the 14th Photographic Reconnaissance Squadron—and a native of Colorado—crashed and was fatally wounded during takeoff on a training mission, becoming the first Coloradan killed in a flying accident at the airfield. On December 13, 1942, base officials changed the name of Colorado Springs Army Air Base to Peterson Army Air Base to honor the fallen Colorado airman.

In November 1943, Peterson Army Air Base transformed into a combat bomber crew training school for ten-man B-24 "Liberator" bomber crews destined for overseas combat assignments. By the time this phase ended in the summer of 1944, hundreds of B-24 crew members had passed through Peterson Field for two to three months of training in strategic bombing. In June 1944, Peterson Field took on fighter pilot training, using P-40N Warhawks. The 72nd Fighter Wing, headquartered at Peterson during this time, oversaw operations at six other fighter training bases in the Southwest United States. Fighter pilot training took place until April 1945, and was winding down when our Bad Love Gang Flying Tigers trainee group arrived on April 21, 1945. Bucky had spoken to the base commander earlier, relating our presidential orders to make this training effective and efficient. The commander knew we were coming and had assigned USAAF Sergeant Lou Smith (no relation to Bucky) to make certain all our needs were met. We drove to the designated hangar, where Smith had five P-40N Warhawks parked on a line, waiting for us. Smith had even arranged for all five planes to be painted with the Flying Tiger shark faces on their noses. Four of the planes were fueled, fully armed, and ready to fly. The fifth was fueled but not armed, ready for the Runt, Meatball, and the Pud to tinker with while the rest of us were out flying. Sergeant Smith enquired, "Is there anything else I can get for you men before you get started?"

Bucky replied, "We want to practice strafing this week. How do you suggest we get that set up to practice with live ammunition?"

"That's no problem, sir. The Lowry Bombing and Gunnery Range is twenty miles southeast of Denver, and encompasses approximately one hundred square miles of land. We've been using that for live munitions training exercises since 1942, at numerous bombing and gunnery targets across that site. It'll take you all of ten minutes to fly there and start shooting away. Tell me your group call sign, and I'll let them know you're coming from Peterson to practice there today and next week. You radio and let them know when you are approaching and leaving. There are tons of targets for you all to shoot at, so knock yourselves out! Any time you need these planes reloaded or refueled, come right back here to this hangar; my crew will get you fueled, locked and loaded, and back in the air. Every night, my maintenance crew will service the planes so they'll be ready for you the next morning. I have been told to give you and your group absolutely everything you need, or face a firing squad at dawn. Just kidding! Oh, by the way... I also brought you these P-40N flight manuals, in case you want to refer to them anytime this week."

We all immediately liked Sergeant Lou Smith's infectious optimism and sense of humor. I felt like a kid in a candy store. This sounded like we had died and gone to P-40 flying heaven! Bucky said, "We are the Panda Bear Squadron; that's our call sign this week, Sergeant."

Smith saluted and said, "You got it, Captain. Go get 'em!"

As Smith headed back into the hangar, the Pud set up his VHF radio equipment in all four of our planes. He said we would have a range of up to 200 miles to communicate with him and each other.

The P-40N had its own radio, we just wanted to have the most modern communications when we went to China. Bucky climbed in the pilot's seat of his plane with Pumpkin, Willy, and I all watching. He spent the next hour going over all the engine and flight controls and gauges, starting the engine and warming up, plus the actions prior to and following takeoff. The P-40 was a taildragger (two wing wheels and a tail wheel) with a fairly long nose and low tail posture. We would have to taxi for takeoff in an "S" pattern to see the runway until we got going and the tail came up so we could see straight ahead. Last but not least, we reviewed the trigger mechanism to fire the six .50-caliber Browning machine guns, three in each wing.

Just before noon, the Peterson Panda Bear squadron fired up all four planes and saluted the Runt, Meatball, and the Pud as we taxied to take off to the north. As we approached the flight line, Bucky first radioed the tower, then radioed the three of us: "This is Panda Leader One to Panda Bear Squadron, we are clear for takeoff."

Pumpkin excitedly radioed back, "This is Panda Paw Two; I'm chuffed to bits, and bloody ready to go up north and shoot some stuff!"

Willy added, "This is Panda Yang Four, and this Panda is ready to go kick some ass!"

I finished the sentiment, "This is Panda Yin Three; let's *light* this candle, and see how fast these bitches can fly and dive!"

And with that, the four of us roared down the runway and took to the air, flying our P-40N Warhawks in a formation. We were on our way to train like mad for the next week over the skies of Colorado.

CHAPTER TWENTY-FOUR:

AREA 51

"There is a mysterious cycle in human events. To some
generations much is given. Of other generations much is expected.
This generation of Americans has a rendezvous with destiny."
—Franklin D. Roosevelt

Friday, April 27, 1945 at 7:00 PM local time,
the Broadmoor Hotel Tavern Restaurant,
Colorado Springs, Colorado

The Bad Love Gang was in rare form at the dinner table on our final
night at the truly amazing Broadmoor Hotel and Resort. At 8:00
AM the following morning, the entire Bad Love Gang—minus Bucky,
Pumpkin, Willy and me—would be zapped back to 1975 Oak Ridge, Tennessee. The four of us were taking our P-40 Warhawks on a flight directly
from Peterson Army Air Base to Area 51 in the remote southwest Nevada
desert, and pulling our planes right up to the hangar that housed the alien
spaceship. Bucky had spoken with Vannevar Bush before dinner, and he
had cleared the way for our Panda Squadron to land there. Vannevar said
they would be expecting us, and there would be a surprise for us there as
well. The four of us were scheduled to be recalled to Oak Ridge at 5:00 PM
on Saturday. We would have several hours to familiarize ourselves with the
alien spaceship before returning to 1975 Tennessee.

Cleopatra and Crisco opined that we needed to stay at the Broadmoor longer. Together they bellowed, "This has been the best vacation *ever!*" Cleopatra recounted some of their highlights of the week. "We had front-row seats to the 'Fantasy on Ice' show, we got to go horseback riding a few times, we went to the Cheyenne Mountain Zoo, we went canoeing and water cycling on the lake, we went swimming in the pool and were pampered at the spa—my skin is sparkling! We took some long walks, too, and this whole property is so beautiful that I felt like I was in Europe somewhere! Then, at the end of every day, we ate like queens and kings; the food has been incredible! At night you go to your comfy, cozy bed and sleep like a baby. I love this mountain air! Everyone here acts like they are your personal genie; your wish is their command! One of the Cadillac touring cars took us to the Royal Gorge in Canon City, Colorado yesterday. That Royal Gorge Bridge was built in 1929, across the canyon carved through the granite there. We got to cross the bridge; it's nine hundred fifty-five feet above the Arkansas River, making it the highest bridge in the world!"

Crazy Ike cut in, "Me and Tater got to be best friends with the Golf Club manager this week. I pretty much lived on the golf course. If I could keep this up a while longer, I might want to skip J-school and go pro!"

Tater in his thick southern drawl disagreed, "Ike is three gallons of crazy in a two-gallon bucket! The only wood that can lower Crazy Ike's score is a pencil; you gotta constantly watch what he writes down on that damn scorecard, every cotton pickin' hole!"

Crazy Ike rebutted, "Listen, Tater; it takes a lot of balls to golf like I do."

"That's right. By my count, you lost at least a hundred balls this week!" Tater shot back. We all roared with laughter.

Pumpkin leapt into the conversation. "Yes, I think Crazy Ike is a few sandwiches short of a picnic, you might say. On one of my flyovers this week, I swear I saw a bloke on the golf course who looked a bit like Ike, kicking a ball out of the rough onto the fairway when no one was looking."

Bucky cried, "You can't see a golf ball from up there!" Pumpkin's face turned bright orange, much like Pinocchio's nose growing long. We all about died laughing again! It was the best demonstration yet of how Pumpkin got his nickname from turning orange when embarrassed or caught in a lie.

"I really like this place," Waldo observed. "All my children got to play, and I didn't have to draw my gun once to shoot anybody. I'd say that was a pretty damn good week, by my reckoning."

I remarked, "Well the Panda Bear Squadron sure got to shoot its fifty-caliber guns like they were going out of style this week. I think we killed at least twenty-five old army Jeeps and trucks, along with a platoon or two of wooden soldiers, on that Lowry gunnery range. Those wooden soldiers never stood a chance against the Peterson Panda Bears!"

The Runt chimed in, "Yeah, Meatball and I have a few ideas to make you guys fly as fast as Bowmar thinks!"

Willy, who had been a huge *Star Trek* fan since it started as a series on TV in 1966, commented, "I guess that means our P-40 Warhawks will fly at warp speed; that might help us catch that UFO when we get to China!"

Continuing our jokes and discussions until we were slap-happy tired, we had a great last night at the Broadmoor. We talked about returning there together in 1975 to see how it would change in 30 years—the blink of an eye, for the Bad Love Gang. I reminded everyone that they would be zapped back to 1975 at 8:00 AM, and that the four of us going to Area 51 would be coming back nine hours later (ten, including the time zone change) at 5:00 PM tomorrow. We all hugged, wishing each other Godspeed and good luck. Waldo group hugged Bucky, Pumpkin, Willy, and me, then said, "Get your asses home safe; that's an order!"

Saturday, April 28, 1945 at 9:00 AM local time,
Peterson Army Air Base, Colorado Springs, Colorado

Sergeant Lou Smith was waiting for us, and had our four P-40 Warhawks fully fueled and ready to fly. We thanked him for all his great help during the past week while we had trained there. Bucky explained that our mission today was classified, but that our flight plan showed us going to Las Vegas Army Airfield. Smith replied, "Captain, whatever you say is good by me, I've never seen four guys train so hard, and fly so many hours in one week, in my whole career. I think you drained our fuel depot and used up almost all of our fifty-caliber ammunition. Whatever you all are up to, God help anyone who comes against you!"

Bucky replied, "You got that right, Sergeant Smith! Good luck to you and thanks again."

Pumpkin had obtained the coordinates to Area 51 from Bucky and had our actual flight plan ready to go. Pumpkin's navigation skills were world class, if not otherworldly. In my opinion, he had a sixth sense when it came to aerial navigation; he would lead the way after we got airborne. Soon, when we would be taking our time travel trip to see General Claire Chennault and volunteer for the Flying Tigers, Pumpkin would navigate the skies for us over south China in June, 1942. The trip today was a roughly 600-mile flight that would take us less than three hours. We fired up our four Warhawks and taxied to the flight line. Bucky cleared our departure with the Peterson Air

Control Tower, then radioed us. "This is Panda Leader One to Panda Bear Squadron; let's wave our wings goodbye as we leave this place. They have been very good to us this past week."

I acknowledged, "That's an affirmative, Panda Leader One. Lead the way!"

We took off south, waving our wings as we departed, then turned to a west-southwest heading for Area 51. We had all grown to love flying the rugged P-40s. Bucky had shown us the full complement of aerobatics, including high-speed dives pushing near to compressibility, rolls, spins, head-on passes, and cutting the throttle forcefully to a stall. If a faster Jap Zero was closing rapidly from behind, a stall might let it fly by to become a target. We were never to turn with a Japanese Oscar or Zero. Instead, we would have to dive to evade and/or fight head on. Our guns were superior in a head-to-head matchup, but we risked failure and/or death in a dogfight with the faster more maneuverable Japanese fighter planes. I had secretly contemplated what I would do if I ever ran out of bullets in battle but had to stay in the fight. It was one of those "what-ifs" that my brain debated and played games with. The past week had been so intense that I had found myself daydreaming as well as dreaming every night about flying the P-40 Warhawk, even when we weren't flying. Bucky had been an amazing fighter pilot instructor for the three of us; for better or worse, we had gained a level of confidence in our abilities as a cohesive squadron of four Panda Bear Flying Tigers.

We were flying at 27,000 feet over the majestic Colorado Rocky Mountains, and the views were spectacular! I got on the radio with a question for Bucky. "This is Panda Yin Three to Panda Leader One, over."

"This is Panda Leader One, I copy. What's up?"

"I was wondering what would happen if the four of us just flew into the base at Indian Springs Airfield (Area 51) unannounced and without authorization."

Bucky replied, "All hell would break loose before we even got close to landing! We would be caught in the crosshairs of vicious antiaircraft fire, and if we made it through that first perimeter of defense, we would be met with an ace squadron of P-51 Mustangs that would eat our lunch big time! The place is a testing ground for the newest and best American fighter planes, in addition to any and all secret aircraft advances. If we made it to the ground anywhere near the hangar where the alien spacecraft is kept, we would die in a hailstorm of snipers' bullets coming from every direction—while simultaneously confronted by crack ground forces. If, by any wild chance, we miraculously made it to the hangar, it is actually *two* hangars: a larger hangar, encompassing a smaller hangar, that encompasses the alien spaceship. A garrison of special ops Marines guards the space between the two hangars. Inside the inner hangar, where we will see the alien ship, the workers all wear white jumpsuits and probably at least half of them are actually armed guards, representing the final layer of defense. You won't see this defensive juggernaut today; we will simply pull our planes up to the outer hangar and be met by someone who will take us to the inner sanctum."

"This is Panda Paw Two, over."

"Go ahead, Pumpkin. What's on your mind?"

Pumpkin replied, "I don't like the odds of getting in there unannounced! I suppose if they didn't kill your arse, then you would be spending the rest of your days at Her Majesty's pleasure." He had explained that this was British slang for spending time in prison.

"Panda Yang Four here; Bubble Butt, how would you envision getting past that elaborate defense network?"

"Easy, Willy," I replied. "I just took Bucky to see the latest James Bond movie, The Man with the Golden Gun, in January. Bond's arch villain in the movie is an assassin named Francisco Scaramanga; his mistress is the sexy actress Maud Adams, playing the role of Andrea Anders. Of course, Bond becomes involved with her to get to Scaramanga. In one of his best lines, Bond says, 'Miss Anders! I didn't recognize you with your clothes on.'" I gave them my best Bond impersonation, and everyone chuckled.

Willy shot back, "I don't get it. And how exactly does that get you past all those defensive layers?"

"Patience, my man; I was getting to that part. If I were going to evade that entire elaborate defensive network at Area 51, I would just walk right through the front door in the broad daylight, as a secret agent who had been authorized and accepted as part of the team working there. Better yet, as a highly intelligent, handsome man or beautiful woman, so we could put it on the big screen!"

"That is some imagination you've got going there, BB!" Willy exclaimed.

Bucky added, "Maybe that isn't as farfetched as it sounds. From some of my discussions with Colonel Clarke, his Venona Project is uncovering Russian spies, men and women working together to steal America's secrets from the Manhattan Project in Los Alamos, New Mexico. An inside job is always better than using brute force!"

We flew for a while, then I clicked on the radio again. "Panda Yin Three to Panda Leader One, over."

"This is Pander Leader One, go ahead, BB."

"I've been thinking about this road trip and our time in Colorado. I was curious: What was in the large envelope that your Mom gave you the night we went to visit them and show them that you were still alive?"

"It is interesting that you asked, BB. I was looking at the contents of that envelope again this morning, right before we left. When she thought I was dead, she assembled all the photos of me and our family together, from the time I was a newborn baby and growing up in Colorado. There were pictures from every year of elementary school and high school, my time attending and graduation from West Point, and pictures of me in the Air Force. She also wrote me a couple of letters after she thought I was gone. She said it had helped her in her grieving process, to somehow stay connected to 'her only child.' She kept some of her favorite pictures, but wanted me to have it all as a remembrance of my life and my family, and to know how valuable life and family are. I am so grateful for all that; even when I go back to the future with all of you, I will still have them with me until I can return again."

I replied, "Your parents are solid, Bucky. Very solid."

Saturday, April 28, 1945 at 11:00 AM local time, Area 51, southwestern Nevada desert

The Bad Love Gang Panda Bear Squadron followed Bucky in for the landing at the Area 51 runway. Bucky taxied right up to the hangar where the alien spaceship was hidden. Military activity bustled and guards were everywhere. A moderate-sized active airbase with a control tower and various buildings, smaller closed hangars harboring other secrets, and barracks had been constructed surrounding the gigantic hangar in front of us. We parked our planes, and as we climbed out of our cockpits and to the ground in a group, our surprise approached us. It was Vannevar Bush, dressed in a black suit. He walked toward us with the striking, stunningly beautiful Indian woman who we had first met at the back of the White Hole Project exotic matter containment room on Friday, April 13th. Nisha Singh was wearing a black dress, looking exactly like she had the day we met her—when Bucky whispered to me that he wanted to take her home, so long as she was on our side.

Vannevar walked up to Bucky and shook his hand, giving him a hug. "That's quite a road trip that you took to get here, Bucky!" I think you and your Bad Love Gang wiped out the best of the Russian spies between here and Georgia! I have some good news for you in that regard, and Nisha has new information regarding your upcoming mission to 1942 China. But first, let's all introduce ourselves."

I stepped up and introduced myself as Kevin "Bubble Butt" or "BB" Schafer, indicating that I had already met Nisha as I gave both him and her handshakes. Vannevar replied, "Yes, BB, you and I met by phone on April 12th. It was you and your friend Bowmar who learned how to use the White Hole Project, as I recall. Then you rescued Bucky from being stuck in time."

"We rescued Bucky, and we also brought Bucky's navigator, standing here next to me, back to 1974 with us." I introduced Darby "Pumpkin" Nelson to Vannevar and Nisha, then continued, "And this is Billy 'Willy' Blanchert, who grew up next door to me in Oak Ridge, Tennessee. Willy and I learned how to fly together, when I was fourteen and he was fifteen. The four of us—Bucky, Pumpkin, Willy, and I—are now officially trained and ready as the Panda Bear Squadron, going to meet General Claire Chennault and briefly volunteer for the Flying Tigers in June 1942 at the request of President Roosevelt. It seems that our mission, which Bucky has code named the Denver Project, is leading us to China to secure the continuing secrecy of this Area 51, and to maintain the integrity and future of the White Hole Project. Bucky, Bowmar and I suspect that we will encounter a sister ship to the one we are about to inspect here, and in some way, become involved with the fate of that sister ship. Maybe we are on some kind of a rescue mission. I guess we'll figure that out when we get there."

Vannevar replied, "BB, you, Bucky and Bowmar have put the pieces of this puzzle together remarkably well. Nisha trained in nuclear physics at the prestigious Indian Institute of Science with the renowned physicists C. V. Raman and Homi J. Bhabha. She briefly worked in Chicago with Compton's team, then was transferred to Oak Ridge. That is when I diverted her from joining Martin Whitaker's Manhattan Project team to helping me with the White Hole Project failure analysis. After you briefly detained her on April 13th, she knew that you and your group were making significant progress. She came directly to me and revealed that she had important information to give me, and that she also worked for the Indian Intelligence Bureau—which is closely aligned with the British, as well as Scotland Yard."

"That's a jolly good show there, old chap! I'm glad to know that we are all on the same side!" Pumpkin exclaimed. It brought a moment of levity to our discussion.

Nisha then stated, "Our Indian Intelligence Bureau has been closely aligned with General Chennault and the amazing work that he has done in the defense of China against the Japanese. I was working in India when we first received the news about a possible alien spaceship crash east of Chennault's air base in Kunming, China in June of 1942. For reference, by the late spring of 1942, the Japanese forces had virtu-ally sealed off China from the ground and sea. They had taken over all of China's eastern seaports, from Shanghai in the north to Hong Kong in the south, and around French Indochina to Burma. They had moved up Burma to seal off China from the west. There was no way to effectively get supplies into China, except by air route from India. Allied military supplies were being flown from the Assam Valley in India to Kunming, China across the Himalayas at altitudes approaching twenty thousand feet. This supply flight route from India to China was called the Hump. Chennault understood the critical importance of keeping the Hump active and open, as well as the demands that it placed on aircrews and airplanes."

I enquired, "What does flying over the 'Hump' have to do with our mission to China?"

Nisha patiently continued, "On Thursday, June 18, 1942 at approximately one PM in Kunming, China, one of the Douglas DC-3 Hump transport planes was on its way from India to land at Chennault's air base in Kunming. The plane was headed east on its initial approach to Kunming at an altitude of about 12,000 feet, and the pilot noted that his electrical systems were malfunctioning. As he raised his eyes from his instruments and looked to the northeast, he saw an incredibly bright light shooting through the sky and disappearing beyond the horizon. A few seconds later, his electrical systems normalized again. The pilot did some calculations and made a rough estimate that the crash site was about halfway between Kunming, China and Guilin, China—probably closer to Kunming. After he landed at Chennault's base in Kunming, he described what he saw to Chennault. Later that afternoon, Chennault sent a plane from Kunming to the vicinity of the crash site, but lost contact with that plane. It never returned. When that DC-3 pilot returned to our base in India the following day, he shared this information. That is when our intelligence bureau got involved."

Pumpkin interjected, "I can definitely come up with a flight plan from either Kunming or Guilin along that line, and narrow down a fairly tight zone where we can look for the crash site."

Bucky then enquired, "What else did your intelligence bureau uncover about all this?"

Nisha answered, "Not much more than what Vannevar has already told you, except that General Chennault traveled to Guilin, China on Sunday, June 21, 1942 for meetings about transitioning the AVG Flying Tigers to formally become part of the US military. Finally, we interviewed many eyewitnesses who claimed to have seen a flying saucer leaving the vicinity, between Kunming and Guilin, China, sometime in the evening of Wednesday, June 24, 1942."

I turned to the other Panda Bears. "Gentlemen, I think that we have successfully narrowed down a timeframe and place to meet with General Chennault in China and conduct our mission." I then focused on Vannevar and enquired, "What is the other 'good news' that you mentioned?"

Vannevar was genuinely excited to give us this bit of news. "We have identified the Russian spy that you saw at the K-25 plant on Friday, April 13th. His Russian name is Borya Krovopuskov, and he is known locally in Oak Ridge as Russ Krovo. What do you want us to do with him?" Vannevar handed Krovo's file to Bucky.

I looked at Bucky; he winked and nodded to me to provide the answer. I replied, "Holy shit! You are awesome, Vannevar! That is spectacular news, because we now have the means to secure the White Hole Project in 1975, when we go back to the future. The Bad Love Gang will be so relieved, knowing Krovo and his thugs are off the streets of Oak Ridge, Tennessee."

"Thanks, BB. Should I arrange to have him arrested by Clarke and his team?" Vannevar asked.

"No, no, not at all; do nothing of the sort, Vannevar. This is not to be shared with Colonel Clarke, or anyone else. Bury your investigation and keep it classified for the next thirty years. Detaining or arresting Krovo now would definitely cause a big ripple in time, and the consequences are impossible to calculate. Bucky and I will give Krovo's file to President Ford in 1975, and let him take Krovo and his modern Russian spy cell out of commission—or selectively spy on them for all they're worth!"

Vannevar smiled at me and stated, "I understand. BB, you and Bucky take the file with you; I now consider the case to be closed. What do you say we all go for a little walk now, and take a look inside this hangar?" I noticed Nisha's face starting to glow with excitement, and she had caught Bucky's eyes with a hint of seductiveness. Bucky had been attracted to her since they met and for the moment, he was buying it. They walked together, chatting as we made our way from our parked P-40 Warhawks to the giant hangar entrance doors, which were heavily guarded. As we were walking and gawking, Pumpkin exclaimed, "This place is *ginormous!*"

There were four armed guards at the entrance to the hangar. As we approached, I noticed a sign on the door that read *Hangar 51: Established June 24, 1942.* When we arrived at the door, Vannevar calmly said to one of the guards, "You can take her now; we are finished with her, for the time being." Two of the guards grabbed Nisha Singh's arms as she cried out, "What are you doing? What is the meaning of this?!"

Vannevar retorted, "You have been spying on us since you arrived in Chicago. I let you get this far so that you would tell us all you knew about what happened in China in June 1942. We may be Americans, but we're not stupid."

She pleaded with Bucky for help. "You have the authority, tell him to let me go! I will help you with your mission! I can help you, Bucky!"

This time, Bucky looked at me. I nodded and winked at him. He then confidently declared, "I have the very best help this world has to offer, standing right here with me. I think we can manage on our own." The guards then took her away as she continued to yell that it was wrong, and a mistake.

Vannevar led the four of us through the outer hangar door, and there were Marines all about guarding the inner hangar. As we reached the second hangar door, he said, "I told you that I would have a surprise waiting for you when you got here."

Bucky replied, "You sure delivered on that one, Vannevar." He looked at me with a smirk and said, "I guess I won't be taking her home with me!" Then he asked Vannevar, "What do you plan to do with her?"

"I'm not exactly sure," Vannevar admitted. "She seems to be spying for our 'friends,' but we need to sort that out. We'll work on that while your Bad Love Gang is making your Denver Project's mark on the annals of time."

Passing through the door of the inner hangar, we beheld the magnificence and reality of the alien spaceship that Bucky had discovered and boarded on June 17, 1942 with our own eyes. To Vannevar, I said, "You can rephrase what you just said; that you'll work on that while we are making our mark on the annals of time *and space!*"

CHAPTER TWENTY-FIVE:

THE ROAD TO CHINA

"The journey of a thousand miles starts with a single step."
—Lao Tzu

Friday, June 20, 1975 at 9:00 PM local time,
the White Hole Project, Oak Ridge, Tennessee

The entire Bad Love Gang—including Waldo's wife, Mary—had gathered together at the White Hole Project to see Bucky, Pumpkin, Willy, the Runt, Meatball, the Pud, and me launch on our time-travel mission to Guilin, China to rendezvous with General Claire Chennault, and volunteer for the AVG Flying Tigers. The Bad Love Gang had all returned to 1975 Oak Ridge, Tennessee from our wildly adventurous 1945 time-travel road trip on Monday, April 28, 1975. The following day, Bucky and I had put a call into the White House switchboard with a message to President Gerald R. Ford, along with our callback phone number: "The Denver Project needs you." Amazingly, President Ford had personally alerted his switchboard after he took the oath of office to be on the lookout for a message regarding the "Denver Project." He instructed them to get that message directly and confidentially to him, as it was of the highest priority. Everything that we told him on Sunday, April 15, of 1945 had come true, exactly as we had "predicted." This had left President Ford with an indelible impres-

279

sion of his encounter with us that day, and considerable curiosity as to exactly when he would next hear from us. Within an hour of our call, the phone rang and it was President Ford's Chief of Staff Donald Rumsfeld. He was brief and to the point, telling us that the president was in critical meetings regarding the fall of Saigon, marking the end of the Vietnam War. He scheduled a confidential call between us and President Ford for the following morning.

That night, on the April 29th, 1975 Tuesday evening news, we had all watched TV at Waldo and Mary's house as reports came pouring in that American military helicopters were evacuating hundreds of US civilians and military support personnel, as well as thousands of South Vietnamese citizens, from Saigon—the day before North Vietnamese forces overran the city. It was the longest day of America's longest war, a frustrating and chaotic US departure from an unpopular war. President Ford, who had convened a cabinet meeting at 9:45 AM on April 29, 1975, announced to them that our original intention was to use C-130 transport aircraft for the evacuation, but that shelling of the airport had precluded that approach and helicopters had been substituted for the evacuation in an effort to prevent panic. The president issued a press statement that the evacuation of Saigon had closed a chapter in the American experience. He said, "I ask all Americans to close ranks, to avoid recrimination about the past, to look ahead to the many goals we share, and to work together on the great tasks that remain to be accomplished."

Watching TV that night and witnessing the fall of Saigon, my music brain automatically played **"We Gotta Get Out of This Place,"** released by The Animals in August 1965. The song peaked at number two on the singles chart in the UK and Canada, and number thirteen on the US *Billboard* Hot 100. It was immensely popular with United

States Armed Forces during the Vietnam War—and it was finally coming true on April 29, 1975!

On Wednesday morning, April 30, 1975, Bucky and I received a private call from President Gerald Ford. He started, "Gentleman, I have been waiting to hear back from you for the past thirty years! Betty and I really did spend our honeymoon on the campaign trail. I was never formally elected to get here, and I did have to use my presidential pardon power after taking office. I guess you guys are back to the future now. What can I do for you, Bucky and Bubble Butt? And by the way, where's Waldo?"

Since I had described Ford's future to him in our meeting at NAS Glenview, I led the conversation from our end. "Waldo is at work at the moment, so it is just me and Bucky with you this morning, sir. It's great to hear from you, President Ford. You really don't sound any different from our discussion in Commander Staples' office at NAS Glenview, on that Sunday afternoon in April 1945. It sounds like yesterday was a tough day for you, with the fall of Saigon?"

The president replied, "Yes, BB, it was a tough and very busy day, but the end of the Vietnam War was at hand. We had to improvise to get everyone out; it was a messy process, just like so much of what goes on here in Washington, DC."

"I understand, Mr. President. We got to know President Roosevelt pretty well, and in one of our meetings with him he told us 'I hate getting stung in the ass! It happens to me nearly every day in this damn world of politics, and I've been president for over twelve years!' Someday, Bucky and I will have to share the story behind that quote with you."

Ford replied, "I love that quote! I can really identify with that right now. So, what do you and the Denver Project need from me?"

I got to the point. "The Denver Project has identified a Russian asset here in Oak Ridge, working at the Oak Ridge National Laboratory since late 1944. His Russian name is Borya Krovopuskov, and he is known locally as Russ Krovo. We estimate that he is now about fifty-five years old, and it is conceivable that he holds the record for heading the oldest, longest-standing Soviet Union sleeper cell spy unit in modern history. He is extremely smart and dangerous. He and his local network in the Oak Ridge and Knoxville areas need to be apprehended in order for the Denver Project to remain safe and undetected. However, once you interrogate him and his family, perhaps you can find out a lot more by spying on his network. Obviously, that is up to your judgement. We would very much like for you personally to give this information to the FBI and/or CIA, and keep us and the Denver Project a protected and continuing national secret."

Ford responded, "You guys continue to amaze me, after all these years! I will get this information to the appropriate people as soon as we hang up, so the Denver Project can continue its work in safety. Let's plan to get you discreetly to the White House sometime soon. It will be my treat! Carry on, and call me anytime that you need me."

With the threat of Russ Krovo and his local Russian spy cell out of the way, and the White Hole Project again secure, we spent the next seven weeks diligently preparing for our time-travel trip to 1942 China. This phase of our mission, although its true scope not entirely clear just yet, was to in some way protect the ongoing secrecy of Area 51—and perhaps by extension, the White Hole Project. At 9:00 PM on Friday, June 20, 1975, with Bowmar at the helm of the White Hole Project control panel and the entire Bad Love Gang watching, Bucky, Pumpkin, Willy, the Runt, Meatball, the Pud, me, and the black box were all zapped back in time to Guilin, China.

Sunday, June 21, 1942 at 9:00 AM local time, outside Seven Star Cave, Guilin, China

The time-travel trip seemed a tad longer this time. I had a vision about the alien spaceship that we had seen at Area 51; it had crashed in front of the Great Wall of China, never mind that the Great Wall was nowhere near where we were going. It was a beautiful clear, moonlit night, and I was flying my P-40 Warhawk overhead. I could see the damaged double-hulled flying saucer below, glowing blue-white against the dark of night. The spaceship was comprised of two saucer-shaped hulls, both glowing, on top of one another. The lower hull was 150 feet in diameter; it was connected to the smaller upper hull (about 100 feet in diameter) by a bluish, glowing, hour-glass shaped central core. There was an open doorway visible, with bright white light emanating into the surrounding woods. An apparently human figure stood in the doorway. In one area, the adjacent lower hull had been damaged and was leaking some glowing blue material. *That's exotic matter!* I thought. As soon as that thought crossed my brain, I hit the ground in Guilin, China and came to my senses. The seven of us collected ourselves and the black box, then headed into Seven Star Cave to meet with the famous General Claire Chennault.

Guilin, China is situated on the west bank of the Li River and borders Hunan to the north. The name *Guilin* means Forest of Sweet Osmanthus, which are the numerous fragrant trees located in the region. The city has one of the most naturally beautiful topographies anywhere in the world. The surrounding fantastical landscape is replete with tall, steep mountains, some of which have shapes likened to upside down ice-cream cones. Their slopes are covered with trees, despite the sharp angles and pull of gravity. The terrain is karstic, terrain dotted with caves created by the excavating effects of underground water on massive deposits of soluble rock, such as limestone, gypsum, and dolomite. General Chennault had welcomed these local caves for their natural coolness in the summer months, and for giving them bombproof operation headquarters in Guilin.

On this day in history, Chennault had set up his operations room in Seven Star Cave, where Lieutenant Colonel Tex Sanders was trying to convince the original "nicely-paid" volunteer AVG Flying Tigers to remain in China, as part of the USAAF military taking over the three AVG squadrons on July 4, 1942. Sanders was offering these battle-hardened, seasoned pilots reserve military commissions rather than regular Army commissions in the Air Corps, in addition to a pay cut. Hardly any of those pilots were biting on this insulting offer; only five AVG pilots agreed to stay on after July 4th. Chennault was sitting in the background, puffing away on Camel cigarettes and listening to Tex Sanders conduct the interviews of his trusted pilots. He understood their negative reactions to a less than satisfactory offer to stay on as Flying Tigers, and to stay in the fight.

Bucky led the way and I was right behind him, anxious to meet this legendary figure of WWII US airborne warfare. We walked up to Chennault, and he looked surprised. "I wasn't expecting more outside officers for another ten-twelve days or so." His voice had a bit of a Cajun twang to it; Chennault was born in Texas, but grew up in Louisiana. We also noticed that he spoke a bit loudly. It seemed he was hard of hearing, so we replied to him a bit loudly. His face was worn and wrinkled, earning him the nickname "Old Leatherface." His moniker would have fit in perfectly with the rest of our Bad Love Gang!

Bucky started by introducing all of us, then stated, "Sir, we are here at the specific request of President Roosevelt on a top-secret mission of US national security."

Chennault said, "Oh, hell, Captain Smith! Every goddamned thing we are doing here is a matter of national security."

I wanted to laugh, but I bit my lip. I already liked this guy for his genuine candor, and what I perceived as practicality—something not always found in the ranks of the military. Bucky handed Chennault the letter from FDR, his presidential seal prominently in place. "General, the president asked that we hand deliver this letter directly to you."

This got Chennault's full and undivided attention. He studied the seven of us and the letter in his hand with curiosity and seriousness, then opened the letter and read Roosevelt's handwritten note.

Dear Claire,

The man standing in front of you is Captain Jack "Bucky" Smith. He and his men have my full presidential authority to conduct their top-secret mission, called the Denver Project. Their mission may define the future of our great nation. Give them everything that they need, the best that you have available, and do it without reservation or hesitation. They have my full trust, just as you have, as well.

Very truly yours,

Franklin

When he finished reading, Chennault declared, "Now, that is not exactly what I was expecting! I am going to treasure this letter for the rest of my days, and I am all ears to hear exactly what you want or need from me—so, fire away."

As we all relaxed just a bit, Bucky explained, "We are here to investigate a potential crash site somewhere between here and Kunming that occurred last Thursday afternoon. What can you tell us about that?"

Chennault replied, "Yes, I am very much aware of that. We still don't have an explanation for what happened out there. There were bright lights seen in the sky, despite the fact that the crash happened at about 1:00 PM Thursday afternoon, in the middle of brightest day-light. Our electricity flickered here in Guilin and in Kunming at the time of the event. One of the DC-3 transport pilots, who had been on approach to land in Kunming at that time, gave me his eyewitness report. He believed the crash occurred at about the midpoint between here and Kunming. That afternoon, I sent one of our youngest vol-unteer pilots—a guy named Allen Wright, flying with the Adam and Eves squadron—on a reconnaissance mission to find the crash site. He unexpectedly encountered Jap fighters as he was radioing us his posi-tion, and we believe that he may have been shot down. He has been missing since Thursday night."

Pumpkin enquired, "Can you give me those last known coordi-nates of Wright's reconnaissance flight, sir?"

"I sure can. What else do you boys need?" Chennault queried back.

Bucky responded, "Sir, we need four of your newest P-40E War-hawks, fully loaded and fueled. Two of our men here, Lieutenants Legrande and Eisen, are trained ground crew. They will need tools to make a few adjustments on the planes. Lieutenant Jacobson is our radio expert. Colonel Schafer, Lieutenant Blanchert, Sergeant Nelson, and I will be flying the Warhawks; we are temporarily volunteering as part of the Panda Bear Squadron. We will be getting our planes ready today and tweaking our flight plan, then leaving for the crash site tomorrow morning. We need a place for the seven of us to sleep tonight, and three bunks here on Monday and Tuesday nights. The four of us pilots will be spending some time at the crash site, provided we can find a place to land nearby. All seven of us are planning to depart back to the States late on Wednesday. We have our own trans-portation for that trip."

"Captain, there very well may be Jap ground patrols combing the vicinity of that crash site. I know that the Chinese have sent ground patrols from Kunming to investigate, plus we know that Japanese fighter planes were in that area late Thursday afternoon, when Allen Wright declared an emergency and went missing," Chennault cautioned.

"Yes, sir, understood. We have some experience with fighting on the ground. We brought Thompson machine guns and our Colt service pistols with us. We could use some grenades for good measure, though. By the way, General, now that we are getting to know each other, you can call us by our nicknames: I'm Bucky, Schafer is Bubble Butt or BB, Nelson is Pumpkin, Billy is Willy, Jacobson is the Pud, Eisen is Meatball, and Legrande is the Runt. The code name for our group is the Bad Love Gang; even though we are volunteering for the Panda Bear Squadron, we are also now known as the Bad Love Tigers."

The Pud quipped, "Yeah, we're the seven stars this cave is named after!"

Chennault chuckled at all that and replied, "That's great. I am always good and ready to dispense with formality, especially the kind that the military doles out! You can call me whatever y'all damn well please. All I really care about in this life is getting the job done—and getting results! I can already tell you boys are all over that! Besides, Roosevelt himself sent you to me, so I need to get my job done. Let's go over to the base and I'll set you up with four planes, armed and fueled, along with auxiliary tanks to extend your range and tools for your ground crew. I like the name Bad Love Tigers; it has a nice ring to it!"

CHAPTER TWENTY-SIX:

WHEN WE FIRST MET

"An invisible thread connects those who are destined to meet."
—Chinese Proverb

Monday, June 22, 1942 at 9:00 AM local time,
Guilin, China Allied Air Base

T he Runt and Meatball had juiced our P-40E Warhawks' 1,150 horsepower, Allison V-1710-39 engines with hotter modern spark plugs, ignition contacts, and wiring; the Runt had concocted what he called "liquid white lightning" to add to our fuel tanks. The Pud had us wired for modern, long-range VHF communications. Pumpkin had fine-tuned his navigational flight plan to narrow our search pattern, based on AVG pilot Allen Wright's final radio transmission when he went down. General Chennault provided Bucky, Pumpkin, Willy, and me with a complement of hand grenades as well as arming the four of us with several extra 30-round box magazines for our Thompson machine guns and ammo for our service pistols. The Bad Love Tigers Panda Bear Squadron fired up our engines at 9:00 AM, saluted our ground crew, and followed Bucky to the runway flight line.

The runway at the Guilin airbase was actually better than we expected, and more than a mile long. The Pud had checked with the local ground control, and we were cleared for take-off. Our radios barked, "This is Panda Leader One to Panda Bear Squadron, follow me into the air. Then we will turn west by southwest, toward Kunming. Panda Paw Two will then take the lead as our navigator. Keep your eyes peeled at all times for hostiles. We are at war with the Japanese; let's be the hunters, rather than the hunted. It's time to complete this mission, and as Panda Paw Two would say, 'Tally-ho!'" With that, the four of us roared down the runway and took off, waving our wings to our ground crew watching us below, cheering us into the air over southern China.

The countryside was beautiful below us. As I daydreamed a bit, it dawned on me to share an important fact with the squadron and ground crew. "This is Panda Yin Three, over, and I have a message for us and our ground crew."

The Pud was the first to respond. "Go ahead, BB. I can read you loud and clear."

"Yeah, I was just thinking and wanted to remind you that all of us, and the black box, are being recalled at precisely 5:00 PM Wednesday, local time here in China. Everyone needs to be ready at that time to return. In addition, if we find the crash site today and things work out that we can land nearby, then the ground crew has it easy, because we'll spend the night out here. But we will keep you posted by radio as much as possible."

"That's a big 10-4 there, Bubble Butt! Just remember, 'Live dangerously, have fun, and don't die,' while you're out there in the China boonies!" the Pud exclaimed.

"You got that right." Willy replied. "I'm thinking to myself, 'What the hell am I doing flying over southern China in 1942? How did I get here, and what was I thinking?'"

I replied, "You can blame me, Willy. It's my fault. But it will be a great story to tell someday!"

"Thanks, Bubble Butt; I feel so much better now!" Willy sarcastically bellowed as everyone else chuckled.

We flew a little farther, then Pumpkin spoke on the radio. "Panda Bear Squadron, we are at the northeast corner of our search grid. We are dropping in altitude, slowing down and going into search mode. Follow my lead; we will fly west to the northwest corner of our search grid, then turn south 180 degrees and fly back east. We will crisscross the entire search zone, going west to east and east to west as we gradually move south across the entire zone. As we go back and forth, let's have me and Panda Leader One search with our eyes always to the south. Panda Yin Three and Panda Yang Four, you search with eyes always to the north. As always, keep your eyes peeled for bandits as well. Call out if you see anything that we to need to investigate closer." Three voices answered, "Roger that, Panda Paw Two."

Near the center of our search zone, the alien spaceship had crash landed in a wooded area difficult to spot from the air. It was the "sister ship" of the now abandoned alien spaceship hidden at Area 51, which had crashed in the southwestern Nevada desert at the exact same time on the opposite side of Planet Earth. Both ships were bound for Earth, arriving simultaneously. For reasons that were under active investigation, they had both lost their intergalactic inertial guidance control from their mother planet on their final approach to Earth. Both crews had done their best to manually override their controls once the problem was apparent, with only partial success. The unplanned ultra-high-velocity approach at both ends of the Earth had shattered their hopes of stealthy, undetected visits to our planet, creating spectacular atmospheric entries and forced "landings." The crew of the spaceship that crashed at Area 51 very quickly knew that their vessel had sustained too much damage to fly again. They elected to use its white hole intergalactic transport drive unit to safely return home, leaving their ship behind. The crew of the alien spaceship that had come down in the southern China forest below us had softened their landing on approach to some degree, and sustained less structural damage. They knew they had been seen, and were very busy working to repair the damage; they desired to make their exit from planet Earth with their ship intact. The loss of one spaceship halfway around the planet in North America was problematic enough for this expedition.

Two miles due south of the alien spaceship crash site was injured AVG Flying Tiger pilot Allen Murray Wright, hunkered down in the woods near a protective hillside. Allen grew up in Dyersburg, Tennessee; like Bucky, he was drawn to adventure since childhood. One summer day, he had gone missing and his grandmother was afraid he had drowned in the nearby river. After nightfall, Allen returned home—having caught a ride that day with a stranger, and going for a tour of the countryside. It was only a harbinger of much bigger adventures to come. He graduated from Dyersburg High School in 1937, attended two years of college, and then enlisted in the US Army Air Corps. While stationed at Cochran Field in Georgia, he would sometimes fly through Dyersburg and buzz his grandmother's house at treetop level, while she was hanging clothes to dry outside. She would throw the wash in the air and run for the house! Pursuing his lust for adventure, Allen volunteered for service in China; he became a flight instructor, training cadets for the Chinese Air Force at Yunnanyizhen. In the spring of 1942, he joined the AVG Flying Tigers, and at age twenty-one, became one of the youngest pilots flying with the Adam & Eves squadron.

On Thursday, June 18, 1942, Allen Wright had been sent on a solo reconnaissance mission by Chennault to investigate a potential crash site between Guilin and Kunming, China. There were no military or civilian targets in the crash site area, so Chennault sent one plane, not expecting any Japanese opposition. At 3:30 PM, mainly by sheer luck, Allen spotted a large white circular object in the reported crash zone, partially hidden by trees in the forest below. In his sudden curiosity as to the nature of this finding, and haste to get a closer look, he forgot to visually scan the skies for potential enemies. Allen slowed, descended, and circled the crash site, growing more intrigued and mesmerized as the alien ship came into better view.

Coming from the east at a higher altitude was Japanese squadron leader, Lieutenant Haruki Takahashi of the 84th Independent Flight Wing, who had been sent to investigate the same reported crash site. Takahashi was flying one of two Japanese Nakajima Ki-43 "Hayabusa" aircraft, also called "Oscars" as well as the "Army Zero," because it had a similar appearance to the more famous Japanese Navy Mitsubishi A6M Zero. With him were two brand-new Kawasaki Ki-45 two-seat, twin-engine fighters, called Dragon Slayers, rounding out the squadron of four planes. The new twin-engine Japanese Dragon Slayer was entering this war theater with Japan's hope that it would become a Tiger Slayer. Takahashi pointed to Allen Wright's circling P-40 below, indicating that the hunt was on and he was taking the lead. Allen really never had a fighting chance.

Takahashi slipped up on his tail undetected, and opened fire while the other three Japanese fighters used their altitude advantage to dive and shoot at the lone American. Allen's engine caught fire, and his plane was peppered with bullet holes. He radioed his last position to the base in Guilin in a panic. He knew if he bailed out that the Japs would probably take shots at him while he dangled from his parachute, so he deftly found a place to ditch his damaged, burning plane, two miles south of the alien crash site. His vanquishers watched his burning plane go down, taking him for dead as they circled back to get a better look at the alien spaceship crash site. Low on fuel, they documented the crash site location and headed back to base. In the meantime, Allen Wright's back was badly sprained on impact, but he was able to climb free of his wrecked and burning P-40 Warhawk, taking his flare gun with him. He had been hiding and hoping for a rescue since his near-death disaster on Thursday afternoon. On Monday at about noon, he heard the beautiful sound of the Bad Love Tigers Panda Bear Squadron flying above and coming his way.

Lieutenant Haruki Takahashi returned to base and was debriefed by his superiors. The Japanese were worried that the Chinese and/or Americans were testing some amazing new military technology that had suffered a misfortune. They wanted to get ground troops to the site to inspect it, but the closest asset was a special purpose Japanese reconnaissance patrol, headed by Imperial Japanese Army Sergeant Akito Kobayashi. His team was covertly patrolling to the east of the crash site. It would take him and his squadron of ten men roughly five days to hike west to the crash site, putting them there on or by Tuesday. They would have one or two days at the most to document their findings. Takahashi, on the other hand, was ordered to prepare a bombing mission of the crash site for Wednesday, June, 24, 1942 and congratulated on his confirmed combat victory over the American AVG Flying Tigers.

Already on the ground west of the crash site was a Chinese Special Forces squadron, headed by Chinese agent Li-Ming "Ming" Sun. She was working for the Central Department of Social Affairs (CDSA) headquartered in northern China, where she had trained and exceled in every measurable parameter. She was on assignment in Kunming, China when the alien ship crashed. Ming spoke Mandarin Chinese, Japanese, English, and at least two other languages; she was brilliant, beautiful, and trained to be deadly.

The Chinese CDSA was concerned that this reported crash was related to some new Japanese secret weapon, and had assigned 1st Lieutenant Chaoxiang Ch'eng and his crack special forces squadron of twelve to get Ming to the crash site, ASAP. Ming's orders were to report her detailed findings so that next steps could be planned. Ming and Chaoxiang were working well together and closing in on the location of the crash.

On our third leg through the middle of the search zone, we were flying east to west. Willy and I scanned the area to the north. AVG Flying Tiger pilot Allen Wright, hiding in the woods below, could hear us approaching and knew this was his chance. Slow to move with his injured back, he came out of his hiding place into a clearing and saw the four of us approaching from the east, just south of his position. He timed it perfectly and shot his flare in our direction.

"Holy shit!" I exclaimed. "Do you see that flare?!"

Willy excitedly replied, "I see it, I see it! I wonder if that is coming from the downed Adam and Eves pilot, Allen Wright?"

"BB, you take the lead and guide us to that location."

I led the squadron lower and directly over Allen. We could see him jumping awkwardly and waving his arms wildly. I was totally focused on Allen Wright below, and actively waving my wings at him. Bucky was the first to notice the alien spaceship crash site, two miles north of Allen's position; he peeled off for a moment to get a closer look at the crash site. Pumpkin radioed the Pud with our exact coordinates, and the Pud said, "We're all sending you high-fives right now, and we will let 'Old Leatherface' know that we found his pilot alive."

Willy radioed, "I found Allen's crashed Warhawk; he had barely overshot a decent place for the four of us to land. Follow me in, and let's go help that guy!"

One by one, the Bad Love Tigers Panda Bear Squadron followed Willy in for a landing in the fairly flat field that Allen Wright had identified in his effort to crash land his heavily-damaged P-40 Warhawk. Allen's plane had overshot the end of the field and come to an abrupt stop in a rugged area. The force of that impact had injured his back. We pulled our Warhawks to the edge of the field near the tree line so that we could hide and camouflage the planes. I radioed the Pud and told him, "The Pandas have landed; I repeat, the Pandas have landed. Yin and Yang are out to find some balance and harmony." We all took our gear, guns and grenades as we exited the planes and went to meet the downed pilot, Allen Wright.

We hiked over to Allen, who was looking a bit worn and tired but thrilled to see us. He had a medium build, dark wavy hair, and thick eyebrows. Allen sported a mustache and spoke with a slight southern accent, which we recognized as being from our home state of Tennessee. He saw that we were all officers and saluted us as we reached him. Bucky introduced all of us, along with our nicknames. We found a place to sit and rest, then gave Allen a canteen of water to drink and a sandwich, plus a candy bar that we had packed. He was famished, and ate and drank between excited statements. "You guys are an incredible sight for sore eyes! I must have sprained my back bad when I crashed on Thursday. It still hurts like hell if I walk too far. In fact, it was hurting bad when I was jumping and waving at you, but I wanted you to see me more than anything!" He shared the story of his surprise ambush by the Japanese fighter squadron late Thursday afternoon, and described their planes. Then he asked, "Did you guys get a look at that flying saucer that crashed a couple miles north of here? That thing is crazy; it glows so bright at night that you can see the glow from here. By the way, are you four new to the AVG? I don't recall ever seeing you before."

Bucky replied, "Yes, Allen, that flying saucer is exactly why we are here. We are part of a top-secret military operation called the 'Denver Project.' We have to get to that spaceship and do what we can to protect its secrecy—and we only have two days to accomplish that objective. We know that there are friendly Chinese patrols on their way from Kunming, in the west. If it works out, we will get you into their hands to return you to the AVG airbase in Kunming. We suspect that the Japanese have also sent ground forces to investigate, and we know that they are planning to bomb the alien ship sometime Wednesday afternoon. We intend to intercept that mission, and terminate their ambitions before they get here. We will be leaving on Wednesday as well. No matter what happens, Allen, you must keep what happens here a secret. Take it to your grave! Our mission, and the Denver Project, are of vital importance to US national security."

"Captain Smith, as far as I am concerned, you and your men are angels sent from heaven. I thought I was gonna die out here. You saved my life, so your secret is good as gold with me! I am a little slow on my feet, with my back hurting so badly, and I sure don't want to slow you down any. I can stay here while you guys do your work. I do recommend that you go spy on that spaceship after dark tonight. You can't miss it; it glows so brightly! Do you have any extra guns or ammo? All I have is my pistol?"

Bucky nodded. "We have an extra clip for your service pistol, and we can give you a couple of our hand grenades. Hopefully you won't need any of that, though. We are going to eat some lunch, then go scout out the areas east and west of the crash to get the lay of the land. That is a great idea you had, to check out the crash site tonight after dark. That's the plan!"

Monday, June 22, 1942 at 8:00 PM local time,
alien spaceship crash site in South China,
between Kunming and Guilin

During the afternoon and before dusk, Bucky, Pumpkin, Willy, and I had thoroughly scouted out the east and west approaches to the alien spaceship crash site. There was a large protective and fairly steep hillside to the north of the site. To the east of the crash zone, the easiest approach to the alien spaceship was through a shallow valley along a creek bed. If any Japanese ground forces were coming from the east, that would be their most likely path to the crash site. We had also thoroughly familiarized ourselves with the way to and from the crash site, as well as Allen Wright's hide-out position; we would know that route day or night. We had camouflaged and hidden our P-40E Warhawks well, positioning them facing out of the woods that lined the field where we landed. They would be ready to go on Wednesday.

Allen was doing fine, feeling a bit better and stronger with the food and hydration that we provided. As dusk fell, he stayed at his hideout while the four of us made our way discreetly to some shrubbery in a grove of trees about forty yards south of the crash site, where we were spying with our binoculars. The sun had set at 7:32 PM local time, so it was dark when we located the ship. As we had seen with our own eyes at Area 51—and I had seen in my vision in the White Hole time tunnel—the alien spaceship directly in front of us was a double hulled flying saucer, glowing brightly against the night in these, dark, remote woods of southern China. The ship's glow lit up the immediate area like a baseball park at night. The spaceship was comprised of two saucer-shaped hulls both glowing white and "on top of one another." The lower hull was 150 feet in diameter and connected to the smaller upper hull, which was about 100 feet in diameter, by a bluish, glowing, hour-glass shaped central core. We knew this central core was lined with exotic matter, similar to the connected upper and lower racetracks at the White Hole Project. In one area, the lower hull had been damaged and looked to be partially repaired, but exotic matter still leaked from a crack in the outer hull. As we looked at the spaceship, Pumpkin whispered, "These blokes must be of British alien descent, because they drive double decker spaceships!" This was a reference to double-decker buses in Pumpkin's home town of London, England, the first of which were horse-drawn and introduced in 1847. This brought some much-needed comic relief, even though we could not laugh out loud.

Suddenly, about 20 feet to the left of the crack in the lower, outer hull, one of the lower hatch entryways flew open in an instant. Brilliant white light emanated from the interior of the ship, spilling out into the dark of night. We stared at the open hatch, and out walked a feminine-shaped alien in the tightly fitting clothing that Bucky had previously described when sharing the details of his first alien encounter with us. She was pulling a small cart, with some type of container and equipment on board. Her head was covered from behind and on the sides with a snug hood, so we couldn't see any hair, but her face was uncovered and we could make out her eyes, nose and mouth. Really, from what we could see, she looked human, just a bit on the thin side—but I had seen thinner models on TV, walking the runways of New York fashion shows.

She turned left out of the hatch, pulled her cart to the crack in the lower, outer hull, and went to work repairing the crack with some of the equipment from her cart. There was a small but bright bluish-white glow coming from the tip of device she was using, and an occasional "spark," but it was definitely not what we would call "welding." It appeared to be rather tedious, and slow going. We watched her work for about 40 minutes, then she took a break. Sitting down next to her cart, she appeared to be taking a drink from something that resembled a thermos bottle. At that moment, as I was watching her relax and take a break from her repair duties, I was overcome with the desire to try to go make contact with her. I removed my Thompson machine gun from my shoulder, then removed my Colt pistol from my holster and handed them both to Bucky. He looked at me and softly whispered, "What the hell are you doing, BB?"

"I'm going to meet her, that's what I'm doing!" I exclaimed in a very determined, serious whisper, looking into Bucky's eyes. Pumpkin and Willy witnessed the exchange as well.

Bucky protested, "If anyone goes, it should be me; I've approached them before."

I answered, "Yeah, that's true...but they were running from you. I'm ten years younger than you; maybe they won't be so intimidated by a teenager."

"They weren't running from me; they were running to get away from the military!" Bucky was a little pissed at me, but I continued to press my case.

"You were running with your Colt pistol in your hand. What if you have a reputation of being a cowboy with them? You did go to high school at the 'home of the Cowboys,' Bucky!"

Bucky was equally mad and trying not to smile as he shot back, "BB, you are just incorrigible! So, what's your plan?"

"I'm gonna hum and maybe sing a little earth tune while I nonchalantly stroll up to her and try to make her acquaintance. Music is the universal language."

Willy blurted out, "That is so you, Bubble Butt! I can totally see you doing that! You're totally crazy, but I can see you doing that! What song is it gonna be?"

I whispered, "I'll let you play 'Name that Tune' while I go for it." Without further debate, I rose from my position, cleared the concealing vegetation we were hiding behind, and started making my way directly to the alien. The night was still and very quiet as I stepped into the clearing carved in the woods by the alien ship's forced landing. I started humming and then gently singing the song **"Stand by Me,"** by Ben E. King. This hugely popular song, one of my all-time favorites, was released in April 1961. It had hit number one on the US R&B chart and number four on the US *Billboard* Hot 100. Ben E. King had left his successful music group, the Drifters, over a contract dispute and was debating going solo versus working in his father's restaurant. One night, while playing his guitar in his bedroom, he adapted the song from a gospel hymn by Charles Albert Tindley, which was based on an Old Testament Psalm and published in 1905. At this moment in the dark, quiet, south China boonies, the song "Stand by Me" was all that stood between me and the female alien I was slowly approaching.

As I got closer, humming and singing, my music brain was taking over. Soon I was half-dancing with a pretend partner, holding my hands open as I sang and moving my head to the music. I even did a little twirl, imagining that I was dancing at a wedding reception. I guess you could say that I was putting on a little a cappella song and dance performance on my approach to the alien. Bucky, Pumpkin, and Willy were mesmerized by my unrehearsed craziness; the alien sat and watched me draw near without making any attempt to return inside the spaceship. When I was six feet away, she stood up and faced me with a subtle but warm smile on her blue face. I immediately stopped my performance and froze. We studied each other in total silence for what seemed like a long time.

At five foot, ten inches tall, I was looking directly into her eyes; we were the same height. Her clothing was made of a shiny, metallic silvery-white material and fit like a glove, covering her body; only her hands and the front of her face showing. Her skin was blue in color, judging by the hue of her exposed face and hands. Her complexion was perfect and if I had to guesstimate her age in earth years, I would say 25–30. Not really knowing what to do next because I was deep in uncharted waters, I said, "Hi, I'm Kevin Schafer, but you can call me Bubble Butt, or BB."

She replied with a veiled smile, "I know you, BB. We've met before. My name is Blue Nova One. I enjoyed your entrance."

Astonished, I had to clear my throat. "You speak English and we have met before?"

She responded, "I don't really speak English, but you can hear me in English." I was having trouble wrapping my brain around that statement, and wished Bowmar was there to respond to that. "I have met you, but you do not yet perceive to have met me. That will change in due time, and you will understand then."

"My team and I are here to help you. You and this ship are in danger," I warned. "The Japanese Air Force is coming to bomb you Wednesday afternoon. We need to get you out of here in less than two days, before that happens. How can I, or we, help you?" While speaking, I noticed some glowing blue exotic matter on the ground below the crack in the outer hull.

"This expedition did not go exactly as planned. We are in agreement with you that our departure is necessary. We have been making repairs to our ship, but your timetable is tight." Blue Nova One then handed me what amounted to a fancy shovel from her cart and said, "I'll keep working on the damage to the exterior, and you can shovel the glowing blue matter into this container." She pointed to the box on the cart.

"I hope... You don't mind having some Earth dirt mixed in with the blue stuff?" I queried as I got started with the shovel. "Why are you alone out here and doing the hard labor, Blue Nova One?"

"Having some Earth dirt, as you say, will be a source of interest back home, so no problem there, BB. Repairing the outer hull is essential for our departure and safe return, and I am the best of our small crew at this function. The males are working on damaged machines inside. We divided the labor to make the repairs most swiftly. I do understand your question; I can be both female and strong, just like our males can be both male and supportive or kindhearted. Our roles are defined by ability and aptitude."

"How would you like to join the Bad Love Gang, Nova?" I teasingly asked as I shoveled the blue exotic matter and dirt into the square container, getting it done efficiently.

"Bubble Butt, you haven't changed a bit since we first met! I know Bucky and Pumpkin over there, behind the bushes, but I don't know the other guy yet. What I do know is that the Bad Love Gang members I have met so far are all certainly unique and fun to be around. And your best-friend, Bowmar... I miss him a lot!"

I was blown away "You knew we were watching from the bushes? You know Bucky, Bowmar, and Pumpkin? What is going on here?" I enquired in rapid-fire fashion.

"Help me with the hull repair over here," she replied. I held the body of the machine she was using while she reached a hard-to-get crack with the tip of her repair wand. She passed the wand methodically and slowly across the edges of the damaged hull, and it was as if the metal was being reconstituted before my eyes. She answered my questions as she worked. "Our perceptions are keen; I knew the four of you were there, and not a threat to me or my repair work out here. When we meet again under different circumstances, you will understand how I know some of you. And so you understand, there is a solid portion of the hull material in that part of the machine you are holding. I am applying the molecular matrix of that material out of the tip of the applicator to complete the sound repair of the hull."

We worked together for a while longer while my mind raced in many directions. I was really enjoying working with Nova. As we completed the hull repairs and sealed all of the blue exotic matter safely inside the square container, Blue Nova One said, "Call your friends over here and introduce me."

I shouted and waved for the group to join me and introduced them all to Blue Nova One. She addressed each of us in an interesting way. "Bucky and Pumpkin, it is great to see you both again; BB will try to explain what that means. Bucky, you were the first Earthling to travel in time. That is historic, and you are fulfilling your destiny. Pumpkin, your amazing navigational skills put you in a class by yourself. Willy, it's nice to meet Goondoggy's brother! You must have inherited all the fear from your parents, because Goondoggy has none; we are still trying to grasp that! Your heart will take you a long way, and your words of caution are needed. BB, your love of strategy and adventure, sense of humor, and music brain are a crazy combination! Maybe I'll take you up on your offer some day."

Before any of us could think to speak, she continued. "Let me give you some help to complete your mission. Your Chinese friends will arrive first, from the west, early tomorrow afternoon. The Japanese aggressors will arrive shortly thereafter from the east, giving you only a brief time to prepare. We have eyes in the sky monitoring the timing and approach of both parties, but despite our methods, we cannot fully predict human behavior. We will make every effort to complete our repairs and leave here by Wednesday, before the Japanese Air Force arrives. I am needed inside now; my work out here is done, but we have much to do inside. Thank you, BB, for your assistance tonight, and thanks to all of you for being here. Goodbye."

We stood there lost in wonder, awed as we said goodbye. Blue Nova One pulled her cart back into the spaceship, and the door closed behind her in a flash. We then returned to Allen Wright, and I briefed the three of them regarding all that was said and my thoughts about how and why she knew us before we knew her.

CHAPTER TWENTY-SEVEN:
BAD LOVE TIGERS

"The more you sweat in practice, the less you bleed in battle."
—Chinese Proverb

Tuesday, June 23, 1942 at 1:00 PM local time,
South China forest, west of alien spaceship crash site

Leaving Allen Wright at his hideout, Bucky, Pumpkin, Willy, and I made our way to a location west of the alien spaceship crash site. Fully armed, we had our walkie talkies and carried an American flag to use when we identified ourselves to the incoming Chinese military patrol. We positioned ourselves at different vantage points and scanned to the west with binoculars, looking for the inbound Chinese ground patrol. We discussed and rehearsed how we would know Ming, but she would be meeting us for the first time. It remained to be seen how Bucky would save her life, but I encouraged Bucky not to think too much about it and react to the circumstances by reflex and with spontaneity. Willy was the first to spot the incoming Chinese Special Forces squadron, led by Chinese Army 1st Lieutenant Chaoxiang Ch'eng and Chinese agent Li-Ming "Ming" Sun. They would have to come up a slight rise to get to our location, so I decided to attach our American flag to a tree branch and wave it back and forth over my head to get their attention.

Lieutenant Chaoxiang Ch'eng was the first of their squadron to see me waving the American flag. Not wanting to take any chances of a deceitfully orchestrated Japanese ambush, Ming insisted that Chaoxiang and his squadron stand back and cover her while she walked up the rise to meet us. In the same fashion, Bucky came into plain view with me while Pumpkin and Willy discreetly covered us. When Ming was 25 yards away, we walked towards her until we were face to face.

Ming was the first to speak. "You are both American officers?"

Bucky responded, "I am glad you speak good English and yes, we are American officers and pilots, working with General Claire Chennault and the Flying Tigers." He introduced us and she introduced herself in return. "We flew to this location yesterday, and have rescued a downed AVG Flying Tiger pilot named, Allen Wright. Our P-40 Warhawks are nearby. This may sound crazy, but there is an alien spaceship that crash landed just west of here; we were sent here to help ensure the safety of that vessel until it could depart. The Imperial Japanese Air Force will be here tomorrow afternoon to bomb this site, and we intend to ruin their plans. However, the Japanese Army has also sent an expeditionary squadron on the ground, coming from the east, and they will be here very soon. We need your help to stop them, and can take you to the place where we expect them to come. We do not have much time to get ready."

Ming replied, "Show me the rest of your men."

Knowing that Ming actually did work for the Chinese, Bucky was able to comply without fear that this was a trap. He called Pumpkin and Willy to come out from hiding. Bucky introduced them and said, "There are four of us, and we have four planes. The other pilot we rescued is injured and in hiding. He was shot down by the Japanese last Thursday, and his plane was destroyed when he crash landed. When we leave here tomorrow to fight the incoming Japanese planes, we will need for you to take our injured pilot back to Kunming with you, and return him to General Chennault's squadron."

Ming waved for Lieutenant Chaoxiang Ch'eng and her Chinese Special Forces squadron to join us. As they came out of cover and up the rise to meet us, Ming enquired, "Can you take us to the alien spaceship crash site? That is why we were sent to this location. My instructions are to document what happened here. Then we will help you to stop the Japanese Army forces coming this way."

Knowing it was fair trade, Bucky answered, "Yes, we will take you directly to the crash site. The aliens have patched the damage to the outer hull of their ship and are now completing repairs inside. Once they complete those repairs, then they will be leaving—hopefully before the Japanese Air Force arrives tomorrow. We really need to move it; I don't want to lose the element of surprise over the Japanese ground forces, and we know they will be here soon. Once you see the spaceship and its location, you can go back to it after we deal with the Japanese. We must repel the incoming Japanese ground troops, or tomorrow will never come!"

Ming agreed. She called her squadron together and explained the plan of action in Mandarin. After speaking to Lieutenant Ch'eng and his men she enquired, "How do you know so much about the status of the Japanese plans?"

Bucky promptly answered, "We have our own sources of intel." He did not want to explain that we had met one of the aliens, much less that she spoke English and gave us intel about the incoming Japanese ground forces! Ming accepted Bucky's straightforwardness and we proceeded east, with our group leading the way to the alien spaceship crash site. Marching to the crash site were eighteen allies: the four of us, Chinese agent Li-Ming "Ming" Sun, 1st Lieutenant Chaoxiang Ch'eng, and his Special Forces squadron of twelve men.

None of us understood Mandarin, but once we arrived at the crash site it was obvious our Chinese friends were awestruck and flabbergasted at the unearthly sight of the spaceship. The Mandarin was flying at warp speed! Ming then let her guard down and warmed up to us, thanking us for bringing them directly to the crash site. "General Chennault and his Flying Tigers are famous warriors here in China; they are revered by our people and by our military. The skies over Kunming are safe because the Flying Tigers make their home there. It will be an honor to fight alongside you against the Japanese. We will prevail, or we will die fighting; we will not stop fighting until our enemy has been destroyed."

She immediately turned to address her squadron. As she spoke to them in Mandarin, I nudged Bucky, with Pumpkin and Willy looking on in anticipation. Using my best John Wayne impersonation and body language I said, "Well, listen here, Pilgrim; when you come against trouble, it's never half as bad if you face up to it. And another thing—when you stop fighting, that's death!"

Pumpkin joined in the moment of fun with his British version of John Wayne, saying, "I'm not the sort of bloke to back away from a fight!"

Willy finished it off with probably his first ever attempt to impersonate John Wayne, but the quote fit him perfectly. "All battles are fought by scared men who'd rather be someplace else."

When Ming finished her Mandarin inspirational session, her team let out a battle cry in unison. Now we were all pumped! She looked at Bucky and said, "We are ready, Captain. Lead the way to the battleground." I then led the way to the east of the crash zone while Bucky walked nearest to Ming and Lieutenant Ch'eng, getting to know them better now that mutual trust had been established. The eighteen of us were all spread out, being careful not to walk in a tight grouping. I led the group to the site of the shallow valley along the creek bed, which we suspected that any Japanese ground forces coming in from the east would use as their most likely path to access the crash site. We were exactly correct in our assessment in that regard, but had missed the ideal window of opportunity.

The Japanese reconnaissance patrol, headed by Imperial Japanese Army Sergeant Akito Kobayashi, was coming toward us from the east along the creek bed. His squadron of ten had doubled in size, with twenty men; they had been joined by another reconnaissance patrol during their five-day hike to get here. They did not have much time to prepare, but one of their forward scouts had seen us first. Kobayashi had sent a sniper to the adjacent hillside, and the rest of his team fanned out within the fairly tight valley to lie in wait and execute their ambush.

It was 3:30 PM and the sun was to our backs in the west. Leading the way, I noticed the sunlight reflecting off a small object roughly seventy-five yards ahead of us (probably the lens of a Japanese soldier's eyeglasses) and immediately held up my right fist for our squadron to halt. Bucky, Ming, and Ch'eng were all standing 10–12 feet apart, with Ch'eng to the far left. In that instant, the Japanese sniper's first shot rang out and a bullet hit Ch'eng in the middle of his chest. Ming and Bucky both saw Ch'eng flail and fall as the sniper quickly chambered the next round, his bolt action rifle instantly ready for his next shot. He had planned to walk his shots, firing from Ch'eng to Ming to Bucky in rapid succession. Bucky instantly realized it was the work of a sniper. Ming paused ever so briefly, then started to turn toward Ch'eng with the thought that she would try to help him. Bucky moved swiftly to his left without a moment's hesitation, and literally dove to tackle Ming. He took her out of the next bullet's path with his arms stretched straight out, just like in his high school football days. The sniper's second bullet grazed the back of Bucky's right shoulder/scapula, and he winced as he and Ming hit the ground together. Ming's and Bucky's eyes met as they landed and she said, "That bullet was meant for me; you saved my life."

"Yes, that was close!" Bucky exclaimed. He touched the back of his right shoulder with his left hand, pulling back to see blood on his fingers. I had seen the muzzle flash of the sniper's second shot, and immediately sprayed that general area with the first 30-round box clip from my Thompson machine gun. All hell broke loose, with everyone in our group taking cover as shots flew in both directions. I started to belly crawl over to Bucky's position and as I did, a small group of Japanese soldiers charged our position like crazy men thinking they were heroes; they were mowed down by heavy fire from our side. Ten minutes into the fight, I reached Bucky. By then, the two sides were at a temporary stalemate with both sides intermittently firing while trying to move closer, into better tactical positions.

When I reached Bucky, I saw the blood on his shoulder. "I understand that you're hard to kill, but why the hell do you keep getting hurt? What the hell is wrong with you?!" I demanded, exasperated.

"Shut-up, BB. You're not helping matters!" he exclaimed with a thin smile. "Listen, BB, I have an idea how to win this battle. But you need to take this order and literally run with it, using your sprinter's legs and Bubble Butt adrenaline."

"OK, Bucky, what do you have in mind?"

He handed me one of our walkie talkies and said, "Take this and run to your plane like you are Jesse Owens. Get your ass in the air, and let me know when you are close. We will start to retreat just before you get here; the Japanese will think they are winning and begin to chase us. Come in from the west, fly down this valley with the sun at your back, and strafe the hell out of those bastards with all six guns blazing, just like we practiced over and over again at the Lowry Bombing and Gunnery Range in Colorado. Once you mow most of them down, we will reverse course and mop up the rest—if they even stay in the fight, knowing that we have air power on our side, especially out here in the middle of nowhere."

"Roger that, Captain Denver!" I replied as I grabbed the walkie talkie. "Give me some cover so I can clear the area and get to the plane!"

Bucky yelled to Willy and Pumpkin, "BB is headed for his plane! Give him cover when I start firing!" Bucky rose up and started spraying the Japanese positions with .45-caliber machine gun bullets, and Willy and Pumpkin did the same. Three Thompson machine guns drenched the enemy's location with lead as I began the sprint to my P-40 Warhawk, parked two miles to the southwest. I knew the way through the forest, recognizing trails that we had identified or established over the past twenty-four hours—especially when I turned south, and came to Allen Wright's hideout.

Allen heard me coming. He met me on the trail and said he could hear the gunfire in the distance. I stopped very briefly to partially catch my breath and explain to Allen that we and our Chinese friends were in a ground battle with the Japanese. Despite his back pain, he understood that we were fighting for our lives and wanted to help. I told him he could direct me out onto the field to take off. I started running again, and Allen followed behind as best he could.

When I got to my P-40 Warhawk, I quickly brushed off the camouflaging branches and leaves before I climbed into the cockpit and fired that mother up! Less than 25 minutes had elapsed since I left the battlefield. My heart was racing, but my mind was focused. The engine started flawlessly; I warmed it up quickly at 1000 rpm, and checked the operation of my flaps. The radiator temperature hit 80 degrees Celsius; I checked the engine and magnetos at higher rpm, and reset the propeller switch to the automatic position. By then, Allen was on the scene. I waved at him with my left arm outside the cockpit, then rocked my forearm and wrist back and forth with a trigger fist, index finger pointing to the field to taxi and go. Allen led me out of the western edge of the forest and onto the field. When he knew I was in the center of the field, he held up his left hand straight up and pointed south with his right arm and hand. I made the turn south as he knelt down and moved his right hand back and forth, pointing south down the field for me to go. Allen and I saluted each other as I made the turn south. When I opened the throttle, the Runt's and Meatball's tweaks to the Allison engine and fuel mixture came to life. I was up and running in an instant, with the engine roaring loud and strong. The tail came up seconds later, and I could see clearly down the field. Once I was in the air, I retracted the landing gear and tailwheel, then raised my flaps. I made a 180-degree turn to the west and then to the north, and was on my way to the battlefield.

Heading north, I radioed Bucky on the battlefield. "Panda Leader One, this is Panda Yin Three, over!"

Bucky's reply barked and crackled back at me. "Panda Yin Three, we have lost some of our Chinese friends, and the battle is intense! What is your ETA to mow these enemy bastards down?"

"I'll be there in five to seven minutes. Make your retreat now; I repeat, make your retreat now!" I found myself yelling into the radio. I passed over the alien spaceship below as I was flying northward. Looking to my right at that moment, I then knew my exact approach east to the creek bed and the valley of the battlefield. I made a 270-degree turn to the west, south, and then back east and was pointed straight down the valley. I shouted at Bucky on the radio again. "Bucky, when you hear my plane approaching from the west, shoot a flare straight up from your position. I will strafe the hell out of everything east of your flare!"

"Got it, BB! Give them the fires of hell, right up the ass!"

Imperial Japanese Army Sergeant Akito Kobayashi, commanding the Japanese squadron, saw his enemy in full retreat running to the west. Thrilled with the imminent prospect of total victory, he screamed out the order to "attack" to his remaining troops; eight were dead or mortally injured, with only Kobayashi and twelve soldiers left to stay in the fight.

With Kobayashi leading the charge, the remaining Japanese troops rose up and gave chase with him, stampeding down the creek bed and yelling at top of their lungs as they ran, shooting at our retreating squadron.

Bucky heard the drone of the P-40 Warhawk Allison engine approaching from the west and stopped for an instant to fire his flare gun straight up, then resumed his retreat for another fifty yards. I saw his flare on my incoming approach and angled my P-40 to make the strafing run. Then Bucky yelled at the squadron, "NOW! TURN AND ATTACK!"

Just as Bucky gave that command on the ground, I opened fire with all six .50-caliber machine guns blazing simultaneously. Our intense strafing practice in Colorado had paid off. Japanese Sergeant Akito Kobayashi looked up, staring hard into the western sun. He couldn't believe his ears; there was the sound of a plane coming directly at him and his remaining troops (who were now exposed and on the run *into* unexpected oncoming trouble), making a low-altitude pass from the west. An instant later, he couldn't believe his eyes. He was staring at the incoming shark mouth and teeth of a Flying Tigers P-40 Warhawk, coming out of the sun with all six wing-mounted .50-caliber machine guns firing in harmony, muzzles flashing steadily. That was his last visual as he and nearly all his remaining team went down in a hailstorm of bullets raining from above.

Bucky, Pumpkin, Willy, Ming, and the remaining five Chinese troops all loudly cheered as I passed over their heads, then watched the decimation of Sergeant Kobayashi and his troops. One or two of the Japanese troops who were well behind Kobayashi and spared from death turned and ran eastward in retreat. The battle was over. Bucky radioed to me, "No need to make a second pass, BB; you did good. Mission accomplished! You can return to base."

Ming actually hugged Bucky and said, "I owe you my life! Thank you for thinking and acting so quickly. What can I do to return the favor?"

Bucky answered, "Two things: Return our pilot Allen Wright safely to Chennault's command at Kunming Air Base, and somehow minimize your description or explanation of the alien spaceship in your official report, swearing your surviving men to secrecy. The Japanese Air Force will be here tomorrow afternoon at about this time to bomb the alien ship. You need to get away from here before then. We will be fighting from the air tomorrow to thwart the Japanese ambitions."

Ming was actually taken by and attracted to Bucky at this point, and agreed. "I will do as you ask, and you have my word of honor. I hope that our paths cross again in the future."

"I am certain of that, Ming," Bucky said with a smile, in complete confidence.

I had circled back toward the landing field and radioed the Pud on the VHF radio while I was still airborne, hoping he was listening: "Panda Pud Five, this is Panda Yin Three; do you read me? Panda Pud Five, this is Panda Yin Three; do you read me?... over."

The Pud responded, "I gotcha, Panda Yin Three. What's your status out there?"

"We made contact with our primary target last night, and eliminated an enemy ground threat today. Tomorrow, we have an air battle to win before heading home. You and the ground crew need to be ready to go as planned tomorrow, and we will see you at the home of the Wildcats," I said, a reference to our high school mascot and Oak Ridge, Tennessee. "Tell the Runt and Meatball that their mechanical work has been outstanding! Chennault's pilot, Allen Wright, will be returning to the Kunming Air Base with some Chinese friends of ours in a few days."

"Roger all that, Panda Yin Three. Remember the last two words of our motto: 'Don't die!'"

"See you tomorrow at home, Pud. Over and out."

Wednesday, June 24, 1942 at 4:15 PM local time, South China
airspace, above and to the east of the alien spaceship crash site

Lieutenant Haruki Takahashi, of the Imperial Japanese Air Force 84th Independent Flight Wing, had been to the alien spaceship crash site one week ago, scoring a victory over AVG Flying Tiger pilot Allen Wright. He had been ordered by his superiors to plan a bombing mission of the strange, downed airship crash site for this day. Imperial Japanese Army Sergeant Akito Kobayashi, commanding the Japanese ground forces approaching the site, had not been heard from since Tuesday morning, as they were getting very close to the crash site. Takahashi had waited until late Wednesday afternoon to give Kobayashi the maximum amount of time to do his work. Coming from the east at an altitude of 15,000 feet, Lieutenant Takahashi was again flying one of two Japanese Nakajima Ki-43 Hayabusa fighter aircraft, also called Oscars. This time there were four brand new Kawasaki Ki-45 two-seat, twin-engine Dragon Slayers with him as fighter escorts to the four Kawasaki Ki-48s. Known among Allied forces as the Lily, the twin-engine medium bombers flew at 10,000 feet altitude, below and slightly ahead of the Ki-45s, rounding out the squadron of ten total planes. Takahashi felt that he had, if anything, over-planned for the mission, since the bombing target was a single large airship of some strange type that had crashed in the middle of nowhere and was of uncertain strategic interest.

Bucky, Pumpkin, Willy, and I had been in the air for over an hour. We were flying in two groups, with Willy and I circling at 75 miles east of the alien ship crash site while Bucky and Pumpkin flew 125 miles to the east of the crash site. All of us were at 20,000 feet altitude, searching below for the Japanese Air Force bombing squadron that we knew would be approaching from the east in the late afternoon. We doubted that they were expecting any opposition whatsoever, and believed that we held the element of surprise. On the other hand, we suspected that we would be outnumbered—which would to some degree mitigate our element of surprise advantage. It was a warm summer day and partly cloudy, which we hoped to take advantage of for cover and hiding. Pumpkin was the first to spot the incoming Japanese bomber squadron with escorting fighter planes.

"This is Panda Paw Two to Panda Bear Squadron, over. There is a squadron of ten enemy bogies approaching from the east, well below us, with four Lily bombers low and six fighters covering above them. Four of the fighters are twin-engine, and I think two single-engine Oscars round out the six. It's time for us to pull a blinder on these bastards!" That was a British phrase for skillfully and flawlessly achieving something difficult.

Bucky immediately radioed back, "Good work, Panda Paw Two! Here's the plan, Panda Bear Squadron. We have the element of surprise, and we are going to take it to the bank today! Panda Paw Two and I will stay out of sight and high above the six trailing Japanese fighter planes that are protecting the bombers, getting in position above and behind them as they go by. Bubble Butt, you and Willy are going to come down out of the western sun and attack the four bombers head-on. Bubble Butt, you take the lead bomber—and take him down on your first pass. Focus on the front of the plane, and don't miss; blow that son of a bitch to smithereens! We want the lead bomber going down in a blaze of glory to strike fear in the hearts of the three other bombers."

"Willy, those four bombers will be flying in a diamond formation, protecting each other. You take the bomber on the left wing of the lead as you cover BB's wing from the right and behind. Your instructions are the same: Focus your gunfire on the front of the bomber ahead of you, and both you and BB pull up at the last moment. You have the advantage of surprise, and coming straight at them out of the sun behind you. Those Ki-48 Lily bombers are only defended by the equivalent of three thirty-caliber machine guns, with one gun in the nose. They can't see you well in the sun and you are closing the distance fast, flying at each other with a closure rate in excess of five hundred miles per hour, coming head on. Don't be afraid; remember all the head-on passes we practiced in Colorado; some of those had closure rates of six hundred miles per hour."

"While BB and Willy are attacking the bombers head on, the six fighters will see them from above. It will be a complete surprise, our planes suddenly materializing before their eyes out of the sun. Their focus will be on BB and Willy, and protecting their bombers. Without the bombers, their mission is done; they can't let that happen. They will split up in some fashion to go after BB and Willy. BB and Willy, after you both pull up from your head on run at the bombers, climb at full power and look up to your east. The fighters will be diving down toward you, head on. Both of you pick a fighter plane to your right as you are climbing and take them on! Pumpkin and I will appear on their tails, coming from above and behind them. We will stay to our right as we come down from our altitude advantage. Pumpkin and I will get at least two of the fighters, because they won't even know we are behind them. If we all do our jobs and use our element of surprise well, we should eliminate four to six of their planes out of the gate—making the rest of this fight fairer. Whatever we do after that, we have to destroy the bombers at all cost. Once they are annihilated, the alien ship is safe."

"One more thing... I suspect those twin-engine fighter escorts are Kawasaki Ki-45 Dragon Slayers. They entered this theater of war at about this time and place in 1942. The Japanese were hoping that they would be Tiger Slayers, but they were no match against the P-40s. Let's send the Japanese Air Force an early message that their Dragon Slayers are nothing more than Tiger food!"

By the time Bucky finished outlining the plan, the entire Japanese squadron had passed below him and Pumpkin, approaching Willy's and my position at a hundred miles out from the alien spaceship crash site. I looked at my watch and it was 4:30 PM local time. We had thirty minutes before we would be zapped back to 1975 Oak Ridge, Tennessee. Pumpkin had radioed the incoming Japanese squadron coordinates to us while Willy and I circled back to attack them with the sun at our backs. We looked to the east and could see the four Kawasaki Ki-48, bombers coming at us in a diamond formation. Willy was on my right wing. I looked over at him, clicking on my radio. "I'm really proud of you, Willy. You're totally out of your comfort zone, by a long shot."

Willy replied, "You owe me one big time, Bubble Butt—if we get out of this alive."

"Pretend we're kids again, playing with our model planes, taking them into battle," I suggested, "and we can't lose!"

"I'll try, BB. Lead the way; let's end this thing now, before I shit my pants!"

Willy and I dropped out of the sun behind us to an altitude of 10,000 feet and headed straight at the Lily bomber squadron. I honed my approach, targeting the nose of the lead plane. Willy did the same from behind my right wing, focusing on the Lily off the lead's left wing. With a closure rate of at least 500 mph and coming on with the sun at our backs, the bombers' nose gunners and pilots had little time to react and were caught by surprise. I put the midway point between the Lily's Plexiglas nose and cockpit in the crosshairs of my gunsight, and made certain not to open fire too soon. It was thrilling and scary at the same time; my adrenaline was going crazy. As the target rapidly filled the middle of my gunsight, I fired with all six .50-caliber machine guns, unleashing intense violence upon the lead bomber, which one second later exploded into a ball of flames. Willy did the same, but had started his firing a tad early; he was forced to pull up with me when he saw the fireball bursting in front of us. Nevertheless, Willy had scored as well, destroying his target's cockpit controls and setting that plane on fire. Its occupants bailed out as their plane plummeted to earth. Our radios barked a slightly burred version of Bucky's voice. "Great shooting, Yin and Yang! Focus on the fighter's now; they're diving straight at you!"

Lieutenant Haruki Takahashi flew one of the two Japanese Nakajima Ki-43 Oscars at an altitude of 15,000 feet and had to wipe his eyes in disbelief at what had just happened. Two of the four bombers they were "protecting" had already been shot down. He ordered the two remaining bombers, which had been slightly thrown off course, to get back and stay on course. He then ordered the four Ki-45 Dragon Slayers to attack the enemy planes; Willy and I were in a steep climb, aiming to meet them head on.

Willy and I climbed with our engines at full throttle. The Runt's and Meatball's tweaks to our Allison engines and fuel mixture were coming into play as we defied gravity in our powerful ascent. Coming down directly at us were four of the twin-engine Dragon Slayers, two for each of us. For a brief moment, the Japanese fighters were unaware that Bucky and Pumpkin were coming down directly behind them, wasting no time closing the distance with the strength of their dives from above. Opening fire just as Takahashi screamed on his radio that two more P-40s had come from nowhere and were on the tails of the four Dragon Slayers. Willy and I opened fire head on at the lead Dragon Slayers with all twelve of our .50-caliber machine guns blasting, while Bucky and Pumpkin lit up the two trailing Dragon Slayers. Twenty-four .50-caliber Warhawk machine guns unleashed a crossfire of hell upon the four Dragon Slayers. All four enemy planes were doomed, falling hopelessly to earth as their crews made every effort to bail out.

As I blasted away at the Dragon Slayer in front of me and it started to smoke and veer off, my guns ran out of ammunition and stopped firing. I suddenly realized that I had partially depleted my ammunition the day before, on my strafing run; now I was completely out! Willy radioed, "BB, my plane has been hit and I'm having trouble with my controls. What should I do?"

I reflexively replied, "See if you can nurse it back to the landing field south of the alien ship. Peel off to the south now, and go for it! I'm out of ammunition. I am going to monitor the battle from above, to try and provide some visual reconnaissance for Bucky and Pumpkin."

"Roger that, BB. I'll do my best to get there, and keep you posted," Willy responded.

I circled above and to the east of the air battle below me. Our opposition was down to two bombers and two fighters. We were down to two battle-worthy Warhawks. I circled to turn west, poured on the power, and got a better view of what was happening. Bucky and Pumpkin were coming down while firing ferociously on the two remaining Ki-48 bombers, while Takahashi and the other Oscar approached them from behind. I yelled a warning into my radio. "Panda Leader One and Panda Paw Two, you both have Oscars hot on your tails! *Get the hell out of there!*"

Bucky barked, "Don't let these bombers go, Pumpkin! Keep pouring your ammo into them until they can't fly anymore!"

Shit, goddammit, shit. There goes Bucky with that hero stuff again, I thought. I pushed to full throttle and aimed my P-40 Warhawk for their position, thinking that maybe I could scare one of the remaining two Japanese planes into veering off. As I approached them from above and to the west, the Oscar on Pumpkin's tail started to smoke. It must have been hit, or was having engine trouble. Either way, it left Pumpkin's tail and went down in a controlled crash just as Pumpkin successfully destroyed the port wing and set fire to the Lily he was targeting. Pumpkin then declared, "I'm out; I'm out of bullets!" He pulled away from the battle in a turning dive.

I could see the remaining battle plainly, in front of and below my trajectory. We were all in a straight sightline to the alien spaceship crash site.

The last of the four Ki-48 bombers in Bucky's gunsights then started billowing heavy black smoke from both engines, and began to spiral downward to earth. Bucky immediately cried out, "I'm out of ammunition now too! I'm taking fire from behind! I'm going to dive to get away; it's my best shot!"

As Bucky put his P-40 into a steep dive, something odd happened. The sight sent a shiver of supernatural chills through my entire body. Lieutenant Haruki Takahashi, piloting his still sound Japanese Nakajima Ki-43 Hayabusa, chose not to follow Bucky's Warhawk to try and finish him off. Instead, he angled his Oscar in a downward trajectory, aiming to make a suicide crash into the alien spaceship.

Kamikaze, meaning divine wind or spirit wind, pilots were a part of Special Japanese Attack Units of military aviators that started their suicide missions in October of 1944 during WWII. As Allied forces advanced towards the Japanese home islands, the Kamikaze pilots flew suicide attacks for the Empire of Japan against Allied naval vessels in the closing days of World War II. In the days before computer guided missiles existed, humans were used to guide bomb-laden planes to their targets in suicide missions; the time-honored tradition of death before defeat was deeply entrenched in Japanese military culture. About 3,800 kamikaze pilots gave their lives for their country in suicide missions in the Pacific theater during the waning days of WWII.

Japanese Lieutenant Haruki Takahashi had been ordered by his Imperial Japanese Army Air Force superiors to destroy the strange spaceship in the southern China forest between the cities of Guilin and Kunming. It was his mission to plan and execute. His entire squadron had been shot to pieces by General Chennault's AVG Flying Tigers (actually the Bad Love Tigers); he could not keep his honor and return empty handed. Two and a half years before the word *kamikaze* would become a feared reality to Allied forces in the Pacific, Takahashi decided to make his last act in that Ki-43 Oscar a kamikaze mission, flying his plane directly into the downed alien spaceship.

Willy had successfully nursed his damaged P-40 Warhawk back to the south of the alien spaceship, and was watching the end of the battle unfold. Bucky and Pumpkin had both pulled out of their dives and could see what was happening as well. I looked at my watch and pushed my P-40 into a steep dive. My rate of descent was extremely rapid, my airspeed dial moving faster than anything we had done in our practice sessions. Bucky was the first of the Panda Bear Squadron to recognize what was happening. He screamed into his radio, "BB! Stop now, pull out! Don't do it!" Willy and Pumpkin yelled, "No, BB, pull up! *Pull up!*"

It was too late for me to respond; I was totally committed and focused on my speed and angle of approach, about to intersect with Takahashi's plane from above and behind him. His plane was no match for the speed of a P-40 Warhawk in a terminal dive. My indicated speed was rapidly approaching 470 mph, and I was feeling the effect of compressibility on my controls. My whole life flashed before my eyes in an instant; I smiled as I recalled a few of Blue Nova One's last words to us, when she said, "We cannot fully predict human behavior." I closed my eyes and felt violent shaking as my propeller made initial contact with the tail of Takahashi's plane.

Bucky, Pumpkin, and Willy witnessed my collision with Takahashi while they were screaming into their radios. The Pud did not hear what happened; he had packed his radio into the black box and was sitting with the Runt and Meatball, ready to go home. At exactly 5:00 PM our time, Bowmar reliably and methodically hit the recall button on the White Hole Project time travel machine control panel. The world went white for the Bad Love Tigers and its ground crew.

Tuesday, June 24, 1975 at 5:00 AM local time,
the White Hole Project, Oak Ridge, Tennessee

As Bowmar, Benzion "Ben" Kaplan, Waldo, and Mary looked on to the padded circular eye of the ground floor White Hole Project time machine racetrack, the time travelers wondrously appeared. The Pud, Meatball, and the Runt were all comfortably sitting in a tight circle, smiling at each other. Bucky, Pumpkin, and Willy were all still screaming some version of "No BB, don't do it!" as they landed, randomly scattered around the circular eye. When they realized they were back, they stopped screaming. Ben quickly ran to Pumpkin and hugged him, saying, "It's OK, Dad. It's OK, you're home now!" Mary said, "Waldo, I hope you don't ever come back screaming like that. I'd be a nervous wreck, and scared to death!"

I looked at Bucky and Willy, who were shocked to see me, and said, "Now that is the definition of a close call."

"You crazy son of a bitch, that was either the bravest or the stupidest thing I ever saw!" Bucky exclaimed.

Willy just shook his head, speechless. He, Bucky, Pumpkin, and Ben all came over and hugged me while I sat there, crying tears of joy and relief.

Wednesday, June 24, 1942 at 8:00 PM local time,
alien spaceship crash site in the south China forest
between Kunming and Guilin, China

With the repairs completed and the alien spaceship judged to be sound, Blue Nova One and her crew took off from their crash site in the south China forest between Kunming and Guilin, China. The launch was spectacular, lighting up the night sky for hundreds of miles in every direction.

From their campsite twenty miles to the west, Chinese agent "Ming" Sun, her five surviving Chinese troops, and AVG Flying Tiger pilot Allen Wright all watched the bright lights in amazement, knowing what they were witnessing. Ming looked at Allen and said in English, "There is a Chinese Proverb that says, 'Man's schemes are inferior to those made by heaven.'"

Thirty miles to the west, one of the surviving Imperial Japanese Air Force pilots who had parachuted and landed safely following the brutal air battle earlier in the day, saw the unexplained, unearthly, bright lights in the dark of night. He thought *Nanakorobi yaoki*. Literally interpreted, the phrase means fall down seven times and stand up eight. In other words, it means when life knocks you down, stand back up; what matters is not the bad things that happened, but what one does after.

AVG Flying Tigers General Claire Chennault was back in Kunming, China and taking a break after a late dinner. Smoking a Camel cigarette outside, he saw the bright lights in the skies to the east. The AVG's Dissolve Day (July 4, 1942) was only ten days away. Looking at the lights, he thought, *I'll take that as a sign of change. Changes are on the horizon, and change is not all bad.*

Watching planet Earth fade below, Blue Nova One readied the white hole intergalactic transport drive unit to safely return home. She smiled as she thought: *Until we meet again.*

EPILOGUE

"You'll never get what you don't ask for."
—Gloria Schewe

Friday, November 28, 1975, the White Hole Project,
Oak Ridge, Tennessee

It was the Friday after Thanksgiving 1975, and the entire Bad Love Gang was gathering together at the White Hole Project to discuss Meatball's return from Jerusalem, Israel and my crazy encounter with my 62-year-old self. Bowmar, Cleopatra, Crisco and I were the first to get there, followed immediately by Bucky, Waldo, and Mary. To make the White Hole Project more music friendly, I had installed a high-end Sony cassette player with Marantz components and Klipsch Heresy speakers, a setup that could blast deafening and unlimited volume into the White Hole vault. Cleopatra, Crisco, Bowmar and I were out on the center stage of the lower racetrack boogieing (with Bucky, Waldo and Mary looking on) to the number one song in the land on Thanksgiving Day 1975: **"That's the Way (I Like It),"** by KC and the Sunshine Band. The song was one of the few chart-toppers in history to hit number one on more than one occasion during a one-month period, as it did between November and December 1975. The song was also a huge international hit as well, reaching number one in Canada and the Netherlands, and the top ten in Australia, Belgium, Norway, and the UK. Disco music was still relatively new and we were gettin' down out on the floor! The only thing we were lacking was a multifaceted silver ball with spotlights on it rotating above our heads.

After everyone arrived, the entire group gathered together to sit on the comfy, padded central stage of the lower White Hole Project racetrack. Meatball filled us all in on his trip to Jerusalem with intermittent tears in his eyes as he spoke. "Hannah Lieb, whom I fell in love with during our rescue mission to Poland, moved with her family to Jerusalem in late 1946 and has lived there since then. She got pregnant the day before we flew them all out of Poland, when she and I went to that idyllic pond together near the country cottage where we were all hiding. I have a thirty-year-old son with her, named Elijah. He's an Israeli Special Defense Forces commando, just a chip off the old block!" Meatball smiled through the tears and we all laughed. "Hannah is now forty-nine years old, and has terminal breast cancer. She never got married this whole time. She is too young to die!" His tears were flowing down his cheeks. "She doesn't have long to live. We have to figure out a way to save her!"

The group was silent as Crisco, Cleopatra and Ben all tried to support and comfort Meatball. I looked at Bucky and Bowmar; they both knew exactly what I was thinking, and nodded in agreement. At a time like this, I couldn't believe how strong my brotherly bond was with the two of them. How lucky I was to have them and the Bad Love Gang as my extended family! Thanksgiving Day 1975 had just been extended into the Friday after.

I stood up and addressed Meatball and the group. "Although I can't promise a miracle, we may have a way to save Hannah. Bowmar, Bucky, and I have been discussing the details of our next time-travel mission over the past couple of months. We would have to move our timetable up a bit, but it's doable."

Meatball looked up at me with anticipation and a sense of relief. "Whatever you've got in mind, if we can rescue Hannah, I am with you a hundred and ten percent!"

Goondoggy agreed. "You know me, I'm ready to go! Let's do it!"

We all loudly yelled, "*Goondoggy!*"

Willy shook his head and said, "There he goes again; that's my brother, always ready and raring to rush into the waiting jaws of death at a moment's notice!" We all laughed with relief, and hope. "So, Bubble Butt... Tell us what your older self said to you when he—you—paid you a visit."

"That's an intriguing question, Willy." I responded. "He—I—was trying to give me some wisdom for the future, without giving the future away. Although he slipped a little bit...maybe that has something to do with trying to rescue Hannah. I'll try to paraphrase some of what I heard sixty-two-year-old-me say.

"**Change and challenge are normal in life; you get to choose how you react. Don't shrink away, but grow from these things.**

"**Most things that happen in life are beyond our control. Control yourself and your own response; you can't control others.**

"**Peace is the opposite of fear.**

"**Learn from the past, plan for the future, live in the moment.**

"**Always seek God's face, not just his hand.**

"**The truth is, the more difficult your situation, the more treasure there is to discover in it.**

"**Life is too short to live it negative.**

"**Know that your best days are ahead.**"

"You said that the older you slipped a little bit. What was said that was a slip?" Willy enquired.

"At the end of our ten minutes together, he said, 'You and the Bad Love Gang will make history in 1975; don't blow it, Bubble Butt!'"

ABOUT THE AUTHOR

Kevin L. Schewe, MD, FACRO, is the proud father of two daughters (Ashley and Christie) and two granddaughters (Gracie and Olivia). He is a native of St. Louis, Missouri and now makes his home in Denver, Colorado. He graduated from the University of Missouri–Columbia with a Bachelor's Degree in Biology, and from the University Missouri Columbia School of Medicine as an M.D. He trained at the Medical College of Wisconsin to become a board-certified Radiation Oncologist. He is a Fellow of the American College of Radiation Oncology (FACRO). Having practiced radiation oncology for 33 years, he continues to serve as Medical Director of Radiation Oncology for Alliance Cancer Care Colorado at Red Rocks in Golden, Colorado (www.accredrocks.com). He is an entrepreneur, having founded a cosmetics company called Elite Therapeutics (www.elitetherapeutics.com) and Bad Love Cosmetics Company. He serves as Chairman of the Board of a micro-cap renewable, green energy and animal feed company called VIASPACE, Inc. (www.viaspace.com).

The first Sunday of June every year is National Cancer Survivor's Day. Dr. Schewe co-chairs a yearly celebration of National Cancer Survivor's Day at the Red Rocks Medical Center in Golden, Colorado. Every year he writes a skit that he and the local doctors perform for the Survivor's Day crowd. The skit always has a musical theme from the 1950s, 1960s, 1970s, 1980s, or one of various Hollywood venues. The doctors are dressed in costumes for their parts and ask questions or pose dilemmas to each other. The answers to those questions or dilemmas are clips from songs, which the doctors lip sync and dance to in front of the crowd. There is a dance contest in the middle of the skit and everyone comes together and dances at the end of the skit. It is great fun and an uplifting celebration of survival for the cancer patients, their families, and loved ones!

Bad Love Tigers is Dr. Schewe's second novel in the *Bad Love Series*. His highly-rated first novel, *Bad Love Strikes*, was released in September 2019 and is an Amazon bestseller. Follow Dr. Schewe on Instagram @ realkevinschewe and at his author website, kevinschewe.com.

COMING SOON

BAD LOVE BEYOND –
The Bad Love Series Continues...

In a race against time and space to rescue Hannah Lieb from the ravages of metastatic breast cancer, Bubble Butt and the Bad Love Gang must find a way to get to their new alien friend, Blue Nova One, hoping that she and her advanced civilization will have a cure for Hannah. Time and space travel are inexorably intertwined as the future, the mid-1970s, the WWII-1940s, and the best recorded music in the history of the universe continue to collide with each other in dramatic fashion!

CPSIA information can be obtained
at www.ICGtesting.com
Printed in the USA
LVHW011414300720
661946LV00003B/162